"What ship?" sent Grimes again. "What ship? Identify yourself, or I open fire."

He grinned when the reply came, "You'd better not."

He said aloud, "Not only human, but our sort of people." He flashed, "This is the Rim Worlds Confederacy's cruiser **Faraway Quest**."

"Imperial Navy's armed scout **Vindictive**. Never heard of Rim Worlds Confederacy. Who the hell are you?"

Grimes grinned again, sent, "Can't we talk this over?"

"Please prepare to receive my boat."

*   *   *

"Captain Sir Dominic Flandry, of the Imperial Navy," Williams announced cheerfully. "Sir Dominic, may I present Commodore John Grimes, of the Rim Worlds Naval Reserve?"

"Your servant, Commodore," said Flandry stiffly.

That'll be the sunny Friday, thought Grimes. "Good to have you aboard, Captain. Or should I say, 'Sir Dominic'?"

AND THAT WAS ONLY THE BEGINNING...

THE DARK DIMENSIONS

A. BERTRAM CHANDLER

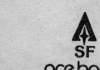

SF
ace books
A Division of Charter Communications Inc.
A GROSSET & DUNLAP COMPANY
51 Madison Avenue
New York, New York 10010

THE DARK DIMENSIONS

Copyright © 1971 by A. Bertram Chandler

An ACE Book

With the author's sincere thanks to Poul Anderson for his loan of Captain Sir Dominic Flandry.

Cover art by Rowena Morrill

1

"I'VE ANOTHER JOB for you, Grimes," said Admiral Kravitz.

"Mphm," grunted Commodore Grimes, Rim Worlds Naval Reserve, "sir." He regarded the portly flag officer with something less than enthusiasm. There had been a time, not so very long ago, when he had welcomed being dragged away from his rather boring civilian duties as Rim Runners' astronautical superintendent, but increasingly of late he had come to appreciate a relatively quiet, uneventful life. Younger men than he could fare the starways, he was happy to remain a desk-sitting space commodore.

"Rim Runners are granting you indefinite leave of absence," went on Kravitz.

"They would," grumbled Grimes.

"On full pay."

Grimes' manner brightened slightly. "And I'll be drawing my commodore's pay and allowances from the Admiralty, of course?"

"Of course. You are back on the active list as and from 0000 hours this very day."

"We can always use the extra money . . ." murmured Grimes.

Kravitz looked shocked. "I never knew that you were so mercenary, Grimes."

"You do now, sir." The Commodore grinned briefly, then once again looked rather apprehensive. "But it's not Kinsolving's Planet again, is it?"

The Admiral laughed. "I can understand your being more than somewhat allergic to that peculiar world."

Grimes chuckled grimly. "I think it's allergic to me, sir. Three times I've landed there, and each time was unlucky; the third time unluckiest of all."

"I've read your reports. But set your mind at rest. It's not Kinsolving."

"Then where?"

"The Outsider."

"The Outsider . . ." repeated Grimes slowly. How many times since the discovery of that alien construction out beyond the Galactic Rim had he urged that he be allowed to take *Faraway Quest* to make his own investigation? He had lost count. Always his proposals had been turned down. Always he could not be spared or was required more urgently elsewhere. Too, it was obvious that the Confederacy was scared of the thing, even though it swam in space that came under Rim Worlds' jurisdiction. The Federation was scared of it, too. "Let well enough alone," was the attitude of both governments.

"The Outsider . . ." said Grimes again. "I was beginning to think that it occupied top place on the list of untouchables. Why the sudden revival of interest?"

"We have learned," Kravitz told him, "from reliable sources, that the Waldegren destroyer *Adler* is on her way out to the . . . *thing*. I needn't tell you that the Duchy of Waldegren is making a comeback, or that Federation policy is that Waldegren will never be allowed to build its fleet up to the old level. But sophisticated weaponry can give a small navy superiority over a large one."

"The Outsiders' Ship, as we all know, is a storehouse of science and technology thousands—millions, perhaps—of years in advance of our own. *Your* Captain Calver got his paws on to some of it, but passed nothing of interest on to us before he flew the coop. Since then we, and the Federation, and the Shaara Empire, and probably quite a few more, have sent expeditions. Every one has ended disastrously. It is possible, probable, even, that this Waldegren effort will end disastrously. But we can't be sure."

"It should not take long to recommission your *Faraway Quest*. She's only just back from the Fleet Maneuvers, at which she was present as an auxiliary cruiser. . . ."

"I know," said Grimes. "I should have been in command of her."

"But you weren't. For all your early life in the

Federation's Survey Service, for all your rank in our Naval Reserve, you don't make a good naval officer. You're too damned independent. You like to be left alone to play in your own little corner. But—I grant you this—whatever sort of mess you fall into you always come up smelling of roses."

"Thank you, sir," said Grimes stiffly.

Kravitz chuckled. "It's true, isn't it? Anyhow, you should be on the spot, showing the flag, before *Adler* blows in. You'll be minding the shop. Play it by ear, as you always do. And while you're about it, you might try to find out something useful about The Outsider."

"Is that all?" asked Grimes.

"For the time being, yes. Oh, personnel for *Faraway Quest*. . . . You've a free hand. Make up the crew you think you'll need from whatever officers are available, Regulars or Reservists. The Federation has intimated that it'd like an observer along. I think I'm right in saying that Commodore Verrill still holds a reserve commission in the Intelligence Branch of their Survey Service. . . ."

"She does, sir. And she'd be very annoyed if she wasn't allowed to come along for the ride."

"I can well imagine. And now we'll browse through The Outsider files and try to put you in the picture."

He pressed a button under his desk, and a smartly uniformed W.R.W.N. officer came in, carrying a half dozen bulky folders that she put on the Admiral's desk. She was followed by two male petty officers who set up screen, projector and tape recorders.

Kravitz opened the first folder. "It all started," he said, "with Commander Maudsley of the Federation Survey Service's Intelligence Branch. . . ."

2

"IT ALL STARTED," said Grimes, "with Commander Maudsley of the Federation Survey Service's Intelligence Branch. . . ."

As soon as he had spoken the words he regretted them. Sonya, his wife, had known Maudsley well. They had been more, much more, than merely fellow officers in the same service. Grimes looked at her anxiously, the reddening of his prominent ears betraying his embarrassment. But her strong, fine-featured face under the high-piled, glossy, auburn hair was expressionless. All that she said, coldly, was, "Why bring that up, John?"

He told her, "You know the story. Mayhew knows the story. I know the story. But Clarisse doesn't. And as she's to be one of my key officers on this expedition it's essential that she be put in the picture."

"I can get it all from Ken," said Clarisse Mayhew.

"Not in such detail," stated Sonya. "We have to admit that my ever-loving husband has always been up to the eyebrows in whatever's happened on the Rim."

"You haven't done so badly yourself," Grimes told her, breaking the tension, returning the smile that flickered briefly over her face.

"One thing that I *like* about the Rim Worlds," murmured Clarisse, "is that the oddest things always seem to be happening. Life was never like this on Francisco. But go on, please, John."

"Mphm," grunted Grimes. "Talking is thirsty work."

He raised a hand, and on silent wheels a robot servitor rolled into the comfortable lounge room. Most people who could afford such luxuries preferred humanoid automatons and called them by human names, but not Grimes. He always said, and always would say, that it was essential that machines be kept in their proper place. The thing that had answered his summons was obviously just a machine, no more than a cylindrical tank on a tricycle carriage with two cranelike arms. It stood there impassively waiting for their orders, and then from a hatch in its body produced a tankard of cold beer for Grimes, Waverley Scotch and soda for Mayhew, iced Rigellian dragon's milk for the ladies.

"Here's to all of us," said Grimes, sipping appreciatively. He looked over the rim of his glass at his guests—at Mayhew, tall, gangling, deceptively

8

youthful and fragile in appearance, at Clarisse, attractively plump in face and figure, her rich brown hair hanging down to waist level. On Francisco, the world of her birth, she had been one of the so-called Blossom People, and still looked the part.

"Get on with it, John," said Sonya after sampling her own drink.

"Very well. It all started, as I've already said, with Commander Maudsley. As well as being a fully qualified astronaut, he was an Intelligence Officer. . . ."

"It didn't start with Maudsley," said Sonya sharply. "No one knows *when* it started."

"Oh, all right. I'll go back a few more years in time. It was suspected for quite a long while that there was *something out there*. Many years ago, long before the Rim Worlds seceded from the Federation, Faraway was a penal colony of sorts. The Survey Service actually manned a ship with the sweepings of the jails and sent her out to find that . . .*something*. What happened to her is not known to this day. After we'd established our own Confederacy, the Federation's Survey Service was still snooping around the Rim—and Maudsley, passing himself off as the master of a star tramp called *Polar Queen,* did quite a lot of work out there. So far as we know he was the first *human* spaceman to set eyes on the Outsiders' Ship. Shortly thereafter he crashed his own vessel coming in to a landing at Port Farewell on Faraway. He was the only survivor. After that he stayed out there. He served in a few of our Rim Runners' ships, but he was practically unemployable. We didn't know then that he was a Survey Service Commander, Intelligence Branch at that, but it wouldn't have made any difference. He finished up as mate of a ship called, funnily enough, *The Outsider*. Her master, Captain Calver, had been master in our employ, but he and his officers made a pile of money out of the salvage of the T.G. Clipper *Thermopylae* and invested it in an obsolescent Epsilon Class tramp, going into business as shipowners. To comply with regulations, Calver had to ship a chief officer with at least a Chief Pilot's Certificate—and Maudsley was the only one that he could find on Nova Caledon.''

''Maudsley was hitting the bottle, almost drinking himself to death. (Forgive me, Sonya, but that's the way that it was.) He talked in his drunken delirium. He talked about the Outsiders' Ship, the finding of which had somehow wrecked his life. Then he committed suicide. . . .''

Grimes paused, looking at his wife. Her face was expressionless. He went on, ''For quite a while after that Calver got by in his *Outsider*. Toward the finish, Sonya was his chief officer— she holds her Master Astronaut's papers, as you know. Trade on the Rim was expanding faster than Rim Runners' fleet and there was plenty of cargo for an independent operator. But, eventually, times got bad for Calver. Rim Runners had sufficient tonnage for all requirements, and a small, one ship company just couldn't compete. It was then that he and his co-owners remembered Maudsley's story, and decided to find the Ship

From Outside for themselves. They knew that there was something out beyond the Rim that could make them impossibly rich. They had Maudsley's sailing directions, such as they were. The Confederacy evinced some slight interest in the matter, and I was able to help out with the loan of a Mass Proximity Indicator—which, in those days, was a *very* expensive hunk of equipment. Even the Federation chipped in. As *you* know, my dear.

"Calver found the Outsiders' Ship. He and his people boarded . . . her? . . .it? A ship? A robot intelligence? A quarantine station? Who knows? But they found the thing. They boarded it. But I'll let Calver speak for himself. This is a recording of the report he made to me."

Grimes switched on the small recorder that was standing ready on the coffee table. He hated himself for raising so many ghosts from Sonya's past—she and Calver had been lovers, he knew—but these ghosts were bound to have been raised during the expedition. Her face was stony, expressionless, as the once familiar voice issued from the little machine.

"Did you ever read a twentieth century Terran author called Wells? He's recommended reading in the 'Fathers of the Future' course they have at most schools. Anyhow, there's one of his stories, a fantasy, called *A Vision Of Judgment*. Wells imagined a Judgment Day, with all living and all who have ever lived called by the Last Trump to face their Maker, to be tried and punished for their sins or, perhaps, to be rewarded for their good deeds.

Everyone has his session of Hell as his naked soul stands in full view of the multitude while the Recording Angel recites the long, long catalog of petty acts of meanness and spite. . . . All the trivial (but not so trivial) shabby things, all the things in which even the most perverted nature could never take pride, and even the spectacular wrongdoings made to look shabby and trivial. . . .

"It was left there, the Outsiders' Ship, out beyond the Rim, in the hope that with the development of interstellar flight techniques it would be discovered. It was left there, in the far outer reaches of this galaxy, to test the fitness of its discoverers to use the treasures of science and technology that it contains, to build ships capable of making the Big Crossing. We passed the test without cracking . . . quite. Had we cracked there is little doubt that we should have been bundled off the premises as unceremoniously as Maudsley must have been, bundled outside with memories of fear and of horror, and of loss, and with some sort of posthypnotic inhibition to stop us from ever talking about it. It's possible, of course, that some of Maudsley's crew did pass the test—but they died with *Polar Queen*."

"The test . . . yes, it's ingenious, and amazingly simple. It's . . . it's a mirror that's held up to you in which you see . . . everything. Yes, *everything*. Things that you've forgotten, and things that you've wished for years that you could forget. After all, a man can meet any alien monster without fear, without hate, after he has met and faced and accepted the most horrible monster of all. . . ."

"Himself."

Grimes switched off, then busied himself refueling and lighting his pipe. He said, through the acrid smoke cloud, "Calver came back, as you've gathered, and then he and his engineers did a few odd things to his ship's Mannschenn Drive, and then they all pushed off to . . . ? Your guess is as good as mine. To the next galaxy but three? The general impression was that they had some sort of intergalactic drive. Calver was decent enough to leave me a pile of things—notes and diagrams and calculations. Unfortunately I'm no engineer. . . ."

"You can say that again!" interjected Sonya.

Grimes ignored this. "Our own bright boys tried to make something of them. They actually rebuilt a Mannschenn Drive unit as allegedly specified, but it just won't work. Literally. Every moving part has absolute freedom to move on bearings that are practically frictionless, but . . ." He grinned. "Mayhew reckons that the thing won't work unless its operator is approved by it. Frankly, I can't approve of a *machine* that thinks it has the right to approve or disapprove of *me*!"

"That's only my theory, John," put in Mayhew.

"But you believe it, don't you? Where was I? Oh, yes. After the Calver affair there was quite a flurry of interest in the Outsiders' Ship. The Federation, with our permission, sent *Starfinder* to nose around. She located quite a few derelicts in the vicinity—a Shaara ship, an odd vessel that must have belonged to some incredibly ancient culture, a Dring cruiser. Then she became a derelict herself. When her Carlotti transmissions suddenly stopped we sent *Rim Culverin* to investigate. The *Culverin's* captain reported that he had boarded *Starfinder* and found all hands very dead; a few had been shot and the rest wiped out by a lethal gas in the air circulation system. Whether or not any of *Starfinder's* people boarded the Outsiders' Ship we don't know. Probably some, at least, did. *Rim Culverin* was ordered not to investigate The Outsider but to tow *Starfinder* in to Lorn. She did just that. Then our big brothers of the Federation tried again, this time with a Constellation Class cruiser, *Orion*. *Orion* blew up with no survivors. *Rim Carronade* was with her and saw it happen. *Orion* had put quite a large boarding party onto—or into—the Outsiders' Ship, and it was after their return to their own vessel that the big bang happened. *Rim Carronade* was damaged herself, with quite a few casualties, and returned to Lorn.''

''All of you here know me. I'm not one of those people who say, in a revoltingly pious voice, that there are some things that we are not meant to know. For years I've been wanting to take my own expedition out to investigate that hunk of alien ironmongery. I've got my chance at last—and I'm just a little scared.''

''And I'm damn glad that I shall have all of you with me.''

3

SHE WAS AN old ship, was *Faraway Quest*, but in first class condition. She had started life as an Epsilon Class tramp, one of those sturdy work-horses of the Federation's Interstellar Transport Commission. Sold to Rim Runners during the days when practically all of the tonnage out on the Rim was at best secondhand, she had been converted into a survey ship. In her, Grimes had discovered and explored the worlds of the Eastern Circuit: Tharn, Mellise, Grollor and Stree. In her he had made the first contact with the antimatter systems to the galactic west.

After secession, the setting up of the Rim Worlds Confederacy, she had been subject to further conversion, this time being fitted out as an auxiliary cruiser. Even though the Rim Worlds Navy now possessed a sizable fleet built to its own specifications, this was still her official status. Nonetheless, Commodore Grimes regarded her as *his* ship.

As Admiral Kravitz had told him, she was practically ready to lift off at once to where The Outsider drifted in the intergalactic nothingness. She was almost fully stored. Her "farm" was in a flourishing state; her tissue culture, yeast and algae tanks were well stocked and healthy. Main and auxiliary machinery were almost fresh from thorough overhaul. Sundry weaponry had been mounted so that she could play her part in the fleet maneuvers, and this Grimes decided to retain. He liked to think of himself as a man of peace these days but was willing to admit that it is much easier to be peaceful behind laser projections and rocket batteries than in an unarmed ship.

The selection of personnel for the expedition posed no great problems. Billy Williams, normally skipper of the deep space tug *Rim Mamelute*, was available. On more than one occasion he had served as Grimes' second-in-command. James Carnaby, second officer with Rim Runners and an outstandingly competent navigator, had just come off leave and was awaiting reappointment. Like Williams, he held a commission in the Reserve, as did Hendrikson, another Rim Runners' second officer, just paid off from *Rim Griffon*. There was Davis, an engineer whom Grimes knew quite well and liked, and who was qualified in all three Drives: Mannschenn, inertial and reaction. There was Sparky Daniels, currently officer in charge of the Port Forlorn Carlotti Station but who frequently pined for a deep space appointment. And there was Major Dalzell of the Rim Worlds Marines. Grimes had heard good reports of this young space soldier and, on being introduced to him, had liked him at once.

There was what Grimes described as a brain 'trust of buffoons from the University of Lorn. There was a team of technicians.

There was an officer of the Intelligence Branch of the Federation's Survey Service—just along, as she said, "to see how the poor live." This, of course, was Commander Sonya Verrill, otherwise Mrs. Grimes, who, in spite of her marriage to a Rim Worlder, had retained both her Federation citizenship and her Survey Service commission.

There were the psionicists—Ken Mayhew, one of the last of the psionic communications officers, and Clarisse, his wife. He was a highly trained and qualified telepath. She, born on Francisco, was a descendant of that caveman artist from the remote past who, somehow, on Kinsolving's Planet, had been dragged through time to what was, to him, the far future. Like her ancestor, Clarisse was an artist. Like him, she was a specialist. Inborn in her was the talent to lure victims to the hunter's snare. Twice, on Kinsolving itself, she had exercised this talent—and on each occasion the hunters had become the victims.

The work of preparing the ship for her voyage went well and swiftly. There was little to be done, actually, save for the rearranging of her accommodations for the personnel that she was to carry, the conversion of a few of her compartments into laboratories for the scientists. Toward the end of the refit Grimes was wishing that on that long ago day when the Rim Worlds had decided that they should have their own survey ship somebody had put up a convincing case for the purchase of an obsolescent Alpha Class liner! Not that there was anything wrong with *Faraway Quest*—save for her relative smallness. And it was not only the civilians who demanded space and yet more space. Officer Hendrikson—who, as a Reserve officer had specialized in gunnery—sulked hard when he was told that he could not have the recreation rooms as magazines for his missiles. (Dr. Druthen, leader of the scientists, was already sulking because he had not been allowed to take them over as workshops.)

Grimes knew that he could not hasten matters, but he chafed at every delay. As long as the *Quest* was sitting on her pad in Port Forlorn far too many people were getting into every act. Once she was up and outward bound he would be king of his own little spaceborne castle, an absolute monarch. Admiral Kravitz had made it clear to him that he would be on his own, that he was to act as he saw fit. It was a game in which he was to make up the rules as he went along.

It was a game that Grimes had always enjoyed playing.

FARAWAY QUEST LIFTED from Port Forlorn without ceremony; it could have been no more than the routine departure of a Rim Runners' freighter. Grimes had the controls; he loved ship handling and knew, without false modesty, that he was a better than average practitioner of this art. In the control room with him were Sonya, Billy Williams, Carnaby, Hendrikson and Sparky Daniels. Also there, as a guest, was Dr. Druthen. Grimes already did not like Druthen. The physicist was a fat slug of a man, always with an oily sheen of perspiration over his hairless skin, always with an annoyingly supercilious manner. He sat there, a silent sneer embodied. Had he been a crew member he would have faced a charge of dumb insolence.

Daniels was at the NST transceiver, a little man who looked as though he had been assembled from odds and ends of wire, highly charged wire at that. Williams—bulky, blue-jowled, with shaggy black hair—lounged in the co-pilot's seat. He slumped there at ease, but his big hands were ready to slam down on his controls at a microsecond's notice. Slim, yellow-haired, a little too conventionally handsome, Carnaby was stationed at the radar with Hendrikson, also blond but bearded and burly, looking as though he should have been wearing a horned helmet, ready to take over if necessary. He managed to convey the impression that fire control was his real job, not navigation.

And Sonya conveyed the impression that she was just along as an observer. She was slim and beautiful in her Survey Service uniform, with the micro-skirt that would have been frowned upon by the rather frumpish senior female officers of the Confederacy's Navy. She was a distracting influence, decided Grimes. Luckily he knew her well; even so he would find it hard to keep his attention on the controls.

"Mphm," he grunted. Then, "Commander Williams?"

"All stations secured for lift-off, Skipper. All drives on Stand By."

"Mr. Daniels, request clearance, please."

"*Faraway Quest* to Tower. *Faraway Quest* to tower. Request clearance for departure. Over."

The voice of the Aerospace Control officer came in reply. "Tower to *Faraway Quest*. You have clearance." Then, in far less impersonal accents, "Good questing!"

Grimes grunted, keeping his face expressionless. He said into his intercom microphone, "Count down for lift-off. Over to you, Commander Williams."

"Ten . . ." intoned Williams. "Nine . . . Eight . . ."

"A touching ritual," muttered Dr. Druthen. Grimes glared at him but said nothing.

"Five . . . Four . . ."

The Commodore's glance swept the control room, missing nothing. His eyes lingered longer than they should have done on Sonya's knees and exposed thighs.

"Zero!"

At the touch of Grimes' finger on the button the inertial drive grumbled into life. The ship quivered, but seemed reluctant to leave the pad. *I should have been expecting this,* he thought. *The last time I took this little bitch out I wasn't inflicted with this excess tonnage of personnel . . .* He applied more pressure, feeling and hearing the faint *clicks* as the next two stages were brought into operation. The irregular beat of the drive was suddenly louder.

"Negative contact, sir," stated Carnaby. "Lifting . . . lifting . . ."

Grimes did not need to look at the instruments. He was flying by the seat of his pants. He could feel the additional weight on his buttocks as acceleration, gentle though it was, augmented gravity. He did not bother to correct lateral drift when the wind caught *Faraway Quest* as soon as she was out of the lee of the spaceport buildings. It did not really matter at which point she emerged from the upper atmosphere of the planet.

Up she climbed, and up, and the drab, gray landscape with the drab, gray city was spread beneath her, and the drab, gray cloud ceiling was heavy over the transparent dome of the control room. Up she climbed and up and beyond the dome; outside the viewports there was only the formless, swirling fog of the overcast.

Up she climbed—and suddenly, the steely Lorn sun broke through, and the dome darkened in compensation to near opacity.

Up she climbed. . . .

"Commodore," asked Druthen in his unpleasantly high-pitched voice, "isn't it time that you set course or trajectory or whatever you call it?"

"No," snapped Grimes. Then, trying to make his voice pleasant or, at least, less unpleasant, "I usually wait until I'm clear of the Van Allen."

"Oh. Surely in this day and age that would not be necessary."

"It's the way that I was brought up," grunted Grimes. He scowled at Sonya, who had assumed her maddeningly superior expression. He snapped at Carnaby, "Let me know as soon as we're clear of the radiation belt, will you?"

The sun, dimmed by polarization, was still directly ahead, directly overhead from the viewpoint of those in the control room, in the very nose of the ship. To either side now there was almost unrelieved blackness, the ultimate night in which swam the few, faint, far nebulosities of the Rim sky; the distant, unreachable island universes. Below, huge in the after vision screen, was the pearly gray sphere that was Lorn. Below, too, was the misty Galactic Lens.

"All clear, sir," said Carnaby quietly.

"Good. Commander Williams, make the usual announcements."

"Attention, please," Williams said. "Attention, please. Stand by for free fall. Stand by for free fall. Stand by for centrifugal effects."

Grimes cut the drive. He was amused to note that, in spite of the ample warning, Druthen had not secured his seat belt. He remarked mildly, "I thought that you'd have been ready for free fall, Doctor."

The physicist snarled wordlessly, managed to clip the strap about his flabby corpulence. Grimes returned his full attention to the controls. Directional gyroscopes rumbled, hummed and whined as the ship was turned about her short axis. The Lorn sun drifted from its directly ahead position to a point well abaft the *Quest's* beam. The cartwheel sight set in the ship's stem was centered on . . . nothingness. Broad on the bow was the Lens, with a very few bright stars, the suns of the Rim Worlds, lonely in the blackness beyond its edge.

Williams looked toward Grimes inquiringly. The Commodore nodded.

"Attention, please," Williams said. "Stand by for resumption of acceleration. Stand by for initiation of Mannschenn Drive."

Grimes watched the accelerometer as he restarted the engines. He let acceleration build up to a steady one G, no more, no less. He switched on the Mannshenn Drive. Deep in the bowels of the ship the gleaming complexity of gyroscopes began to move, to turn, to precess, building up speed. Faster spun the rotors and faster and their song was a thin, high keening on the very verge of audibility. And as they spun they precessed, tumbling out of the frame of the continuum, falling down and through the dark dimensions, pulling the vessel and all aboard her with them.

The Commodore visualized the working of the uncanny machines—as he always did. It helped to take his mind off the initial effects: the sagging of all colors down the spectrum, the wavering insubstantiality of the forms, the outlines of everything and everybody, the distortion of all the senses, the frightening feeling of déjà vu. He said, making a rather feeble joke of it, "This is where we came in."

The others might be paid to laugh at their commanding officer's witticisms, but Dr. Druthen made it plain that he was not. He looked at Grimes, all irritated and irritating inquiry. "Came in *where*?" he demanded.

Sonya laughed without being paid for it.

Grimes glared at his wife, then said patiently to the scientist, "Just a figure of speech, Doctor."

"Oh. I would have thought that 'this is where we are going out' would have been more apt." Druthen stared out through the viewport, to the distorted Galactic Lens. Grimes, seeing what he was looking at, thought of making his usual remark about a Klein flask blown by a drunken glassblower, then thought better of it. He found it hard to cope with people who had too literal minds.

"And talking of going out," went on Druthen, "why aren't we going out?"

"What do you mean, Doctor?"

"Correct me if I'm wrong, Commodore, but I always understood that the Outsiders' Ship lay some fifty light years out beyond the outermost Rim sun. I'm not a spaceman, but even I can see that we are, at the moment, just circumnavigating the fringe of the galaxy."

Grimes sighed. He said, "Finding The Outsider is like trying to find a tiny needle in one helluva big haystack. At the moment we are, as you have said, circumnavigating the Lens. When we have run the correct distance we shall have the Lead Stars in line or almost in line. I shall bring the Leads astern, and run out on them for fifty light years. *Then* I shall run a search pattern. . . ."

Druthen snorted. What he said next revealed that he must have acquainted himself very well with Grimes' history, his past record. He said sardonically, "What a *seamanlike* like way of doing it, Commodore. But, of course, you're an honorary admiral of the surface Navy on Tharn, and your Master Mariner's Certificate is valid for the oceans of Aquarius. I would have thought, in my layman's innocence, that somebody would have laid a marker buoy, complete with Carlotti beacon, off The Outsider years ago."

"Somebody did," Grimes told him tersely. "No less than three somebodies did. According to last reports those buoys are still there, but none of them is functioning as a Carlotti transmitter. None of them ever did function for longer than three days, Galactic Standard.''

"Steady on trajectory, Skipper," announced Williams.

"Thank you, Commander. Set normal deep space watches," replied Grimes. Slowly he unbuckled himself from his chair. It was customary for the captain of a ship, at this juncture, to invite any important passengers to his quarters for an ice-breaking drink or two. He supposed that Druthen was a passenger of sorts—he had signed no Articles of Agreement—and, as leader of the scientific team he was important enough. Too important.

"Will you join me in a quiet drink before dinner, Doctor?" Grimes asked.

"Too right," replied Druthen, licking his thick lips.

Sonya's eyebrows lifted, although her fine-featured face showed no expression.

5

DRUTHEN DRANK GIN, straight, from a large glass. Sonya sipped a weak Scotch and soda. Grimes drank gin, but with plenty of ice and a touch of bitters. Druthen managed to convey the impression of being more at home in the Commodore's day cabin than its rightful occupants. He talked down at Grimes and Sonya. It was obvious that he considered himself to be the real leader of the expedition, with the astronautical personnel along only as coach drivers.

Patronizingly he said, "Your trouble, Grimes, is that you're too old fashioned. You don't move with the times. I really believe that you'd have been happy in the days of wooden ships and iron men."

"You can say that again," agreed Grimes. He

was pleased to note that Sonya was not taking sides against him, as she usually did when the conversation got on to these lines. He went on, "Then, the shipmaster wasn't at the mercy of his technicians to the extent that he is now."

"And you really believe that . . ." Druthen's pale eyebrows were almost invisible against the unhealthy pallor of his skin, but it was obvious that they had been raised. "But why, my dear Grimes, must you persist in this passion for the archaic? To take just one glaring example—the invention and subsequent development of the Carlotti deep space communications system should have put every over glamorized but unreliable psionic communications officer out of a job. And yet I was amazed to discover that you carry a representative of that peculiar breed aboard this very vessel."

"Ken Mayhew—Commander Mayhew—is an old friend and shipmate. . . ."

"Sentiment, Grimes. Sentiment."

"Let me finish, Druthen." Grimes was childishly pleased to note that the physicist had been offended by the omission of his title. "Let me finish. Commander Mayhew is outstanding in his own field. As long as I have him on board, as well as the Carlotti gadgetry, I shall never be at the mercy of a single fuse. Throughout this voyage he will be in continuous touch, waking and sleeping, with his juniors at the PC Station at Port Forlorn. Too. . . ." But Grimes suddenly decided not to come out with what he had been going to say.

"Go on, Commodore."

I always like to keep at least one ace up my

sleeve thought Grimes. He said nothing further about Mayhew's abilities, but went on, "Too, it's just possible that we shall be able to make use of his wife's talents."

Druthen laughed sneeringly. "What sort of outfit *is* this? A telepath and a ghost raiser considered essential to the success of a *scientific* expedition." He raised a pudgy hand. "Hear me out. I've done my homework Grimes. I've read the reports written by you and about you. I know that you experienced some odd hallucinations on Kinsolving's Planet—but surely you can distinguish between the objective and the subjective. Or can't you?"

"He can," put in Sonya. "And I can. I was there too, one of the times."

"And on the second occasion," said Grimes nastily, "we had a scad of scientists along."

"Agreed," remarked Druthen smugly. "But second-raters, all of them. On the first occasion—correct me if I'm wrong—it was an expedition organized by a group of religious fanatics. On the third occasion there was, with the Commodore and you, Mrs. Grimes, a shipload of fellow spacemen and—women. So. . . ."

Grimes managed to keep his temper. "So it all never happened, Doctor?"

"That is my opinion, Commodore." He refilled his glass without invitation. "Frankly, I maintain that *this* expedition should have been under the command of a hardheaded scientist rather than a spaceman who has shown himself to be as superstitious as the old-time seamen regarding whom he is such an expert.''

Grimes grinned mirthlessly. "But I am in command, Doctor."

"That is quite obvious. For example, this wasting of time by running to bring your famous Lead Stars in line rather than steering directly for the last reported position of The Outsider."

Grimes laughed. "As long as I'm in command, Dr. Druthen, things will be done my way. But I will tell you why I'm doing things this way. The Outsider . . . wobbles. Unpredictably. Sometimes it is this side of the Leads, sometimes the other. Sometimes it is further in, toward the Rim, sometimes it is further out. In the unlikely event of its being in the vicinity of the position at which I shall bring the Lead Stars in line it will be within the detection range of several planet-based observatories. It just might be there, but the chances are that it will not be. So I stand out, and out, until I've run my distance, and then if I've picked up nothing on the mass proximity indicator I just cruise around in circles, through an ever expanding volume of space. Quite simple, really."

"Simple!" snorted Druthen. He muttered something about people who must have learned their navigation in Noah's Ark. He splashed more gin into his glass. Grimes was pleased to see that the bottle was empty.

Sonya made a major production of consulting her wristwatch. She said, "It's time that we got dressed for dinner."

Surlily, Druthen took the hint. He finished his drink, got up clumsily. "Thank you, Commodore. Thank you, Mrs. Grimes. I suppose I'd better freshen up myself. No, you needn't come with me. I can find my own way down."

When the door had shut behind him Grimes looked at Sonya, and she looked at him. Grimes demanded, of nobody in particular, "What have I done to deserve this?"

"Plenty," she told him. Then, "Pour me a drink, a stiff one. I just didn't want to be accused of setting that bastard a bad example."

He complied. "I don't think that anybody could possibly."

She laughed. "You're right." Then, "But don't underestimate him, John. He wasn't the only one doing his homework before we lifted off. I did, too, while you were getting the ship ready. I was able to get my paws on his dossier. To begin with, he's brilliant. Not quite a genius—although he likes to think that he is—but not far from it. He is also notorious for being completely lacking in the social graces."

"You can say that again!"

"But . . . and it's an interesting 'but'. But this he turns to his advantage. When he wants to pick anybody's brains he goes out of his way to annoy them—and, as like as not, they spill far more beans than they would do normally."

"Mphm," grunted Grimes, feeling smugly pleased with himself. "Mphm."

"He resents all authority. . . ."

"Doesn't he just!"

"He feels that he has not received his just due."

"Who doesn't? But since when was this a just universe?"

"In short, he's dangerous."

"Aren't we all in this rustbucket? Aren't we all?" he refilled his glass from the whiskey bottle. "Here's tae us. What's like us? De'il a yin!"

"And thank all the odd gods of the galaxy for *that*," she riposted.

6

THE RUN OUT to the departure position was uneventful and reasonably pleasant. It could have
been more pleasant; spacemen welcome company
aboard their ships whom they can impress with
their shop talk. But the scientists and technicians
each had their own mess and, obedient to Druthen,
kept themselves to themselves. It could have been
unpleasant, Grimes conceded, if Druthen had
forced his company upon Sonya and himself. He
was content to let well enough alone.

Meanwhile, he could and did enjoy the society
of Mayhew and Clarisse, of Billy Williams, of
young Major Dalzell, of the other officers. But
during the drink and talk sessions it was hard to
keep the conversation away from the purpose of

their expedition, from the findings and the fates of earlier expeditions.

Why had Calver been successful (if he had been successful)? Why had those before him and after him met disaster? "There's only one way to find out, Skipper," Williams had said cheerfully. "We'll just have to see what happens to *us!* And if you're around, the fat always gets pulled out of the fire somehow!"

"There has to be a first time for everything," Grimes told his second in command with grim humor. "There'll be a first time when the fat won't be pulled out of the fire."

"She'll be right," Williams told him. "Mark my words, Skipper. She'll be right."

And all of them studied the sailing directions, such as they were, until they knew them by heart. "Put Macbeth and Kinsolving's sun in line," the long dead Maudsley had told somebody. "Put Macbeth and Kinsolving's sun in line, and keep them so. That's the way that we came back. Fifty light years, and all hands choking on the stink of frying lubricating oil from the Mannschenn Drive . . ." And for fifty light years Calver had run, but with the Lead Stars in line astern. He had logged the distance, but found nothing. He had initiated a search pattern, and at last he had been successful. Those following him had not experienced the same difficulties—but each successive Ship had been fitted with an improved model of the mass proximity indicator. Calver's instrument had been no more than a prototype, capable of detection at only short ranges.

On the ship sped, running the Rim, and Carnaby checked and rechecked the fixes that he got from the Carlotti beacons set along the very edge of the galaxy. They were not very accurate fixes; the navigational aids had been positioned to assist vessels running under Mannschenn Drive from known world to known world, not a ship out where no ship, normally, had any business to be. But Carnaby was a good navigator, possessing the valuable quality of intuition. He could look at a spider's web of intersecting lines and mutter, "That can't be right." He could look at another one and say, "That could be right." Now and again he would state, "This *is* right."

He said firmly, "This *is* right."

Grimes and Williams were with him in the control room. The Commodore did not hesitate. "All right, Commander Williams," he ordered. "You know the drill."

Williams spoke into the most convenient intercom microphone. "Attention, attention. All bridge officers to Control. All hands stand by for shutdown of Mannschenn Drive, free fall and centrifugal effects." Throughout the ship the alarm bells that he had actuated were ringing.

Sonya came in, followed by Hendrikson and Daniels. Each of them went to a chair, strapped himself securely. Druthen came in, bobbing up through the hatch like some pantomime monster. His normally pale face was flushed. He sputtered, "What is the meaning of this, Commodore? We were in the middle of a most important experiment."

"And we, Doctor, are in the middle of a most important piece of navigation."

"There should have been warning."

"There was warning. Three hours ago the announcement was made that the adjustment of trajectory would be at about this time."

"Sir, we shall overrun . . ." warned Carnaby.

"Get into a chair, Druthen!" snapped Grimes.

The scientist, moving surprisingly fast for one of his build, complied, sat there glowering.

"Inertial drive—off!" Grimes ordered.

"Inertial drive—off!" repeated Williams.

The irregular throbbing slowed, ceased. There were weightlessness and loss of spacial orientation.

"Mannschenn Drive—off!"

Down in the Mannschenn Drive room the spinning, precessing gyroscopes slowed to a halt, their thin, high whine dropped to a low humming, a rumble, then was silenced. Sight and hearing were distorted; the time sense was twisted. Grimes heard Sonya whisper, "Odd, very odd. This is the first time I've seen double. Is it *me*, or is something wrong with the Drive?"

"Did you see double?" asked Carnaby, with professional interest. "*I* didn't, Commander Verrill."

She laughed shakily. "It must have been a manifestation of wishful thinking, or something. It was only my husband, the Commodore, that I saw two of. . . ." She was recovering fast. "And did you see two of *me*, John?"

"One is ample," he replied.

But he had not seen even one of her. The woman who, briefly, had occupied Sonya's seat had not been Sonya, although it was somebody who once had been as familiar to him as Sonya was now.

"I would have thought," commented Druthen, "that you people would have been accustomed by now to the psychological effects of changing rates of temporal precession."

"It's just that we haven't lost our sense of wonder, Doctor," Grimes told him.

He looked out through the viewport. The Lens was there, looking as it should look when viewed in the normal continuum, a glowing ellipsoid against the absolute blackness. Visible against the pearly mistiness were the Rim Suns, sparks upon the face of the haze. Carnaby was busy with his instruments. "Yes," he muttered, "that's Kinsolving all right. Its spectral type can't be confused with anything else . . . Macbeth must be obscured, directly in line with it . . . yes . . . ."

"Set trajectory, Mr. Carnaby?" asked Grimes.

"Yes, sir. You may set trajectory."

"Good." Grimes gave the orders decisively. *Faraway Quest* turned on her directional gyroscopes until the Kinsolving sun was directly astern. Inertial and Mannschenn Drives were restarted. She was on her way.

"I saw two of you again, John," said Sonya in a peculiarly flat voice.

Druthen laughed sneeringly.

And Grimes asked himself silently, *Why did I see her?*

7

EVER SINCE THE first ships, captains have had
their confidants. Usually this role is played by a
senior officer, but very rarely is it the second-in-
command. Ship's doctors, with their almost
priestly status, have enjoyed—and still do so
enjoy—the status of privileged listeners. But it
was not *Faraway Quest's* doctor whose company
Grimes sought when he wished to talk things out.
It was Mayhew.

Grimes sat with the psionic communications
officer in the cabin that had been put to use as the
ship's Psionic Communications Station. As a general rule PCOs used their own living quarters for
this purpose, but PCOs did not often carry their
wives with them. On this voyage Mayhew was

accompanied by Clarisse. Clarisse did not think that the psionic amplifier—the so-called "dog's brain in aspic"—was a pleasant thing to have in plain view all the time, to live with and to sleep with. So Lassie—the name by which Mayhew called his disembodied pet—was banished to a spare cabin that was little more than a dogbox anyhow.

Those wrinkled masses of cerebral tissue suspended in their transparent tanks of nutrient solution gave most people the horrors, and the Commodore was no exception. As he talked with Mayhew he was careful not to look at Lassie. It was hard, in these cramped quarters, to avoid doing so.

"We're on the last leg, Ken," he remarked.

"Yes, John."

"Have you picked anything up from anybody—or anything?"

"I've told Lassie to keep her telepathic ears skinned for any indication that the Waldegren destroyer is in the vicinity. So far—nothing."

"Mphm. Of course, she mightn't have any telepaths on board. Let's face it, Ken, you're one of the last of a dying breed."

"We aren't quite extinct, John, as well you know. Too, everybody transmits telepathically, to a greater or lesser extent. People like myself and Clarisse are, essentially, trained, selective receivers."

"I know." Grimes cleared his throat. "You must have been receiving quite a few things from the personnel of this vessel. . . ."

Mayhew laughed. "I can guess what's coming next. But, as I've told you on quite a few past occasions, I'm bound by my oath of secrecy. We just don't pry, John. If we did pry—and if it became known, as it certainly would—we'd find ourselves the most popular guests at a lynching party. And, in any case, it's not done."

"Not even when the safety of the ship is involved?"

"The old, old argument. All power corrupts, and absolute power corrupts absolutely. I'll not be a party to your corruption."

But Grimes was persistent. "Even when you're not actually prying you must pick a few things up, without trying to, without meaning to. . . ."

"Well, yes. But it's just—how shall I put it?—background noise. Here's a good analogy for you, and one that you'll understand. After all, you're the Rim Worlds' own authority on Terran sea transport from Noah's Ark to the dawn of the Space Age. Think of the early days of radio—or wireless telegraphy as it was then called. Telegraphy, not telephony. Messages tapped out in Morse code, with dots and dashes. There'd be one of the old time Sparkses on watch, his earphones clamped over his head, listening. He'd hear the crash and crackle of static; he'd hear relatively close stations booming in, and thin, mosquito voices of distant ones. But—the only one that he'd actually hear would be the one that he wanted to hear."

"Go on."

"It's like that with Clarisse and myself. We hear

41

a horrid jumble of thoughts all the time but ignore them. But if there were the faintest whisper from the Waldegren ship or from The Outsider we'd do our damnedest to read it loud and clear.''

''Yes, I see, But. . . .''

''Something's worrying you, John.''

''You don't have to be a telepath to realize that.''

Mayhew scowled. ''Unless you can convince me that the ship—or anybody aboard her—is in danger I'll not pry.''

''Not even on me?''

''With your permission I might. But what seems to be the trouble? Tell me out loud. I'll not put on my thoughtreading act unless I have to.''

''It was during the alteration of trajectory. You know as well as any of us that there are all kinds of odd psychological effects when the Mannschenn Drive is stopped or restarted.''

''Too right.''

''This time they were odder than usual. To two of us, at least. To Sonya and myself.''

''Go on.''

''Sonya . . . saw two of me. No, she wasn't seeing double. There was only one of anybody and anything else in the control room.''

''Interesting. I'd have thought that one of you would be ample. And what did you see?''

''Whom did I see, you should have said. I was looking at Sonya. But it was not Sonya whom I saw. Years ago I knew a woman called Maggie Lazenby. She was a specialist officer in the Survey Service, an ethologist, with a doctorate in that science, and commander's rank. Very similar to Sonya in appearance. She married a bloke called Mike Carshalton. He's an admiral now, I believe.''

"Local girl makes good. If she'd married you she'd only be Mrs. Commodore—and a commodore of the Reserve at that.''

"I *like* being a commodore of the Reserve. I don't think I'd like being an admiral. But—it was all rather oddish. . . .''

Mayhew laughed. "You, of all people, should be used to the odd things that happen out on the Rim. Don't tell me that you've forgotten the Wild Ghost Chase, in this very ship!''

"Hardly. It was during that when Sonya and I decided to get hitched. But I just don't like these odd things happening at this time.''

"Getting choosy in your old age.''

"Who's old? But what I'm driving at is this. There's some sort of tie-in with the Outsiders' Ship and Kinsolving's Planet. After all, this business of the Lead Stars—Macbeth and Kinsolving in line. Kinsolving—*and* Macbeth. Years ago, long before our time, there was that odd business on one of the Macbeth planets. A ship from nowhere, old, derelict. A gift horse for the colonists, who didn't look the gift horse in the mouth carefully enough. It came from nowhere and it went back to nowhere—with a few hundred men and women aboard.''

"Yes. I've read the story.''

"So . . .'' murmured Grimes softly.

"So what?''

"I was hoping you'd have some sort of a clue.''

"I only work here, John."

"But you're a sensitive."

"A selective sensitive. Do you think it would help if I . . . pried?"

"Go ahead. It's my mind."

"Then . . . relax. Just relax. Don't think of anything in particular. . . ."

Grimes tried to relax. He found that he was looking at that obscenely named animal brain in the transparent container. He tried to look elsewhere, but couldn't. And *it* was aware of him. A dim, wavering image formed in his mind—that of a large, furry dog of indeterminate breed, a friendly dog, but a timid one. What was in his mind's eye was far better than what was in his physical eye, and he was grateful for it. He saw his hand go out and down to pat, to stroke the visionary dog. He saw the plumed tail waving.

Maggie had liked dogs with a sentimentality rare in one qualified in her science. Maggie would like this dog—if she were here. But she was not. She was who knew how many light years distant, and probably very happy as an admiral's lady. But what of all the other Maggies? What of the Maggie whom he had met again, briefly, in that other universe, the doorway into which he had stumbled through on Kinsolving's Planet? How many universes were there—and how many Maggies?

He was jerked back to reality with a start.

Mayhew's voice was coldly censorious. He said, "I wish that you hadn't asked me to do this, John. It's time you realized how bloody lucky you are."

"Eh, what?"

"Lucky I said—and mean. Lucky being married to Sonya. *Her* temporal precession hallucination was just *you,* in duplicate. Yours was an old flame. You're still hankering after her."

"Some men are naturally monogamous, Ken...."

"And some, like you, are not." He laughed. ";Oh, well, it takes all sorts to make a universe. Forgive me if I sounded shocked, but I'd always thought of you and Sonya as being as close as it's possible for two nontelepaths to be. Even a mind reader can be wrong."

"Why shouldn't a man have bread *and* cake?" asked Grimes reasonably. "But the odd part is that Sonya and Maggie are as alike as two slices from the same loaf. They'd pass for sisters. Almost as twin sisters."

Mayhew allowed himself to smile. "I suppose you're in love with a type, John, rather than a person. Oh, well."

Grimes changed the subject. "And how do you find our scientific passengers? Dr. Druthen, I'm sure, regards you and Clarisse as sort of commissioned teacup readers."

"He would. But that's one mind, John, that I wouldn't care to pry into. The man just oozes bigotry. He's a second-rater, and although he'd hate to admit it, he knows it. That accounts for his attitude toward the universe in general. He has this driving ambition to be on top, no matter what the cost to other people."

"And you haven't pried?"

"No. I have not pried. But every trained tele-

45

path is something of a psychologist—not that one needs to be one to figure out what makes a man like Druthen tick.''

''Mphm.'' Slowly Grimes filled and lit his pipe. ''Well, thanks, Ken. There're one or two things I'd like to check in Control. I'll see you later.''

He let himself out of the little cabin and then, by way of the axial shaft, made his way to the control room. He chatted there for a while with Billy Williams, then went to his own quarters to join Sonya for a drink or two before dinner.

''Why are you looking at me like that?'' she asked him.

''There are times,'' he told her, ''when I realize how lucky I am.''

8

THERE WERE TIMES—rather more frequent than he cared to admit—when Grimes was lucky. This was one of them. Part of his luck, perhaps, was in having a really outstanding navigator aboard his ship. Carnaby's last captain had said of him, "He could find a black cat in a coal mine at midnight in three seconds flat." This was not far from the truth.

There had been no need whatsoever for *Faraway Quest* to run a wearisome search pattern after the fifty light year plunge outward from the Lead Stars. Carnaby had applied this course correction and that course correction, each time a matter of seconds rather than of minutes or degrees, had played a complicated game of three dimensional—or four dimensional, even—noughts and crosses in the plotting tank, had overworked the ship's computer to such an extent that Williams had said to Grimes, "If the bloody thing had a *real* brain it would go on strike!"

And then the mass proximity indicator had picked up a target just inside its one light year maximum range. Almost directly ahead it was, a tiny spark, a minute bead on the thin, glowing filament that was the extrapolated trajectory. It was time to slow down, although there was no danger of collision. Two solid bodies cannot occupy the same space at the same time—but when one of those solid bodies is proceeding under Mannschenn Drive it is in a time of its own.

Grimes took over personally as the range closed. The tiny spark in the screen slowly expanded to a globe, luminescent, with other tiny sparks in orbit about it. There could be no doubt as to what it was.

The Mannschenn Drive was shut down and *Faraway Quest* proceeded cautiously under inertial drive only, a run of about twelve hours at one G acceleration. The Commodore stayed in Control, smoking, drinking coffee, nibbling an occasional sandwich. His officers, their control room watches completed, stayed on with him. Sonya was there, of course, and so were Mayhew and Clarisse. Major Dalzell was there for most of the time, and even Druthen, uninvited, came up.

The Outsiders' Ship was within radar range now, it and the derelicts circling it. It was within radar range and it could be seen visually at last, a tiny, not very bright star in the blackness where no star had any right to be. The powerful telescope was trained on it, adjusted, and its picture glowed on the forward vision screen. It was. . . . There was only one word for it. It was fantastic. It shone with a light of its own, a cold luminosity, bright but not harsh. It was not a ship so much as a castle out of some old fairy tale, with towers and turrets, cupolas and minarets and gables and buttresses. It should have looked absurd, but it did not. It should have looked grotesque, and it did, but for all the grotesquerie it was somehow . . . right. Its proportions were the only possible proportions.

Grimes stared at the picture, the somehow frightening picture, as did the others. He felt Sonya's hand tighten on his shoulder. The very humanness of the gesture helped him, brought him back to the prosaic reality of the control room of his own ship. There were things to be done.

"Mr. Carnaby," he snapped, "let me have the elements of a stable orbit about this . . . *thing*. Mr. Hendrikson, see if you can ascertain how many derelicts there are in this vicinity. Plot their orbits."

"And have the weaponry in a state of readiness, sir?" asked Hendrikson hopefully.

"Use your tracking system for plotting those orbits," Grimes told him coldly. "It can be used for other things besides gunnery, you know."

Daniels, the radio officer, had not waited for specific orders. He was dividing his attention between the normal space time equipment and the Carlotti transceiver. He reported to Grimes: "I think there's the faintest whisper on the Carlotti, sir. I have it on broad band, but I'll try to get a bearing."

Grimes looked at the pilot antenna, at the elipsoid Mobius strip rotating about its long axis and quivering, hunting, on its universal mount. There was something there, *something*, but it didn't know quite where. He was about to get up from his chair to join Daniels at the communications equipment when, to his annoyance, Druthen remarked, "So you got us here, Commodore." The tone of his voice implied more than mild surprise.

"Yes. I got us here. Excuse me, I'm busy. . . ."

"Sir. . . ." It was the navigator.

"Yes, Mr. Carnaby?"

"All ready, sir. But we'd better not bring her in closer than a couple of miles. That *thing* has the mass of a planetoid."

"Mphm." Carnaby was exaggerating, of course. It was one of his failings. Even so . . . an artificial gravitational field? A distortion of the framework of space itself?

"Sir, I think I have something . . ." broke in Daniels.

"Commander Williams, take over the pilotage, please. Be careful not to run into any of the derelicts that Mr. Hendrikson is using for his make-believe target practice!"

"Good-oh, Skipper."

Grimes unsnapped his seat belt, strode swiftly to the vacant chair beside Daniels, buckled himself in just as the inertial drive was stopped and the ship went into free fall. He saw that the pilot antenna had stopped hunting, was now steady on a relative bearing almost dead astern of *Faraway Quest,* a bearing that slowly changed as Williams began to put the ship into her orbit.

Yes, he could hear a whisper, no more than a faint, faraway muttering, even though the volume control was turned full on. He could not distinguish the words. He did not think that the speaker was using Standard English. He regretted, as he had done before, that he was and always had been so distressingly monolingual.

"New German, I think . . ." Daniels said slowly.

"Sonya," called Grimes, "see if you can get the drift of this!"

But when she joined her husband and Daniels the set was silent again. Perhaps, thought Grimes, Mayhew might be able to pick something up. It was not necessary for him to say it aloud.

"Yes, sir," the telepath almost whispered, "there *is* something, somebody. No, it's not the Waldegren warship you're expecting. . . .It's . . . it's. . . ."

"Damn it all, Commander, who the hell is it?" demanded Grimes.

Mayhew's voice, as he replied, held reproof. "You've broken the very tenuous contact that I'd just begun to make."

"Sorry. But do your best, Commander Mayhew."

"I'm . . . trying. . . ."

"Orbit established, Skipper," reported Williams.

"No dangerous approach to any of the other

orbits, sir," reported Carnaby and Hendrikson, speaking as one.

"Yes, yes. Commander Mayhew?"

"I'm trying . . . to try." Mayhew's expression was both very faraway and more than a little pained. "But . . . so much interference. There's somebody we know . . . and there are strangers. . . ."

"Are they in these derelicts? Aboard The Outsider?"

"No, sir. If they were close, I should know. But they are distant still. But please, please try not to interrupt any more. . . ."

"Let him go into his trance and get on with the clairvoyance," sneered Druthen.

"Shut up, Doctor! Do you want to be ordered out of Control?" snarled Grimes.

The scientist subsided.

"Please . . ." pleaded Mayhew.

Then there was silence in the control room, broken only by the sibilant whisperings of such machines as, with the ship now in free falling orbit, were still in operation. The soughing of fans, the whining of generators, the very occasional sharp click of a relay. . . .

"Metzenther . . ." muttered Mayhew.

Grimes and Sonya exchanged glances. They were the only two, apart from the psionic communications officer, to whom the name meant anything.

"Trialanne. . . ." He was vocalizing his thoughts for Grimes' benefit. "Metzenther, Trialanne. . . . Where are you bound?" He seemed to find the answer amusing. "No, *we* haven't any company yet, apart from a half dozen or so derelict ships. . . . Be seeing you. . . . Or shall we . . .? *I* wouldn't know, I'm not a physicist or a mathematician. . . . And can *you* pick up anybody else . . .? We think we heard a Waldegren ship on our Carlotti. . . . And *I* got the faintest mutter from somebody else. . . . No, not a telepath, just unconscious broadcasting. . . . A servant of some empire or other. . . . Not *yours,* by any chance . . . ? No . . .?"

"And are we to have the pleasure of meeting that big, blonde cow again?" demanded Sonya coldly.

"She was quite attractive, in a hefty sort of way," Grimes told her.

"You *would* think so."

Mayhew grinned. "I rather think, Commander Verrill, that we shall shortly experience the pleasure of renewing our acquaintance with the ex-Empress Irene, and Captain Trafford, and all the rest of *Wanderer's* people."

"But they're on a different time track," said Sonya. "And thank all the odd gods of the galaxy for that!"

"Mphm," grunted Grimes. "Mphm." He gestured toward the viewport through which the Outsiders' Ship was clearly visible. "But here, I think, is where all the time tracks converge."

"I hope you're wrong," said Sonya. "I hope you're wrong. But I'm rather afraid that you're not."

"He's not," confirmed Mayhew.

9

"MPHM." GRIMES MADE a major production of filling and lighting his foul pipe. "How long before your odd friends get here, Commander Mayhew?"

"*My* friends, sir?"

"Yes. Your friends. Metzenther and his everloving. You telepaths always seem to stick together." Grimes grinned. "Frankly, I regarded that ex-Empress woman and her bunch of Imperial Navy throwouts as a pain in the arse. . . ."

Mayhew grinned back. "They thought about you and Commander Verrill in rather the same way."

"Good. But when do they get here?"

The psionic communications officer shut his eyes, concentrated. He said slowly, "In about three hours fifteen minutes Standard.''

''That gives us time . . . Commander Williams, I think you'll find one or two Confederate ensigns in the flag locker. You'll want one with wire stiffening, and a pole with a magnetic base. We'll plant our colors on the . . . The Outsider. I doubt if the legality of the claim will be recognized in a court of interstellar law, but it will give us some sort of talking point.

''Meanwhile, probably quite a few of you are wondering what this is all about. *You* know, Commander Williams, and Mayhew knows, but none of the rest of you will have heard the full story. It'll be as well if I put you in the picture.'' He turned to Williams. ''You'd better get your flag planting under way, Commander, just in case Mayhew's ETA is out. And could you lend Commander Williams a couple or three hands for the job, Major Dalzell? And Mr. Daniels, I shall want everything I say put through on the intercom. Thank you.''

Williams and Dalzell left the control room. Grimes cleared his throat. He said into the microphone that Daniels handed him, ''Attention, all hands. Attention, all hands. This is important. You will all have seen, in the public information screens, our objective, the Outsiders' Ship. Most of you will have realized that we are now in orbit about it. Shortly you will see a landing party jetting off from this vessel toward The Outsider. They will be planting a flag on it. The reason for this is that we shall soon be having company. This will not be the Waldegren warship that we have been expecting—although she, probably, will be along before very long.''

"A few years ago," Grimes continued, "I was instructed to take *Faraway Quest* out to investigate some strange, drifting wreckage—wreckage that, obviously, had not originated in *this* universe. It was the remains of a lifeboat that had belonged to a ship called *Star Scout,* and this *Star Scout* had been a unit of the Imperial Navy. The only empire that *we* know is the Empire of Waverley, and its navy is officially called the Imperial Jacobean Navy. So. . . ."

"So we were stooging around, trying to find a few further clues, when this ship, quite literally, appeared from nowhere. Her name was *Wanderer.* She was quite heavily armed, the equivalent to one of our destroyers, but she was privately owned. She had been the yacht of the Empress Irene. She was still owned by the ex-Empress Irene, who was married to her Captain. She carried only a small crew—this Irene woman was mate, as well as owner; a Mr. Tallentire, who had been a gunnery officer in the Imperial Navy was second mate, and his wife, Susanna, had been lady-in-waiting to the Empress, and was now radio-officer-cum-purser. The psionic communications officer was—and still is—a Mr. Metzenther, almost the double of *our* Commander Mayhew. This Metzenther had—has—an Iralian wife called Trialanne. We don't have any Iralians on this time track. They were all wiped out by a plague. Bronheim was the engineer. He, too, had an Iralian wife— Denelleen. . . ."

"Not now he doesn't," Mayhew said soberly. "I've been catching up on past history with Metzenther. Do you mind if I take over, sir?"

"Go ahead, Commander."

"Mayhew speaking. As you all will, by this time, have gathered, I am in psionic touch with the yacht *Wanderer*. She was thrown, somehow, onto this time track when she attempted the passage of the Horsehead Nebula. She was pursued by two New Iralian cruisers—the New Iralians being insurgents. She was carrying Iralian passengers, some of whom were in sympathy with the rebels. With our help she shook off pursuit, and then tried to get back into her own universe by running back through the Nebula. She was overtaken, but came out on top in the running fight. But the rebels among the passengers tried to take over the ship. Denelleen was one of them. . . . Anyhow, the mutineers were defeated. And that's about all."

"That was *then*," said Grimes. "What are these people doing here *now*?"

"You may remember, sir," Mayhew told him, "that when we last met them they were on charter to an organization called GLASS—Galactic League Against Supression and Slavery. They're still on charter to GLASS. GLASS has the idea that the science and technology in the Outsiders' Ship will be useful to them in their work."

"So *they*: the ex-Empress, GLASS and all the rest of 'em have an Outsiders' Ship in *their* universe. So—as I've already guessed—it's not a different one, but the same one as we have. So the time tracks meet and mingle right here." The Commodore laughed. "Who else shall we meet, I wonder. . . ."

Sonya said flatly, "Williams has planted the flag."

"And so we, more or less legally, own *it*," said Grimes. He added softly, "Unless *it* owns us."

"Rubbish!" sneered Druthen.

Grimes ignored the man.

10

"I JUST MIGHT," suggested Daniels diffidently, "be able to establish Carlotti contact with *Wanderer*. I think that the time tracks will almost have converged by now."

"Mphm," grunted Grimes, giving thought to the possibility. Technologically his universe and the universe of the ex-Empress Irene were almost twins. At the time of his previous encounter with the so-called yacht she had possessed Carlotti equipment almost identical to his own. "Mphm." Then, "No, Mr. Daniels. Concentrate on that Waldegren destroyer. She's our main worry." He looked out through the view port and was relieved to see that Williams and the two marines, silvery figures trailing luminous blue exhausts, were almost back to the ship.

"Looks like being quite a party," commented Sonya. "The big, fat blonde, Irene, with her playmates, *and* our dear friends from Waldegren. . . ."

"No friends of mine," growled Grimes. "I was at the Battle of Dartura. . . . Remember?"

"Long before my time, dearie," she commented.

"Commodore! Sir!" broke in Carnaby. "A target, on the radar!"

"Not one of the derelicts, Mr. Carnaby?"

"No. It just appeared out of nothingness. It's closing on us, fast."

"Mr. Hendrikson—all weapons to bear. Do not open fire without orders. Mr. Daniels, try to establish contact. Commander Mayhew—is it *Wanderer*?"

"No, sir."

"Then who the hell . . . or *what* the hell . . . ?"

"Locked on, sir," reported Hendrikson.

"Good."

"Range still closing, but less rapidly. We should have her visually in a few seconds." said Carnaby.

"Thank you. Commander Williams, the telescope."

"Aye, aye, Skipper!"

"No contact, sir," murmured Daniels. "But I *can* hear the Waldegren ship again. She's still distant."

"I've got her in the telescope," drawled Williams. "Odd looking bitch . . . she's on the screen now, if you care to take a butcher's."

Grimes took a "butcher's hook," reflecting that

life was already sufficiently complicated without his second-in-command's rhyming slang. The strange ship was there, exactly in the center of the circle of blackness, a silver moth pinned against the backdrop of the night. As she approached, her image expanded rapidly. She was a gleaming disc—but, Grimes realized, he was looking at her head on—from which sprouted a complexity of antennae. And then, slowly, she turned, presenting her profile. Apart from that veritable forest of metallic rods she was not unlike the Survey Service courier that had been Grimes' first command long ago, so very long ago, one of the so-called "flying darning needles." As yet she had made no hostile move. But, assuming that she was alien, captained by a nonhuman or, even, by a nonhumanoid, would a hostile move be recognized as such before it was too late?

Grimes flashed a glance at Hendrikson, hushed intently over his console. *He* was ready; possibly rather too ready. He looked back at the screen. He thought, he was almost sure, that the lines of the strange vessel showed a human sense of proportion. He snapped at Daniels, "Haven't you raised her yet?"

"I'm . . . I'm trying sir. I've tried every frequency known to civilized Man, and a few that aren't . . . Ah! Got it!"

There was a babble of sound from the speaker of the NST transceiver. Alien gibberings? No. . . . It sounded more like human speech, but horridly distorted, garbled.

Daniels spoke very slowly and distinctly into his

microphone. "Rim Worlds Confederacy's cruiser *Faraway Quest* to unknown vessel. *Faraway Quest* to unknown vessel. Come in, please. Come in, please. Over."

In reply came the meaningless gabble.

Daniels was patient, carefully adjusting his tuning. "*Faraway Quest* to unknown vessel. Please identify yourself. Please identify yourself. Over."

"A shi? A shi?"

What ship? What ship? It could be, thought Grimes.

"A shi? A shi? Dringle na puss. Gleeble."

Tickle my puss? Hardly.

"We'll try visual," said Grimes. "Pass me the key, will you? I don't think that my Morse is too rusty."

Williams passed him the Morse key on its long lead. Grimes took it in his right hand, his thumb on the button. He sent a series of "A"s, the general calling sign. He assumed that somebody, by this time, would have the *Quest's* big searchlight trained on the stranger. He kept his attention on the image in the telescope screen.

Yes, he, whoever (or whatever) he was seemed to know Morse. The acknowledgment, the long flash, the Morse "T," was almost blindingly obvious.

"What ship?" sent Grimes. "What ship?"

From the other came a succession of "A"s. Grimes replied with "T". Then, "What ship?" he read. "What ship?"

So . . . so was the stranger repeating parrot fashion, or was he being cagey?

"What ship?" sent Grimes again. "What ship?"

"What ship?" he received.

He sent, not too slowly but carefully, making sure that each word was acknowledged, "Identify yourself, or I open fire."

He grinned when the reply came, "You'd better not."

He said aloud, "Not only human, but our sort of people." He flashed, "This is the Rim Worlds Confederacy's cruiser *Faraway Quest*. You are intruding into our sector of space. Please identify yourself."

"Imperial Navy's armed scout *Vindictive*. Rim Worlds Confederacy's Navy not listed in Jane's. Never heard of Rim Worlds Confederacy. Who the hell are you?"

"Commander Williams," said Grimes, "*Jane's Fighting Ships* is in the computer's library bank. Check *Vindictive*, will you? And the Imperial Navy."

"Will do, Skipper. But the only Imperial Navy *we* have is the Waverley one."

"I know. But check it, anyhow." Again his thumb worked rhythmically on the key. "This is *Faraway Quest*. This is Rim Worlds space. You are intruding."

"You are intruding."

Grimes grinned again, sent, "Can't we talk this over?"

For long seconds there was no reply. Carnaby reported that the stranger was no longer closing the range, was maintaining her distance. Hendrikson announced, unnecessarily, that his weaponry was still in a state of readiness.

Daniels asked, "Can I have the key, sir? If I have a yarn with her radio officer I shall be able to find out what frequencies to use. . . ."

And then *Vindictive* started flashing again. "Request permission to board."

"One man only," Grimes replied.

More time passed. Then, "Please prepare to receive my boat."

Oh, no, thought Grimes. *Oh, no.* The dividing line between a boat and a torpedo is a very narrow one. He was satisfied by now that *Vindictive's* people were humans; but the human race has a long record of viciousness and treachery, far too often actuated by the very highest motives.

"One man in a suit," he sent, "will meet one man in a suit, midway between our two vessels. They will return to *Faraway Quest* together. You may close the range between ships to ten miles. Do not forget that all my weapons are trained on you, and that my gunnery officer has a very itchy trigger finger." He said aloud, "And I have a very sore thumb."

"Agreed," sent *Vindictive* at last. "Closing. Please remember that you are a big target."

"Commander Mayhew," asked the Commodore, "can you pick up anything, anything at all, from those people?"

"Faintly . . ." replied the telepath slowly. "Very faintly. I sense suspicion, distrust. They will fire if they think that they are about to be fired upon."

"And so will we. And now—who's for the space walk? Don't all answer at once."

66

There was no shortage of volunteers, but Mayhew's rather high voice was distinctly heard above the others. "There's only one possible choice, sir. Me. When I get close to whoever *they* send I should be able to read his thoughts more easily. And Clarisse can look after the shop in my absence."

"Mphm. Very well, Ken. Get suited up. And— look after yourself."

"I always have done, John, all the years that you've known me." He said nothing to Clarisse, but it was not necessary. Accompanied by Williams he left the control room.

"Please let me know when you are ready," flashed *Vindictive*.

"Willco," replied Grimes.

11

"I SUPPOSE THAT it has occurred to you," said Sonya, "that this *Vindictive,* of which no mention is made in *our* version of *Jane's Fighting Ships,* could be from that Irene woman's universe. After all, she is supposed to be a unit of the Imperial Navy."

"The thought had flickered across my mind," admitted Grimes, "even though I'm not, and never have been, an intelligence officer." In spite of the absence of gravity he contrived to lay back in his chair. "We rather gathered, the last—and the only, so far—time that we met the ex-Empress that her employers, these GLASS people, were regarded by the Imperial Government as more than somewhat of a nuisance. Shit stirrers, if you'll pardon the expression."

"I've heard worse. Continue."

"So it is reasonable to suppose that if GLASS want to get their paws on The Outsider and The Outsider's secrets, the Imperial Navy could be sent out to make sure that they didn't. But. . . ."

"What is your 'but'?"

"But I don't think that *Vindictive* was built by the same technology as Irene's *Wanderer*. *Wanderer*, like *Faraway Quest*, had all sorts of odd lumps and bumps on her hull, but she didn't look like a deep space hedgehog. Too, neither *Wanderer* nor ourselves experienced any trouble in initiating either Carlotti or NST radio telephone hookups."

"H'm. I suppose we could get Clarisse to ask that man Metzenther, aboard *Wanderer*, if they're being followed. Not that you can call it being followed when the pursuer gets there hours before the pursued."

"That, my dear, is very sound tactics, when you can manage it."

Williams' voice came over the intercom. "Commander Mayhew suited up an' in the after airlock."

Then, over the transceiver that was operating on the suit frequencies, Mayhew reported, "All ready, sir."

Grimes flashed the signal to *Vindictive*, read the reply, "The Captain is on his way."

"A do-it-yourself-trust-nobody type," commented the Commodore. "Tell Commander Mayhew to shove off."

He felt a slight twinge of anxiety—but, after all, Mayhew was a spaceman as well as a telepath, and

Williams would have given him a thorough briefing. It would be simple enough; just switch on the suit's reaction unit and steer straight for the other ship, keeping eyes skinned for the blinker that would be flashing from *Vindictive's* captain's helmet. But did this peculiar Empire in some peculiar universe observe the same rules of spacemanship as were observed in Grimes' continuum?

Obviously it did. All the lights of *Vindictive* went out, as had all the lights showing from *Faraway Quest*. This would make it easier for the spacewalkers; each of them now would see only the little, but bright beacon toward which he was steering.

Carnaby had the radar on short range, was tracking both space suited men. He was speaking into the microphone of the transceiver. "That's fine, Commander. Steady. . . . Steady as you go . . . . Better shut off your propulsion. . . . Be ready for a retro-blast. . . ."

Grimes, staring through the viewport, could see the two blinking lights almost as one, so nearly in line were they. Surely Mayhew hadn't much further to go. . . .

"Brake, Commander," came Carnaby's voice. "Brake! Yes, he's braking too. Now . . . just a nudge ahead . . . that's it!"

And from the transceiver's speaker came Mayhew's whisper. "Contact. Contact established. He's tough, Commodore. Hard to get inside. . . . But . . . I can assure you that he intends no treachery."

Grimes took the microphone. "Does he know

that you're . . . prying?"

"I don't think so."

"Can he hear you? Me?"

"No, sir. I'm careful that our helmets don't come into contact."

"Good. Go through the motions of searching him for any weapons that he may have outside his suit. Then you can touch helmets and talk to him."

"Very good, sir."

There was a silence that seemed to drag on and on. At last Mayhew said, "Be ready to receive us on board, Commodore."

Williams called up from the after airlock to say that Mayhew and the man from *Vindictive* were aboard, and that he was bringing them up to Control. Grimes found himself wondering what his visitor would be like. He was an officer in the armed forces of an empire—and Empire sounded far more glamorous than Federation or Confederacy. *He's probably got a title,* thought Grimes idly, *and a string of letters after his name half a light year long.* He glanced around his control room, missing nothing. All of his officers were in correct uniform, although some of them were more than a little untidy in appearance. Druthen, of course, was his usual slovenly self—but he was a mere civilian, a passenger.

Williams came up through the hatch. "Commander Mayhew, Skipper," he announced cheerfully. Mayhew, still suited up but carrying his helmet under his left arm, followed Williams. "And Captain Sir Dominic Flandry, of the Imperial Navy. Sir Dominic, may I present Commodore

John Grimes, of the Rim Worlds Naval Reserve?'' Commander Williams was plainly enjoying himself.

Grimes looked at Flandry. He was not at all sure if he liked what he saw. The Captain of *Vindictive* was a tall man, and conveyed the impression of slimness even in his bulky spacesuit. The suit itself was gleaming black with gold trimmings. The helmet that Flandry carried tucked under his arm was also black, with a wreath of golden oak leaves on its visor, with, as an ornate badge, a golden eagle with outspread wings gripping a conventionalized planetary globe in its talons. His face was harsh, with a fierce beak of a nose, and the pencil line black moustache over the sensual mouth should have looked foppish—but somehow didn't. The glossy black hair was touched with gray at the temples. The eyes were a pale blue, and very bleak.

''Your servant, Commodore,'' said Flandry stiffly.

That'll be the sunny Friday when you're any man's servant, thought Grimes. He said, ''Good to have you aboard, Captain. Or should I say, 'Sir Dominic'?''

''Either will do, Commodore.'' Flandry's sharp eyes were flickering around the control room, missing nothing, missing nobody. They lingered for a few seconds on Clarisse—and for longer on Sonya. *Of course,* thought Grimes, *she would be wearing that indecent micro-skirted Federation uniform.* Flandry said, ''You carry a mixed crew, Commodore.''

"Mphm. Yes. Although the ladies are specialist officers. Mrs. Mayhew. . . ." Clarisse unbuckled herself from her chair, came forward. "This is Captain Flandry, of *Vindictive*. Captain Flandry, this is Mrs. Mayhew, our assistant psionic communications officer . . ."

"Psionic communications? A telepath . . . and I take it that Commander Mayhew, whom you sent out to meet me, is your chief psionic communications officer. . . ."

He looked at Clarisse again, and suddenly she flushed. Flandry laughed. "Sorry," he said. "Sorry, my dear. I should have had the sense to keep my thoughts under proper control." But he did not sound sorry, and Clarisse, although embarrassed, did not look at all resentful.

"And this is Commander Verrill, of the Federation's Survey Service. She is acting as the Federation's observer on this expedition."

"And not a telepath, I take it," murmured Flandry. He looked as though he were undressing Sonya with his eyes—not that she needed much undressing, thought Grimes, in that apology for a uniform. And he did not like the way that she was looking back at the Imperial captain.

Grimes introduced his other officers, and then Druthen. He said, "And now, Sir Dominic, I suggest that we withdraw to my quarters for discussion. Commander Williams, please accompany us. Commander Mayhew, Mr. Daniels—please let me know at once if either of you hear anything further from *Wanderer* or Adler."

"*Wanderer*?" asked Flandry, with a lift of one eyebrow.

"One of yours, possibly. She's the private yacht of the ex-Empress Irene."

"Then *not* one of ours," laughed the other. "We don't have an empress. We never have had an empress. I, sir, have the honor . . ." and he made it sound a dubious honor . . . "of serving His Imperial Majesty Edouard XIV. And this *Adler*?"

"A destroyer sailing under the flag of the Duchy of Waldegren."

"The Duchy of Waldegren? Never heard of it."

The officers were looking at Grimes and his visitor curiously. The Commodore decided that they had better continue their discussion in greater privacy. He said, "This way, please, Sir Dominic."

On the way to his suite he noticed that Flandry did not handle himself very well in free fall. So, probably, *Vindictive* ran to some sort of artificial gravity, and when in orbit her officers did not have to cope with the problems of weightlessness. He decided to get one of his engineers aboard the armed scout if it were at all possible. There must be quite a few technologies aboard her well worth copying.

The sliding door opened as Grimes approached it. He stood to one side, waving the others into his day cabin ahead of him. Flandry moved clumsily, shuffling his feet, in their magnetically soled boots, on the deck.

Grimes said, "This is Liberty Hall. You can spit on the mat and call the cat a bastard."

Sonya looked at him coldly. "This is the first time I've heard you say that for quite some time, John. I'd hoped you'd forgotten it."

Flandry flashed her a smile. "It *is* a vivid figure of speech, Commander Verrill. Have you known the Commodore for a long time?"

"Yes. I'm married to him."

"Commodore Grimes, have you any *unmarried* ladies among your crew as attractive as the two ladies I have already met?"

"No, I haven't." Then, in a less surly tone of voice, "Sit down, Captain. And perhaps you will take a drink with us. . . ."

"I'll be glad of the drink—but this suit's not made for sitting in. And when in a strange ship, quite possibly a hostile ship, I prefer to keep it on."

"As you please, Captain Flandry. And you'll have to take my word for it that the drinks aren't drugged or poisoned." Grimes pulled himself into his own chair, strapped himself in. Sonya followed suit. Williams was about to do likewise when Grimes told him to look after the refreshments. Efficiently the Commander produced bulbs of the drink required. Flandry asked for Scotch.

"Your health, Captain Sir Dominic!"

"Your health, Commodore Grimes." Again there was that sardonic smile. "But should I, as a loyal servant of His Imperial Majesty, be drinking your health?"

"And why the hell shouldn't you be?" demanded Grimes crustily.

"And why should I, Commodore—if you *are* a commodore. Oh, I'll let you have your rank. Even pirates must have officers."

"Pirates? What the hell are you getting at?"

"Pirates." Flandry's voice was harsh. "Pirates, setting themselves up as petty kings on the fringes of a disintegrating Empire. Laying their grubby paws on Imperial property, even planting their absurd flag on it. Tell me, Commodore Grimes, what genius thought up that black banner with a golden wheel on it? What does it signify?"

Grimes didn't answer the question directly. He snapped. "*Imperial* property? I suppose you're referring to that heap of alien ironmongery that somebody left in *our* back yard. The Outsiders' Ship, as we call it, lies within Rim Worlds' territorial space."

"Does it? And who, or what, are the Rim Worlds? The Outsider, as we call it, was first discovered by Admiral Lord Wolverhelm, who commanded the *Fringe Sweep*."

Grimes eyed Flandry cautiously. He thought, *The bastard's enjoying himself. He's trying to make us lose our tempers.* He said, "Neither the Federation nor the Confederacy runs to 'sirs' and 'lords.' The Empire of Waverley does, of course—but it would never dream of sending an expedition out here without our permission."

"Odd name for a ship—the *Fringe Sweep* . . ." commented Williams.

"That, sir, was the designation of the mission," Flandry told him coldly.

"In any case," put in Sonya, who had been silent for too long, "the Outsiders' Ship was first discovered by Commander Maudsley of the Federation's Survey Service. But the Federation recognizes the territorial rights of the Confederacy."

"Somebody," grinned Flandry, "is going to have a good laugh over this conversation." He lifted a gloved hand to tap the collar of his suit, just below the throat. Grimes thought with no surprise, *A concealed microphone.* "In the unlikely event of my not getting back to my ship, all that's being said is being recorded aboard *Vindictive*. It is also being relayed to our nearest base. My masters will already have come to the conclusion that I have blundered into a nest of pirates. . . ."

"Watch it, mate," growled Williams. "Watch it!"

In a blur of motion Flandry snapped on his helmet. His voice, only slightly distorted, issued from a diaphragm. He said, "This suit, gentlemen—and Commander Verrill—is proof against anything that you can throw at me. Probably I should not survive a nuclear blast—but neither would you. And now, if you will excuse me, I must return to my own vessel. I strongly advise that nobody try to stop me."

Grimes said dryly, "As I recollect it, Captain, the main purpose of this meeting was that we should talk things over. I suppose that you can hear what I'm saying inside that gaudy carapace of yours."

"Of course. Say what you must say."

"Well, Captain Flandry, we haven't talked things over. You've jumped to conclusions, assumed that I'm a pirate king or some such. If I were, I'd not be content with the rank of commodore! It's a wonder that you didn't see that wheel of ours on the black flag as a skull and crossbones! Just try to understand this. As far as *we* are concerned, *you* are the intruder.''

"And how can that be, Commodore?''

"Been out on the Rim before, Captain Flandry? Or the Fringe, as you people call it?''

"Nobody comes out here but outlaws.''

"And yourself, of course. And that Admiral Lord what's-his-name before you. But we live on the Rim. We *know* that here, at the very edge of the expanding universe, the walls between the alternate time tracks are very thin indeed, at times nonexistent. We have good reason to believe that the Outsiders' Ship has warped the continuum about itself so that this small volume of space is common ground for ships—and people—from all the universes. . . .''

"You tell a good fairy story, Commodore.''

The intercom buzzed sharply; then Carnaby's voice came through the speaker. "Commodore, sir. *Wanderer* has just broken through! And Mr. Daniels thinks that *Adler* is very close. She is reporting back to her base in some sort of code.''

"Reinforcements, Commodore Grimes?'' asked Flandry coldly.

Briefly Grimes was tempted to say yes. But that could have been dangerous. This Flandry, feeling himself to be outnumbered, would be quite capable of ordering his ship to lash out with all weapons like a vicious cornered animal. "No,'' he said slowly. "No. Just old friends—or acquaintances, rather—and old enemies.''

"Commodore, sir!'' It was Carnaby again. "Mr. Daniels says there's *another* ship using a Carlotti transmitter!''

"Cor stone me Aunt Fanny up a gum tree!''

marveled Williams. "How many *more* are goin' to turn up at the Vicar's flamin' afternoon tea party?"

"So," said Flandry, "we seem to have met at the crossroads of the universe. If you are to be believed, that is. . . . But I think you will agree that I should return to my own vessel."

"If I were in your shoes I should be saying the same," agreed Grimes. "Commander Williams, escort Captain Flandry to the airlock."

"And how shall I keep in touch—assuming, of course, that I wish to do so? By flashing lamp?"

"Get your radio officer to talk to mine on the blinker. Perhaps, between the pair of them, they'll be able to cook something up."

"I'll tell him now." Grimes could see, through the frontal transparency of Flandry's helmet, the man's lips moving, but he could hear nothing. Then: "Before I go, just one more question. These people in *Wanderer* . . . are they friendly or hostile?"

"They could be either. And, to save you the trouble of asking another question, I haven't a clue as to who or what this other strange ship is."

"If this is the Rim," said Flandry, "you're welcome to it." He bowed stiffly to Sonya. "Although life out here seems to have its compensations."

Then he followed Williams out to the axial shaft.

12

GRIMES AND SONYA hurried back to the control room.

As Carnaby had told him, *Wanderer* had arrived. She was hanging there in the blackness, slim, sleek and deadly looking, no more than a couple of cables from *Faraway Quest*. Typical, thought Grimes, of Irene Trafford or the ex-Empress Irene or whatever she called herself these days. But the Commodore, over the years, had become more of a merchant officer than a naval officer in his outlook and just could not see the point of exposing a vessel, any vessel, to unnecessary hazard.

Anyhow, there she was, and close, too close. Grimes thought of actuating his inertial drive to put more distance between himself and the armed yacht—but, damn it all, he was here first. Why should he shift?

The screen of the NST transceiver glowed into life. Colors swirled, coalesced; and then Grimes was looking into the control room of the other ship. Yes, there was Irene, big and brassy as ever, with the careful touch of nonuniform color, the crimson cravat with the white polka dots, added to her otherwise correct attire. Before she became empress, she had been a tough mate in the Dog Star Line, and this outfit, in Grimes' universe as well as in hers, was notorious for its rough and ready star tramps. She had been mate in the Dog Star Line, and was determined that nobody should ever be allowed to forget it. Beside her sat Benjamin Trafford, officially master of *Wanderer*. The little, wiry, sandy-haired man was as neat and correct as he would have been had he still been serving in the Imperial Navy. And behind them Grimes saw the dark, dapper Tallentire, alert at his fire control console; and with him was Susanna: tall, slender and with high-piled and glossy auburn hair. There was Metzenther who, if he shaved off his beard, would be almost the double of Grimes' Mayhew. There was Trialanne, the Iralian woman: frail, willowy, beautiful, looking as though she had been blown from translucent glass by a master craftsman who was also a superb artist.

And there was a stranger, a most undistinguished looking man of medium height, dressed in a drab, gray coverall suit. Normally one would not look at him twice. But in *Wanderer's* control room he was a sparrow among hawks and drew attention. Grimes decided suddenly, *He's hard and dangerous, whoever he is.* . . .

"Commodore Grimes," said Irene in the voice that was almost a baritone.

"Your servant, ma'am," replied Grimes politely—after all, she had been an empress—while, behind him, Sonya snorted inelegantly.

"Come off it, Commodore. Nature never intended you to be a courtier."

"You can say that again," remarked Sonya quietly.

"Commodore Grimes, may I ask what the hell you and your spaceborne junk heap are doing in *our* universe?"

"I might ask the same question of you, Mrs. Trafford."

"Just because I jumped time tracks once—and that accidentally—you needn't think that I make a habit of it."

"Neither do I," said Grimes flatly. This was not quite true, but Irene and her people would not know this.

"And what's that odd looking ship like a tin sea urchin? You must know. We saw a man in a spacesuit jetting off from your vessel to her."

"One of yours, isn't she? Her captain says that she's the Imperial Navy's armed scout *Vindictive*."

"*Not* one of ours," said Trafford firmly. "We *do* have a *Vindictive*, Commodore, but she's a light cruiser. I should know. I've served in her."

"Irene," asked that drab, too ordinary man in a voice that matched his appearance, "would you mind putting me in the picture? Who *are* these people?"

"Mr. Smith," said the big blonde, "allow me to present Commodore Grimes, of the Rim Worlds Naval Reserve. In *his* cockeyed continuum the Rim Worlds are self-governing. And Commander Sonya Verrill, who is also Mrs. Grimes, of the Federation's Survey Service. Their Federation is roughly analogous to our Empire. The only other person I know is Mr. Mayhew, who is *Faraway Quest's* psionic communications officer.

"And this gentleman, Commodore, is Mr. Smith, managing director of GLASS. We have been chartered by him to lay claim to and to investigate the Outsiders' Ship."

"The Outsiders' Ship," Grimes told her firmly, "is in the territorial space of the Rim Worlds Confederacy. Furthermore, we have planted our flag on it."

"According to Space Law," stated Irene, "the mere planting of a flag is not sufficient for laying claim to any planet, planetoid, satellite or whatever. For a claim to be valid a self-sustaining colony must be established. I doubt very much if you have gone so far as that. In any case, the Outsiders' Ship is within Imperial territorial space."

"And *which* Empire, madam?" demanded a sardonic voice.

Daniels whispered, "I've managed a hookup with *Vindictive,* sir. That was Captain Flandry."

"Who the hell was that?" demanded Irene.

"The captain of *Vindictive*," Grimes replied. "But let us continue our discussion of the finer points of Space Law. As I see it, that *thing* is neither a planet, a planetoid nor a satellite. It is a derelict. . . ."

"It could be held to be a satellite," insisted Irene. "An artificial satellite. . . ."

"A satellite must have a primary."

"Oh, all right, you bloody space lawyer. It's a derelict. But have you put a prize crew on board? Have you got a towline fast to it?"

"My flag. . . ."

"You know what you can do with that!"

In the little screen Trafford looked both shocked and embarrassed. Tallentire tried to hide a grin. Smith did not try to hide his.

"Mphm," grunted Grimes disapprovingly; and, "What charming friends you have, Commodore," commented Flandry.

"Acquaintances, Captain," Grimes told him.

"As you wish. But might I suggest, sir, that all three parties convene to discuss matters in a *civilized* fashion?"

"That could be worth considering," admitted Grimes reluctantly.

"And might I urge that we do it as soon as possible, if not before? As yet our three ships haven't opened fire on each other—but who knows what might happen when the other two vessels in the vicinity put in an appearance?"

"He's talking sense," said Sonya.

"*What* other two vessels?" demanded Irene. "We only know of the Waldegren destroyer, *Adler*. Who is the other one?"

"I wish I knew," sighed Grimes.

"Well, Commodore?" snapped Flandry. Grimes was sorry that Daniels had not been able to arrange a visual as well as an audio hookup. He would have liked to have been able to read the other's expression.

"Well, Commodore?" echoed Irene.

"Your place or mine?" asked Grimes, with an attempt at humor.

"Neutral territory," said Flandry. "While all the nattering was going on my first lieutenant sent a boarding party to that odd, dome-shaped derelict about 10 kilometers beyond *Vindictive* from your viewpoint. Its late owners were oxygen breathers, although not human. All its life-support systems were intact, and are now functioning. . . ."

"A Shaara ship," stated Grimes.

"The *Shaara*?" asked Irene and Flandry simultaneously. And then Flandry demanded, "And who the hell are they when they're up and dressed?"

"Never mind," said Grimes. "The Shaara ship will do very nicely."

13

THE SHAARA DERELICT was a good place for a meeting. The ship was in good order and condition; her interior lighting glowed brightly; her humming fans kept the clean, untainted air in circulation. How long had they been doing so? Not for too long. The mosslike growth in the hydroponics tanks that the Shaara used for atmospheric regeneration was neither running wild nor withering for lack of the organic wastes that were its food. But of her crew: of the Queen-Captain, the Princess-Officers, the Drones, the Workers, there was no sign—not even so much as a dry exoskeleton. The logbook was still on its ledge in the control room; but no human could hope to read that straggling script.

She was a latter day *Mary Celeste*. She was one of several *Mary Celestes* in orbit about The Outsider.

Boats from the three ships had rendezvoused at the airlock of the derelict. Grimes himself had piloted *Faraway Quest's* pinnace. With him he had Sonya and Mayhew. Irene had brought with her Trialanne and Stanley Smith, the man from GLASS. Flandry was accompainied only by a simian young officer, almost as broad as he was tall, whom he introduced as Ensign Bugolsky.

This, of course, was when they were all assembled in the Shaara ship's control room, standing among the equipment and instruments, some familiar (although modified to suit arthropodal claws instead of human hands) and some weirdly alien. There were cradles of flimsy-looking webbing but no seats. As the vessel was in free fall, to stand was no hardship.

Flandry, resplendent in his black and gold space armor, removed his helmet. The others removed theirs. Grimes didn't like the way that the man looked at Irene and Trialanne. He most certainly didn't like the way that the man looked at Sonya. And he disapproved most strongly of the way in which the three women looked at Flandry. Mental undressing can be a two-way process.

"And now," announced Flandry with a wide grin, "I declare this meeting open."

"Not so fast, Captain," Grimes told him. "As the senior officer present I feel that that should be my privilege."

"Senior officer? But *I* represent the Imperium."

"*What* Imperium?" demanded Irene nastily.

"Commodore!" Mayhew's usually soft voice was sharp with urgency. "Commodore! Sir!"

Grimes waved him aside. "Later, Commander Mayhew—unless my ship's in danger. She's not? Good. Then let's get this business settled first." He turned to the others. "I'm not overly rank conscious, and I'm insisting on my seniority only because Rim Worlds' sovereignty is involved. To begin with—we are in Rim Confederacy's territorial space. Secondly, I outrank everybody present in this control room. . . ."

"In a pig's arse you do!" flared Irene.

"But I do, madam. I concede that you *were* an empress, but you're not now. Legally speaking you're only the chief officer of *Wanderer*. . . ."

"And the owner of *Wanderer*, Grimes! Which is more than you can say regarding yourself and your precious rustbucket!"

"And *I* still claim," stated Flandry, "that *Wanderer* and *Faraway Quest* are no better than pirates, attempting to steal Imperial property."

"It's a great pity that GLASS is not operative in *your* universe," said Smith in a flat voice. "But since we are discussing legalities, I feel that I, as the charterer of Mrs. Trafford's vessel, should have some voice in the matter."

"Irene!" Trialanne was trying to gain the attention of the ex-Empress. "Irene!"

"Pipe down, damn you! Can't you see I'm busy?"

"Obviously," said Sonya coldly, "it would be pointless to put it to the vote who should be chair-

89

man of this meeting. Everybody is quite convinced that he has a more valid claim than anybody else. I could say—and, come to that, I *do* say—that I represent the Federation, but I have no desire to be yet another complication. . . ."

"But a very charming one," murmured Flandry, flashing that dazzling grin.

"Thank you, Sir Dominic."

"Very charming, and, I feel, highly competent. For the record, I do not recognize the Interstellar Federation. Nonetheless, I feel that Mrs. Grimes—or, if you prefer it, Commander Verrill—should preside over this meeting. She appears, in spite of her marriage . . ." he made it sound as though he meant "disastrous marriage" . . . "to be the nearest thing we have to a neutral. Will you, then, take charge, Commander Verrill?"

She smiled at him. "Thank you, Sir Dominic. I will." She raised her voice slightly. "To begin with, all of you, this situation calls for straight thinking. We are met together in what is, to all of us, an alien ship. We represent, between us, three different cultures, at least four different governments. But we are all—and I include you, Trialanne—human. . . ."

"So *you* say," growled Irene.

Sonya ignored this, went on. "As an aid to straight thinking, recapitulation will be in order. We are all of us *here*, all of us *now*—that much is obvious. But it should be obvious, too, that The Outsider, the Outsiders' Ship, warps normal space time. It exists simultaneously in our universe, and in yours, Sir Dominic, and in yours,

Irene—and yet it is from outside all our universes. . . ."

Somebody was grabbing Grimes' arm, the pressure evident even through the thick sleeve of his suit. It was Mayhew. The telepath was pointing to the hatch which gave access to the control room from the body of the ship. Through it a helmeted head was rising slowly.

"I—we—were trying to tell you!" muttered Mayhew.

"Tell me *what*?" growled Grimes.

In reply the other shrugged—no easy feat in a space suit—infuriatingly. *Bloody prima donna!* thought Grimes. *But it can't be all that important. Probably somebody from one of the ships with some trivial message.*

"It could be," Sonya was continuing, in a schoolmistress' voice, "that we are all of us here on sufferance. . . ."

The shoulders of the new arrival were now visible, but the faceplate of his helmet was almost opaque. Grimes stared at those armored shoulders. They carried the broad gold stripe of a commodore, the winged wheel of the Rim Worlds Navy. Who the hell could it be? Lannigan? DuBois? Why should either of them be sent out here to interfere with him, Grimes? And this interloping commodore had somebody with him, wearing commander's badges of rank, and the stylized star cluster of the Federation. . . .

Sonya's voice trailed off into silence. She had seen the newcomers at last. So had all the others.

The stranger put gloved hands to his helmet,

twisted, lifted. He stared at Grimes—and Grimes stared at him. It was long seconds before Grimes recognized him. One is used to seeing one's own face in a mirror, but one spends very little (if any) time studying solidographs of oneself. Dimly, Grimes was aware that the other stranger, standing to one side and a little behind the commodore, had removed her helmet. He didn't really notice her until she spoke.

"This is a surprise, John," said Maggie Lazenby.

Flandry laughed. "Getting back to our original argument—just which of you two gentlemen is the senior?"

14

"MPHM," GRUNTED Grimes.

"Mphm," grunted Grimes.

Slowly he opened the pouch at his belt, took from it his tobacco tin and his battered pipe. Carefully he filled the pipe, returned the tin to the pouch, brought out a lighter. He lit the pipe. He squinted at Grimes through the swirl of blue, acrid smoke.

Slowly he opened the pouch at his belt, took from it his tobacco tin and his battered pipe. Carefully he filled the pipe, returned the tin to the pouch, brought out a lighter. He lit the pipe. He squinted at Grimes through the swirl of blue, acrid smoke.

Sonya made a major production of a lung-wracking cough.

Maggie said, "Let the man have his little pleasures—and his aid to cerebration."

Sonya demanded, "What are *you* doing with *him*?"

Maggie replied, "I could ask you the same, duckie."

Grimes demanded, "How the hell did *you* get here?"

Grimes replied, "The same way as you." He gestured toward the nearest hexagonal viewport with the hand that held the pipe.

Grimes stared out into the blackness. There had been three vessels there: Flandry's *Vindictive,* Irene's *Wanderer,* his own *Faraway Quest.* Now there were four. He asked, "And what is the name of *your* ship?"

"*Faraway Quest,* of course. She was *Delta Puppis* before the Federation flogged her to us."

"Mphm," grunted Grimes again, feeling a twinge of envy. His *Faraway Quest* was an ex-Epsilon Class tramp. He turned to Mayhew. "You might have kept me better informed, Commander."

"Sir, both Trialanne and I tried to tell you as soon as this other *Faraway Quest* broke through. I couldn't tell you anything before then as she does not carry a psionic communications officer."

"Unfortunately, no," agreed Grimes II. "I tried to convince my masters that a good PCO is worth ten thousand times his weight in Carlotti transceivers—but *they* know best." He added after a pause, "I can never understand this craving to put oneself at the mercy of a single fuse. . . ."

"And how many times have you heard *that* before, Maggie?" asked Sonya.

"I've lost count," said Maggie Lazenby.

"But this question of seniority . . . ?" hinted Flandry, obviously determined to extract the utmost in amusement from the situation.

"*I* am the senior," stated both Grimeses.

"I was here first," said Grimes I.

"Mine is the larger ship," said Grimes II.

Grimes I laughed. "This is bloody absurd, Grimes. Before we get involved in any futile arguments would you mind putting me—us—into your picture?"

"I'll try, Grimes. My masters decided that it was time that somebody took another expedition out to the Outsiders' Ship, and I was given the job. Maggie—you *do* know Maggie, of course . . .?"

"I do. And so does Sonya."

"And I know Sonya. Quite a family party, isn't it? But where was I? Oh, yes. Maggie, although she's married to me, has retained her Federation citizenship and her commission in the Federation's Survey Service. She's along as an observer for the Federation."

"As Sonya is. But go on."

Grimes II carefully relit his pipe. "Well, we rather suspected that there would be other ships, in addition to the known derelicts, in orbit about The Outsider. But we were certainly surprised to find that one of those other ships, like mine, was named *Faraway Quest*. Your second-in-command, Commander Williams, was even more surprised. It must have been a shock to him to see my face

95

looking out of the screen when we started nattering over the NST radio. It put him in rather a dither. There he was, conditioned to say, 'Yes, sir; no, sir,' to Commodore Grimes. . . .''

"That doesn't sound like Williams!" said Grimes II.

"Well, as a matter of fact he called me 'Skipper.' But he was in a fine tangle of conflicting loyalties. He suggested that I'd better make contact with you to get things sorted out, and told me where I'd find you. And now, Commodore Grimes, suppose you introduce your friends to me. . . .''

"Certainly, Commodore Grimes," said Grimes who, in a dazed sort of way, was beginning to enjoy himself. "Irene, Trialanne, this, as you see, is Commodore Grimes, who obviously is from a time track not too far divergent from my own. And the lady is Commander Lazenby, of the Federation's Survey Service, and also Mrs. Grimes. Commodore, may I present Mrs. Trafford, who is chief officer *and* owner of the so-called yacht *Wanderer,* and Trialanne, one of her PCOs. Oh, yes, before I forget—Mrs. Trafford is also the ex-Empress Irene.''

"I am honored," said Grimes II, with a stiff little bow.

"You bloody well should be," growled Irene.

"And Mr. Smith, the managing director of GLASS, charterer of *Wanderer*. GLASS is an acronym for GALACTIC LEAGUE AGAINST SUPPRESSION and SLAVERY. It is, I imagine, a severe pain in the neck to quite a few governments in Irene's universe. . . .''

"We try to be just that," agreed Smith modestly.

"And this, Commodore, is Captain Sir Dominic Flandry, of the Imperial armed scout *Vindictive*. The young gentleman with him is Ensign Bugolsky."

Flandry smiled, but his eyes were cold, wary. "I am glad to meet you, Commodore. And *you*, Commander Lazenby."

You would be, thought Grimes.

"In one way your arrival, sir, is welcome. Until now I have been inclined to doubt your alter ego's stories of alternate time tracks and all the rest of it. But now . . ." Flandry shrugged. He went on, "You are welcome to join our discussion."

"What discussion?" asked Grimes II.

"As to who can lay claim to The Outsider."

"You will agree with me," said Grimes I, "that it lies within Rim Confederacy's territorial space."

"Of course," said Grimes II.

"But *whose* Rim Confederacy?" demanded Flandry and Irene simultaneously. "Yours or his?"

"It's *my* flag that's planted on it," stated Grimes I stubbornly.

"You and your bloody flag!" snarled Irene.

"As I see it," said Grimes II judiciously, "this is a matter to be decided between Commodore Grimes and myself."

"Definitely," said Grimes I.

"We're *surrounded* by the bastards," muttered Irene. Then, to Flandry, "You'll not stand for that, Sir Dominic?"

"*You*," said Sonya, "can fight it out between yourselves which Empire has a claim to ownership."

Flandry flashed a charming smile at Irene. "I really think, ma'am, that we imperialists should stick together."

"GLASS has never approved of imperialism," stated Smith. "In any case, *Wanderer* is on charter to my organization."

"I seem to remember," said Sonya coldly, "that quite some time ago it was decided that I should preside over this meeting. Even though my husband has been duplicated, I have not. Therefore I suggest that we carry on from where we left off."

"And just why were you so honored, Sonya?" asked Maggie curiously.

"Because I, as an officer of the Federation's Survey Service, am the only one who can claim neutral status."

"But I, too, am an officer of the Federation's Survey Service, dearie."

"Commodore Grimes!" Mayhew called excitedly.

Both Grimeses turned to look at him.

"Yes, Commander?" asked Grimes I.

"*Faraway Quest*. . . . She's . . . gone!"

"I was in touch with Clarisse," confirmed Trialanne. "But the contact has been broken."

From Flandry's suit radio came a small, tinny voice. "Captian, sir, *Faraway Quest,* the first *Faraway quest,* has vanished."

There was no need for Grimes to stare out through the viewport, but he did so. There, hanging in nothingness, were the three ships, three only: *Vindictive, Wanderer* and what must be the other *Quest,* the wrong *Quest.*

He turned to look at the elaborately grotesque Outsider with something akin to hatred. "That bloody thing!" he muttered. "That bloody thing!" And he thought, *My ship, my people . . . where are they? Where—or when—has It thrown them?*

The Iralian woman said softly, "Commodore, *It* is not responsible. Your vessel's Mannschenn Drive was restarted just before she vanished. So I am told by Mr. Tallentire, aboard *Wanderer.*"

"Trialanne! Mayhew! Get in touch with Clarisse. Find out what's happening!"

"Don't you think that I'm bloody well trying already?" snarled Mayhew. "Damn your ship. It's my woman I'm worried about!"

"Sorry, Ken," said Grimes. "I needn't tell you to do your best, and better. . . ."

"Mutiny?" asked Grimes II quietly.

"Be your age, Commodore!" flared Grimes I. "With a handpicked crew, like mine, it's impossible."

"The passengers weren't handpicked, John," Sonya told him somberly. "At least, not by you."

Mayhew, his face white and strained, whispered, "The blame is mine, John. I should have disregarded the Rhine Institute's code of ethics. I should have pried."

"But you didn't. And I didn't order you to. . . ." He looked around him at the faces of the others in the control room. All realized the gravity of the situation.

Grimes II broke the silence. He said, "Much as I

hate to leave the Outsiders' Ship to these . . . outsiders, my *Faraway Quest* is at your disposal, Commodore. After all, we may as well keep this in the family.''

"Mutiny is a crime," stated Irene. "All law-abiding citizens should combine to capture and to punish the criminals. I am with you. I am sure that I speak for my officers."

"And count me in," said Flandry, not without a touch of regret.

"Thank you," Grimes said. "Thank you. All of you."

"And where," asked Maggie Lazenby, "do we go from here?"

15

WHERE DID THEY go from there?

Where had *Faraway Quest* gone?

And where was that Waldegren destroyer, *Adler*?

But the discussion, the consideration of these problems was better than the rather childish squabbling as to who had prior claim to the Outsiders' Ship.

It was decided that Grimes, Sonya and Mayhew should take passage in the second *Faraway Quest*, and that Flandry should accompany them. Flandry's own ship, *Vindictive*, was unsuitable for the pursuit of the original *Quest*. She had faster than light drive, of course, and faster than light deep space communications equipment, but neither of these operated on the principles of the Mann-schenn Drive or the Carlotti beacon. She could proceed from Point A to Point B at least as fast as *Faraway Quest* or *Wanderer,* but until she reemerged into normal space time she would be completely out of touch with them.

Vindictive, therefore, would remain in orbit about The Outsider as a guard ship. Flandry impressed upon her acting captain that he was to counter any hostile move made by *Adler,* should she put in an appearance, without hesitation, but that he was to be careful in his dealings with *Faraway Quest I* should she return. As long as there was any possibility that her rightful crew were still alive, as prisoners, as hostages, their safety must be considered at all times.

All this took time, but not too much time. And then Flandry, with his aide, returned briefly to his own vessel, while Irene and her party made their way back to *Wanderer,* while Grimes I in his pinnace followed his other self, in his pinnace, to *Faraway Quest II.* The stowage of this extra boat in the *Quest's* cargo hold presented no great problems. By the time that it was secured Captain Flandry was alongside, at the airlock, and was being admitted.

And then the control rooms of *Wanderer* and *Faraway Quest* were manned. Grimes sat in one of the spare acceleration chairs, with Mayhew to one side of him and Sonya to the other, and with Flandry beside Sonya. He watched the other Grimes enviously. *He* still had a ship of his own. He looked curiously at the officers at their stations—

and they looked curiously at him and at Sonya and at Flandry. He felt that he almost knew them. Almost certainly their counterparts lived in his continuum; he must have met some of them, however briefly. The communications officer, beside whom Mayhew had taken a seat. . . . Surely that was young Carradine, who held the same rank in Rim Runners in Grimes' universe. . . .

Grimes II was giving his orders unhurriedly, decisively; they were acknowledged smartly. In the little screen of the NST transceiver, Captain Trafford in *Wanderer's* control room was doing likewise. Then Trafford said, facing the iconoscope, ''All machinery on full stand by, Commodore.''

''Thank you, Captain,'' replied Grimes II, just a fraction of a second before Grimes I could do so. (*I'll have to watch myself,* he thought. *I'm only a passenger*. . . .)

''Execute on the count of zero.''

''Aye, aye. Execute on the count of zero.''

''Five . . .'' intoned Grimes II. ''Four . . . Three . . . Two . . . One . . . Zero!''

From below came the high, undulating whine of the Mannschenn Drive, and with it the temporal disorientation, the sense of unreality. Grimes looked at Sonya and asked himself, with wry humor, *How many of me is she seeing now?* The picture of *Wanderer's* control room faded from the NST transceiver screen, was replaced by that in the screen of the Carlotti set. Beyond the viewports the brightly lit *Vindictive* and the distant Shaara derelict faded into invisibility—but the cold-gleaming intricacy of the Outsiders' Ship persisted stubbornly.

It is in every space, thought Grimes. *It is in every time. But how is it that nobody else has ever reported this phenomenon?* He answered his own question. *Dead men and missing men do not tell tales.*

And then, suddenly, things were normal—or as normal as they ever are, as they ever can be while the Drive is in operation.

Flandry looked at Grimes. His face was pale. He said, "So this is your Mannschenn Drive. I think I prefer our Standing Wave."

"You get used to it," Grimes told him.

"Speak for yourself," snapped Sonya.

But Grimes II—after all, this was his ship—was taking charge. "Mr. Carradine," he ordered, "keep your ears skinned for the faintest whisper from *anybody* on the main Carlotti. Grab a bearing if you can. Mr. Danby, let me know if you see even the merest flicker in the MPI. And you, Commander Mayhew, I needn't tell *you* what to do. I'm sorry that this ship doesn't run to psionic amplifier, but Mr. Metzenther and Trialanne in *Wanderer* have one."

Flandry said something about trying to find a black cat in a coal mine at midnight. Grimes II laughed. "Yes, Captain, that just about sums it up. And once we do find it we may not be much better off. For any physical contact to be made between ships while the Mannschenn Drive is operating there must be exact synchronization of temporal precession rates. There have been devices whereby one vessel can induce synchronization in the Mannschenn Drive unit of another vessel with her own. But most ships today—certainly all warships—are fitted with special governors which make this impossible unless the captain so desires."

"And when do you start accelerating, Commodore? I'm finding all this free fall rather boring."

"As soon as we know where to accelerate to."

Flandry shrugged. The gesture, now that he was out of his space suit and attired in a close-fitting, beautifully tailored, black and gold uniform, was much more effective.

Irritated, Grimes II asked sharply, "And do *you* have any ideas, Captain Flandry?"

"Why, yes. People don't hijack ships just for the fun of it. We don't have any Duchy of Waldegren in *my* universe—but, from what I have gathered, the Waldegrenese are baddies. The people who have seized the *Faraway quest,* the first *Faraway Quest* that I was aboard, are also baddies. Could this hijacked *Faraway Quest* be making a rendezvous with *Adler?*"

"What do *you* think, Commodore?" asked Grimes II.

"I think that Captain Flandry could be right, Commodore," replied Grimes I.

"Of course I'm right," said Flandry.

"Mphm," grunted Grimes II thoughtfully. He turned to his navigator. "Mr. Danby," he said, "run up a trajectory for Waldegren. We'll just have to assume that she's coming out by the most direct route, the same as we did from *Faraway. . . .*"

"No," Grimes told him. "She's running out on the Leads astern, the same as we did."

"The *Leads*?" demanded Grimes II.

"Yes. Macbeth and the Kinsolving sun in line."

"You have some most peculiar ideas about navigation on *your* time track, Commodore. However, this *Adler* also belongs to your time track, so. . . . All right, Mr. Danby, do as the carbon copy Commodore Grimes says. And Mr. Carradine, inform *Wanderer* of our intentions."

Carbon copy . . . thought Grimes indignantly. But, original or not, this was not his ship. He—or his own version of himself—was not giving the orders. He could only suggest and be thankful that this other Grimes did not seem to be as pigheaded as he, more than once, had been accused of being.

Briefly the Mannschenn Drive was shut down, and the big, directional gyroscopes rumbled, hummed and then whined as the ship turned about her short axis. Directly ahead—overhead from the viewport of those in Control—the dim, misty Galactic Lens swam into view and was almost immediately distorted beyond recognition as the interstellar drive was restarted. The irregular throbbing beat of the inertial drive made itself felt, and there was gravity again, and weight, and up and down.

"Now we're getting someplace," murmured Flandry a little smugly.

Grimes glared at him and was even more annoyed when he saw that Sonya was looking at the Imperial Captain with what could have been admiration.

IT WAS NOT a long pursuit, and it ended in stale-mate.

Falling through the non-space, non-time between the dimensions were the four ships: *Adler, Wanderer,* both versions of *Faraway Quest.* Trajectories had been matched, in spite of the initial efforts of *Adler* and *Faraway Quest I* to throw off their pursuers; but it was only those two vessels that had synchronized temporal precession rates.

Back toward The Outsider they ran, all four of them, a mismatched squadron. And they would run past their objective, and go on running, until somebody did something, somehow, to break the deadlock.

Meanwhile, Grimes had learned that his crew was safe, although they were now prisoners. At last, at long last, and with assistance from Metzenther and Trialanne, Mayhew had been able to reestablish his *rapport* with Clarisse. It had not been easy, but after many hours of concentrated effort the three telepaths had been able to drag her mind up out of its drugged sleep to a condition of full awareness. She was able, then, to supply the details of Druthen's take-over of the ship. It had been done with surprising ease, merely by the introduction of an instantaneously anesthetic gas into the air circulatory system. In theory, this should have been impossible. Alarms should have sounded; pumps and fans should have stopped; baffle plates should automatically have sealed off the ducts. But Druthen was a scientist, and his people were scientists and technicians. He had a very well equipped laboratory at his disposal. And, most important of all, Mayhew and Clarisse had obeyed that commandment of the Rhine Institute: Thou shalt not pry into the mind of a shipmate.

"It's no use crying over spilt milk, Ken," Grimes told his psionic communications officer. "At least we know that Clarisse and the others are unhurt. . . ."

"What the hell's the use of having these talents if you don't use 'em?" wondered Flandry, all too audibly.

"Some of us," Grimes told him coldly, "subscribe to ethical codes."

"Don't we all, Commodore? Do unto others as

they would do unto you—but do it first!"

"Captain Flandry is right, John," said Sonya.

Yes, thought Grimes, *I suppose the bastard is right. And, come to that, I've tried often enough, and sometimes successfully, to get PCOs to pry for me. . . . Like Spooky Deane, who loved his gin—or my gin. . . . Even so. . . .*

Anyhow, there was now telepathic communication between the two *Faraway Quests,* and communication regarding which neither Druthen nor the captain of *Adler* was aware. Not that it would have worried them much if they had known about it. Clarisse was locked up in the quarters that she had shared with her husband. There was little that she could tell him, and nothing that she could do. She could not communicate with the other prisoners, who were nontelepaths. She could not even pry into the minds of Druthen and his people—and neither could Mayhew and Metzenther and Trialanne. The scientist had, somehow, succeeded in stimulating Mayhew's psionic amplifier—it could, of course, have been just a side effect of the anesthetic gas that had been used during the takeover—and the continual howling of that hapless, disembodied dog's brain blanketed all stray thoughts. Trained telepaths could punch their signals through the psionic interference, but that was all.

In any case, Druthen was willing enough to talk.

He, fat and slovenly as ever, glowered out at Grimes from the screen of the Carlotti transceiver. Grimes stared back at him, trying to keep his own face emotionless. It was all wrong that he should be looking into his own control room this way, from outside, that he should see the nerve center of his own ship in the hands of strangers, of enemies. With Druthen were two of the scientist's own people, and in the background were three uniformed men: large, blond, obviously officers of the Waldegren Navy.

The senior among them, a full commander by his braid, came to stand beside Dr. Druthen. Druthen seemed to resent this, tried to push the officer out of the field of the iconoscope. He muttered, "Nehmen Sie mal Ihre Latschen weg."

The other replied, "Sie sind zwar dick genug für zwei, aber Sie haben nur für einen Platz gezahlt Rücken Sie weiter."

Sonya laughed. Grimes asked her, "What's the joke?"

"Just that they don't seem to love each other. Druthen told the commander to get his big feet out of his way, and the commander told *him* that even though he's big enough to fill two seats he's only paid for one. . . ."

"Paid?" asked Grimes.

"Obviously. He's bought his way into the Duchy of Waldegren."

"Ja," agreed the Waldegren commander. And then, speaking directly to Grimes, "And you the captain of this ship were? But. . . ." His eyes widened. "*Vich* of you der kapitan vas?"

"I suppose we're twins, of a sort," grinned Grimes I. "The gentleman standing behind me is Commodore Grimes, commanding *Faraway Quest.* And I am Commodore Grimes, commanding *Faraway Quest*—the *Faraway Quest* aboard which you, sir, are trespassing."

"But I am the captain now," stated Druthen, smugly.

Grimes ignored this. He asked coldly, "Where are my people?" (There was no point in letting Druthen and the officers of the prize crew know that he was already fully informed on that subject.)

"Do you want them back?" countered Druthen, with an infuriating expression of deliberate incredulity.

"Yes. And my ship."

Druthen laughed sneeringly. "You don't want much, Commodore. Or should I say, ex-Commodore? Your masters will not be very pleased with you. The ship—*I* keep. Doubtless the Duchy will pay me a fair price for her. The crew. . . . They are useful hostages. You and your allies dare make no hostile move for fear of hurting them." The fat face was suddenly gloating, evil. "And, perhaps, I can use them to persuade you to call off this futile chase. Suppose I have them thrown, one by one, unsuited, out of the airlock . . . ?"

"Herr Doktor!" snapped the commander. "Enough. That I will never countenance. I am an officer, not an executioner."

"Sie glauben wohl Sie sind als Schiffsoffizier was besonderes!"

"Hau'ab!" The commander struck rather than pushed Druthen away from the screen. Those in the control room of *Quest II* watched, fascinated, a brief scuffle in the control room of the other ship.

And then the senior officer of the prize crew was addressing them again. "Herr Commodore, my apologies. But I my orders must follow, even when I am told to cooperate with *schwein. Aber,* my word I give. I, Erich von Donderberg, promise you that your crew will be treated well as long as I in this ship am."

"Thank you, Commander," said Grimes stiffly.

Druthen, with one eye puffed and almost shut, bleeding from the corner of his mouth, reappeared.

"Officers!" he spat. "Gold-braided nincompoops, survivals from a past age who should have become extinct millennia ago! I'm cutting you off, Grimes. I want the transceiver so that I can call Captain Blumenfeld in *Adler.* There'll be some changes made in the composition of this so-called prize crew!'

The screen went blank.

"What now?" asked Flandry. "You know these Waldegren people. I don't."

"They're naval officers," said Grimes at last. "They're professional naval officers. They can be ruthless bastards—but they do, at times, subscribe to a rather antique code of honor. . . ."

"I concur," said Grimes II.

"Would you mind," asked Grimes I, "passing the recording of this rather odd interview on to *Wanderer?* Irene and her people may have some comments."

"Certainly, Commodore."

"And you should be able to let us know, Ken, if Druthen is able to persuade Captain Blumenfeld to let him play the game his way?"

"I'll try," said Mayhew doubtfully. "I'll try. With Clarisse alert and with Metzenther and Trialanne to help us. . . . Yes, I should manage."

"And so," commented Flandry, "we just, all of us, go on falling through sweet damn' all until somebody condescends to make something happen."

"That's the way of it," agreed Grimes.

17

THEY, ALL OF them, went on falling through sweet damn' all.

They swept past the Outsider's Ship, which was still dimly visible, although the derelicts in orbit about it were not. Neither was Flandry's *Vindictive*. The Imperial Captain complained rather bitterly that he was unable to communicate with his ship. Both Grimeses growled, simultaneously, that it was the fault of his culture for developing neither psionic communications nor the Carlotti system. Both Mrs. Grimeses were inclined to commiserate with Flandry. Relations aboard *Faraway Quest II* were becoming strained. Aboard *Wanderer* there were not the same problems. There was only one of each person, and there were no outsiders.

Out they fell, the four ships, out into the ultimate night.

Druthen and Captain Blumenfeld made an occasional attempt at evasion, which was countered with ease by the pursuers. Once Blumenfeld, using the Carlotti equipment, tried to reason with Grimes—either or both of him—and with Irene, who had been hooked into the conversation.

Blumenfeld was an older and stouter version of von Donderberg, and he was more of the politician and less of the space officer. His accent was not so heavy. He appeared in the screens of *Faraway Quest II* and *Wanderer* by himself, a fatherly-grandfatherly, almost—figure, smoking an elaborate pipe with a porcelain bowl. It was a pity that his cold, very cold, blue eyes spoiled the effect.

"Come now, Commodore," he said, "we are both reasonable men. And you, Kaiserin, are a reasonable lady. What do any of us gain by this pointless chase?"

"You gain nothing," Grimes told him. "Furthermore, you are intruding in Rim Worlds' territorial space. I order you, legally, to hand my ship and my personnel back to me, and also Dr. Druthen and his people so that they may be dealt with by our courts. . . ."

"*You* order, Commodore?" asked the other Grimes softly.

"Yes. I order, Commodore. *Faraway Quest I* is mine, and Druthen and his accomplices will be my prisoners."

"Speak up, Commodores," put in Blumenfeld jovially. "Do I detect a slight dissension in your ranks? And you, Kaiserin, do you acknowledge the right of these gentlemen to give orders? And you, Captain Sir Dominic Flandry? What is your view?''

"We'll settle our own differences after you have been disposed of,'' growled Irene.

"I second that,'' said Flandry.

Captain Blumenfeld puffed placidly at his pipe. Grimes wondered what tobacco it was that he was smoking. The man seemed to be enjoying it. At last he said, through a wreathing blue cloud, ''My patience is not inexhaustible, Commodore. Or Commodores. I am addressing, however, whichever one of you it is who commanded the *Faraway Quest* aboard which I have placed my prize crew. The good Herr Doktor Druthen has made certain proposals to me regarding the prisoners. I was horrified, and told him so, in no uncertain terms. But . . .'' There was a great exhalation of smoke. ''But . . . I have thought about what he said to me. I still do not like it.'' He shrugged heavily.

"Nonetheless, my loyalty is to the Duchy, not to citizens of a Confederacy that the Duchy still has not recognized. It may—note that I say 'may,' Commodore, not 'will'—it may be expedient to use those prisoners as a lever to force a certain degree of compliance from you.'' Again he shrugged. ''I shall not like doing it—assuming, that is, that I am obliged to do it. And I shall not resort to painful or . . . messy methods. Just a simple shooting, to be watched by all of you. And then, after a suitable interval, another. And then, if it is necessary, another." He smiled coldly. "But there is no real urgency. You will be given time to think it over, to talk it over. Three days' subjective time, shall we say? Call me on this frequency. Over. And out."

The screen went blank, but the other screen, that showing *Wanderer's* control room, stayed alive.

"Well?" demanded Irene harshly. "Well?"

"Suppose," said Grimes, "just suppose that I do knuckle under, to get my people back, my ship back. Suppose that I, as the ranking officer of the Rim Worlds Confederacy, do allow him prior rights to The Outsider. . . . What about *you* and *you*, Commodore Grimes, and *you*, Captain Flandry?"

"I shall abide by your decision, John," said the other Grimes.

"Speaking for the Federation," said Sonya, "I shall be with you."

"You beat me to it," said Maggie Lazenby.

"I'll have to think about it," stated Irene.

"As tour charterer," Smith told her, "I have *some* say. A great deal of say. I sympathize with Commodore Grimes. But it's a matter of evaluation. Are the lives of a handful of people of greater importance than the lives of the millions of oppressed men and women and children who look to GLASS for help?"

"Anybody mind if I shove in my two bits' worth?" asked Flandry. "I owe allegiance neither to the Federation nor to the Confederacy and certainly not to GLASS. I swore an oath of fealty to the Emperor." He looked at Irene's face in the screen, and added, "*My* Emperor. But my sympathies are with the Commodore."

"Thank you, Sir Dominic," said Grimes.

"Wait till you see the bill. Furthermore, sir, I would remind you that you have at your disposal equipment and personnel which I have not. The same applies to you, ma'am. You have your espers. Can't you make full use of them?"

"I would remind you, Sir Dominic," said Mayhew, "that my wife is among the prisoners aboard the *Quest*."

"All the more reason why you should pull your finger out. All of you."

You arrogant bastard, thought Grimes.

"Sir Dominic's talking sense," said Sonya. "*We* have the telepaths. *Adler* hasn't. Furthermore, one of *our* telepaths is aboard *your Quest,* John. There must be something that Clarisse can do to help herself. And the others."

"It's all we can do to get through to her," objected Mayhew. "There's too much interference from Lassie. . . ."

Sonya muttered something about a poodle's brain in aspic. Then she said, "Why don't you silence the bitch? Lassie, I mean. There's three of you here: Metzenther and Trialanne aboard *Wanderer,* and yourself. You told us once—remember?—that thoughts can kill."

"I . . . I couldn't, Sonya. . . ."

"Damn it all!" exploded Grimes. "Do you put that animal brain before your wife? What sort of man are you?"

"But . . . but Lassie's so . . . helpless."

"So is Clarisse, unless we do something to help her—and fast. It is *essential* that she be able to keep us informed as to what Druthen is thinking, and von Donderberg . . . and with that psionic interference snuffed out you should be able to keep us informed as to Captain Blumenfeld's intentions. You must do it, Ken."

"Yes," agreed the telepath slowly. "I . . . must. Metzenther and Trialanne will help. They have already told me that."

"Then go to it," ordered Grimes.

Not for the first time he thought, *They're odd people. Too bloody odd. But I suppose when you live inside your pet's brain, and it lives inside yours, you feel more intensely for and about it than any normal man feels for his dog. . . . They'll be guilt involved, too. . . . You'll blame yourself for its absolute helplessness. . . .*

He watched Mayhew stumbling out of the control room, his features stiff, too stiff. He saw the sympathy on the face of Grimes II, and rather more than a hint of a sneer on that of Flandry.

Grimes II looked at his watch. He said, "There's nothing much that we can do, Commodore, until your Commander Mayhew reports results. I suggest that we all adjourn for dinner."

"An army marches on its stomach," quipped Flandry. "I suppose that the same saying applies to a space navy."

"I've never known John to miss a meal," Sonya told him, "no matter what the circumstances."

Women . . . thought Grimes—both of him.

"You said it," agreed Maggie Lazenby.

18

THIS WAS THE first proper, sit down meal that anybody had enjoyed for quite a while. Not that
Grimes really enjoyed it. He was used to eating at
the captain's table—but at the head of the board.
To see himself sitting there, a replica of himself,
was . . . odd. He derived a certain wry pleasure
from the fact that this other Grimes, like himself,
was not one to let conversation interfere with the
serious business of feeding. He did not think,
somehow, that Maggie appreciated this trait any
more than Sonya did.

There were five of them at the Commodore's
table. Grimes II was at the head of it, of course,
with Maggie Lazenby at his right and Sonya at his
left. Grimes I sat beside Maggie, and Flandry be-

side Sonya. The Imperial Captain was a brilliant conversationalist, and the two women were lapping it up. He made his own time track sound so much more glamorous than the time tracks of the two Grimeses—which, in any case, differed only very slightly from each other. He made the two Commodores seem very dull dogs in comparison with his flamboyant, charming self. And, in spite of the nonstop flow of outrageous anecdotes, his plate was clean before any of the others.

The meal, Grimes admitted, was a good one. Grimes II kept an excellent table, and the service, provided by two neatly uniformed little stewardesses, matched the quality of the food. There was wine, of which Grimes II partook sparingly, of which the others partook not so sparingly. Grimes thought, with disapproval, *That man Flandry is gulping it down as though it were lager . . .* then realized that he was doing the same.

At last they were finished, sipping their coffee. Grimes—both of him—pulled out his pipe. His wife—both of her—objected, saying, "John! You *know* that the air conditioners can't cope with the *stink!*" Flandry, sleek and smug, lit a cigar that one of the stewardesses brought him. The ladies accepted lights from him for their cigarillos.

Grimes, from the head of the table, looked at Grimes with slightly raised eyebrows. He said, "I'm going up to Control, Commodore, to enjoy my pipe in peace. The officer of the watch mightn't like it, but he daren't say so. Coming?"

"Thank you, Commodore."

He (they) excused himself (themselves). got to

his (their) feet. Flandry and the wives were enjoying liqueurs with their coffee and hardly noticed their going. Grimes II led the way out of the dining saloon, which, as a public room in a much larger ship, was luxurious in comparison with that aboard *Faraway Quest I.* Indoor plants, the lush, flowering vines of Caribbea twining around every pillar. Holograms, brightly glowing, picture windows opening onto a score of alien worlds. Grimes paused before one that depicted a beach scene on Arcadia. Maggie was an Arcadian. He looked closely to see if she were among the naked, golden-skinned people on the sand and in the surf. But what if she was? He grunted, followed his counterpart into the axial shaft.

The control room seemed bleak and cold after the warm luxury of the dining saloon. The officer of the watch got to his feet as the two Commodores entered, looked doubtfully from one to the other before deciding which one to salute. But he got it right. Outside the viewports was—nothingness. To starboard, Grimes knew, were his own ship and *Adler,* and beyond them was Irene's *Wanderer*— but unless temporal precession rates were synchronized they would remain invisible. One of the Carlotti screens was alive. It showed a bored looking Tallentire slumped in his chair, his fingers busy with some sort of mathematical puzzle.

"Any word from our tame telepaths yet, Mr. Grigsby?" asked Grimes II.

"No, sir. Commander Mayhew did buzz me to tell me that he and the people aboard *Wanderer* are still trying but aren't getting anywhere."

"Mphm." Grimes slumped into an acceleration chair, motioning to Grimes to follow suit. He (they) filled and lit his (their) pipes. "Mphm."

"There must be a way," said Grimes thoughtfully.

"There always is," agreed Grimes. "The only trouble is finding it."

The two men smoked in companionable silence. Grimes I was almost at ease but knew that he would be properly at ease only aboard his own *Faraway Quest*. He looked around him, noticing all the similarities—and all the differences. From the control room he went down, in his mind, deck by deck. And then . . . and then the idea came to him.

"Commodore," he said, "I think I have it. Do you mind if I borrow your O.O.W.?"

"Help yourself, Commodore. This is Liberty Hall. You can spit on the mat and call the cat a bastard."

Grimes winced. So that was the way it sounded when he said it. He caught the attention of the watch officer. "Mr. Grigsby. . . ."

"Sir?"

"Ask Commander Mayhew to come up here, will you?"

"Aye, aye, sir."

The young man spoke into a telephone, then said, "He's on his way."

"Thank you."

When Mayhew came in the two Commodores were wrapped in a pungent blue haze. "Sir?" asked the telepath doubtfully, looking from one to the other. "Sir?"

"Damn it all, Ken," growled Grimes. "*You* should know which one of us is which."

"There was a sort of . . . mingling."

"Don't go all metaphysical on me. I take it that you've made no headway."

"No. We just can't get through to Lassie. And it takes effort, considerable effort, to maintain Clarisse in a state approaching full awareness."

"But you are getting through to her."

"Yes."

"Good. Now tell me, Ken, *where* is she? Yes, Yes—I know bloody well that she's aboard my *Faraway Quest*—but where aboard the *Quest*? In your living quarters—or in your watch room?"

"In . . . in the watch room, sir. She hates Lassie, as you know, but she went to the watch room to maintain better communications when we left the ship to go aboard the Shaara derelict. The watch room is fitted up as a living cabin, and Druthen and his crowd left her there after the take-over."

"That makes things easier, a lot easier. Now, get in touch with your cobbers aboard *Wanderer*. . . ."

"I already am." Mayhew's voice was pained.

"Punch this message through, the three of you. *Stop Lassie's life-support system.*"

"You can't mean. . . ."

"I do mean. It's the only way to quiet that helpless hound of yours. With that source of telepathic interference wiped out we might be able to learn something. After all, it's only short range work. You don't need an amplifier."

"But. . . ."

"*Do it!*"

"All right, Sir." Mayhew's face was white and strained. "But you don't understand. If I could do it myself, kill Lassie, I mean, it wouldn't be as bad. Because . . . because Clarisse has always hated Lassie. She'll . . . she'll enjoy it. . . ."

"Good for her," said Grimes brutally. "And have Mr. Metzenther inform Captain Trafford of what's going on."

He visualized Clarisse's slim fingers switching off the tiny pumps that supplied oxygen and nutrient fluid to the tank in which floated that obsenely naked brain—but only a dog's brain—and, suddenly, felt more than a little sick.

He said, "I think I'll go below, Commodore."

"As you please, Commodore," replied Grimes II. "I shall stay up here. There should be information coming through at any time now. If things start happening, this is my place."

"Too right," agreed Grimes. "And there's an old saying about two women in the same kitchen. Two shipmasters in the same control room would be at least as bad."

19

HE MADE HIS way down from the control room to
the deck upon which the master's quarters and the
V.I.P. suite—in which he and Sonya had been
housed—were situated. The general layout was
very similar to that of his own ship. There was no
extra accommodation in this compartment; everything was on a larger scale.

Absentmindedly he paused outside the door that
had above it, in gold lettering, CAPTAIN. It was
ajar. He had started to enter when he realized his
error, but too late for him to pull back. He could
see through into the bedroom. His wife was there,
sitting up in bed, reading. The spectacles that she
was wearing enhanced her nakedness.

His wife?

But she might have been.

On another time track she was.

"Come in," she not quite snapped. "Don't dither around outside."

He went in.

She put down her book and looked at him gravely, but there was a quirk at the corners of her mouth. She was very beautiful, and she was . . . different. Her breasts were not so full as Sonya's but were pointed. Her smooth shoulders were just a little broader.

She said, "Long time no see, John."

He felt a wild, impossible hope, decided to bluff his way out—or in. He asked gruffly, "What the hell do you mean?"

She replied, "Come off it, John. She's put her mark on you, just as I've put my mark on him. Once you were identical, or there was only one of you. That must have been years ago, round about the time that we had the fun and games on Sparta. Remember?"

Grimes remembered. It had been very shortly after the Spartan affair that he and Maggie had split brass rags.

"Furthermore," she went on, "my ever-loving had the decency to buzz down to tell me that he'd be in Control all night, and not to wait up for him . . ."

"But Sonya. . . ."

"Damn Sonya. Not that I've anything against her, mind you. We've known each other for years and have always been good friends. But if you must know, John, she and I have just enjoyed a girlish natter on the telephone, and she's under the impression that you're sharing *my* John's sleepless vigil.''

Get the hell out of here, you lecherous rat! urged the rather priggish censor who inhabited an odd corner of Grimes' brain.

"Don't just stand there," she said.

He sat down at the foot of the wide bed.

"John! Look at me."

He looked. He went on looking. There was so much that he remembered vividly, so much that he had almost forgotten.

"Have I got Denebian leprosy, or something?"

He admitted that she had not. Her skin was sleek, golden gleaming, with the coppery pubic puff in delicious contrast, the pink nipples of her breasts prominent. He thought, *To hell with it. Why not?* He moved slowly toward her. Her wide, red mouth was inviting. He kissed her—for the first time in how many years? He kissed her and went on kissing her, until she managed to get her hands between their upper bodies and push him away.

"Enough . . ." she gasped. "Enough . . . for the time being. Better shut the outer door . . . and snap on the lock. . . ."

He broke away from her reluctantly. He said, "But suppose *he* . . ." he could not bring himself to say the name "*. . . comes down from Control. . . .*"

"He won't. I know him. I should, by this time. The only thing in his mind will be the safety of his precious ship." She smiled. "And, after all, I am an ethologist, specializing in animal behavior, the human animal included. . . ."

Grimes asked rather stiffly, "I suppose you knew that I would be coming in?"

"I didn't know, duckie, but I'd have been willing to bet on it. The outer door was left ajar on purpose."

"Mphm." Grimes got up, went into the day cabin, shut and locked the door. He returned to the bedroom.

She said, "You look hot. Better take off your shirt."

He took off his shirt. It was a borrowed one, of course. And so was the pair of trousers. So were the shoes. (He had boarded this ship, of course, with only the usual long johns under his space suit.)

Borrowed clothing, a borrowed wife. . . .

But was it adultery?

Grimes grinned. What were the legalities of the situation? Or, come to that, the ethics?

"What the hell are you laughing at?" she demanded.

"Nothing," he told her. "Everything."

She said, "I'll do my best to make this a happy occasion."

It was. There was no guilt, although perhaps there should have been. There was no guilt—after all, Grimes rationalized, he had known Maggie for years; he (or one of him) had been married to her for years. It was a wild, sweet mixture of the soothing familiar and the stimulating unfamiliar. It was—right.

They were together on the now rumpled bed, their bodies just touching, each of them savoring a fragrant cigarillo.

Grimes said lazily, "After all that, I'd better have a shower before I leave. I don't suppose I—*he*—will mind if I use his bathroom. . . ."

She said, "There's no hurry. . . ."

And then the telephone buzzed.

She picked up the handset. "Mrs. Grimes . . ." she said drowsily, with simulated drowsiness. "Yes, John. It's me, of course. Maggie. . . . Yes, I *did* lock the door. . . ." She covered the mouthpiece with her hand, whispered, "Get dressed, and *out*. Quickly. I'll try to stall him off." Speaking into the telephone again, "Yes, yes. I know that I'm the Commodore's wife and that nobody would dream of making a pass at me. But have you forgotten that *wolf*, Sir Dominic Flandry, who's aboard at *your* invitation, duckie, is *prowling* around your ship seeking whom he may devour? And you left me all by myself, to sit and *brood*, or whatever it is you do up there in your bloody control room. . . . No, Sir Dominic didn't make a pass at me, but I could tell by the way he was looking at me. . . . All right, then. . . ."

Grimes was dressed, after a fashion. As he walked fast toward the door, he saw that Maggie was punching the buttons for another number on the ship's exchange. She called over her shoulder, "Wait a moment!"

"Sorry. See you later."

He went out into the alleyway. He hesitated outside the door to his own quarters. Dare he face

Sonya? It would be obvious, too obvious, what he had been doing, and with whom.

The door opened suddenly—and Grimes was staring at Flandry, and Flandry was staring at him, staring and smiling knowingly.

"You bastard!" snarled Grimes, swinging wildly. The punch never connected, but Flandry's hand around Grimes' right wrist used the momentum of the blow to bring Grimes sprawling to the deck.

"Gentlemen," said Grimes II coldly. "Gentlemen—if you will pardon my misuse of the word—I permit no brawling aboard my ship."

Grimes I got groggily to his feet assisted by Flandry. They looked silently at the Commodore. He looked at them. He said, "Such conduct I expected from you, Captain Flandry. But as for you, Commodore Grimes, I am both surprised and pained to learn that your time track is apparently more permissive than mine."

At last Grimes felt the beginnings of guilt. In a way it was himself whom he had cuckolded, but that was no excuse. And what hurt was that during this night's lovemaking it had been his own counterpart, himself although not himself, who had been the odd man out. He knew how this other Grimes must be feeling.

He thought, *I wish I were anywhere but here*.

He said, "Believe me, Commodore, I wish I were anywhere but here." Then he grinned incredulously, looking like a clown with that smile on a face besmeared with lip rouge. "And why the hell shouldn't I be?"

"If I had any say in the matter you would be, Commodore. You *and* Captain Sir Dominic Flandry." He made it sound as though the honorific were a word of four letters, not three.

"You just might have your wish, Commodore. Tell me, have you received any reports from Commander Mayhew and the other PCOs?"

"This is no time to. . . ."

"But it is. The success of our mission, the safety of our ships; these matters, surely, are of overriding importance. . . ."

"He's right, you know," said Sonya, who had appeared in the doorway, looking as though butter would not melt in her mouth.

"Shut up!" snapped Grimes. "You keep out of it."

"He's right, you know," said Maggie, cool and unruffled, who had just joined the party.

"Shut up!" snapped Grimes II. "You keep out of it."

"He's right, you know," drawled Flandry.

Grimes II snarled wordlessly. Then, "As a matter of fact, your Mayhew and his mates did get Clarisse to . . . to turn off the amplifier. They're trying to sort out the psionic impressions that they're getting from *Adler* and your *Faraway Quest,* now that the interference has been . . . switched off. I was thinking of calling you to let you know, but there was no urgency, and I thought you needed your sleep. Ha, ha."

"So now we work out a plan of campaign . . ." murmured Grimes I.

"Yes. In the control room. It'll be some time

133

before I feel like setting foot in my own quarters again. And might I suggest that you two officers and gentlemen get yourselves looking like officers, at least, before you come up.''

Grimes looked doubtfully at Sonya. Then he turned to Flandry. "Do you mind if I make use of your toilet facilities, Sir Dominic?''

"Be my guest, Commodore.'' Then, in almost a whisper, "After all, I was yours—and you were his.''

Grimes didn't want to laugh, but he did. If looks could have killed he would have died there and then. But women have no sense of humor.

20

WANDERER AND *Faraway Quest II* synchronized temporal precession rates, and *Wanderer* closed with the *Quest,* laying herself almost alongside her. It was a maneuver typical of Irene's spacemanship—or spacewomanship—and when it was over Grimes I looked closely at Grimes II's head to see if his counterpart had acquired any additional gray hairs. He thought wryly, *Probably Maggie and I have put a few there ourselves. . . .* It was essential, however, that the meeting of the leaders be held aboard one of the ships; *Adler* would do her best to monitor a conversation conducted over the Carlotti transceivers.

So there they all were in *Faraway Quest's* control room: the two Grimeses, their wives, Sir

Dominic, Irene, Trafford, Smith (inevitably), Mayhew and Metzenther. Somehow Grimes I found himself in the chair.

Slowly and carefully, he filled and lit his pipe. (The other Grimes produced and lit a cigarette. *Subtle*, thought Grimes. *Subtle. I didn't think you had it in you, John . . .*) After he had it going well he said, "All right. I think we can take it as read that our PCOs have silenced the dog, and that they— including, of course, Clarisse—are now doing some snooping into the minds of our mutual enemies. Correct?"

"Correct, sir," answered Mayhew.

"Good. Then report, please, Commander."

The telepath spoke in a toneless voice. "Clarisse is well, although her mind is not yet operating at full capacity. As far as she can determine, as far as we can determine, all the other members of *Faraway Quest's* crew are unharmed. As yet.

"Insofar as their captors are concerned, we have found it advisable to concentrate on key personnel: Dr. Druthen, Captain Blumenfeld and Commander von Donderberg, who is still the senior prize officer aboard *Quest*. Dr. Druthen is not quite sane. He is ambitious. He thinks that the Duchy of Waldegren will appreciate his brilliance, whereas the Confederacy does not. His mother, who exercised considerable influence over him during his formative years, was an expatriate Waldegrener. Druthen, too, has strong sadistic tendencies. Had it not been for the restraining influence of von Donderberg the lot of the prisoners

would have been a sorry one. He is still urging
Blumenfeld to use them to blackmail us into giving
him a free hand with The Outsider.

"Now, von Donderberg. The impression you
gained from that talk with him over the Carlotti
radio is a correct one. Like many—although not
all—naval officers, he regards himself as a spaceman first and foremost. The prisoners happen to be
wearing the wrong uniform, but they, as far as he is
concerned, are also spacemen. He hates Druthen,
and Druthen hates and despises him."

"Finally, Captain Blumenfeld. Once again, sir,
you summed him up rather neatly. He is essentially a politician, with a politician's lack of conscience. He would stand on his mother's grave to
get two inches nearer to where he wants to be. As a
spaceman he is, at best, merely competent—but
the success of this mission would put him at least
two steps up the promotion ladder. He would play
along with Druthen if he thought that he could get
away with it, but realizes that maltreatment, or
even murder of *Faraway Quests'* rightful crew
could lead to an outbreak of hostilities between the
Duchy and the Confederacy. He knows that his
government would welcome this rather than
otherwise, but fears, as they fear, that the Confederacy's Big Brother might step in. Should he get
the 'all clear' from Waldegren—we gained the impression that the Duchy's political experts are hard
at work evaluating the possibility of Federation
intervention—he will tell Druthen to go ahead."

"Meanwhile, he is hoping that there will be dissension in our ranks. That was why he gave us time

to think things over; not long, but long enough."
He looked at Smith. "As you know, at least one of
us present puts his own interests before the well-
being of *Faraway Quest's* crew."

"Mphm." Grimes puffed thoughtfully at his
pipe. Then, "Do you concur, Mr. Metzenther?"

"Yes, Commodore. Commander Mayhew has
summarized the findings of all four of us."

"And now you know," said Grimes II, who did
not seem to be enjoying his cigarette, "what are
you going to do about it? Not that you can do
much. You haven't a ship of your own, even
though. . . ."

"Even though I'm carrying on as though this
were my own ship?" asked Grimes. "In a way, she
is. Just as. . . ."

"She's not. And neither is Maggie."

"Shut up!" snapped the wife referred to. "Shut
up! This is no time to let your personal feelings get
in the way of important business."

"You should have thought of that last night,"
her husband told her.

Flandry laughed.

"Just what has been going on aboard this
rustbucket?" asked Irene curiously, looking at Sir
Dominic speculatively.

"It's a pity that you weren't here," he told her,
while Sonya looked at him nastily.

"Just a slight domestic problem," said Grimes
airily.

"Some people's idea of what's *slight* . . ."
snarled Grimes II.

"Don't forget that I, too, am an injured party."

Flandry laughed again.

"Please . . ." pleaded Grimes. "Please. We're getting no place at all with this petty squabbling." He turned to Mayhew. "You've given us the general background. It's obvious that we have to do something before Blumenfeld gives Druthen the okay, or before Druthen acts off his own bat. I've already thought of something that we—that Clarisse especially—can do. I take it that there are writing materials in your watch room aboard *my Quest*?"

"Of course."

"And writing materials are also drawing materials. . . ."

"Yes. But to call up some peculiar deities or demons at this juncture could make the situation worse than it is now."

"Who mentioned deities or demons?" Grimes saw that Flandry, Irene and Trafford were looking at him curiously, as were his alter ego and Maggie Lazenby. He said slowly, "I suppose I'd better put you in the picture. Clarisse is more than a mere telepath. She is descended from a caveman artist who, displaced in time, was found on Kinsolving's Planet many years ago. He, it seems, had specialized in painting pictures of various animals which, consequently, were drawn into the hunters' traps. Clarisse inherited his talent. . . ."

"Impossible," said Grimes II flatly.

"Not so, Commodore. I've seen it happen. Ken Mayhew has seen it happen. So has Sonya."

"It's true," she agreed soberly.

"So Clarisse could be a sort of Trojan horse . . ." murmured Flandry.

"You're getting the idea. Of course, there's one snag. Each time that she's . . . performed she's been under the influence of some hallucinogenic drug."

"And the rest of you," sneered Smith.

"No. Most definitely not. The main problem now is to get her suitably high."

"That's no problem," said Mayhew. A great load seemed suddenly to have dropped from his thin shoulders. He had something to do at last—something to help to save Clarisse. "That's no problem. Two telepaths who are married have more, much more in common than any pair of nontelepaths. There is far greater sensitivity, far more . . . sharing than in any common marriage. If *I* get high on anything at all, so will Clarisse. If I go on a trip, so will she."

"Good," murmured Grimes. "Good. So buzz the quack and tell him what you need to put your mind in the proper state. Try to get instructions through to Clarisse. All she has to do is sketch us, one by one, and we'll be with her. . . ." He looked rapidly around the control room. "Not you, Ken. I'm sorry, but you'll be too muzzy with dope. What about you, Mr. Metzenther? Good. And you, Flandry? And myself, and Sonya. . . ."

"Count me in," Irene said gruffly. "I still don't believe it, but if it works I'd like to be in the party."

"And me," said Trafford, although not overenthusiastically. "Tallentire can look after the ship."

Smith did not volunteer.

Maggie Lazenby was about to, Grimes thought,

but lapsed into silence as her husband looked at her long and coldly.

And Grimes II said, "I'll not be sorry to see some of you off my vessel and back aboard your own ships."

21

THIS SHOULDN'T BE happening, thought Grimes. *Magic—and what else can it be called? in the control room of an interstellar ship. . . .* But this was the Rim, where the laws of nature, although not repealed, were not enforced with any stringency. This was beyond the Rim.

He looked at Mayhew as the telepath regarded dubiously the little glass of some colorless fluid that he was holding. "This," the too jovial ship's doctor had assured him, "will give you hallucinations in glorious technicolor and at least seven dimensions. . . ." Grimes looked at Mayhew, and everybody else looked at Mayhew. The PCO quipped, "Now I know how Socrates must have felt."

"Get on with it, Ken," urged Grimes.

"I'm drinking this muck, not you. All right, then. Down the hatch." He suited the action to the words.

His prominent Adam's apple wobbled as the draught went down. He licked his lips, enunciated slowly, "Not . . . bad. Not . . . too . . . bad." An odd sort of vagueness crept over his face. His eyes went out of focus. He wavered on his feet, groped almost aimlessly for a chair, slumped down into it.

Grimes whispered to Metzenther, "Clarisse—is she ready? Are you and Trialanne standing by to help?"

"Of course, Commodore."

Mayhew said with surprising clarity, "The black lambs of Damballa. But they shouldn't. No."

Never mind the bloody black lambs, thought Grimes testily.

"Clarisse . . ." Mayhew's voice was very soft, almost inaudible. "Clarisse. You shouldn't have killed Lassie."

"Damn Lassie," muttered Grimes.

"A man's best friend is his . . . is his . . . is his . . .? But the black lambs. And no sheep dog. Yes."

Metzenther looked toward Grimes. He whispered reassuringly, "It'll not be long now, Commodore. She's started on her pictures. And they won't be of black lambs. Black sheep, more likely."

"You can say that again," grunted Grimes II.

Grimes I allowed himself a smile. Let Metzenther enjoy his play on words, and let the other Grimes make what he liked of it. It didn't matter. He would soon be back aboard his own ship. He looked down at the Minetti automatic pistol that he was holding, ready, in his right hand. (Luckily, his counterpart shared his taste in personal weaponry—as in other things.) He, he was sure, would be the first to be pulled aboard the *Quest*. After all, he knew Clarisse, had known her before Mayhew had. He took one last look around at the other members of the boarding party. All were armed. Sonya, Trafford and Metzenther wore holstered laser handguns; and Irene, two ugly looking pistols of .50 caliber. Flandry had something that looked as though it had been dreamed up by an illustrator of juvenile science fiction thrillers.

Grimes remembered the two occasions on which he had seen Clarisse at work. He recalled, vividly, that bare, windswept mountaintop on Kinsolving, with the black sky overhead, the Galactic Lens a misty shimmer low on the horizon. He visualized, without any effort on his part, the floodlit easel with its square of canvas, the pots of pigment, the girl, naked save for a scanty scrap of some animal pelt, working with swift, sure strokes on her brushes.

Sudden doubt assailed him.

Those had been ideal conditions. Would conditions aboard the hijacked *Faraway Quest* be as ideal?

Mayhew seemed to be completely out, sprawled loosely in his chair, his eyes closed, his mouth slack. A thin dribble of spittle crawled down his chin. Had the telepath taken too much of whatever concoction it was that the doctor had prepared? Was Clarisse similarly unconscious?

Metzenther smiled reassuringly at the Commodore, whispered, "Any time now. . . ."

Flandry, overhearing, snorted his disbelief.

Grimes turned to admonish him, and. . . .

Flandry was gone.

22

FLANDRY WAS GONE.

Grimes wondered why there had been no miniature clap of thunder as the air rushed in to fill the
vacuum caused by his abrupt departure. Had the
exactly correct volume of atmosphere been tele-
ported from the room in which Clarisse was imprisoned to fill the space that the Imperial Captain
had occupied? What did it matter, anyhow? Magic
is an art, not a science.

Flandry was gone—and who next?

Grimes was more than a little hurt. He had
known Clarisse for years. Sonya had known her
for almost as long. And yet she called a stranger to
her. She had met Sir Dominic only once; he must
have made an impression on her.

He turned to the others. "Well, it seems to be working. But why *him*?"

"Why not?" asked Sonya sweetly. "He's resourceful. He's tough."

"And he's out of *my* hair," added Grimes II. He did not say aloud that he hoped that other people would soon be out of his hair. He did not need to.

Mayhew, still unconscious in his chair, twitched. He looked as though he were having a bad dream.

"Is she all right?" demanded Grimes of Metzenther.

"Yes, Commodore," answered the telepath. "Yes." He looked as though he had been about to say more but had decided against it.

"Can't you tell her to get the rest of us shifted across?"

"I . . . I will try. But you must realize that teleportation is a strain upon the operator."

"Damn it all, this is urgent."

"I know, Commodore. But . . . she will not be hurried."

"Druthen, von Donderberg. . . . Do *they* know that Flandry is aboard the ship?"

"No. And with von Donderberg actually in charge everything—including the prisoners' meals—is very much to timetable. There is little chance that Clarisse and Sir Dominic will be disturbed."

Disturbed? thought Grimes. An odd choice of words. . . .

"You must be patient, Commodore," said Metzenther.

Grimes was never to know if it was his own imagination, or if the telepath had deliberately planted the picture in his mind. But he *knew* what was happening, what had happened. He saw Clarisse, her clothing cast aside the better to emulate her savage forebears, working at the sketch she was making on a signals pad. She saw the picture growing out of her swift, sure stylus strokes, the depiction of Sir Dominic. What subconscious desires had been brought to the surface by the drug that Mayhew had taken, the effects of which he had shared with her?

And then. . . .

And then Flandry was with her.

Flandry, the unprincipled, suddenly confronted with a beautiful, naked, available and willing woman.

If Metzenther had not put thoughts, impressions into Grimes' brain he had read the Commodore's mind. He said, telepathically, "Mayhew will never know. We shall make sure of that."

"But . . . but how can she?" asked Grimes silently.

He got the impression of quiet laughter in reply. "How could you? How could Sonya? How could Maggie? Some of us—even you, Commodore—have regarded this straying into other continua as a sort of a holiday. A pubic holiday. . . . Forgive me. That just slipped out. And Clarisse has been under strain as much as any of us, more than most of us. What's more natural than that she should greet her deliverer in the age-old manner? Are you jealous, Commodore?"

149

"Frankly, yes," thought Grimes. He grinned ruefully. "What the hell do you find so amusing?" asked Sonya sharply.

"Oh, er . . . I was just wondering where Sir Dominic had finished up. As we both of us know, this talent of Clarisse's is rather . . . unreliable."

"You have an odd sense of humor," she told him. She was beginning to look anxious.

There were no pictures in Grimes' mind now. He was rather thankful for that. But still he did not know how long it would be before Clarisse resumed her magical activities. He knocked his pipe out into one of the large ashtrays that were placed all around the control room. He refilled it. He lit it.

"Please, John," said Clarisse, "not in here. It's dreadfully stuffy."

She was, as he had visualized her, naked. She was standing at the desk, adding the last touches to the sketch she had made of Grimes. Flandry was seated on the bunk. He was fully clothed.

But. . . .

"Wipe the lipstick off your face, Sir Dominic," said Grimes coldly.

23

CLARISSE IGNORED THE exchange. She tore the sheet upon which she had portrayed Grimes off the pad, put it to one side. She started a fresh sketch. The Commodore peered over her smooth, bare shoulder as she worked. The likeness was unmistakable.

"Now!" she whispered intently.

Grimes was almost knocked off his feet as Irene materialized. She exclaimed cheerfully, "Oops, dearie! Fancy meeting *you* here!" And then, to Clarisse, "Hadn't you better put something on, ducks? All these *men*. . . ."

"I work better this way," she was told.

"Ssshh!" hissed Grimes. "This cabin . . . bugged. . . ."

"It was," remarked Flandry, in normal conversational tones. "And very amateurishly, if I may say so."

"So you did, at least, take precautions before. . . ." Grimes began.

"Before *what*?" asked Flandry, smiling reminiscently. "I always take precautions, Commodore."

Clarisse blushed spectacularly, over her entire body. But she went on sketching.

Sonya appeared, looking around her disapprovingly. *What's been going on here?* she asked silently. Then it was Trafford's turn, and finally Metzenther's. The little cabin was uncomfortably crowded. Grimes didn't like the way that his wife was sitting close beside Flandry on the bunk. She, obviously, didn't like the way that he was being pressed between Irene's flamboyance and Clarisse's nudity. Somebody knocked over the tank in which the psionic amplifier was housed. It did not break, but the cover came off it, allowing the stagnant nutrient solution to spill on the deck. It smelled as though something had been dead for a very long time.

Sonya sniffed. "And now what do we do?" she demanded. "I'd suggest that Clarisse get dressed, but I realize that it's almost impossible in these circumstances."

"This is *your* ship, Commodore," said Flandry.

"Mphm. When is your next meal due, Clarisse?"

"I . . . my watch . . . with my clothes. On the bunk. . . ."

Flandry rummaged in the little pile of garments

and found the timepiece. He announced, "It is 1135 hours, this ship's time."

"Twenty-five minutes," said Clarisse.

"So we wait," said Grimes. "It'll not be for too long. Then we overpower whoever brings the tray and any other guards and take over."

Flandry laughed jeeringly. "Brilliant, Commodore. Really brilliant. And if anybody fires into this dogbox he'll get at.least four of us with one shot."

"Have you any better ideas, Captain?"

"Of course," Flandry replied smugly. "If I am not mistaken, those weapons being toted around by Sonya, Captain Trafford and Mr. Metzenther are laser pistols. They are not used much in my continuum, but you people seem to like them. A laser pistol can be used as a tool as well as a handgun. A cutting tool. . . ."

"So we break out, rather than wait to be let out."

"A truly blinding glimpse of the obvious, sir."

Trafford was nearest the door. "Go ahead, please, Captain," said Grimes.

The little man unholstered his weapon. He pulled out a slender screwdriver that had been recessed in the butt of it. Carefully, not hurrying, he made adjustments to the power settings. He replaced the screwdriver.

Grimes took a pencil from Clarisse. He managed to shove his way through the crowd to stand beside Trafford. He drew a rough circle on the smooth, painted metal panel of the door. He said, "The lock should be there, Captain. If you burn around it. . . ."

"I'll try, Commodore."

The narrow beam of intensely bright light shot from the muzzle of the pistol. Metal became blue white incandescent immediately but was reluctant to melt. The structural components of a starship are designed to withstand almost anything. Trafford removed his finger from the trigger, used the screwdriver to make further adjustments. Then he tried again.

Grimes had foreseen what was going to happen. After all, as Flandry had pointed out, this was *his* ship. Grimes should have warned the others, but this chance to see the silly grin wiped off Sir Dominic's face was not one to be passed over.

The air in the watch room became stiflingly hot, and acrid with the fumes of burning paint and metal. And then. . . .

And then there were bells ringing, some close and some distant, filling the echoing shell of *Faraway Quest* with their clangor. A klaxon added its stridency to the uproar. From the nozzles of the spray system jetted a white foam that blanketed everything and everybody. Flandry cursed, but he could never hope to match Irene's picturesque obscenities and blasphemies.

The door sagged open.

Grimes, pistol in hand, shoved past Trafford, out into the brightly lit alleyway. Sonya, looking like a figure roughly hacked from white foam plastic, was behind him, then Trafford, then Irene. Metzenther staggered out supporting Clarisse, who looked as though she had just emerged from a bubble bath.

"You bloody fool," gasped Flandry, who was

last to emerge. "You bloody fool! You should have known. . . ."

"I did know," snapped Grimes. "Pipe down, damn you!"

The fire-extinguishing foam was pouring out into the alleyway. Grimes motioned to the others to follow suit, dropped to his knees, let the cool, not unpleasantly acrid froth almost cover him. How long would it be before the fire-fighting party was on the scene? When *Quest's* own crew had been running the ship scant seconds would have elapsed; but Druthen and his scientists and technicians were not spacemen, and at least one of the three officers put aboard from *Adler* would be remaining in the control room.

Somebody, somewhere, switched the alarms off. So they realized that there was a fire. And without that incessant noise it was possible to think, to give orders.

"Keep covered," said Grimes. "They'll not see us until it's too late." He added, in a disgruntled voice, "The bastards are certainly taking their time. Billy Williams and his crowd would have had the fire out half an hour ago!"

"Glumph," replied Sonya through a mouthful of foam.

They were here at last, rounding the curve in the alleyway: a tall figure in a space suit, the spiked helmet of which made it obvious that he was a member of the Waldegren Navy, four men in civilian space armor, pushing a wheeled tank.

"Lasers only," whispered Grimes. "Fire!"

Lasers are silent—but they are dreadfully lethal. Grimes hated to have to do it—but the fire fighters must be given no chance to warn Druthen and von Donderberg in Control. Druthen's men were hijackers, and their lives were already forfeit. The universal penalty for this crime is death. The Waldegrener was acting under orders, but he had no business aboard Grimes' ship. What happened to him was just his bad luck.

Grimes stood up slowly in the waist-high foam. He looked at the five silent figures. They were dead all right, each of them with his armor neatly pierced in half a dozen places. There was no blood, luckily, and luckily nobody had employed the effective slashing technique, so the suits were still reasonably intact.

Five of them, he thought, trying hard to fight down his nausea. *Seven of us. Flandry can wear the Waldegren space suit—it'll fit him. Then myself. And Sonya. Irene? Metzenther? Trafford? Clarisse?*

He said, "Get the armor off them. It's a made-to-order disguise."

Trafford, Flandry and Sonya went to work. The smell of charred meat and burned blood was distressingly evident. Suddenly, Sonya beckoned to Grimes. He went to look, down at the stripped figure. It was a woman. She was, she had been one of the junior technicians. Grimes remembered her. He had referred to her, in his thoughts, as a hard-faced little bitch. Feeling sorry for this would not help her now.

He walked slowly back to where Clarisse was standing, patches of foam slipping slowly down her smooth skin, others still clinging to the salient points of her body. He whispered, pointing, ''You know her?''

''Yes.''

''Wear her suit. Speak into the suit radio, using her voice. . . . You can do that?''

''Of course.''

''Report that the fire is under control. Should Druthen or von Donderberg feel uneasy about anything you, as a telepath, will know the right things to say to put their minds at rest. Say that we are returning topside to report as soon as the fire is out. Get it?''

''Yes.''

''Then get suited up.''

She obeyed him, assisted by Sonya and Irene. She spurned their suggestion that she should wear the dead woman's long johns. Grimes didn't blame her, although he winced at the thought of the unlined inside of the suit chafing her unprotected skin.

Then Grimes, too, stripped to his skimpy underwear, could not bring himself to put on a dead man's next-to-the-skin union suit. Neither could Sonya. But the corpse robbing worried neither Irene nor Flandry.

The bodies were concealed in the congealing foam, which hid, too, the tools taken from the belt pouches of the fire party. Those same pouches served as holsters for the weapons of Grimes and his people. It was decided that Trafford and Metzenther, who had been unable to disguise themselves, would stay in the watch room. They would be safe enough there, especially since Metzenther should be able to give ample advance warning of the approach of any hostile persons.

Then, speaking in a voice that was not her own, Clarisse said into her helmet microphone, "Sadie Hawkes reporting to Dr. Druthen. The fire's out. Nothing serious. That stupid bitch was burning papers for some reason or other."

"Is she hurt?" Druthen's voice did not betray much, if any, concern.

"Naw, Doc. We just slapped her round a little, is all."

Von Donderberg's voice came through the speakers. "Lieutenant Muller."

"Sorry, Commander," Clarisse told him. "The Lieutenant slipped on the foam an' caught his helmet a crack. His transceiver's on the blink."

"Where is the prisoner now?" inquired Druthen.

"We left her in her bubble batch to cool down. Ha, ha."

"Ha, ha," echoed Dr. Druthen.

Ha, ha, thought Grimes nastily.

24

GRIMES LED THE way into the control room. (After all, this was his ship.) He was followed by Flandry, whose right hand hovered just over the butt of his energy pistol, then by Sonya, then by Irene. Clarisse caught up the rear.

Druthen and von Donderberg swiveled in their chairs to face the returning fire-fighting party. The scientist was fatly arrogant. The Waldegrener looked more than a little frayed around the edges. *It's your own fault*, thought Grimes. *If you aren't fussy about the company you keep. . . .*

Grimes and the others stood there. Druthen and von Donderberg sat there. Grimes knew that he should act and act fast, but he was savoring this moment. Druthen, an expression of petulant impatience growing on his face, snarled, "Take your bloody helmets off! Anybody'd think there was a smell in here." His words, although distorted by the suit diaphragms, were distinct enough.

"There is," replied Grimes. "You."

The scientist's face turned a rich purple. He sputtered, "Mutinous swine! Von Donderberg, you heard! *Do* something!"

Von Donderberg shrugged. There was a flicker of amusement in his blue eyes.

Grimes said, "Mutiny, Dr. Druthen? I am arresting *you* for mutiny and piracy." He fumbled for his Minetti, but the little pistol, unlike the heavier weapons carried by the others, was not suitable for use by a man wearing space armor with its clumsy gloves.

But Flandry's odd-looking weapon was out, as were Sonya's and Irene's pistols. Druthen stared at them helplessly, von Donderberg in a coldly calculating manner. "You will note, Herr Doktor," remarked the Waldegren officer, "that there are neat holes in those space suits, holes that could have been made by laser fire at short range." He seemed to be speaking rather louder than was really necessary. "It would seem that our prisoners somehow have escaped and have murdered my Lieutenant Muller and four of your people." He turned to face Grimes. "You will surrender."

"I admire your nerve," Grimes told him.

"That is not one of the prisoners!" exclaimed Druthen. "It's that bastard Grimes! But that's impossible!"

"It's not, Doctor. It's not." The Commodore

was really enjoying himself. "You sneered at me—remember—for carrying a practicing witch on my Articles of Agreement. . . ."

The practicing witch screamed, "John! The Carlotti set! It's on! *Adler's* seeing and hearing everything!"

And *Adler's* temporal precession rate was synchronized with that of *Faraway Quest*. No doubt her cannon and projectors were already trained upon their target. No doubt boarding parties were already suited up and hurrying into the warship's airlocks.

Grimes swore. His gloating could easily have ruined everything. He dived for the Mannschenn Drive remote controls. He heard pistol fire as somebody, Irene probably, switched off the Carlotti transceiver in an effective but destructive manner. Von Donderberg got in his way, grappled him. The Waldegrener was a strong man and agile, whereas Grimes was hampered by his armor. His body was a barrier between the Commodore and the Mannschenn Drive control console. Brutally, Grimes flailed at him with his mailed fists, but von Donderberg managed to get a firm grip on both his wrists. Grimes tried to bring his knee up, but he was too slow and the foul blow was easily avoided.

It was Irene who settled matters. (After all, this was not *her* ship.) Her heavy pistols barked deafeningly, the slugs just missing Grimes (intentionally, he hoped) and von Donderberg. The face of the control panel splintered; otherwise the immediate results were unspectacular.

But down in the Mannschenn Drive room the

duty technician watched aghast as the great, gleaming rotos ran wild, precessing faster and faster yet, tumbling down and into the dark dimensions uncontrolled and uncontrollably. Beyond the control room viewports, the image of *Adler* glowed with impossible clarity against the blackness, then flickered out like a snuffed candle flame. Throughout the ship, men and women stared at familiar surroundings and fittings that sagged and fluoresced, that wavered on the very brink of the absolute nothingness. Belatedly, alarm bells started to ring, but their sound was a thin, high shrilling, felt rather than heard.

Abruptly, shockingly, normalcy returned as the Drive shut itself off. Colors, forms and sounds were suddenly . . . drab. The irregular throbbing of the inertial drive was harsh and irritating.

Grimes, still straining against von Donderberg, snapped, "Shut that bloody thing off!" Apart from the Waldegren Commander and his surviving officer—wherever *he* was—there were no spacemen among those who had hijacked the ship. Free fall would not worry Grimes and his boarding party overmuch, but it would be, at the very least, an inconvenience to the planet lubbers.

The annoying vibration ceased. *What next?* Grimes asked himself. It was hard to think clearly. That blasted von Donderberg was still putting up a fight, and Sonya and Clarisse, who had come to the Commodore's aid, were more of a hindrance than a help. "Irene!" he called. "Check the indicator! Are all AT doors shut?" (The airtight doors should have automatically at the first signs of main drive malfunction.)

162

"Yes," she replied at last.

"There's a switch by itself in a glass-fronted box. . . . It's labeled LOCK. . . ."

"Got it. . . ."

"Then throw it!"

Grimes heard the little crash of shattering glass, heard Irene say, "Locked."

Sonya had a space suited arm across von Donderberg's throat. The man was starting to choke; his face was turning blue, his eyes were protruding. Suddenly he relinquished his hold on Grimes' wrists. The two women hustled him to an acceleration chair, forced him down into it. They held him there while Irene, using a length of flex that she had found somewhere, lashed him into the seat. Druthen had already been similarly dealt with by Irene and Flandry.

"Mphm," grunted Grimes. The situation was, for the time being, under control. Slowly he removed his gloves, then took his pipe from one of the pouches at the belt of his space suit. He filled it and lit it, ignoring Sonya's "Not *now*!" He stared at Druthen, demanded, "Where are the prisoners?"

"Find out!" came the snarled reply.

From the intercom speakers came a growing uproar. "Doctor Druthen, what's happened?" "We're shut in, let us out of here!" "Doctor, there's no gravity!"

"We can do without that," said Grimes. Sonya switched off the system. Then, "Where are the prisoners, Druthen?"

Again the scientist snarled, "Find out!"

"And that is just what we intend to do, Herr

Doktor," remarked Flandry. He pulled that complicated looking weapon from a makeshift holster at his belt, looked at it thoughtfully, said regretfully, "Not quite subtle enough. . . ." From another pouch he took out a knife, drew it from its sheath. It was only small, but it gleamed evilly. "Perhaps a little judicious whittling . . ." He murmured. "Where shall I start?"

Von Donderberg, who had recovered his voice, croaked, "Remember that you an officer and gentleman are. A civilized man."

"Who says that I'm civilized, Commander? Come to that—who dares say that either you or the learned Herr Doktor are civilized? You, sir, are a pirate. He is either a mutineer or a hijacker or both—but this is no time to discuss legalities. H'm. Your hands are nicely secured to the arms of your chair. Doctor. Perhaps if I pry off your fingernails, one by one. . . ."

"Flandry, you wouldn't!" expostulated Grimes.

"Wouldn't I, Commodore? You may watch."

"But I know where they are," said Clarisse. She added tartly, "What the hell's the good of having a professional telepath around if you don't make use of her?"

"Why must you spoil everything?" asked Flandry plaintively.

Von Donderberg laughed mirthlessly and Druthen fainted.

25

Yes, Clarisse knew where they were. It was an obvious enough place anyhow, the empty cargo compartment, right aft, in which Grimes had intended to stow whatever fantastic artifacts could be plundered from the Outsiders' Ship. Sonya, taking with her the electronic master key that would allow her passage through the locked airtight doors, went to release them. She was accompanied by Irene and would pick up Trafford and Metzenther on the way. She assured Grimes that if she encountered any of Druthen's people she would shoot if she had to. Irene growled that *she* would shoot, period. But there was not much risk. Metzenther would be able to give them ample warning of what hostile action, if any, awaited them in any compartment that they were about to enter.

Grimes switched on the second Carlotti transceiver—luckily the ship was fitted with two of the sets—and raised *Faraway Quest II* without any difficulty. She was no longer ahead, relatively speaking. *Adler* had turned, and *Quest II* and *Wanderer* had turned with her, and all three ships were racing back toward The Outsider on a reciprocal of their original trajectory.

"So you've got your ship back, Commodore," commented the other Grimes, looking out from the little screen. "Your Commander Mayhew, and Trialanne aboard *Wanderer*, have been keeping us informed."

"There's a little mopping up yet, Commodore," said Grimes. "But it shouldn't take long. I suggest that you and *Wanderer* slow down to allow me to catch up."

"*Wanderer* can if she likes, Commodore, but I'm not going to. *Adler's* going like a bat out of hell, and has the heels of us. Mayhew tells me that she's using some experimental accelerator, for the first time. Unluckily he's a mechanical and mathematical moron, so he can't get anything but absolute gibberish from the mind of *Adler's* engineer officer. But I know that it's Blumenfeld's intention to race us to The Outsider and then to seize and to hold it against all comers, waiting for reinforcements."

"What about *Vindictive?* Captain Flandry's ship?"

"What, indeed?" echoed Flandry.

"We can't warn her," said Grimes II. "That stupid culture she comes from has never developed the Carlotti system, or used tele-paths. . . ."

"I resent that," snarled Flandry.

Grimes II seemed to notice him for the first time. "Sorry, Captain. I didn't realize that you were listening. But can *you* warn your ship?"

"No, I can't. But my men have very itchy trigger fingers."

"They'll need 'em. But switch on your other set, Commodore. Mr. Smith in *Wanderer* would like a word with you."

"I can't, Commodore. Will you tell Mr. Smith that his Mrs. Trafford switched off my other set rather permanently? The same applies to the remote control panel of my Mannschenn Drive."

"Then switch over to *Wanderer*. I'll just stick beak."

Grimes made the necessary adjustments, found himself looking at Smith. Tallentire was well in the background.

"Commodore," said Smith, "you realize that neither we nor the other Commodore Grimes can afford to wait until you have effected repairs and adjusted trajectory. *Adler* must be stopped. I, as the charterer, have assumed effective command of *Wanderer*. I do not see either Captain Trafford or Mrs. Trafford in your control room. Could you ask them to speak with me?"

"They're not available at the moment," said Grimes.

"They bloody well are!" Irene contradicted him.

Suddenly the control room had become

crowded with people: Sonya, Irene, Trafford, Metzenther, Billy Williams, Carnaby, Hendrikson, Major Dalzell and Daniels. Williams reported to Grimes, "Commander Davis and his juniors have gone straight to the engine room, Skipper. They'll let you know as soon as they can get her started up." He went to where Druthen and von Donderberg were lashed in their chairs. "An' what shall we do with these drongos?"

"Take 'em away and lock 'em up, as soon as we can get round to it."

"Captain Trafford; Mrs. Trafford," came Smith's insistent voice from the Carlotti speaker.

"Yes!" snapped Irene.

"You and Captain Trafford should be aboard this ship. But you're not. So I had no option but to order Mr. Tallentire to press the chase."

"You . . . *ordered*?"

"Yes. I ordered."

"He *is* the charterer," pointed out Trafford.

"All right. He's the bloody charterer. And so what?"

"Blumenfeld must be stopped," insisted the little captain. "Waldegren, in any continuum, cannot be allowed to get its hands on The Outsider's secrets."

"You'll never stop us now!" bragged von Donderberg.

"Shut up, you!" growled Billy Williams.

Irene turned back to the Carlotti transceiver, "All right, Smith. Press the chase. But, as owner, I appoint Mr. Tallentire master—until Captain Trafford's return. Mr. Tallentire will act as *he* sees fit. Get it?"

"As you wish." Smith managed to convey the impression of being supremely unconcerned.

"I will talk with Mr. Tallentire now."

Tallentire's face replaced that of Smith in the screen. He looked far from happy. "Yes, ma'am?"

"You are acting captain. Put the interests of the ship before those of Mr. Smith. Press the chase. Make use of your weaponry as requisite. You will revert to your normal rank as soon as we are back on board. That's all."

Somehow a junior engineer had managed to insert himself into the crowded control room. He elbowed his way toward Grimes. "Sir, Commander Davis told me to tell you that you can start inertial and Mannschenn Drives as soon as you like. He's been trying to raise you on the intercom, but the line is dead."

"It's switched off," Grimes admitted. "But we'll get it working again to the engine room. . . ." Daniels had anticipated him, handed Grimes a microphone. "Commodore here, Commander Davis. The remote control panel of the Mannschenn Drive is . . . out of order. You'll just have to get your instructions by telephone. Good." He turned to Carnaby. "Get ready to put the ship on the reciprocal heading—straight for The Outsider. We may be a little late for the start of the party, but we should be there before it's over . . ."

Flandry, Irene and Trafford looked at him with some animosity. "It's all right for *you*," growled the ex-Empress. "You've got a ship now, and we haven't."

"Can you get us back to where we belong?" Flandry asked Clarisse, a little desperately.

"I . . . I don't know . . ." she admitted. "I've never tried *sending* anybody anywhere before."

"You'd better try now," Grimes told her. "Or as soon as we have things sorted out." He didn't want Sonya and Flandry in the same ship.

26

THE COMMODORE'S QUARTERS still retained the distasteful traces of Druthen's occupancy, but the cleaning up could wait. Grimes forced himself to ignore the untidiness—no less than his own, but *different*—the scars left by smoldering cigarette ends on table tops; the sticky rings that showed where slopping over glasses had been set down. Sonya had wanted to do something about it at once, if not before, but Grimes had restrained her. "It is essential," he said firmly, "that Sir Dominic, Irene, Captain Trafford and Mr. Metzenther be returned to their own ships as soon as possible. . . ."

"And it is equally essential—to me, anyhow—that Ken be brought back here as soon as possible," Clarisse told him.

"Mphm. I see your point. But first of all both Captain Flandry's *Vindictive* and Captain Trafford's *Wanderer* must be put in a state of full fighting efficiency, so as to be able to cope with *Adler*. I would suggest that you deal with Sir Dominic first."

"Thank you," said Flandry.

"It will be a pleasure, Captain. Well, Clarisse?"

"I don't know how it *can* be done . . ." muttered the girl. "I don't know *if* it can be done. . . ."

"Rubbish!" snorted Irene. "If you can pull, you can push. It's as simple as that."

"Then why don't *you* try it?"

"It's just not my specialty, dearie. I'm just a rough and tough ex-mate out of the Dog Star Line."

"To say nothing of being a rough and tough ex-empress," commented Sonya acidly. "Shut up, unless you have something constructive to contribute."

"What I said *was* constructive."

"Like hell it was."

"Ladies, ladies . . ." murmured Flandry soothingly. Then, to Clarisse. "As I see it, your talent works this way. You're in the right, drug-induced frame of mind. You paint or draw a picture of whatever animal or person you wish to pull into the trap or ambush, concentrate—and the result is instant teleportation. . . ."

"You've oversimplified a little, Dominic, but that's about it."

"All right. Now suppose you sketched, to the best of your ability, the inside of my control room aboard *Vindictive*. . . ."

"I've never been aboard your ship, Dominic."

"But you've been inside my mind."

Oh, thought Grimes. *Have you, indeed? But I suppose that a telepath wants more than mere physical contact*. . . .

"Yes."

"This is what I want you to do. You must order from the ship's doctor whatever hallucinogen it is you need. And then, when you are ready, I'll visualize the control room of my ship, in as exact detail as possible, and you put it down on paper. . . ."

"And what," asked Grimes, "if *Vindictive's* control room is brought to Captain Flandry, instead of the other way round? I seem to recall a law of physics that I learned as a child: Two solid bodies cannot occupy the same space at the same time."

"Let me finish, Commodore. After she has drawn the control room she will put me in it . . . ."

"Yes, Dominic," whispered Clarisse. "I think it will work. I'm sure it will work."

"As long as somebody's sure about something . . ." grumbled Grimes. "Now, I think that we have some neo-mescalin in our medical stores. It was you who insisted that we carry some. . . ."

"That is correct. If you will have it sent up . . .?"

Grimes called the doctor on the intercom, and then Billy Williams in Control. "Commander Williams," he said, "unless it is a matter of utmost urgency we are not, repeat not, to be disturbed."

"You won't be, Skipper. We're the also-ran in

this race—an' I'm afraid that *Adler's* the odds on favorite! Of course, *Vindictive* might pip her at the post.''

"We're trying to insure that she does," said Grimes, breaking off the conversation.

Slowly, without embarrassment, Clarisse removed her clothing, ignoring Irene's, "Is that necessary?" and Sonya's, "You're only jealous." She took the small glass of opalescent fluid that Grimes handed her, drained it. In her nudity she was more witch than mere woman. She was . . . untouchable. (But that bastard Flandry hadn't found her so, thought Grimes.) Her face was solemn, her eyes looking at something very far away. And yet it was Sir Dominic at whom she was looking. At whom? Through whom? Beyond whom?

She was stooping slightly over the table upon which a sheet of paper had been spread, upon which the colored pens had been laid out. With her gaze still intent upon Flandry she commenced to draw with swift, sure strokes. The picture was taking shape: acceleration chairs, consoles, screens, the remote controls of machinery and weaponry, all subtly unlike anything that *Quest's* and *Wanderer's* people had ever seen before. *Different ships, different long splices,* thought Grimes, recalling an ancient Terran seafaring proverb. *Different universes, different interstellar drives. . . .*

Tension was building up in the Commodore's day cabin as the naked Clarisse stared at Flandry in his glittering uniform; as Flandry stared at Clarisse. As far as he was concerned, as far as she was concerned they were alone. Under her weaving hands the sketch was becoming three dimensional, real. Were the lights dimming? Was the irregular beat of the inertial drive, the thin, high whining of the Mannschenn Drive becoming fainter? Was the deathly cold of interstellar space pervading the ship?

There is one law of nature that is never broken—magic notwithstanding: *You can't get something for nothing*. A transfer of a solid body across a vast distance was about to take place. Such a transfer, whether by wheels, wings or witchcraft, involves the use of energy. There was energy in many usable forms available within the hull of *Faraway Quest*. It was being drawn upon.

Grimes stared at the picture on the table. The lights—red, green, blue and amber—on the panels of the consoles were glowing, and some of them were blinking rapidly. The darkness beyond the viewports was the utter blackness of intergalactic space. Something swam slowly into sight beyond one of the big transparencies—the dome-shaped Shaara derelict.

And then. . . .

And then there was a man there, standing in the middle of the hitherto deserted control room, the details of his face and figure growing under the witch artist's flying fingers. It was unmistakably Flandry, and he was stark naked save for his belt and his holstered pistol.

Grimes looked up from the sketch to stare at the

emptiness where Flandry had been standing. He was . . . gone. But not entirely; his uniform, a small bundle of black and gold, of rainbow ribbons, was all that remained of him.

Irene said—was it to Sonya or to Clarisse?— "At least you've something to remember him by, dearie."

Clarisse, her face cold and hard, snatched the sheet with the sketch off the table, screwed it up into a ball, threw it toward the disposal chute. She did not miss. She moved swiftly around the table, picked up the empty uniform, then stuffed it down the chute after the crumpled paper. Grimes made as though to stop her—after all, an analysis of the cloth from which Flandry's clothing had been cut could have told a great deal about the technology of his culture—then decided against it. He would be able to swap information with Sir Dominic after *Adler* had been disposed of. Nonetheless, he was sorry that he had not said goodbye properly to the man, thanked him for all his help. (But Flandry had helped himself, in more ways than one. . . .)

The witch girl was ready to resume operations. A fresh sheet of paper was on the table. She said nothing aloud to Metzenther, but the two telepaths must have been in communication. He came to stand beside her, was obviously feeding into her mind the details of *Wanderer's* control room. Again the detailed picture grew.

Irene asked. "Would you mind if I kept my clothes on. Clarisse? Public nudism never appealed to me."

Sonya said, cattily, "I don't think female

nakedness interests her."

Nor did it. When Irene vanished she left nothing behind—and neither did Trafford nor Metzenther.

And now, at last, Clarisse was working for herself. For the last time the lights dimmed, the temperature dropped, the shipboard sounds were muffled. Grimes looked at the flattering portrait of Mayhew that had appeared, then at Sonya. He said, "I think we'll see what's happening topside, my dear." And, as Mayhew materialized, just as they were leaving, "It's good to have our ship to ourselves again."

27

THEY HAD THEIR ship to themselves again, but she was a ship alone. Far ahead of them now were their allies—allies only as long as it was expedient for them to be so—and their enemies. There was communication still with *Faraway Quest II* and with *Wanderer,* by Carlotti radio and through the telepaths. There was no word from *Vindictive;* but as Irene, Trafford and Metzenther were safely back aboard their own vessel, it could be assumed that Flandry was safely back in his.

Grimes, pacing his control room (three steps one way, three steps the other unless he wished to make complicated detours around chairs and banked instruments) was becoming more and more impatient. For many years he had thought of himself as a man of peace—but in his younger days, in the Federation's Survey Service, he had specialized in gunnery. If there was to be a fight he wanted to be in it. Apart from anything else, should he not be present at the moment of victory over *Adler* his prior claim to The Outsider would be laughed at by Irene, by Smith, by Flandry and even by his other self. And his engines were not developing their full capacity.

The emergency shutdown of the Mannschenn Drive had affected the smooth running of that delicate, complex mechanism. It was nothing serious, but recalibration was necessary. Recalibration can be carried out only on the surface of a planet. And even if there had been any planets in the vicinity—which, of course, there were not—Grimes could not afford the time.

So *Faraway Quest* limped on, while, at last, the reports started coming in from ahead of her. *Wanderer* thought the *Vindictive* was engaging *Adler*. One of the officers aboard *Faraway Quest II* had broken the code that *Adler* was using in her Carlotti transmissions to base, and Grimes II reported that Blumenfeld was screaming for reinforcements.

Wanderer and *Faraway Quest II* were now within extreme missile range of the engagement but had not yet opened fire. To do so they would have to revert to normal space time. Metzenther, aboard *Wanderer*, reported through Clarisse that he and Trialanne were monitoring the involuntary psionic transmissions of the personnel of both ships presently engaged in the fighting, and that

Flandry was emanating confidence, and Blumen-feld a growing doubt as to the outcome of the battle. Each ship, however, was finding it difficult to counter the unfamiliar weapons being used by the other, and each ship was making maximum use of the cover of the derelicts in orbit about The Outsider.

Wanderer had emerged into the normal continuum and had launched missiles.

Faraway Quest II was engaging *Adler* with long range laser.

Somebody had scored a direct hit on the Outsiders' Ship itself.

And that was all.

28

THE CARLOTTI TRANSCEIVER was dead insofar as *Wanderer, Faraway Quest II* and *Adler* were concerned. There were no psionic transmissions from *Wanderer,* no unintentional emanations from the crews of the other ships.

What had happened? Had the allies launched their Sunday punch against *Adler,* and had *Adler's* retaliatory Sunday punch connected on all three of them? It was possible, Grimes supposed, just barely possible—but wildly improbable.

"Are you sure you can pick up absolutely nothing?" he demanded of Mayhew and Clarisse. (There are usually some survivors, even when a ship is totally destroyed, even though they may not survive for long.)

"Nothing," she replied flatly. And then—"But I'm picking up an emanation. . . . It's more an emotion than actual thought. . . ."

"I get it too," agreed Mayhew. "It's . . . it's a sense of strong disapproval."

"Mphm. I think that I'd disapprove strongly if *my* ship were shot from under me," said Grimes.

"But . . . but it's not *human* . . ." insisted the girl.

"Mr. Carnaby," Grimes barked at his navigator. "What do you get in the MPI? Is the Outsiders' Ship still there?"

"Still there, sir. And, as far as I can make out, only four vessels in orbit about her. . . . There could be a cloud of wreckage."

Possibly a couple of the derelicts, thought Grimes. Possibly *Adler,* or *Wanderer,* or the other *Quest,* or *Vindictive.* Possibly a large hunk blown off the Outsiders' Ship herself. Possibly anything.

He said, "We will stand in cautiously, proceeding under Mannschenn Drive until we are reasonably sure that it is safe to reenter normal space time. Meanwhile, Mr. Hendrikson, have all weaponry in a state of instant readiness. And you, Major Dalzell, have your men standing by for boarding operations. Commander Williams, see that the boats are all cleared away."

"What is a killer ape?" asked Clarisse suddenly.

"This is hardly the time or place to speculate about our probable ancestry!" snapped Grimes.

"I am not speculating, Commodore. It is just that I picked up a scrap of coherent thought. It was as though a voice—not a human voice—said,

'Nothing but killer apes. . . .' "

"It's a pity we haven't an ethologist along," remarked Grimes. And where was Maggie Lazenby, the Survey Service ethologist whom he had known, years ago, whom he knew, now—but when *was* now?—as the other Grimes, captain of the other *Faraway Quest?* Where was Grimes? Where was Irene? Where was Flandry? He didn't worry about Blumenfeld.

He went to look at the MPI screen. It was a pity that it showed no details. But that large, rapidly expanding blob of luminescence must be The Outsider; those small sparks the derelicts. Carnaby said, in that tone of voice used by junior officers who doubt the wisdom of the procedures of their superiors, "We're *close,* sir."

"Yes, Mr. Carnaby. Mphm." He took his time filling and lighting his pipe. "All right, you may stand by the intercom to the engine room. Stop inertial drive. Half-astern. Stop her. Mannschenn Drive—stop! Mr. Hendrikson—stand by all weapons!"

And there, plain beyond the viewports, was The Outsider coldly luminescent, unscarred, not so much a ship as a castle out of some fairy tale told when Man was very young: with towers and turrets, cupolas and minarets and gables and buttresses, awe-inspiring rather than grotesque. And drifting by, tumbling over and over, came one of the derelicts, the Shaara vessel aboard which the conference had been held. It had been neatly bisected, so that each of its halves looked like one of those models of passenger liners in booking agents' display windows, cut down the midship line to show every deck, every compartment.

"We will continue to orbit The Outsider," said Grimes. "We will search for survivors."

"Commodore," said Mayhew. "There are no survivors. They are all . . . gone."

"Dead, you mean?"

"No, sir. Just . . . gone."

29

THE WERE ... GONE: *Wanderer* and *Adler*, *Faraway. Quest II* and *Vindictive*. They were gone, without a trace, as though they had never been. (But had they ever been?) There was wreckage in orbit about The Outsider—the shattered and fused remains of the Dring cruiser: a whirling cloud of fragments that could have come only from that weird, archaic and alien ship that had never been investigated, that would never now be investigated. And Grimes' flag, the banner of the Rim Worlds Confederacy that he had planted on the Outsiders' Ship, was gone too. This was a small matter and was not noticed until, at last, Grimes decided to send away his boarding party. Until then the search for survivors had occupied all his attention.

Faraway Quest had the field to herself.

"We will carry on," said Grimes heavily, "with what we came out here to do." And his conscience was nagging him. Surely there was *something* that he could have done for Flandry, for Irene, for the other Grimes. All of them had helped him. What had he done to help them? What had he done to help Maggie? But space was so vast, and space time, with its infinitude of dimensions, vaster still; and the lost ships and their people were no more than microscopic needles in a macrocosmic haystack. Too, he told himself, some clue to their fates might be found within that enormous, utterly alien hull.

So it was that Grimes, suited up, stood in the airlock of the *Quest* with Sonya and Williams and Major Dalzell. The Outsider had . . . permitted the ship to approach much closer than she had before; there would be no need to use the boats for the boarding party. The door slowly opened, revealing beyond itself that huge, gleaming construction. It looked neither friendly nor menacing. It was . . . neutral.

Grimes made the little jump required to break magnetic contact between boot soles and deck plating, at the same time actuating his suit propulsion unit. He knew, without turning to watch, that the others were following him. Swiftly he crossed the narrow moat of nothingness, turning himself about his short axis at just the right time, coming in to a landing on an area of The Outsider's hull that was clear of turrets and antennae. He felt rather than heard the muffled clang as his feet hit the flat metal surface. Sonya came down beside him, then Williams, then Dalzell.

The commodore looked up at his ship, hanging there in the absolute blackness, faint light showing from her control room viewports, a circle of brighter light marking the reopened airlock door. He could see four figures jumping from it—the sergeant of marines and three privates. Next would be Mayhew, with Engineer Commander Davis, Brenda Coles, the assistant biochemist and Ruth Macoby, assistant radio officer. It was a pity, thought Grimes, that he had not crewed his ship with more specialist officers; but it had been assumed, of course, that Dr. Druthen and his scientists and technicians would fill this need. But Druthen and his people, together with von Donderberg and his surviving junior officer, were prisoners in the empty cargo hold in which *Faraway Quest's* crew had been confined.

"We're being watched," whispered Sonya, her voice faint from the helmet transceiver.

They were being watched. Two of the antennae on the border of the clear area were turning, twisting. They looked unpleasantly like cobras poised to strike.

"Not to worry," Grimes assured her. "Calver mentioned the very same thing in *his* report."

The sergeant and his men were down now. The eight humans were tending to huddle. "Break it up!" Dalzell was barking. "Break it up! We're too good a target like this!"

"So is the ship, Major." Grimes told him.

"Sorry, sir." The young marine did not sound

very penitent. "But I think we should take all precautions."

"All right," said Grimes. "Scatter—within reason." But he and Sonya stayed very close together.

Mayhew, Davis, Coles and Macoby came in. The telepath identified Grimes by the badges of rank on his space suit, came to stand with him and Sonya.

"Well, Ken?" asked the Commodore.

"It . . . it knows we're here. It . . . it is deciding. . . ."

"If it doesn't make its mind up soon," said Grimes, "I'll burn my way in."

"*Sir!*" Mayhew sounded horrifed.

"Don't worry," Sonya told him. "It's opening up for us."

Smoothly, with no vibrations, a circular door was sliding to one side. Those standing on it had ample time to get clear of the opening, to group themselves about its rim. They looked down into a chamber, lit from no discernible source, that was obviously an airlock. From one of its walls, rungs spaced for the convenience of human beings extruded themselves. (And would those rungs have been differently spaced for other, intelligent, space-faring beings? Almost certainly.)

Grimes reported briefly by his suit radio to Hendrikson who had been left in charge. He knew without asking that Mayhew would be making a similar report to Clarisse. Then he said, "All right. We'll accept the invitation." He lowered himself over the rim, a foot on the first rung of the ladder.

The Outsider's artificial gravity field was functioning, and *down* was down.

There was ample room in the chamber for all twelve of them. They stood there silently, watching the door slide back into place over their heads. Dalzell and his marines kept their hands just over the butts of their handguns. Grimes realized that he was doing the same. He was wearing at his belt a pair of laser pistols. He spoke again into his helmet microphone. His companions could hear him, but it became obvious that they were now cut off from communication with the ship. Captain Calver, he remembered, had reported the same phenomenon. It didn't really matter. Mayhew said that he could still reach Clarisse and that she could reach him.

"Atmosphere, Commodore," said the biochemist, looking at the gauge among the other gauges on her wrist. "Oxygen helium mixture. It would be safe to remove our helmets."

"We keep them on," said Grimes.

Another door in the curving wall was opening. Beyond it was an alleyway, a tunnel that seemed to run for miles and flooded with light. As was the case in the chamber there were no globes or tubes visible. There was nothing but that shadowless illumination and that long, long metallic tube, like the smooth bore of some fantastically huge cannon.

Grimes hesitated only briefly, then began to stride along the alleyway. Sonya stayed at his side. The others followed. Consciously or unconsciously they fell into step. The regular crash of their boots on the metal floor was echoed, reechoed, amplified. They could have been a regiment of the Brigade of Guards, or of Roman legionaries. They marched on and on, along that tunnel with no end. And as they marched the ghosts of those who had been there before them kept pace with them—the spirits of men and of not-men, from only yesterday and from ages before the Terran killer ape realized that an antelope humerus made an effective tool for murder.

It was wrong to march, Grimes dimly realized. It was wrong to tramp into this . . . this temple in military formation, keeping military step. But millennia of martial tradition were too strong for him, were too strong for the others to resist (even if they wanted to do so). They were Men, uniformed men, members of a crew, proud of their uniforms, their weapons and their ability to use them. Before them—unseen, unheard, but almost tangible—marched the phalanxes of Alexander, Napoleon's infantry, Rommel's Afrika Korps. Behind them marched the armies yet to come.

Damn it all! thought Grimes desperately, *we're spacemen, not soldiers. Even Dalzell and his Pongoes are more spacemen than soldiers.*

But a gun doesn't worry about the color of the uniform of the man who fires it.

"Stop!" Mayhew was shouting urgently. "Stop!" He caught Grimes' swinging right arm, dragged on it.

Grimes stopped. Those behind him stopped, in a milling huddle—but the hypnotic spell of marching feet, of phantom drum and fife and bugle, was broken.

"Yes, Commander Mayhew?" asked Grimes.

"It's . . . Clarisse. A message. . . . Important. I couldn't receive until we stopped marching. . . ."

"What is it?" demanded Grimes.

"The . . . ship . . . and Clarisse and Hendrikson and the others. . . . They're prisoners again!"

"Druthen? Von Donderberg?"

"Yes."

Grimes turned to his second-in-command. "You heard that, Commander Williams?"

"Yair. But it ain't possible, Skipper. Nary a tool or a weapon among Druthen an' his mob. We stripped 'em all to their skivvies before we locked 'em up, just to make sure."

"How did it happen'?" Grimes asked Mayhew sharply.

"The . . . the details aren't very clear. But Clarisse thinks that it was a swarm of fragments, from one of the blown up derelicts, on an unpredictable orbit. The *Quest* was holed badly, in several places . . . including the cargo hold. Mr. Hendrikson opened up so the prisoners could escape to an unholed compartment."

"Any of us would have done the same," said Grimes slowly. He seemed to hear Sir Dominic Flandry's mocking laughter. "But what's happening now?"

"Von Donderberg has all the *Quest's* weapons trained on The Outsider, on the airlock door. If we try to get out we shall be like sitting ducks."

"Stalemate . . ." said the Commodore. "Well, we've a breathable atmosphere in here—I hope. So that's no worry. There may even be water and food suitable for our kind of life. . . ."

"But they're coming after us. The airlock door has opened for them! They're here now!"

"Down!" barked Dalzell, falling prone with a clatter. The others followed suit. There were dim figures visible at the end of the tunnel, dim and very distant. There was the faraway chatter of some automatic projectile weapon. The Major and his men were firing back, but without apparent success.

And at the back of Grimes' mind a voice—an inhuman voice, mechanical but with a hint of emotion—was saying. *No, no. Not again. They must learn. They must learn.*

Then there was nothingness.

30

GRIMES SAT ON the hilltop, watching Clarisse work.

She, clad in the rough, more-or-less cured pelt of a wolflike beast, looked like a cavewoman, looked as her ancestors on this very world must have looked. Grimes looked like what he was—a castaway. He was wearing the ragged remnants of his long johns. His space suit, together with the suits of the others who had been so armored, was stowed neatly in a cave against the day when it would be required again—if ever. Other members of the party wore what was left of their uniforms. They were all here, all on what Grimes had decided must be Kinsolving's Planet, twenty men and thirteen women.

And, some miles away, were Druthen and von Donderberg and their people. They were still hostile—and in their tribe were only five women, two of them past childbearing age. They had their weapons still—but, like *Faraway Quest's* crew, were conserving cartridges and power packs. Nonetheless, three nights ago they had approached Grimes' encampment closely enough to bring it within range of their trebuchet and had lobbed a couple of boulders into the mouth of the main cave before they were driven off by Dalzell and his marines.

All of them were on Kinsolving's Planet.

It was Kinsolving's Planet ages before it had been discovered by Commodore Kinsolving, ages before those mysterious cavemen had painted their pictures on the walls of the caves. (Perhaps the ancestors of those cavemen were here now. . . .) The topography was all wrong. But by the time that Man pushed out to the rim of the galaxy, old mountain ranges would have been eroded would have sunk, seas would roll where now there were plains, wrinklings of the world's crust would bring new, towering peaks into being.

But that feeling of *oddness* that Grimes had known on his previous visit (previous, but in the far distant future) to this planet still persisted. On Kinsolving *anything* could happen, and most probably would.

Was it some sort of psionic field induced by the Outsiders' Ship? Or had The Outsider been drawn to that one position in space by the field? Come to that—who (or what) were *the Outsiders?* Do-gooders? Missionaries? Beings whose evolution had taken a different course from that of Man, of the other intelligent races of the galaxy?

And we, thought Grimes, *are descendants of the killer ape, children of Cain. . . . What would we have been like if our forebears had been herbivores, if we had not needed to kill for food—and to protect ourselves from other predators? What if our first tools had been tools, peaceful tools, and not weapons? But conflict is essential to the evolution of a species. But it could have been conflict with the harsh forces of Nature herself rather than with other creatures, related and unrelated. Didn't some ethologist once refer to Man as the Bad Weather Animal?*

But They, he thought, as he watched Clarisse, squatting on her hunkers, scratching industriously away with a piece of chalky stone on the flat, slate surface of the rock, *but They have certainly thrown us back to our first beginnings. We didn't pass the test. First of all there was the naval battle—and I wonder what happened to* Wanderer, Vindictive, *the other* Quest *and* Adler. . . *First of all there was the naval battle, and then the brawl actually within the sacred precincts. Calver and his crew must have been very well behaved to have been accepted, nonetheless. Perhaps, by this time, the stupid pugnacity is being bred out of Man, perhaps Calver was one of the new breed. . . .*

"Stop brooding!" admonished Sonya sharply.

"I'm not brooding. I'm thinking. I'm still trying to work things out."

"You'd be better employed trying to recall every

possible, smallest detail of your beloved *Quest*. Clarisse knows damn' all about engineering, and if she's to succeed she must have all the help we can give her.''

"*If* she succeeds. . . ."

"John!" Her voice betrayed the strain under which she was living. "I'm not cut out to be an ancestral cavewoman, or any other sort of cavewoman. I was brought up to wear clean clothes, not filthy rags, to bathe in hot water, not a stream straight off the ice, to eat well-cooked food, not greasy meat charred on the outside and raw inside. . . . Perhaps I'm too civilized—but this is no world for me." She paused. "And here we are, all of us, relying on the wild talent of a witch, a teleporteuse, who's been at least half poisoning herself by chewing various wild fungi which might—or might not—have the proper hallucinogenic effect . . ." She laughed bitterly. "All right—the artists in her ancestry did have the power to pull food animals to them. She has it too, as well we know. But will it work with a complex construction such as a spaceship?"

"It worked," Grimes told her, "with complex constructions such as human beings. And Clarisse is no more an anatomist or a physiologist than she is an engineer."

"Commodore," Mayhew was calling. "Clarisse needs your help again!"

Grimes got to his feet. Before he walked to where the artist was at work he slowly looked from his vantage point around his little kingdom. To the north were the jagged, snowcapped peaks, with their darkly forested foothills. To the south was the sea. To east and west were the rolling plains, with their fur of coarse, yellowish grass, their outcroppings of stony hillocks and boulders. From behind one of the distant hills drifted the blue smoke of Druthen's fires.

"Commodore!" called Mayhew again.

"Oh, all right."

He walked over the rocky hilltop to that slab of slate, to where Davis, Williams, Hendrikson and Carnaby were clustered around Clarisse. The sketch of *Faraway Quest* was taking shape, but it was vague, uncertain in outline. How many attempts had there been to date? Grimes had lost count. Earlier drawings had been obliterated by sudden vicious rain showers, had been rubbed out in fits of tearful anger by the artist herself. Once, and once only, it had seemed that a shimmering ship shape, almost invisible, had hung in the air for a microsecond.

Grimes looked at the faces of his officers, his departmental heads. All showed signs of strain, of overmuch concentration. Williams, who was responsible for maintenance, must have been making a mental tally of every rivet, every welded seam in the shell plating. Davis would have been visualizing machinery; Hendrikson, his weapons; Carnaby, his navigational instruments.

But. . . .

But, Grimes suddenly realized, none of them had seen, had *felt* the ship as a smoothly functioning whole.

"Ready?" he asked Clarisse.

"Ready," she replied in a tired, distant voice.

And Grimes remembered. He remembered the

first commissioning of *Faraway Quest* and all the work that had gone into her, the maintenance and the modifications. He relived his voyage of exploration to the Galactic East: his landings on Tharn, Grollor, Mellise and Stree. He recalled, vividly, his discovery of the antimatter systems to the Galactic West, and that most peculiar voyage, during which he and Sonya had come together, which was made as part of the research into the Rim Ghost phenomena.

All this he remembered, and more, and his mind was wide open to Clarisse as she scratched busily away with her rough piece of chalk—and hers was open to him. It was all so vivid, too vivid for mere imagination, for memory. He could actually have been standing in his familiar control room. . . .

He was standing in his familiar control room.

But that was impossible.

He opened his eyes, looked around in a slow circle.

He saw the jagged, snowcapped peaks to the north, with their darkly forested foothills. He saw the glimmering sea to the south. To east and west were the rolling plains, with their fur of coarse, yellowish grass, their outcroppings of stony hillocks and boulders. From behind one of the distant hills drifted the blue smoke of Druthen's fires.

But. . . .

But he was seeing all this through the wide viewports of *Faraway Quest*.

He walked, fast, to the screen of the periscope, adjusted the controls of the instrument so that he had an all-round view around the ship. Yes—his people, his crew were there, all of them staring upward. He did not need to increase the magnification to see the wonder on their faces.

"Mphm," he grunted. He went to the panel on which were the controls for the airlock doors. He punched the necessary buttons. The illuminated indicators came on. OUTER DOOR OPEN. INNER DOOR OPEN. RAMP EXTRUDING—to be replaced by RAMP DOWN.

Meanwhile. . . .

He put his eyes to the huge binoculars on their universal mounting. Druthen and von Donderberg must have seen the sudden appearance of the ship. She would mean a chance of escape for *them*. Yes, there they were, two dozen of them, running. The sun glinted from the weapons they carried—the guns with their hoarded ammunition, their carefully conserved power packs.

It was a hopeless sortie; but desperate men, more than once have achieved miracles.

Grimes sighed, went to the gunner's seat of the bow 40 millimeter cannon. He put the gun on manual control. It would be the best one for the job; a noisy projectile weapon has far greater psychological effect than something silent and much more deadly. He flipped the selector switches for automatic and H.E. He traversed until he had the leaders of the attackers in the telescopic sights. Druthen was one of them, his bulk and his waddling run unmistakable. Von Donderberg was the other.

Grimes sighed again. He was genuinely sorry for the Waldegrener. In many ways he and Grimes

201

were the same breed of cat. Only Druthen then. . . .
He shifted his sights slightly. But the explosion of
a high explosive shell might kill, would probably
injure von Donderberg. Solid shot? Yes. One
round should be ample, if Grimes' old skill with
firearms still persisted. And it would be a sepctacu-
lar enough deterrent for the survivors of Druthen's
party.

Still Grimes hesitated. The hijackers would be
marooned on Kinsolving; nothing would make him
change his mind about that. But even if they didn't
deserve a chance their children, their descendants
did.

And, on a primitive world such as this, the more
outstandingly bad bastards contributing to the
gene pool the better.

Again he flipped the ammunition selector
switch, then lowered his sights. He stitched a neat
seam of bursting incendiary shells across the
savannah, well ahead of Druthen and von Donderberg. The long grass was highly and satisfactorily
flammable. The raiding party retreated in panic.
By the time that those of them who possessed
space armor got back to their camp to put it on, no
matter how they hurried, *Faraway Quest* would be
gone.

"All aboard, Skipper," reported Williams from
behind Grimes. "Take her up?"

"Take her up, Commander Williams," ordered
the Commodore.

31

"SET TRAJECTORY, SIR?" asked Carnaby.

Grimes looked out through the viewports, toward the opalescent sphere that was Kinsolving, toward the distant luminosity of the Galactic Lens.

"We have to go *somewhere*, John," said Sonya sharply.

"Or somewhen," murmured Grimes. He said, in a louder voice, "We'd better head for where The Outsider was, or will be, or is. We have unfinished business."

But it didn't really matter. For the time being, nothing really mattered.

He had his ship again.

THE RIM GODS

A. BERTRAM CHANDLER

SF

ace books

A Division of Charter Communications Inc.
A GROSSET & DUNLAP COMPANY
51 Madison Avenue
New York, New York 10010

THE RIM GODS

Copyright © 1968 by A. Bertram Chandler

The four parts of this book appeared individually during 1968 in *Galaxy* magazine.

An ACE Book

4 6 8 0 9 7 5 3
Manufactured in the United States of America

For itchy-footed Susan

Part One

"AND WHO," DEMANDED Commodore Grimes, "will it be this time?" He added, "Or *what?*"

"I don't know, sir, I'm sure," simpered Miss Walton.

Grimes looked at his new secretary with some distaste. There was no denying that she was far more photogenic then her predecessor, and that she possessed a far sweeter personality. But sweetness and prettiness are not everything. He bit back a sarcastic rejoinder, looked again at the signal that the girl had just handed him. It was from a ship, a vessel with the unlikely name of *Piety*. And it was not a word in some alien language that could mean *anything*—the name of the originator of the message was Terran enough. Anglo-Terran at that. William Smith. And after that prosaic apellation there was his title—but that was odd. It was not the usual Master, Captain, Officer Commanding or whatever. It was, plainly and simply, Rector.

Piety. . . Rector. . . . That ship's name, and that title of rank, had an archaic ring to them. Grimes had always been a student of naval history, and probably knew more about the vessels that had sailed Earth's oceans in the dim and distant past than anybody on the Rim Worlds and, come to that, the vast majority of people on the home planet itself. He remembered that most of the ancient sailing ships had been given religious names. He remembered, too, that rector had once been the shipmaster's official title.

So what was this ship coming out to the Rim, giving her ETA, details of last clearance, state of health on board and all the rest of it? Some cog, some caravel, some galleass? Grimes smiled at his own fancy. Nonetheless, strange ships, very strange ships, had drifted out to the Rim.

"Miss Walton . . ." he said.

"Yes, Commodore," she replied brightly.

"This *Piety* . . . see what details Lloyd's *Register* has on her."

"Very good, sir."

The Commodore—rugged, stocky, short, iron-gray hair over a deeply tanned and seamed face, ears that in spite of suggestions made by two wives and several mistresses still protruded—paced the polished floor of his office while the little blonde punched the buttons that would actuate the Port

Forlorn robot librarian. Legally, he supposed, the impending arrival of the *Piety* was the port captain's pigeon. Grimes was Astronautical Superintendent of Rim Runners, the Confederacy's shipping line. But he was also the officer commanding the Rim Worlds Naval Reserve and, as such, was concerned with matters of security and defense. He wished that Sonya, his wife, were available so that he could talk things over with her. She, before her marriage to him, had held the rank of Commander in the Intelligence branch of the Interstellar Federation's Survey Service and, when it came to mysteries and secrets of any kind, displayed the aptitudes of a highly intelligent ferret. But Sonya, after declaring that another week on Lorn would have her climbing up the wallpaper, had taken off for a long vacation—Waverley, Caribbea, Atlantia and points inward—by herself. She, when she returned, would be sorry to have missed whatever odd adventures the arrival of this queerly named ship presaged—and Grimes knew that there would be some. His premonitions were rarely, if ever, wrong.

He turned away from the banked sceens and instruments that made his office look like an exceptionally well fitted spaceship's control room, walked to the wide window that took up an entire wall, which overlooked the port. It was a fine day—for Lorn. The almost perpetual overcast was thin enough to permit a hint of blue sky to show through, and the Lorn sun was a clearly defined disk rather than the usual fuzzy ball. There was almost no wind. Discharge of *Rim Leopard*, noted, seemed to be progressing satisfactorily. There was a blue flare of welding arcs about the little spacetug *Rim Mamelute*, presently undergoing her annual survey. And there, all by herself, was the ship that Grimes—to the annoyance of his wife—often referred to as his one true love, the old, battered *Faraway Quest*. She had been built how many (too many) years ago as a standard *Epsilon* Class tramp for the Interstellar Transport Commission. She had been converted into a survey ship for the Rim Worlds' government. In her, Grimes had made the first landings on the inhabited planets to the Galactic East, the worlds now referred to as the Eastern Circuit. In her he had made the first contact—but not a physical one—with the anti-matter systems to the Galactic West.

And would the arrival of the good ship *Piety* lead to her recommissioning? Grimes hoped so. He liked his job—it was interesting work, carrying both authority and responsibility—but he was often tired of being a deskborne commodore, and had always welcomed the chance to take the old *Quest* up and out into deep space again. As often in the past he had a hunch, a strong one. Something was cooking, and he would have a finger in the pie.

Miss Walton's childish treble broke into his thoughts. "Sir, I have the information on *Piety*. . . ."

"Yes?"

"She was built as *Epsilon Crucis* for the Interstellar Transport Commission fifty Terran standard years ago. She was purchased from them last year, Terran reckoning, by the Skarsten Theological Institute, whose address is listed as Nuevo Angeles on Francisco, otherwise known as Beta Puppis VI. . . ."

"I've visited Francisco," he told her. "A pleasant world, in many ways. But an odd one."

"Odd? How, sir?"

"I hope I'm not treading on any of your corns, Miss Walton, but the whole planet's no more than a breeding ground for fancy religions."

"I'm a Latter Day Reformed Methodist myself, sir," she told him severely. "And that's not fancy."

"Indeed it's not, Miss Walton." *And I'm a cynical, more or less tolerant agnostic,* he thought. He went on, "And does Lloyds condescend to tell us the category in which this renamed *Epsilon Crucis* is now listed? A missionary ship, perhaps?"

"No, sir. A survey ship."

"Oh," was all that Grimes could say.

Two days later Grimes watched, from his office window, *Piety* come in. Whatever else this Rector William Smith might or might not be he was a good ship handler. There was a nasty wind blowing across the spaceport, not quite a gale, but near enough to it; nonetheless the ship made a classic vertical descent, dropping to the exact center of the triangle formed by the berth-marker beacons. It was easy enough in theory, no more than the exact application of lateral thrust, no more than a sure and steady hand on the remote controls of the Inertial Drive. No more—and no less. Some people get the feel of ships; some never do.

This *Piety* was almost a twin to Grimes's own *Faraway Quest*. She was a newer (less old) ship, of course, but the design of the *Epsilon* Class tramps, those trusty workhorses of the Commission, had changed very little over the years. She sat there in her assigned berth, a gray, weathered spire, the bright scarlet beacons still blinking away just clear of the broad vanes of her tripedal landing gear. From her stem a telescopic mast extended itself, and from the top of the metal staff a flag broke out, whipped to quivering rigidity by the wind. The Commodore picked up his binoculars through which to study it. It was not, as he had assumed it would be, the national ensign of Francisco, the golden *crux ansata* and crescent on a scarlet ground; even with the naked eye he could see that. This was a harshly uncompromising standard: a simple white cross on a black field. *It must be*, decided Grimes, *the houseflag of the Skarsten Institute*.

The after air lock door opened and the ramp extended from it, and to it drew up the beetle-like cars of the various port officials—port captain, customs, immigration, health. The boarding party got out of their vehicles and filed up the gangway, to where an officer was waiting to receive them. They vanished into the ship. Grimes idly wondered whether or not they would get a drink, and what the views of these Skarsten people were on alcohol. He remembered his own visit to Francisco, as a junior officer in the Federation's Survey Service, many years ago. Some of the religious sects had been rigidly abstemious, maintaining that alcohol was an invention of the devil. Others had held that wine symbolized the more beneficent aspects of the Almighty. But is was hardly a subject worthy of speculation. He would find out for himself when, after the arrival formalities were over, he paid his courtesy call on the ship's captain.

He went back to his desk, busied himself with the paper work that made a habit of accumulating. An hour or so later he was interrupted by the buzzing of his telephone. "Grimes here!" he barked into the instrument. "Commodore Grimes," said a strange voice. It was a statement rather than a question. "This is William Smith, Commodore, Rector of *Piety*. I request an appointment."

"It will be my pleasure, er, Rector." Grimes glanced at his watch. It was almost time for his rather dreary coffee and sandwich lunch. It was not the sort of meal that one asked visitors to share. He said, "Shall we say 1400 hours, our time? In my office?"

"That will do very nicely, sir. Thank you."

"I am looking forward to meeting you," said Grimes, replacing the handset in its rest. *And shall I send Miss Walton out for some sacramental wine?* he asked himself.

William Smith was a tall man, thin, with almost all of his pale face hidden by a bushy black beard, from above which a great nose jutted like the beak of a bird of prey. His eyes under the thick, black brows were of a gray so pale as to be almost colorless, and they were cold, cold. A plain black uniform covered his spare frame, the buttons concealed by the fly front of the tunic, the four bands of black braid on the sleeves almost invisible against the cloth. There was a hint of white lace at his throat.

"I have been told, sir," he said, sitting rigidly in his chair, "that you are something of an expert on the queer conditions that prevail here, on the Rim."

"Perhaps, Rector," said Grimes, "you will tell me first the purpose of your visit here."

"Very well, sir." The man's baritone voice was as cold and as colorless as his eyes. "To begin with, we have the permission of your government, your Rim Worlds Confederacy, to conduct our pressing need of a new Revelation, a new Sinai. . . ."

"A survey, Rector? The Rim Worlds have been very well surveyed—even though I say it myself."

"Not our kind of survey. Commodore. I shall, as you would say, put you in the picture. We of the Skarsten Institute are Neo-Calvinists. We deplore the godlessness, the heresy that is ever more prevalent throughout the galaxy—yes, even upon our own planet. We feel that Mankind is in sore and pressing need of a new Revelation, a new Sinai. . . ."

"And you honestly believe that you will find your Sinai here, out on the Rim?"

"We believe that we shall find our Sinai. If not here, then elsewhere. Perhaps, even, beyond the confines of this galaxy."

"Indeed? But how can I help you, Rector?"

"You, we were told, know more about the odd distortions of the Continuum encountered here than anybody else on these planets."

"Such is fame." Grimes sighed and shrugged. "Very well, Rector, you asked for it. I'll tell you what little I know. To begin with, it is thought by many of our scientists that here, at the very edge of the expanding galaxy, the fabric of time and space is stretched thin. We have long become used to the phenomena known as Rim Ghosts, disconcerting glimpses into alternative universes."

"I believe that you, sir, have personally made the transition into their universes."

"Yes. Once when the Federation's Survey Service requested our aid in the investigation of the Rim Ghost phenomena. No doubt your people have read the Survey Service report."

"We have."

"The second time was when we, the Confederacy, took our own steps to deal with what we decided was a very real menace—an alternative universe in which our worlds were ruled by particularly unpleasant mutants, with human beings in a state of slavery. And then there was Captain Listowel, who was master of the first experimental lightjammer. He tried to exceed the speed of light without cheating—as *we* do with our Mannschenn Drive—and experienced quite a few different time tracks."

"And tell me, sir, did you or this Captain Listowel ever feel that you were on the point of being granted the Ultimate Revelation?''

''Frankly, no, Rector. We had our bad moments—who in Space, or anywhere else, doesn't?—and anyone who has indulged in time track switching often wonders, as I do, about the reality, the permanence of both himself and the universe about him. For example, I have vague memories of ships that were equipped with only reaction drive for blast-offs and landings and short interplanetary hauls. Absurd, isn't it, but those memories are there. And my wife—I'm sorry you can't meet her, but she's off on a trip—seems to have changed. I have this half recollection of her when she first came out to the Rim, which is there in my mind alongside the real one—but what is real? She was working for the Federation's Intelligence Service then. Anyhow, in one memory she's small and blond, in one she's tall and blonde, and in one she's tall and red-headed, as she is today, Damn it—that's *three* memories!''

''Women have been known to change their hair styles and colorations, Commodore.''

''Right. I wouldn't be at all surprised if she returns with her crowning glory a bright green! But that doesn't explain the coexistent memories.''

''Perhaps not.'' Smith's voice was bitter as he went on. ''But it seems such a waste of opportunities. To have been privileged to visit the many mansions of our Father's house, and to come back only with confused recollections of the color of a woman's hair!''

''And quite a few scars, Rector. Physical and psychological.''

''No doubt.'' The man's voice was unpleasantly

ironic. "But tell me, sir, what do you know of Kinsolving's Planet?"

"Not much. I suppose that we shall settle it if we're ever faced with a population explosion, which is doubtful."

"I am referring, sir, to the man who appeared there, the Stone Age savage from the remote past."

"Yes, that was a queer business. Well before my time. Nothing like that has happened there in recent years, although there is still an uneasy, brooding atmosphere about that world that makes it undesirable as a piece of real estate. The original theory is that somehow the—the loneliness of the people out here on the Rim, hanging, as it were, by their fingernails over the abyss of the Ultimate Night, became focused on that one particular planet. Now the theory is that the fabric of Time and Space is stretched extremely thin there, and that anything or anybody is liable to fall through, either way. The rock paintings are still in the caves, but there haven't been any new ones and the paint is never wet any more."

"The Stone Age savage," said Smith, "eventually became a Franciscan citizen, and a Neo-Calvinist. He died at a very ripe old age, and among his effects was the manuscript of his life story. His great-granddaughter presented it to the Institute. It was thought, at first, that it was a work of fiction, but the surviving relatives insisted that it was not. And then I, when I made a voyage to Earth, was able to obtain access to the Survey Service records."

"And so?" asked Grimes.

"So Kinsolving's Planet is to become our new Sinai," Smith told him.

"You'd better go along, Grimes," Admiral Kravitz told him, "just to see fair play. Anyhow, it's all been arranged. You will be recalled to the active list—pay, etc., as per regulations—and ship out in this *Piety* of theirs as Rim Worlds' government observer."

"But why me, sir? If I were taking my own ship, if the old *Quest* were being recommissioned, with myself in command, it'd be different. But I don't like being a passenger."

"You'll not be a passenger, Grimes. Captain— sorry, *Rector*—Smith has indicated that he'll appreciate having you along as a sort of pilot. . . ."

"In a ship full of sky pilots—and myself a good agnostic!" He saw the bewildered expression on the Admiral's face and explained his choice of words. "In the old days, before there were any *real* sky pilots, seamen used to refer to ministers of religion as such."

"Did they, now? And what would those tarry-breeked ruffians of whom you're so fond have thought of a captain calling himself 'Rector'?"

"In the early days of sail they'd have thought nothing of it. It was the master's usual title."

"I doubt if anybody'll ever call *you* 'Bishop,' " remarked the Admiral. "Anyhow, you'll be aboard primarily to observe. And to report. In the unlikely event of anything occurring that will affect Rim Worlds' security you are to take action."

"Me—and what squad of Marines?"

"We could send a detachment of the Salvation

Army with you,'' joked the Admiral.

"I doubt that they'd be allowed on board. As far as I can gather, these Neo-Calvinists are somewhat intolerant. Only on a world as tolerant as Francisco would they have been allowed to flourish."

"Intolerant, yes," agreed Kravitz. "But scrupulously honest. And moral."

"In short." said Grimes, "no redeeming vices."

"*Piety* lifts ship at 1800 hours tomorrow, Commodore Grimes," said the Admiral. "You will be aboard."

"Aye, aye, sir," replied Grimes resignedly.

Grimes had never enjoyed serving in a "taut ship" himself, and had never commanded one. Nonetheless, he respected those captains who were able to engender about themselves such a state of affairs. *Piety*, as was obvious from the moment that he set foot on the bottom of the ramp, was a taut ship. Everything was spotless. Every metal fitting and surface that was supposed to be polished boasted a mirror-like sheen. All the paintwork looked as though it was washed at least twice daily—which, in fact, it was. The atmosphere inside the hull bore none of the usual taints of cookery, tobacco smoke or—even though there was a mixed crew—women's perfume. But it was too chilly, and the acridity of some disinfectant made Grimes sneeze.

The junior officer who met him at the head of the ramp showed him into the elevator cage at the foot of the axial shaft. Grimes thanked him and assured the presumably young man—the full beard made it hard to determine his age—that he knew his way around this class of vessel. A captain, no matter what he calls himself or is called, is always accommodated as closely as possible to the center of control. The elevator worked smoothly, noiselessly, carrying the Commodore speedily up to the deck just below the control room. There, as in his own *Faraway Quest,* was the semi-circular suite of cabins. Over the door was a brass plate with the title RECTOR.

As Grimes approached this entrance it slid open. Smith stood there and said formally, "Welcome aboard, Commodore."

"Thank you, Rector."

"Will you come in, sir?"

There were other people in the day cabin: a tall, stout, white-headed and -bearded man dressed in clothing that was very similar to Smith's uniform; a woman in a longsleeved, high-necked, ankle-length black dress, her hair completely covered by a frilly white cap. They looked at Grimes, obviously dispproving of his gold-braided, brass-buttoned, beribboned finery. That did not get up.

"Commodore Grimes," said Smith. "Presbyter Cannan. Sister Lane."

Reluctantly the Presbyter extended his hand. Grimes took it. He was not surprised that it was cold. Sister Lane nodded slightly in his general direction.

Smith gestured stiffly toward a chair, sat down himself. Grimes lowered himself to his own seat incautiously. He should have known that it would be hard. He looked curiously at the two civilians. The Presbyter was an old edition of Rector Smith. The sister . . . ? She had him puzzled. She belonged to a type that been common enough on Francisco when he had been there—the Blossom People, they had called themselves. They preached and practiced a sort of hedonistic Zen, and claimed that their use of the wide range of drugs available to them put them in close communication with the Cosmic All. Prim she was, this Sister Lane, prim and proper in her form-concealing black, but the planes of her face were not harsh, and her unpainted lips were full, and there was a strange gentleness in her brown eyes. Properly dressed —or undressed—thought Grimes, she would be a very attractive woman. Suddenly it was important that he hear her voice.

He pulled his battered pipe out of his pocket, his tobacco pouch and lighter. He asked, addressing her, "Do you mind if I smoke?"

But it was the Presbyter who replied. "Certainly we mind, sir. As you should know, we are opposed to the use of any and all drugs."

"*All* drugs?" murmured the woman, with a sort of malicious sweetness. Her voice was almost a baritone, but it could never be mistaken for a male one.

"There are exceptions, Sister Lane," the old man told her harshly. "As you well know."

"As I well know," she concurred.

"I take it," said Grimes, "that nicotine is not among those exceptions."

"Unfortunately," she stated, "no."

"You may leave us, Sister," said Presbyter Cannan. "We have no further business to discuss with you."

"Thank you, sir." She got gracefully to her feet, made a curtsey to Cannan, walked out of the door. Her ugly clothing could not hide the fluid grace of her movements.

"Your Nursing Sister, Rector?" asked Grimes when she was gone.

"No," answered Cannan. And, *Who's running this ship?* thought Grimes irritably. But evidently the Presbyter piled on more gravs than did the ship's lawful master.

Smith must have noticed the Commodore's expression. "Sister Lane, sir," he explained, "is a member of the Presbyter's staff, not of mine."

"Thank you, Rector." Grimes rewarded him with what was intended to be a friendly smile. "I'm afraid that it will take me some time to get your ranks and ratings sorted out."

"I have no doubt," said Cannan, "that it must be confusing to one who relies upon gaudy fripperies for his authority rather than inner grace."

"Your baggage must be aboard and stowed by now, Commodore," Smith said hastily. He turned to his spiritual superior. "May I suggest, sir, that you and your people retire to your quarters? Lift-off"—he glanced at his watch—"will be in fifteen minutes."

"Very well, Rector." The old man got up, towering over the two spacemen. Smith got up. Grimes remained seated until Smith returned from seeing the Presbyter out.

He said, "I'd better be getting below myself. If you could have somebody show me to my stateroom, Rector."

"I was hoping, Commodore, that you would be coming up to Control for the lift-off."

"Thank you, Rector Smith. It will be my pleasure."

Smith led the way out of his quarters, up the short ladder that brought the two men to the control room. Grimes looked about him. The layout was a standard one: acceleration chairs before which were banks of instruments, sceens, meters, chart tank, mass proximity indicator, Carlotti Beacon direction finder. All seemed to be in perfect order, and much of the equipment was new. Evidently the Skarsten Theological Institute did not believe in spoiling the ship for a ha'porth of tar.

The Rector indicated a chair, into which Grimes strapped himself, then took his own seat. The officers were already at their stations. All those bearded men, thought the Commodore, looked too much alike, and their black-on-black insignia of rank made it hard to tell who was what. But this wasn't *his* ship, and she had managed to come all the way out from Francisco without mishap.

The departure routine went smoothly enough, with the usual messages exchanged between control room and spaceport control tower. The Inertial Drive started up, and there was that brief second of weightlessness before the gentle acceleration made itself felt. The ship lifted easily, falling upward to the cloud ceiling. Briefly Grimes was able to look out through the viewports at Port

Forlorn and at the dreary countryside spread out around the city like a map. And then there was nothing but gray mist outside—mist that suddenly became a pearly, luminescent white and then vanished. Overhead was a steely sun glaring out of a black sky, its light harsh even though the ports were polarized.

There was free fall for a little while, and then the gyroscopes swung the ship's head to the target star. The Inertial Drive came on again, its irregular throbbing beat a bass background for the thin, high keening of the Mannschenn Drive. Ahead, save for the iridescent spiral that was the target sun, there was only blackness. Lorn was to starboard—a vast, writhing planetary amoeba that was falling astern, that was shrinking rapidly. And out to port was the Galactic Lens, distorted by the temporal precession field of the Drive to a Klein flask blown by a drunken glass-blower.

Grimes wondered, as he had wondered before, if anybody would ever come up with another simile. But this one was so apt.

Grimes didn't like this ship.

She was beautifully kept, efficiently run, and with her cargo spaces converted to passenger accommodation she comfortably housed her crew and all the personnel from the Skarsten Institute. But she was . . . cold. She was cold, and she was too quiet. There was none of the often ribald laughter, none of the snatches of light music that lent warmth to the atmosphere of a normal vessel. There were, he noted, playmasters in all the recreation rooms; but when he examined the spools of the machine in the senior officers' mess he found that they consisted entirely of recordings of sermons and the gloomier hymns. The library was as bad. And, socially, there was complete segregation of the sexes. Deaconesses and sisters were berthed aft, and between them and the male crew and passengers were the storerooms and the "farm."

The food was not bad, but it was plain, unimaginative. And there was nothing to drink but water, and even that had a flat taste. The conversation at table was as boring as the provender. Too, Grimes was annoyed to find out that the Rector did not sit at the head of the board in the senior officers' mess; that place of honor was reserved for the Presbyter. And he talked, almost non-stop, about the Institute's internal politics, with the ship's captain interjecting an occasional quiet affirmative as required. The chief officer, surgeon and purser gobbled their meals in silence, as did Grimes, very much the outsider at the foot of the table. They were served by a young stewardess who would have been pretty in anything but that ugly, all-concealing black, who seemed to hold the domineering old man—but nobody else—in awe.

After the evening meal Grimes made his excuses and retired to his cabin. It was little more than a dogbox, and was a comedown after his suite aboard the *Quest*. He was pleased that he had brought his own reading matter with him, and pleased that he had exercised the forethought to make provision for his other little comforts. Before doing anything else, he filled and lit his pipe and then, moving slowly and easily through the blue haze of his own creation, unclipped the larger of his cases from its rack, pulled it out and opened it. He was lifting out the shirts that had acted as shock-proof packing for certain breakables when he heard a light tap at his door. He groaned. A passenger is bound by ship's regulations as much as is any crew member. But he was damned if he was going to put out his pipe. "Come in," he called.

She came in. She pulled the ugly white cap off her lustrous brown hair, tossed it on to the bunk. Then she turned back to the door, snapped on the spring lock. She tested its security, smiled, then flopped down into the one chair that the cabin possessed.

Grimes looked at her, with raised eyebrows. "Yes, Sister Lane?" he asked.

"Got a smoke, spaceman?" she growled.

"There are some cigars . . ." he began doubtfully.

"I didn't expect pot. Although if you have any . . . ?"

"I haven't." Then Grimes said virtuously, "In any case, such drugs are banned on the Rim Worlds."

"Are they? But what about the cigar you promised me?"

Grimes got a box of panatellas out of his case, opened it, offered it to her. She took one, accepted his proffered light. She inhaled luxuriously. She said, "All I need now is a drink."

"I can supply that."

"Good on you, Admiral!"

There was the bottle of absolute alcohol, and there was the case with its ranked phials of essences. "Scotch?" asked Grimes. "Rum? Brandy? Or . . . ?"

"Scotch will do."

The Commodore measured alcohol into the two glasses over the washbasin, added to each a drop of essence, topped up with cold water from the tap. She murmured, "Here's mud in your eye," and gulped from hers as soon as he handed it to her.

"Sister Lane," said Grimes doubtfully.

"You can call me Clarisse."

"Clarisse. . . . Should you be doing this?"

"Don't tell me that you're a wowser, like all those Bible-punchers."

"I'm not. But this is not my ship. . . ."

"And it's not mine, either."

"Then what are you doing here?"

"It's a long story, dearie. And if you ply me with liquor, I might just tell it to you." She sighed and stretched. "You've no idea what a relief it is to enjoy a drink and a talk and a smoke with somebody who's more or less human."

"Thank you," said Grimes stiffly.

She laughed. "Don't be offended, duckie." She put up her hands, pulled her hair back and away from her face. "Look at my ears."

Grimes looked. They were normal enough organs—save for the fact that were pointed, and were tufted with hair at the tips.

227

"I'm only more or less human myself," she told him. "More rather than less, perhaps. You know about the man Raul, the caveman, the Stone Age savage, who was pulled, somehow, from the remote past on Kinsolving's Planet to what was then the present. He was my great-grandfather."

"He was humanoid," said Grimes. "Not human."

"Human-schuman!" she mocked. "There is such a thing as parallel evolution, you know. And old Raul was made something of a pet by the scientists back on Earth, and when he evinced the desire to father a family the finest genetic engineers in the Galaxy were pressed into service. No, not the way that you're thinking. Commodore. You've got a low mind."

"Sorry."

"I should think so. Just for that, you can pour me another drink."

And Grimes asked himself if his liquor ration would last out until his return to Lorn.

"What are you doing here?" he asked bluntly. "In *this* ship?"

"At this very moment I'm breaking at least ninety-nine percent of the regulations laid down by the Presbyter and enforced by the Rector. But I know what you mean." Her voice deepened so that it was like Grimes's own. "What is nasty girl like you doing in a nice place like this?"

"I wouldn't call you nasty," said Grimes.

"Thank you, sir. Then stand by for the story of my life, complete and unexpurgated. I'll start off with dear old great-granddaddy, the Noble Savage. He was an artist, you know, in his proper place and time, one of those specialists who practiced a form of sympathetic magic. He would paint or draw pictures of various animals, and the actual beasts would be drawn to the spot, there to be slaughtered by the hunters. He said that it worked, too. I can remember, when I was a little girl, that he'd put on demonstrations. He'd draw a picture of, say, the cat—and within seconds pussy would be in the room. Oh, yes—and he was a telepath, a very powerful transceiver.

"After many years on Earth, where he was latterly an instructor at the Rhine Institute, he emigrated, with his wife and children, to Francisco, where he was psionic radio officer in charge of the Port Diego Signal Station. It was there that he got religion. And with all the religions to choose from, he had to become a Neo-Calvinist! His family was converted with him—and I often wonder how much part his undeniable psychic powers played in their conversion! And the wives of his sons had to become converts, and the husbands of his daughters—yea, even unto the third and fourth generations."

She grinned. "One member of the fourth generation kicked over the traces. Me. From the Neo-Calvinists to the Blossom People was a logical step. Like most new converts I overdid things. Drinks, drugs, promiscuity—the works. The Neo-Calvinists picked me up, literally, from the gutter and nursed me back to health in their sanatorium—and, at the same time, made it quite clear that if I was predestined to go to Hell I should go there. And then, when they checked up on great-grandfather's autobiographical papers, they realized that I was predestined for something really important—especially since I, alone of his descendants, possess something of his powers."

"You mean that you can . . . ?"

There was a violent knocking on the door, and a voice shouting, "Open up! Open up, I say!"

"They know I'm here," muttered Clarisse sullenly. She got out of her chair, operated the sliding panel herself.

Rector Smith was standing outside, and with him was a tall, gaunt woman. She stared at Sister Lane in horror and snarled, "Cover your nakedness, you shameless hussy!"

Clarisse shrugged, picked up the ugly cap from where it was lying on the bunk, adjusted it over her hair, tucking all loose strands out of sight.

"Will you deal with Sister Lane, Deaconess?" asked Smith.

"That I shall, Rector."

"Miss Lane and I were merely enjoying a friendly talk," said Grimes.

"A friendly talk!" The Deaconess' voice dripped scorn. "Smoking! Wine-bibbing! You—you gilded popinjay!"

Smith had picked up the bottle of alcohol, his obvious intention being to empty it into the washbasin. "Hold it!"

Smith hesitated. Unhurriedly Grimes took the bottle from his hand, restoppered it, put it in the rack over the basin.

Then the Rector started to bluster. "Sir. I must

remind you that you are a guest aboard my ship. A passenger. You are obliged to comply with ship's regulations."

"Sir," replied Grimes coldly, "I have signed no articles of agreement, and no ticket with the back covered with small print has been issued to me. I am surprised that a shipmaster should have been so neglectful of the essential legalities, and were you in the employ of the company of which I am astronautical superintendent I should find it my duty to reprimand you."

"Not only a gilded popinjay," observed the Deaconess harshly, "but a space lawyer."

"Yes, madam, a space lawyer—as any master astronaut should be." He was warming up nicely. "But I must remind you, both of you, that I do have legal standing aboard this vessel. I am here in my capacity as official observer for the Rim Worlds Confederacy. Furthermore, I was called back to active duty in the Rim Worlds Naval Reserve, with the rank of Commodore."

"Meaningless titles," sneered the Deaconess. "A Commodore without a fleet!"

"Perhaps, madam. Perhaps. But I must remind you that we are proceeding through Rim Worlds' territorial space. And I must make it plain that any interference with my own personal liberties—*and* the infliction by yourselves of any harsh punishment on Miss Lane—will mean that *Piety* will be intercepted and seized by one of our warships." He thought, *I hope the bluff isn't called.*

Called it was.

"And just how, Mr. Commodore Grimes, do

you propose to call a warship to your aid?'' asked
the woman.

''Easily, Deaconess, easily,'' said Clarisse
Lane. ''Have you forgotten that I am a telepath—
and a good one? While this ship was on Lorn I
made contact with Mr. Mayhew, Senior Psionic
Radio Officer of the Rim World Navy. Even
though we never met physically we became close
friends. He is an old friend and shipmate of the
Commodore, and asked me to keep in touch to let
him know if Commodore Grimes was in any
danger.''

''And you will tell him, of course,'' said Grimes,
''if *you* are subjected to any harm, or even discom-
fort.''

''He will *know*,'' she said quietly.

''Yes,'' agreed Grimes. ''He will know.''

He was familiar with telepaths, was Grimes,
having commenced his spacefaring career before
the Carlotti direction finding and communications
systems began to replace the psionic radio officers
with its space- and time-twisting beamed radia-
tions. He was familiar with telepaths, and knew
how it was with them when, infrequently, one of
them found a member of the opposite sex with the
same talents attractive. Until this happened—and
it rarely did—they would lavish all their affection
on the disembodied canine brains that they used as
amplifiers.

Rector Smith was the first to weaken. He muttered, ''Very well, Commodore.''

''And is this harlot to go unpunished?'' flared
the Deaconess.

"That's right, she is," Grimes told her.

She glared at him—and Grimes glared back. He regretted deeply that this was not his ship, that he had no authority aboard her.

"Rector Smith . . ." she appealed.

"I'm sorry, Deaconess," Smith told her. "But you have heard what these people have told us."

"And you will allow them to flout your authority?"

"It is better than causing the success of our mission to be jeopardized." He stiffened. "Furthermore, I order you not to lay hands upon Sister Lane, and not to order any of the other sisters to do so."

"And I suppose she's to be free to visit this— this vile seducer any time that she sees fit."

"No," said Smith at last. "No. That I will not sanction. Commodore Grimes claims that I cannot give orders to him, but my authority is still absolute insofar as all other persons aboard this vessel are concerned. Sister Lane will not be ill-treated, but she will be confined to the women's quarters until such time as her services are required."

"The Presbyter shall hear of this," said the woman.

"Indeed he shall. I shall be making my own report to him. Meanwhile, he is not, repeat not, to be disturbed." He added, "And those are *his* orders."

"Very well, then," snapped the Deaconess. And to Clarisse Lane, "Come."

"It was a good try, Commodore," said the girl, looking back wistfully at her unfinished drink, her still smoldering cigar. "It was a good try, but it could have been a better one, as far as I'm concerned. Good night."

It was a good try, thought Grimes. *Period.* He had gone as far as he could go without undermining the Master's—the Rector's—authority too much. As for the girl, he was sure that she would not, now, be maltreated, and it would do her no harm to revert to the abstemious routine of this aptly named ship.

"Good night," he said.

"May I have a word with you, sir?" asked Smith when the two women were gone.

"Surely. Stick around, Rector. This is Liberty Hall; you can spit on the mat and call the cat a bastard."

Smith looked, but did not voice, his disapproval of the figure of speech. He shut the door, snapped the lock on. Then, with a penknife taken from his pocket, he made a little adjustment to one of the securing screws of the mirror over the washbasin.

"Bugged?" asked Grimes interestedly.

"Of course—as is every compartment in the ship. But there are speakers and screens in only two cabins—my own and the Presbyter's. His Reverence, I know, took sleeping pills before retiring, but he might awaken."

"I suppose the ladies' showers are bugged, too?" asked Grimes.

A dull flush covered what little of the Rector's face was not hidden by his beard. He growled. "That, sir, is none of your business."

"And what, sir, is *your* business with me?"

"I feel, Commodore Grimes, that you should know how important that unhappy woman is to the success of our mission; then, perhaps, you will be less inclined, should the opportunity present itself again, to pander to her whims." Smith cleared his throat; then he went on. "This business upsets me, sir. You will know, as you, yourself, were once a shipmaster, how unpleasant it is to have to assert your authority."

"And talking," said Grimes, who had his telepath moments, "is thirsty work."

"If you would be so kind, sir," said Smith, after a long moment of hesitation. "I believe that brandy has always been regarded as a medicine."

Grimes sighed, and mixed fresh drinks. He motioned Smith to the single chair, sat down on the bunk. He thought of shocking the other man with one of the more obscene toasts, but merely said, "Down the hatch." The Rector said, "I needed that."

"Another, Rector Smith?"

"No, thank you, sir."

You want me to twist your arm, you sanctimonious bastard, thought Grimes, but I'm not going to do it. He put the bottle of alcohol and the little case of essences away. "And now," he said, "about Miss Lane. . . ."

"Yes, Sister Lane. As she has told you, she was one of us. But she backslid, and consorted with the fornicaters and wine-bibbers who call themselves the Blossom People. But even this was in accordance with the Divine scheme of things. Whilst consorting with those—those pagans she became accustomed to the use and the abuse—but surely the use is also abuse!—of the psychedelic drugs. Already she possessed considerable psychic powers, but those vile potions enhanced them.

"You will realize, sir, that it would have been out of the question for any of our own Elect to imperil his immortal soul by tampering with such powerful, unseen and unseeable forces, but—"

"But," said Grimes, "Clarisse Lane has already demonstrated that she is damned, so you don't mind using her as your cat's-paw."

"You put it very concisely, sir," agreed Smith.

"I could say more, but I won't. I just might lose my temper. But go on."

"Sister Lane is not entirely human. She is descended from that Raul, the Stone Age savage who was brought to Earth from Kinsolving's Planet. Many factors were involved in his appearance. It could be that the very fabric of the Continuum is worn thin, here on the Rim, and that lines of force, or fault lines, intersect at that world. It could be, as the Rhine Institute claimed at the time, that the loneliness and the fear of all the dwellers on the colonized Rim Worlds are somehow focused on Kinsolving. Be that as it may, it happened. And it happened too that, in the fullness of time, this Raul was accepted into the bosom of our Church.

"Raul, as you may know, was more than a mere telepath. Much more. He was a wizard, one of those who, in his own age, drew animals to the hunters' spears by limning their likenesses on rock."

Grimes interrupted. "Doesn't the Bible say, somewhere, that thou shalt not suffer a witch to live?"

"Yes. It is so written. But we did not know of the full extent of Raul's talents when he was admitted into our Fold. We did not know of them until after his death, when his papers came into our possession."

"But what are you playing at?" demanded Grimes. "Just what you are playing at in *our* back garden?" He had the bottle out again, and the little phial of cognac-flavored essence, and was mixing two more drinks. He held out one of them, the stronger, to Smith, who absentmindedly took it and raised it to his lips.

The Rector said, "Sir, I do not approve of your choice of words. Life is not a game. Life, death and the hereafter are not a game. We are not playing. We are working. Is it not written. "Work, for the night is coming? And you, sir, and I, as spacemen, know that the night is coming—the inevitable heat death of the Universe. . . ." He gulped more of his drink.

"You should visit Darsha some time," said Grimes, "and their Tower of Darkness. You should see the huge clock that is the symbol of *their* God." He added softly, "The clock is running down."

"Yes, the clock is running down, the sands of time are running out. And there is much to be done, so much to be done. . . ."

"Such as?"

"To reestablish the eternal verities. To build a

237

new Sinai, to see the Commandments graven afresh on imperishable stone. And then, perhaps, the heathen, the idolators, will take heed and tremble. And then, surely, the rule of Jehovah will come again, before the End."

Grimes said reasonably enough, "But you people believe in predestination, don't you? Either we're damned or we aren't, and nothing we do makes any difference."

"I have learned by bitter experience," Smith told him, "that it is impossible to argue with a heretic—especally one who is foredoomed to eternal damnation. But even you must see that if the Commandments are given anew to Man then we, the Elect, shall be elevated to our rightful place in the Universe."

"Then God save us all," said Grimes.

Smith looked at him suspiciously, but went on. "It is perhaps necessary that there should be a sacrifice, and, if that be so, the Lord has already delivered her into our hands. No, sir, do not look at me like that. *We* shall not kill her, neither by knife nor fire shall we slay her. But, inevitably, she will be the plaything of supernal powers when she, on the planet of her ancestral origin, her inherited talents intensified by drugs, calls to Jehovah, the true God, the God of the Old Testament, to make Himself known again to sinful men."

There were flecks of white froth on Smith's beard around his lips, a dribble of saliva down the hair on his chin. His eyes were glaring and bloodshot. Grimes thought, *in vino veritas*. He said, with a gentleness he did not feel, actuated only by self-interest, "Don't you think that you've had enough, Rector? Isn't it time that we both turned in?"

"Eh, what? When'm ready. But you understand now that you must not interfere. *You must not interfere.*"

"I understand," said Grimes, thinking, *Too much and, not enough.* He found a tube of tablets in his suitcase, shook one into the palm of his hand. "Here," he said, offering it. "You'd better take this."

"Wha's it for?"

"It'll sweeten the breath and sober you up. It'll be too bad for you if the Presbyter sees the state you're in." *And too bad for me,* he thought.

" 'M not drunk."

"Of course not. Just a little—unsteady."

"Don't really need . . . But jus' to oblige, y'understan'."

Smith swallowed the tablet, his Adam's apple working convulsively. Grimes handed him a glass of cold water to wash it down. It acted almost immediately. The bearded man shuddered, then got steadily to his feet. He glared at Grimes, but it was no longer a fanatical glare. "Good night, sir," he snapped.

"Good night, Rector," Grimes replied.

When he was alone he thought of playing back the record of the evening's conversations, but thought better of it. For all he knew, Smith might be able to switch the hidden microphone and scanner back on from his own quarters—and the less he knew of the tiny device hidden in the starboard equalet of his white mess jacket, the better.

He got out of his clothes and into his bunk, switched off the light; but, unusually for him, his sleep was uneasy and nightmare-ridden. He supposed that it was Clarisse Lane's fault that she played a leading part in most of the dreams.

The voyage wore on, and on, and even as the ever-precessing gyroscopes of the Mannschenn Drive tumbled and receded down the dark infinities, so did the good ship *Piety* fall through the twisted Continuum. On one hand was the warped convoluted Galactic Lens and ahead, a pulsating spiral of iridescent light against the ultimate darkness, was the Kinsolving sun.

And this ship, unlike other ships of Grime's wide experience, was no little man-made oasis of light and warmth in the vast, empty desert of the night. She was cold, cold, and her atmosphere carried always the faint acridity of disinfectant, and men and women talked in grave, low voices and did not mingle, and never was there the merest hint of laughter.

Clarisse Lane was not being maltreated— Grimes made sure of that—and was even allowed to meet the Commodore for a daily conversation, but always heavily chaperoned. She was the only telepath in the ship, which, while the interstellar drive was in operation, depended entirely upon the Carlotti equipment for deep space communication. But the Rector and the Presbyter did not doubt that she was in constant touch with Mayhew back at Port Forlorn—and Grimes did not doubt it either. She told him much during their meetings—things about which she could not possibly have known if there had not been a continual interchange of signals. Some of this intelligence was confirmed by messages addressed to Grimes and received, in the normal way, by the ship's electronic radio officer.

So they were obliged to be careful, these Neo-Calvinists. The chosen instrument for their experiment in practical theology was now also an agent for the Rim Worlds Confederacy. "But what does it matter?" Smith said to Grimes on one of the rare occasions that he spoke at length to him. "What does it matter? Perhaps it was ordained this way. Your friend Mayhew will be the witness to the truth, a witness who is not one of us. He will see through her eyes, hear with her ears, feel with every fiber of her being. The Word propagated by ourselves alone would be scoffed at. But there will be credence given it when it is propagated by an unbeliever."

"If anything happens," said Grimes.

But he couldn't argue with these people, and they couldn't argue with him. There was just no meeting of minds. He remembered a theory that he had once heard advanced by a ship's doctor. "Long ago," the man had said, "very long ago, there was a mutation. It wasn't a physically obvious one, but as a result of it Homo Sapiens was divided into two separate species: *Homo credulens*, those capable of blind faith in the unprovable, and *Homo incredulens*, those who aren't. The vast majority of people are, of course, hybrids."

Grimes had said, "And I suppose that all the pure *Homo incredulens* stock is either atheist or agnostic."

"Not so." The doctor had laughed. "Not so. Agnostic—yes. But don't forget that the atheist, like the theist, makes a definite statement for which he can produce no proof whatsoever."

An atheist would have been far less unhappy aboard this ship than a tolerant agnostic like Grimes.

But even the longest, unhappiest vogage comes to an end. A good planetfall was made—whatever they believed, *Piety's* people were excellent navigators—and, the Mannschenn Drive switched off, the Inertial Drive ticking over just enough to produce minimal gravitational field, the ship was falling in orbit about the lonely world, the blue and green mottled sphere hanging there against the blackness.

The old charts—or copies of them—were out, and Grimes was called up to the control room. "Yes," he told Smith, stabbing a finger down on the paper, "that's where the spaceport was. Probably even now the apron's not too overgrown for a safe landing. Captain Spence, when he came down in *Epsilon Eridani,* reported creepers over everything, but nothing heavy."

"It is a hundred and fifty standard years since he was here," said Smith. "At least. I would suggest one of the beaches."

"Risky," Grimes told him. "They shelve very steeply and according to our records violent storms are more frequent than otherwise." He

turned to the big screen upon which a magnification of the planet was appearing. "There, just to
the east of the sunrise terminator. That's the major
continent—Farland, it was called—where the
capital city and the spaceport were situated. You
see that river, with the S bend? Step up the magnification somebody. . . ."

Now there was only the glowing picture of the
island continent, filling all the screen, and that
expanded, so that there was only the sprawling,
silvery S, and toward the middle of it, on either
bank, a straggle of buildings was visible.

"The spaceport should be about ten miles to the
west," said Grimes.

"Yes," agreed Smith, taking a long pointer to
the screen. "I think that's it."

"Then make it Landing Stations, Rector," ordered Presbyter Cannan.

"Sir," demurred Smith, "you cannot put a big
ship down as though she were a dinghy."

"Lord, oh Lord," almost prayed the Presbyter.
"To have come so far, and then to be plagued by
the dilatoriness of spacemen!"

I wish that this were my control room, thought
Grimes.

But *Piety's* crew worked well and efficiently,
and in a very short space of time the intercom
speakers were blatting strings of orders: "Secure
all for landing stations!" "All idlers to their quarters!" and the like. Gyroscopes hummed and
whined and the ship tilted relative to the planet
until its surface was directly beneath her, and the
first of the sounding rockets, standard equipment

for a survey expedition but not for landing on a world with spaceport control functioning, were fixed.

Parachutes blossomed in the upper atmosphere and the flares, each emitting a great steamer of smoke, ignited. Somebody was singing. It was the Presbyter.

> *"Let the fiery, cloudy pillar*
> *Guide me all my journey through. . . ."*

Even Grimes was touched by the spirit of the occasion. What if this crazy, this impious (for so he was beginning to think of it) experiment did work? What would happen? What would be unleashed upon the worlds of men? Who was it—the Gnostics?—who had said that the God of the Old Testament was the Devil of the New? He shivered as he sat in his acceleration chair.

She was dropping steadily, was *Piety*, following the first of her flares. But there was drift down there—perhaps a gale in the upper atmosphere, or a jet stream. The Inertial Drive generators grumbled suddenly as Smith applied lateral thrust. Down she dropped, and down, almost falling free, but under the full control of her captain. On the target screen, right in the center, highly magnified, the cluster of ruins that had been a spaceport was clearly visible, tilting like tombstones in a deserted graveyard, ghastly in the blue light of the rising sun.

Down she dropped, plunging through the wisps of cirrus, and there was a slight but appreciable rise of temperature as skin friction heated the metal of her hull. Smith slowed the rate of descent. The Presbyter started muttering irritably to himself.

There was no longer need for magnification on the screen. The great rectangle of the landing field was clearly visible, the vegetation that covered it lighter in color—eau de Nile against the surrounding indigo—than the brush outside the area. The last of the flares to have been fired was still burning there, its column of smoke rising almost vertically. The growth among which it had fallen was slowly smoldering.

Grimes looked at Smith. The man was concentrating hard. Beads of perspiration were forming on his upper cheeks, running down into his beard. But this was more important than an ordinary landing. So much hinged upon it. And, perhaps, malign (or benign) forces might be gathering their strength to overset the ship before her massive tripedal landing gear reached the safety of the planetary surface.

But she was down.

There was the gentlest of shocks, the faintest of creakings, the softest sighing of shock-absorbers. She was down, and the Inertial Drive generators muttered to themselves and then were quiet. She was down, and the soughing of the fans seemed to make the silence all the more silent.

Presbyter Cannan broke it. He turned in his chair to address Grimes. "Commodore," he asked as he pointed toward a distant peak, a black, truncated cone against the blue sky, "Commodore

Grimes, what is the name of that mountain?"

"I . . . I don't know, sir."

"*I* know." The old man's voice was triumphant. "It is Sinai."

Had this been any other ship there would have been a period of relaxation. There were wild pigs and rabbits to hunt, descendants of the livestock abandoned by the original colonists. There were the famous caves, with their rock paintings, to visit. But the animals, their fear of Man long forgotten, came out of the undergrowth to stare curiously at the vessel and at the humans who busied themselves around her, opening side ports to allow the egress of the three pinnaces, already stocked with what would be required for the final stages of the expedition. And nobody was remotely interested in the caves.

Grimes managed to see Clarisse Lane. The ship was almost deserted now, so he was able to make his way down into the women's quarters without being challenged and stopped. He found her little cabin, hardly more than a cell. She was not locked in, not restrained in any way. She was sitting in her chair, a somber figure in her black dress, staring into nothingness. Her full lips moved almost imperceptibly as she vocalized her thoughts.

With a sudden start she realized that Grimes was standing before her. She whispered, "I—I was talking to Ken."

"To Mayhew?"

"Yes."

Saying goodbye, he thought. He said, "Clarisse, you don't have to go through with this."

"I am going through with it, Commodore."

"You don't have to," he insisted. "You're in touch with Mayhew. And he'll be in touch with *Rim Sword*. The Admiral told me that she'd be standing by in this sector. She's probably on her way here now. We can stall off those fanatics until she comes in."

She said, "I'm going through with it."

"But why? Why?"

"Because I want to."

"But you're not really one of them."

"I'm not."

"Sister Lane!" It was the Deaconess. "You asked for a few moments of privacy—and now I find you with this—this lecher! But come. The boat is waiting."

"I'll come with you." said Grimes.

"You will not," snapped the woman. "A place has been reserved for you in the pinnace carrying the Presbyter and the Rector. They had decided that it is meet that an infidel shall witness the handing down of the Law."

Clarisse Lane followed the Deaconess from the cabin. Grimes trailed along behind them. They went down to the main air lock, down the ramp to the overgrown apron, stumbling over the tough, straggling vines on their way to the boats. The sun was dropping fast to the western horizon. There was a hint of chill, a smell of dusk in the still air. There was the scent of growing things, and a faint hint of corruption.

Smith beckoned to Grimes from the open door of the leading pinnace. He made his way slowly toward it, walking carefully. He clambered up the retractable steps into the crowded cabin that stank of perspiration and damp, heavy clothing. He found a seat, wedged between two junior officers.

The door hissed shut. The Inertial Drive generator throbbed and snarled. Grimes could not see out of the ports, but he knew that the boat was airborne, was moving. There was no conversation in the cabin, but a metallic male voice reported from the speaker on the pilot's console, "Number Two following." After a pause a harsh female voice said, "Number Three following."

How long the flight lasted Grimes did not know; he was unable to raise his arm to look at his watch. But it seemed a long time, and it seemed a long time that they sat there after they had landed, waiting for the other boats to come down. But at last the door opened and a thin, icy wind whined through the aperture. The Presbyter was out first, then Smith, and eventually Grimes, in the middle of a huddle of officers and civilians.

The plateau was smooth, windswept, an expanse of bare rock. To one side of it were the three pinnaces, and in front of them the men were drawn up in orderly ranks, with only the Presbyter standing apart. In the middle of the circular area were the women, a ragged huddle of somber black.

Grimes's attention was caught by a blue spark far below, not far from the still gleaming, serpentine river. Had *Rim Sword* landed? No. It was only the control room windows of *Piety* reflecting the last rays of the setting sun.

There was a subdued murmuring as the women walked to stand to one side of the men. No, not all the women. Two remained in the center of the plateau. One was the Deaconess, tall and forbidding. The other was the Clarisse Lane. They had stripped her. She was wearing only a kilt cut roughly from the hide of some animal, clothing like that which had been worn by her ancestresses on this very planet. She was shivering and was hugging her full breasts to try to keep out the cold.

Stark, incongruous, and easel stood there, supporting a frame square of black canvas, and there was a battery-powered floodlight to illuminate it. At its foot were pots of pigment, and brushes. Raul, the forefather of this girl, had called animals with his paintings. What would she call? What could she call?

"Drink!" said the Deaconess, her voice and clear over the thin whine of the bitter wind. "Drink!" She was holding out a glass of something. Clarisse took it, drained it.

Suddenly the sun was gone, and there was only the glare of the floodlight. Overhead was the almost empty black sky, and low to the east was an arc of misty luminescence that was the slowly rising Galactic Lens. The wind seemed to be coming straight from intergalactic space.

The Deaconess stalked over the rocky surface to take her stand beside the Presbyter, leaving the girl alone. Hesitantly Clarisse stooped to the pots and brushes, selected one of the latter, dipped it into paint, straightened, stood before the easel.

She stiffened into immobility, seemed to be waiting for something.

They were singing, then, the black-clad men and women drawn up in their stiff ranks before the pinnaces. They were singing. "Cwn Rhonda," it was, and even Grimes, who had always loved that old Welsh hymn tune, found it hard to refrain from joining in. They were singing, the rumbling basses, the baritones, the high tenors and the shrill sopranos.

> Guide, me, oh Thou great Jehovah,
> Pilgrim through this barren land!
> I am weak, but Thou art mighty,
> Hold me with Thy powerful hand!

They were singing, and the girl was painting. With deft, sure strokes she was depicting on the black canvas the figure of a god, white-bearded, white-robed, wrathful. She was painting, and the men and women were singing, and the air was full of unbearable tension and the wind was now howling, tugging at their clothing, buffeting them. But the easel in its circle of harsh light stood steady and the girl worked on. . . .

There was the dreadful *crack* of lightning close at hand, too close at hand, the *crack* and the dazzle, and the pungency of ozone, and the long, long streamer of blue fire licking out from above their heads and culminating on the plain far below, at the spaceport.

There was the burgeoning fireball where the ship had been.

There was the dreadful laughter, booming above the frenzy of the wind, and the metallic crash and clatter as the pinnaces, lifted and rolled over the rim of the plateau, plunged to destruction down the steep, rocky mountain slope.

And *They* were there—the robust, white-bearded deity, a lightning bolt clutched and ready in his right hand, and the naked, seductively smiling goddess, and the other naked one with her bow and her leashed hounds, and she in the white robes, carrying a book, with the owl perched on her shoulder. The lame smith was there, with his hammer, and the sea-god, with his trident, and he with the red beard and the helmet and the body armor and the sword.

Somebody screamed, and at least a score of the men and women had fallen to their knees. But the Presbyter stood his ground.

"Who are you?" he shouted. "Who are you?"

"Little man," the great voice replied, "we were, we are and we always shall be."

Grimes realized that he was laughing uncontrollably and saying, over and over to himself, "Not Sinai, but Olympus! Not Sinai, but Olympus!"

There was another supernal clap of thunder and the dark came sweeping back.

They sat around in miserable little groups on the bare mountaintop.

The Presbyter was gone, nobody knew where or how, and the Deaconess, and Smith, and perhaps a dozen of the others. It had been a long night, and a cold one, but the sun had risen at last, bringing some warmth with it.

Grimes, in shirt and trousers, stood with Clarrise Lane, who was wrapped in his jacket.

"But what happened?" he was asking. "What happened? What did you do?"

She said, "I . . . I don't know. I suppose that I do have some sort of power. And I suppose that I am, at heart, one of the Blossom People. Our religious beliefs are a sort of vague pantheism. . . . And, after all, the Father of the Gods is very similar in His attributes to the patriarchal gods of later religions. . . ." She looked at the sky. "It's lucky that I'm a telepath as well as being . . . whatever it is that I am. *Rim Sword* will be here very shortly. I hope it's soon. I have a feeling that when some of our fanatical friends recover they'll be blaming me for everything."

"*When* they recover," said Grimes. "It will take *me* a long time." He added, "But I don't think you'd better return to Francisco with them."

"Ken," she told him, "has already got the formalities under way that will make me a Rim Worlds citizen."

"The obivous one?"

"Yes."

"And are you going to get married in church?" he asked. "It should be interesting."

"Not if I can help it," she told him.

And so, in due course, Grimes kissed the bride and, at the reception, toasted the newlyweds in imported champagne. He did not stay long after that. He was too much the odd man out—almost all the other guests were married couples, and such few women as were unattached made little or no appeal to him. He was missing Sonya, still away on her galactic cruise. Somehow he missed her less at home, lonely though it was without her. There was still so much of her in the comfortable apartment: her books, the pictures that she had chosen, the furniture that had been specially designed to her taste.

Having left the party early, he was at his office, at the spaceport, bright and early the following morning. He received, personally, the urgent Carlottigram from *Rim Griffon*, on Tharn. He smiled as he read it. He had been deskbound for too long, and his recent voyage in the oddly named *Piety* had aggravated rather than assuaged the itching of his feet. Captain Timms, one of the Rim Runners' senior masters, was due back from annual leave within a few days and, at the moment, there was no appointment open for him. So Timms could keep the chair warm while Grimes took passage to Tharn; the scheduled departure date of *Rim Dragon* for that planet fitted in very nicely with his plans.

"Miss Walton," he said happily to the rather vapid little blonde secretary, "this is going to be a busy morning. Telephoning first, and then correspondence every which way. . . . To begin with, get me the General Manager. . . ."

Part Two

HER INERTIAL DRIVE throbbing softly, all hands at landing stations, all passengers save one strapped in their acceleration couches (a sudden emergency requiring the use of the auxiliary reaction drive was unlikely, but possible), the starship *Rim Dragon* dropped slowly down to Port Grimes on Tharn. The privileged passenger—although in his case it was a right rather than a privilege—was riding in the control room instead of being incarcerated in his cabin. Commodore John Grimes, Astronautical Superintendent of Rim Runners, said nothing, did nothing that could be construed as interference on his part. Legally speaking, of course, he was no more than a guest in the liner's nerve center; but at the same time he could and did excerise considerable authority over the space-going employees of Rim Runners, made the ultimate decisions in such matters as promotions and appointments. However, Captain Wenderby, *Rim Dragon's* master, was a more than competent ship-handler and at no time did Grimes feel impelled to make any suggestions, at no time did his own hands start to reach out hungrily for the controls.

So Grimes sat there, stolid and solid in his acceleration chair, not even now keeping a watchful eye on the briskly efficient Wenderby and his briskly efficient officers. They needed no advice from him, would need none. But it was easier for them than it had been for him, when he made his own first landing on Tharn—how many years ago? Too many. There had been no spaceport then, with spaceport control keeping the master fully informed of meteorological conditions during his entire descent. There had been no body of assorted officials—port captain, customs, port health and all the rest of it—standing by awaiting the ship's arrival. Grimes, in fact, had not known what or whom to expect, although his robot probes had told him that the culture of the planet was roughly analogous to that of Earth's Middle Ages. Even so, he had been lucky in that he had set *Faraway Quest* down near a city controlled by the priesthood rather than in an area under the sway of one of the robber barons.

He looked out of one of the big viewports. From this altitude he could see no signs of change—but change there must have been, change there had been. On that long ago exploration voyage in the old *Quest* he had opened up the worlds of the Eastern Circuit to commerce—and the trader does more to destroy the old ways than either the gunboat or the missionary. In this case the trader would have been the only outside influence: the Rim Worlds had always, fortunately for them, been governed by cynical, tolerant agnostics to whom gunboat diplomacy was distasteful. The Rim Worlders had always valued their own freedom too highly to wish to interfere with that of any other race.

But even commerce, thought Grimes, *is an interference. It makes people want the things that they cannot yet produce for themselves: the mass-produced entertainment, the labor-saving machines, the weapons.* Grimes sighed. *I suppose that we were right to arm the priesthood rather than the robber barons. In any case, they've been good customers.*

Captain Wenderby, still intent on his controls, spoke. "It must seem strange, coming back after all these years, sir."

"It does, Captain."

"And to see the spaceport that they named after you, for the first time."

"A man could have worse monuments."

Grimes transferred his attention from the viewport to the screen that showed, highly magnified, what was directly astern of and below the ship. Yes, there it was. Port Grimes. A great circle of gray-gleaming concrete, ringed by warehouses and administration buildings, with cranes and gantries and conveyor belts casting long shadows the ruddy light of the westering sun. (*He* had made the first landing on rough heathland, and for a long, heart-stopping moment had doubted that the tripedal landing gear would be able to adjust—to the irregularities of the surface.) And there was *Rim Griffon*, the reason for his voyage to Tharn. There was the ship whose officers refused to sail with each other and with the master. There was the mess that had to be sorted out with as few firings as possible—Rim Runners, as usual, was short of spacefaring personnel.

There was the mess.

It was some little time before John Grimes could get around to doing anything about it. As he should have foreseen, he was a personality, a historical personality at that. He was the first outsider to have visited Tharn. He was responsible for the breaking of the power of the barons, for the rise to power of the priesthood and the merchants. Too, the Rim Confederacy's ambassador on Tharn had made it plain that he, and the government that he represented, would appreciate it if the Commodore played along. The delay in the departure of a very unimportant merchant vessel was far less important than the preservation of interstellar good relations.

So Grimes was wined and dined, which was no which was. He was taken on sight-seeing tours, and was pleased to note that progress, although inevitable, had been a controlled progress, not progress for its own sake. The picturesque had been sacrificed only when essential for motives of

hygiene or *real* efficiency. Electricity had
supplanted the flaring natural gas jets for house-
and street-lighting—but the importation and evolution of new building techniques and materials
had not produced a mushroom growth of steel and
concrete matchboxes or plastic domes. Architecture still retained its essentially Tharnian character, even though the streets of the city were no
longer rutted, even though the traffic on those
same streets was now battery-powered cars and
no longer animal-drawn vehicles. (Internal com-
bustion engines were manufactured on the planet,
but their use was prohibited within urban limits.)

And at sea change had come. At the time of
Grimes's first landing the only oceangoing vessels
had been the big schooners; now sail was on its
way out, was being ousted by the steam turbine.
Yet the ships, with their fiddle bows and their
figureheads, with their raked masts and funnels,
still displayed an archaic charm that was altogether lacking on Earth's seas and on the waters
of most Man-colonized worlds. The Commodore,
who was something of an authority on the history
of marine transport, would dearly have loved to
have made a voyage in one of the steamers, but he
knew that time would not permit this. Once he had
sorted out *Rim Griffon's* troubles he would have to
return to Port Forlorn, probably in that very ship.

At last he was able to get around to the real
reason for his visit to Tharn. On the morning of his
fifth day on the planet he strode purposefully
across the clean, well-cared-for concrete of the
apron, walked decisively up the ramp to *Rim Grif-*

fon's after air lock door. There was a junior officer waiting there to receive him; Captain Dingwall had been warned that he would be coming on board. Grimes knew the young man, as he should have; after all, he had interviewed him for a berth in the Rim Runners' service.

"Good morning, Mr. Taylor."

"Good morning, sir." The Third Officer was painfully nervous, and his prominent Adam's apple bobbled as he spoke. His ears, almost as outstanding as Grimes's own, flushed a dull red. "The Old—" The flush spread to all of Taylor's features. "Captain Dingwall is waiting for you, sir. This way, sir."

Grimes did not need a guide. This *Rim Griffon*, like most of the older units in Rim Runners' fleet, had started her career as an *Epsilon* Class tramp in the employ of the Interstellar Transport Commission. The general layout of those tried and trusted Galactic workhouses was familiar to all spacemen. However, young Mr. Taylor had been instructed by his captain to receive the Commodore and to escort him to his, Dingwall's, quarters, and Grimes had no desire to interfere with the running of the ship.

Yet.

The two men rode up in the elevator in silence, each immersed in his own thoughts. Taylor, obviously, was apprehensive. A delay of a vessel is always a serious matter, especially when her own officers are involved. And Grimes was sorting out his own impressions to date. This *Rim Griffon* was obviously not a happy ship. He could feel it—just as he could see and hear the faint yet unmistakable signs of neglect, the hints of rust and dust, the not yet anguished pleading of a machine somewhere, a fan or a pump, for lubrication. And as the elevator cage passed through the "farm" level there was a whiff of decaying vegetation; either algae vats or hydroponic tanks, or both, were overdue for cleaning out.

The elevator stopped at the captain's deck. Young Mr. Taylor led the way out of the cage, knocked diffidently at the door facing the axial shaft. It slid open. A deep voice said, "That will be all, Mr. Taylor. I'll send for you, and the other officers when I want you. And come in, please, Commodore Grimes."

Grimes entered the day cabin. Dingwall rose to meet him—a short, stocky man, his features too large, too ruddy, his eyes too brilliantly blue under a cockatoo-crest of white hair. He extended a hand, saying, "Welcome aboard, Commodore." He did not manage to make the greeting sound convincing. "Sit down, sir. The sun's not yet over the yardarm, but I can offer you coffee."

"No thank you, Captain. Later, perhaps. Mind if I smoke?" Grimes produced his battered pipe, filled and lit it. He said through the initial acid cloud, "And now, sir, what *is* the trouble? Your ship has been held up for far too long."

"You should have asked me that five days ago, Commodore."

"Should I?" Grimes stared at Dingwall, his gray eyes bleak. "Perhaps I should. Unfortunately I was obliged to act almost in an ambassadorial capacity after I arrived here. But now I am free to attend to the real business."

"It's my officers," blurted Dingwall.

"Yes?"

"The second mate to begin with. A bird-brained navigator if ever there was one. Can you imagine anybody, with all the aids we have today, getting lost between Stree and Mellise? *He* did."

"Legally speaking," said Grimes, "the master is responsible for everything. Including the navigation of his ship."

"I navigate myself. Now."

And I can imagine it, thought Grimes. *"Do I have to do everybody's bloody job in this bloody ship? Of course, I'm only the Captain. . . ."* He said, "You reprimanded him, of course?"

"Darn right I did." Dingwall's voice registered pleasant reminiscence. "I told him that he was incapable of navigating a plastic duck across a bathtub."

"Hmm. And your other officers?"

"There're the engineers, Commodore. The Interstellar Drive chief hates the Inertial Drive chief. Not that I've much time for either of 'em. In fact I told Willis—he's supposed to run the Inertial Drive—that he couldn't pull a soldier off his sister. That was after I almost had to use the auxiliary rockets to get clear of Grollor—"

"And the others?"

"Vacchini, Mate. He couldn't run a pie cart. And Sally Bowen, Catering Officer, can't boil water without burning it. And Pilchin, the so-called purser, can't add two and two and get the

same answer twice running. And as for Sparks . . .
I'd stand a better chance of getting an important
message through if I just opened a control viewport and stood there and shouted."

The officer who is to blame for all this, thought
Grimes, *is the doctor. He should have seen this
coming on. But perhaps I'm to blame as well.
Dingwall's home port is Port Forlorn, on Lorn—
and his ship's been running between the worlds of
the Eastern Circuit and Port Farewell, on Faraway, for the past nine standard months. And Mrs.
Dingwall* (Grimes had met her) *is too fond of her
social life to travel with him. . . .*

"Don't you like the ship, Captain?" he asked.

"The *ship's* all right," he was told.

"But the run, as far as you're concerned, could
be better."

"And the officers."

Couldn't we all, Captain Dingwall? Couldn't we
all? And now, just between ourselves, who is it
that refused to sail with you?"

"My bird-brained navigator. I hurt his feelings
when I called him that. A very sensitive young
man is our Mr. Missenden. And the Inertial Drive
chief. He's a member of some fancy religion called
the Neo-Calvinists. . . ."

"I've met them," said Grimes.

"What I said about his sister and the soldier
really shocked him."

"And which of them refuse to sail with each
other?"

"Almost everybody has it in for the second
mate. He's a Latter Day Fascist and is always

trying to make converts. And the two chiefs are at each other's throats. Kerholm the Interstellar Drive specialist, is a militant atheist—"

And I was on my annual leave, thought Grimes, *when this prize bunch of square pegs was appointed to this round hole. Even so, I should have checked up. I would have checked up if I hadn't gotten involved in the fun and games on Kinsolving's Planet.*

"Captain," he said, "I appreciate your problems. But there are two sides to every story. Mr. Vacchini, for example, is a very efficient officer. As far as he is concerned, there could well be a clash of personalities. . . ."

"Perhaps," admitted Dingwall grudgingly.

"As for the others. I don't know them personally. If you could tell them all to meet in the wardroom in—say—five minutes, we can go down to try to iron things out."

"You can try," said the Captain. "I've had them all in a big way. And, to save you the bother of saying it, Commodore Grimes, they've had me likewise."

Grimes ironed things out. On his way from Lorn to Tharn he had studied the files of reports on the captain and his officers. Nonetheless, in other circumstances he would have been quite ruthless—but good spacemen do not grow on trees, especially out toward the Galactic Rim. And these were good spacemen, all of them, with the exception of Missenden, the second officer. He had been born on New Saxony, one of the worlds that had been part of the short-lived Duchy of Waldegren, and one of the worlds upon which the political perversions practiced upon Waldegreen itself had lived on for years after the downfall of the Duchy. He had been an officer in the navy of New Saxony and had taken part in the action off Pelisande, the battle in which the heavy cruisers of the Survey Service had destroyed the last of the self-styled commerce raiders who were, in fact, no better than pirates.

There had been survivors, and Missenden had been one of them. (He owed his survival mainly to the circumstance that the ship of which he had been Navigator had been late in arriving at her rendezvous with the other New Saxony war vessels and had, in fact, surrendered after no more than a token resistance.) He had stood trial with other war criminals, but had escaped with a very light sentence. (Most of the witnesses who could have testified against him were dead.) As he had held a lieutenant commander's commission in the navy of New Saxony he had been able to obtain a Master Astronaut's Certificate after no more than the merest apology for an examination. Then he had drifted out to the Rim, where his New Saxony qualifications were valid; where, in fact, qualifications issued by any human authority anywhere in the galaxy were valid.

Grimes looked at Missenden. He did not like what he saw. He had not liked it when he first met the man, a few years ago, when he had engaged him as a probationary third officer—but then, as now, he had not been able to afford to turn spacemen away from his office door. The Second Officer was tall, with a jutting, arrogant beak of a nose over a wide, thin-lipped mouth, with blue eyes that looked even madder than Captain Dingwall's, his pale, freckled face topped by close-cropped red hair. He was a fanatic, that was obvious from his physical appearance, and in a ship where he, like everybody else, was unhappy his fanaticism would be enhanced. *A lean and hungry look,* thought Grimes. *He thinks too much; such men are dangerous.* He added mentally, *But only when they think about the wrong things. The late Duke Otto's* Galactic Superman, *for example, rather than Pilgren's* Principles of Interstellar Navigation.

He said, "Mr. Missenden . . ."

"Sir?" The curtly snapped word was almost an insult. The way in which it was said implied, "I'm according respect to your rank, not to *you.*"

"The other officers have agreed to continue the voyage. On arrival at Port Forlorn you will all be transferred to more suitable ships, and those of you who are due will be sent on leave or time off as soon as possible. Are you agreeable?"

"No."

"And why not, Mr. Missenden?"

"I'm not prepared to make an intercontinental hop under a captain who insulted me."

"Insulted you?"

"Yes." He turned on Dingwall. "Did you, or did you not, call me a bird-brained navigator?"

"I did, Mr. Missenden," snarled Captain Dingwall. "And I meant it."

"Captain," asked Grimes patiently, "are you

prepared to withdraw that remark?''

"I am not, Commodore. Furthermore, as master of this ship I have the legal right to discharge any member of my crew that I see fit.''

"Very well," said Grimes, "As Captain Dingwall has pointed out I can only advise and mediate. But I do possess some authority; appointments and transfers are my responsibility. Will you arrange, Captain, for Mr. Missenden to be paid, on your books, up to an including midnight, local time? Then get him off your Articles of Agreement as soon as possible, so that the second officer of *Rim Dragon* can be signed on here. And you, Mr. Missenden, will join *Rim Dragon*."

"If you say so," said Missenden, Sir.''

"I do say so. And I say, too, Mr. Missenden, that I shall see you again in my office back in Port Forlorn."

"I can hardly wait, Sir."

Captain Dingwall looked at his watch. He said, "The purser already has Mr. Missenden's payoff almost finalized. Have you made any arrangements with Captain Wenderby regarding his second officer?"

"I told him that there might be a transfer, Captain. Shall we meet at the Consul's office at 1500 hours? You probably know that he is empowered to act as shipping master insofar as our ships on Tharn are concerned."

"Yes, sir," stated Dingwall. "I know."

"You would," muttered Missenden.

The transfer of officers was nice and easy in theory—but it did not work out in practice. The purser, Grimes afterward learned, was the only person aboard *Rim Griffon* with whom the second officer was not on terms of acute enmity. Missenden persuaded him to arrange his pay-off for 1400 hours, not 1500. At the appointed time the purser of the *Griffon* was waiting in the Consul's office, and shortly afterward the purser and the second officer of *Rim Dragon* put in their appearance. The *Dragon's* second mate was paid off his old ship and signed on the Articles of his new one. But Missenden had vanished. All that *Griffon's* purser knew was that he had taken the money due him and said that he had a make a business call and that he would be back.

He did not come back.

Commodore Grimes was not in a happy mood. He had hoped to be a passenger aboard *Rim Griffon* when she lifted off from Port Grimes, but now it seemed that his departure from Tharn for the Rim Worlds would have to be indefinitely postponed. It was, of course, all Missenden's fault. Now that he had gone into smoke all sorts of unsavory facts were coming to light regarding that officer. During his ship's visits to Tharn he had made contact with various subversive elements. The Consul had not known of this—but Rim Runners' local agent, a native to the planet, had. It was the police who had told him, and he had passed the information on to Captain Dingwall. Dingwall had shrugged and growled, "What the hell else do you expect from such a drongo?" adding, "As long as I get rid of the bastard he can consort with Aldebaranian necrophiles for all I care!''

Quite suddenly, with Grimes's baggage already loaded aboard *Rim Griffon*, the mess had blown up to the proportions of an interstellar incident. Port Grimes's Customs refused outward clearance to the ship. The Rim Confederacy's Ambassador sent an urgent message to Grimes requiring him to disembark at once—after which the ship would be permitted to leave—and to report forthwith to the Embassy. With all this happening, Grimes was in no fit state to listen to Captain Wenderby's complaints that he had lost a first class second officer and now would have to sail shorthanded on completion of discharge.

The Ambassador's own car took Grimes from the spaceport to the Embassy. It was a large building, ornately turreted, with metal-bound doors that could have withstood the charge of a medium tank. These opened as the Commodore dismounted from the vehicle, and within them stood saluting Marines. *At least*, thought Grimes, *they aren't going to shoot me. Yet.* An aide in civilian clothes escorted him to the Ambassador's office.

The Honorable Clifton Weeks was a short, fat man with all of a short, fat man's personality. ''Sit down, Commodore,'' he huffed. Then, glowering over his wide, highly polished desk at the spaceman. ''Now, sir. This Missenden character. What about him? Hey?''

''He seems to have flown the coop,'' said Grimes.

''You amaze me, sir.'' Week's glower became even more pronounced. ''You amaze me, sir. Not by what you said, but by the way in which you said it. Surely you, even you, have some appreciation of the seriousness of the situation?"

"Spacemen have deserted before, in foreign ports. Just as seamen used to do—still do, probably. The local police have his description. They'll pick him up, and deport him when they get him. And we'll deport him, too, when he's delivered back to the Confederacy."

"And you still don't think it's serious? Hey?"

"Frankly, no, sir."

"Commodore, you made the first landing on this planet. But what do you know about it? Nothing, sir. Nothing. You haven't lived here. I have. I know that the Confederacy will have to fight to maintain the currently favorable trade relations that we still enjoy with Tharn. Already other astronautical powers are sniffing around the worlds of the Eastern Circuit."

"During the last six months, local time," said Grimes, "three of the Empire of Waverley's ships have called here. And two from the Shakespearean Sector. And one of Trans-Galactic Clippers' cargo liners. But, as far as the rulers of Tharn are concerned, the Confederacy is still the most favored nation."

"Who *are* the rulers of Tharn?" barked the Ambassador.

"Why, the priesthood."

The Ambassador mumbled something about the political illiteracy of spacemen, then got to his feet. He waddled to the far wall of his office, on which was hung a huge map of the planet in Mercator projection, beckoned to Grimes to follow him. From a rack he took a long pointer. "The island continent of Ausiphal . . ." he said, "And here, on the eastern seaboard, Port Grimes, and University City. Where we are now."

"Yes. . . ."

The tip of the pointer described a rhumb line, almost due east. "The other island continent of the northern hemisphere, almost the twin to this one. Climatically, politically—you name it."

"Yes?"

The pointer backtracked, then stabbed viciously. "And here, well to the west of Braziperu, the island of Tangaroa. Not a continent, but still a sizable hunk of real estate."

"So?"

"So Tangaroa's the last stronghold of the robber barons, the ruffians who were struggling for power with the priests and merchants when you made your famous first landing. How many years ago was it? Hey?"

"But what's that to do with Mr. Missenden?" Grimes asked. "And me?" he added.

"Your Mr. Missenden," the Ambassador said, "served in the navy of New Saxony. The people with whom he's been mixing in University City are Tangaroan agents and sympathizers. The priesthood has allowed Tangaroa to continue to exist—in fact, there's even trade between it and Ausiphal—but has been reluctant to allow the Tangaroans access to any new knowledge, especially knowledge that could be perverted to the manufacture of weaponry. Your Mr. Missenden would be a veritable treasure house of such knowledge.''

''He's not *my* Mr. Missenden!'' snapped Grimes.

''But he is, sir. He is. *You* engaged him when he came out to the Rim. *You* appointed him to ships running the Eastern Circuit. *You* engineered his discharge on this world, even.''

''So what am I supposed to do about him?''

''Find him, before he does any real damage. And if you, the man after whom the spaceport was named, are successful it will show the High Priest just how much we of the Confederacy have the welfare of Tharn at heart.''

''But why *me*? These people have a very efficient police force. And a man with a pale, freckled face and red hair will stand out like a sore thumb among the natives.''

The Honorable Mr. Weeks laughed scornfully. ''Green skin dye! Dark blue hair dye! Contact lenses! And, on top of all that, a physical appearance that's common on this planet!''

''Yes,'' admitted Grimes. ''I might recognize him, in spite of a disguise. . . .''

''Good. My car is waiting to take you to the High Priest.''

The University stood on a rise to the east of the city, overlooking the broad river and, a few miles to the north, the sea. It looked more like a fortress than a seat of learning, and in Tharn's turbulent past it had, more than once, been castle rather than academy.

Grimes respected the Tharnian priesthood, and the religion that they preached and practiced made sense to him than most of the other faiths of Man. There was something of Buddhism about it, a recognition of the fact that nothing *is*, but that everything is flux, change, a continual process of becoming. There was the equation of God with Knowledge—but never that infuriating statement made by so many Terran religions, that smug. "There are things that we aren't meant to know." There was a very real wisdom—the wisdom that accepts and rejects, and that neither accepts nor rejects just because a concept is *new*. There was a reluctance to rush headlong into an industrial revolution with all its miseries; and, at the same time, no delay in the adoption of techniques that would make the life of the people longer, easier and happier.

Night had fallen when the Embassy car pulled up outside the great gates of the University. The guard turned out smartly—but in these days their function was merely ceremonial; no longer was there the need to keep either the students in or the townsfolk out. On all of Tharn—save for Tangarora—the robber barons were only an evil memory of the past.

A black-uniformed officer led Grimes through long corridors, lit by bright electric bulbs, and up stairways to the office of the High Priest. He, an elderly, black-robed man, frail, his skin darkened by age to an opaque olive, had been a young student at the time of the first landing. He claimed to have met the Commodore on that occasion, but

Grimes could not remember him. But he was almost the double of the old man who had held the high office then—a clear example of the job making the man.

"Commodore Grimes," he said. "Please be seated."

"Thank you, your Wisdom."

"I am sorry to have interferred with your plans, sir. But your Mr. Weeks insisted."

"He assured me that it was important."

"And he has . . . put you in the picture?"

"Yes."

The old man produced a decanter, two graceful glasses. He poured the wine. Grimes relaxed. He remembered that the Tharnian priesthood made a point of never drinking with anybody whom they considered an enemy, with nobody who was not a friend in the true sense of the word. There was no toast, only a ceremonial raising of goblets. The liquor was good, as it always had been.

"What can I do?" asked Grimes.

The priest shrugged. "Very little. I told Mr. Weeks that our own police were quite capable of handling the situation, but he said, 'It's *his* mess. He should have his nose rubbed in it.' " The old man's teeth were very white in his dark face as he smiled.

"Takes out of school, your Wisdom." Grimes grinned. "Now I'll tell one. Mr. Weeks doesn't like spacemen. A few years ago his wife made a cruise in one of the T-G clippers—and, when the divorce came though, married the chief officer of the liner she traveled in."

The High Priest laughed. "That accounts for it. But I shall enjoy your company for the few weeks that you will have to stay on Tharn. I shall tell my people to bring your baggage from the Embassy to the University."

"That is very good of you." Grimes took another sip of the strong wine. "But I think that since I'm here I shall help in the search for Mr. Missenden. After all, he is still officially one of our nationals."

"As you please, Commodore. Tell me, if you were in charge how would you set about it?"

Grimes lapsed into silence. He looked around the office. All of the walls were covered with books, save one, and on it hung another of those big maps. He said, "He'll have to get out by sea, of course."

"Of course. We have no commercial airship service to Tangaroa, and the Tangaroans have no commerical airship service at all."

"And you have no submarines yet, and your aerial coast guard patrol will keep you informed as to the movements of all surface vessels. So he will have to make his getaway in a merchant vessel. . . . Would you know if there are nay Tangaroan merchantmen in port?"

"I would know. There is one—the *Kawaroa*. She is loading textiles and agricultural machinery."

"Could she be held?"

"On what excuse, Commodore? The Tangaroans are very touchy people, and if the ship is detained their consul will at once send off a radio message to his government."

"A very touchy people, you say . . . and arrogant. And quarrelsome. Now, just suppose that there's a good, old-fashioned tavern brawl, as a result of which the master and his officers are all arrested. . . ."

"It's the sort of thing that could easily happen. It has happened, more than once."

"Just prior to sailing, shall we say? And then, with the ship immobilized, with only rather dim-witted ratings to try to hinder us, we make a thorough search—accommodations, holds, machinery spaces, storerooms, the works."

"The suggestion has its merits."

"The only snag," admitted Grimes, "is that it's very unlikely that the master and all three of his mates will rush ashore for a quick one just before sailing."

"But they always do," said the High Priest.

As they always had done, they did.

Grimes watched proceedings from the innkeeper's cubbyhole, a little compartment just above the main barroom with cunning peepholes in its floor. He would have preferred to have been among the crowd of seamen, fishermen and watersiders, but his rugged face was too well known on Tharn, and no amount of hair and skin dye could have disguised him. He watched the four burly, blue- and brass-clad men breasting the bar, drinking by themselves, tossing down pot after pot of the strong ale. He saw the fat girl whose dyed yellow hair was in vivid contrast to her green skin nuzzle up to the man who was obviously the Tangaroan captain. He wanted none of her—and Grimes sympathized with him. Even from his elevated vantage point he could see that her exposed overblown breasts were sagging, that what little there was of her dress was stained and bedraggled. But the man need not have brushed her away so brutally. She squawked like an indignant parrot as she fell sprawling to the floor with a display of fat, unlovely legs.

One of the other drinkers—a fisherman by the looks of him—came to the aid of beauty in distress. Or perhaps it was only that he was annoyed because the woman, in her fall, had jostled him, spilling his drink. Or, even more likely, he was, like the woman, one of the High Priest's agents. If such was the case, he seemed to be enjoying his work. His huge left hand grasped the captain's shoulder, turning him and holding him, and then right fist and left knee worked in unison. It was dirty, but effective.

After that, as Grimes said later, telling about it, it was on for young and old. The three mates, swinging their heavy metal drinking pots, rallied to the defense of their master. The fisherman picked up a heavy stool to use as his weapon. The woman, who had scrambled to her feet with amazing agility for one of her bulk, sailed into the fray, fell to a crouching posture, straightening abruptly, and one of the Tangaroan officers went sailing over her head as though rocket-propelled, crashing down on to a table at which three watersiders had been enjoying a quiet, peaceful drink. They, roaring their displeasure, fell upon the hapless foreigner with fists and feet.

The police officer with Grimes—his English was not too good—said, "Pity break up good fight. But must arrest very soon."

"You'd better," the Commodore told him. "Some of your people down there are pulling knives."

Yes, knives were out, gleaming wickedly in the lamplight. Knives were out, but the Tangaroans—with the exception of the victim of the lady and her stevedoring friends—had managed to retreat to a corner and there were fighting off all comers, although the captain, propped against the wall, was playing no great part in the proceedings. Like the fisherman, the two officers had picked up stools, were using them as both shields and weapons, deflecting flung pots and bottles with them, smashing them down on the heads and arms of their assailants.

The captain was recovering slowly. His hand went up to fumble inside the front of his coat. It came out, holding something that gleamed evilly—a pistol. But he fired it only once, and harmlessly. The weapon went off as his finger tightened on the trigger quite involuntarily, as the knife thrown by the yellow-haired slattern pinned his wrist to the wall.

And then the place was full of University police, tough men in black tunics who used their clubs quite indiscriminately and herded all those present out into the waiting trucks.

Quietly, Grimes and the police officer left their

observation post and went down the back stairs. Outside the inn they were joined by twelve men—six police and six customs officals, used to searching ships. Their heels ringing on the damp cobblestones, they made their way through the misty night to the riverside, to the quays.

Kawaroa was ready for sea, awaiting only the pilot and, of course, her master and officers. Her derricks were stowed, her moorings had been singled up, and a feather of smoke from her tall, raked funnel showed that steam had been raised. She was not a big ship, but she looked smart, well maintained, seaworthy.

As Grimes and his party approached the vessel they saw that somebody had got there ahead of them, a dark figure who clattered hastily up the gangway. But there was no cause for hurry. The ship, with all her navigating officers either in jail or in the hospital, would not be sailing, and the harbor master had already been told not to send a pilot down to take her out.

There was no cause for hurry. . . .

But what was that jangling of bells, loud and disturbing in the still night? The engine room telegraph? The routine testing of gear one hour before the time set for departure?

And what were those men doing, scurrying along to foc'sle head and poop?

Grimes broke into a run, and as he did so he heard somebody shouting from *Kawaroa's* bridge. The language was unfamiliar, but the voice was not. It was Missenden's. From forward there was a *thunk!* and then a splash as the end of the severed headline fell into the still water. The last of the flood caught the ship's bows and she fell away from the wharf. With the police and customs officers, who had belatedly realized what was happening, well behind him, Grimes reached the edge of the quay. It was all of five feet to the end of the still-dangling gangway and the gap was rapidly widening. Without thinking. Grimes jumped. Had he known that nobody would follow him he would never have done so. But he jumped, and his desperate fingers closed around the outboard man-ropes of the accommodation ladder and somehow, paying a heavy toll of abrasions and lacerations, he was able to squirm upward until he was kneeling on the bottom platform. Dimly he was aware of shouts from the fast receding dock. Again he heard the engine room telegraph bells, and felt the vibration as the screw began to turn. So the after lines had been cut, too, and the ship was under way. And it was—he remembered the charts that he had looked at—a straight run down river with absolutely no need for local knowledge. From above sounded a single, derisory blast from *Kawaroa's* steam whistle.

Grimes was tempted to drop from his perch, to swim back ashore. But he knew too much; he had always been a student of maritime history in all its aspects. He knew that a man going overboard from a ship making way through the water stands a very good chance of being pulled under and then cut to pieces by the screw. In any case, he had said that he would find Missenden, and he had done just that.

Slowly, painfully, he pulled himself erect, then walked up the clattering treads to deck level.

There was nobody on deck to receive him. This was not surprising; Missenden and the crew must have been too engrossed in getting away from the wharf to notice his pierhead jump. So . . . He was standing in an alleyway, open on the port side. Looking out, he saw the harbor lights sliding past, and ahead and to port there was the white-flashing fairway buoy, already dim, but from mist rather than distance. Inboard there was a varnished wooden door set in the white-painted plating of the 'midships house, obviously the entrance to the accommodation. Grimes opened it without difficulty—door handles will be invented and used by any being approximating to human structure. Inside there was a cross alleyway, brightly illuminated by electric light bulbs in well fittings. On the after bulkhead of this there was a steel door, and the mechanical hum and whine that came from behind it told Grimes that it led to the engine room. On the forward bulkhead there was another wooden door.

Grimes went through it. Another alleyway, cabins, and a companionway leading upward. At the top of this there were more cabins, and another companionway. And at the top of this . . . the captain's accommodation, obviously, even though the word on the tally over the door was no more than a meaningless squiggle to Grimes.

One more companionway—this one with a functional handrail instead of a relatively ornate balustrade. At the head of it was a curtained doorway. Grimes pushed through the heavy drape, found himself in what could only be the chart room, looked briefly at the wide chart table upon which was a plan of the harbor, together with a pair of dividers and a set of parallel rulers. The Confederacy, he remembered, had at one time exported quite large consignments of these instruments to Tharn.

On the forward bulkhead of the chart room, and to port, was the doorway leading out to the wheelhouse and bridge. Softly, Grimes stepped through it, out into the near-darkness. The only light was that showing from the compass periscope, the device that enabled the helmsman to steer by the standard magnetic compass, the binnacle of which was sited up yet one more deck, on what had been called on Earth's surface ships the "monkey island." There was the man at the wheel, intent upon his job. And there, at the fore end of the wheelhouse, were two dark figures, looking out through the wide windows. One of them, the taller one, turned suddenly, said something in Tangaroan. As before, the voice was familiar but the language was not.

The question—intonation made that plain—was repeated, and then Missenden said in English, "It's you! How the hell did you get aboard? Hold it, Commodore, hold it!" There was just enough light for Grimes to see the pistol that was pointing at his midriff.

"Turn this ship around," ordered Grimes, "and take her back into port."

"Not a chance." Missenden laughed. "Especially when I've gone to all the trouble to taking her out of port. Pity old Dingwall wasn't here to see it. Not bad, was it, for a bird-brained navigator? And keep your hands up where I can see them.''

"I'm unarmed," said Grimes.

"I've only your word for it," Missenden told him. Then he said something to his companion, who replied in what, in happier circumstances, would have been a very pleasant contralto. The girl produced a mouth whistle, blew a piercing blast. In seconds two burly seamen appeared on the bridge. They grabbed Grimes and held him tightly while she ran practiced hands over his clothing. It was not the first time that she had searched a man for weapons. Then they dragged him below, unlocked a steel door and threw him into the tiny compartment beyond it. The heavily barred port made it obvious that it was the ship's brig.

They locked him in and left him there.

Grimes examined his surroundings by the light of the single dim bulb. Deck, deckhead and bulkheads were all of steel—but had they been of plyboard it would have made no difference: that blasted girl had taken from him the only possession that could possibly have been used as a weapon, his pocketknife. There was a steel-framed bunk, with a thin mattress and one sleazy blanket. There was a stained washbasin, and a single faucet which, when persuaded, emitted a trickle of rusty water. There was a bucket—

plastic, not metal. Still, it could have been worse. He could sleep, perhaps, and he would not die of thirst. Fully clothed, he lay down on the bunk. He realized that he was physically tired; his desperate leap for the gangway had taken something out of him. And the ship was moving gently now, a slight, soporific roll, and the steady hum and vibration of the turbines helped further to induce slumber. There was nothing he could do, absolutely nothing, and to lose valuable sleep by useless worry would have been foolish.

He slept.

It was the girl who awakened him.

She stood there, bending over him, shaking his shoulder. When he stirred she stepped sharply back. She was holding a pistol, a revolver of Terran design if not manufacture, and she looked as though she knew how to use it; and she was one of those women whose beauty is somehow accentuated by juxtaposition to lethal ironmongery. Yes, she was an attractive wench, with her greenish, translucent skin that did not look at all odd, with her fine, strong features, with her sleek, short-cut blue hair, and her slim yet rounded figure that even the rough uniform could not hide. She was an officer of some sort, although what the silver braid on the sleeves of her tunic signified Grimes could not guess. Not that he felt in the mood for guessing games; he was too conscious of his own unshaven scruffiness, of the aches and pains resulting from his athletics of the previous night and from the hardness of the mattress.

She said, in fair enough English, "Your Mr. Missenden would see you."

"He's not *my* Mr. Missenden," replied Grimes testily. Why did everybody ascribe to him the ownership of the late second officer of *Rim Dragon*?

"Come," she said, making an upward jerking motion of the pistol barrel.

"All right," grumbled Grimes. "All right."

He rolled off the narrow bunk, staggered slightly as he made his way to the washbasin. He splashed water over his face, drank some from his cupped hands. There was no towel. He made do with his handkerchief. As he was drying himself he saw that the door was open and that a seaman was standing beyond it. Any thoughts that he had entertained of jumping the girl and seizing her gun—if he could—evaporated.

"Follow that man," she ordered. "I will follow you."

Grimes followed the man, through alleyways and up companionways. They came at last to the bridge. Missenden was there, striding briskly back and forth as though he had been at sea all his life. In the wheelhouse the helmsman was intent on his own task. Grimes noted that the standard compass periscope had been withdrawn and that the man was concentrating upon the binnacle housing the ocean passage compass. So they still used that system. But why shouldn't they? It was a good one. He looked out to the sea, up to the sky. The morning was calm, but the sun was hidden by a thick, anti-cyclonic overcast. The surface of the sea was only slightly ruffled and there was a low, confused swell.

"Missenden," called the girl.

Missenden stopped his pacing, walked slowly to the wheelhouse. With his dyed hair and skin he looked like a Tharnian, a Tangaroan, and in his borrowed uniform he looked like a seaman. He also looked very pleased with himself.

"Ah, Commodore," he said, "welcome aboard. You've met Miss Ellevie, I think. Our radio officer."

"You'd better tell Miss Ellevie to send a message to the High Priest for me, Mr. Missenden."

Missenden laughed harshly. "I'll say this for you, Commodore, you do keep on trying. Why not accept the inevitable? You're in Tangaroan hands; in fact you put yourself in their—our—hands. The Council of Barons has already been informed, and they have told me that they want you alive. If possible."

"Why?" asked Grimes bluntly.

"Use your loaf, Commodore. First, it's possible that we may be able to persuade you to press for the establishment of trade relations between the Confederacy and Tangaroa. You do pile on quite a few G's in this sector of the galaxy, you know. Or should I say that you do draw a lot of water? And if you play, it could be well worth your while."

"And if I don't play?"

"Then we shall be willing to sell you back to your lords and masters. At a fair price of course. A squadron of armed atmosphere fliers? Laser weapons? Missiles with nuclear warheads?"

"That's for *your* lords and masters to decide."

Missenden flushed and the effect, with his green-dyed skin, was an odd one. He said to the girl, "That will do, Ellevie. I'll let you know when I want you again." He walked out to the wing of the bridge, beckoning Grimes to follow. When he turned to face the Commodore he was holding a pistol in his right hand.

He said, "Don't try anything. When I was in the navy of New Saxony I was expert in the use of hand guns of all descriptions. But I'd like a private talk. Ellevie knows English, so I sent her below. The man at the wheel may have a smattering, but he won't overhear from where we are now."

"Well?" asked Grimes coldly.

"We're both Earthmen."

"*I* am, Mr. Missenden."

"And I am, by ancestry. These Tharnians are an inferior breed, but if they see that *you* can be humiliated—"

"—they'll realize that *you* aren't the Galactic Superman you set yourself up to be."

Missenden ignored this, but with an effort. He said, "My position in this ship is rather . . . precarious. The crew doesn't trust me. I'm captain, yes—but only because I'm the only man on board who can navigate."

"But can you?"

"Yes, damn you! I've read the textbooks—it was all the bastards gave me to read when I was holed up down in the secret compartment. And anybody who can navigate a starship can navigate one of these hookers! Anyhow . . . anyhow, Commodore, it will be better for both of us if we maintain the pretense that you are a guest rather than a prisoner. But I must have your parole."

"My parole? What can I do?"

"I've heard stories about you."

"Have you? Very well, then, what about this? I give you my word not to attempt to seize the ship."

"Good. But not good enough. Will you also give your word not to signal, by any means, to aircraft or surface vessels?"

"Yes," agreed Grimes after a short hesitation.

"And your word not to interfere, in any way, with the ship's signaling equipment?"

"Yes."

"Then, Commodore, I feel that we may enjoy quite a pleasant cruise. I can't take you down yet; I relieved the lookout for his breakfast. You'll appreciate that we're rather shorthanded—as well as the Old Man and the three mates half the deck crew was left ashore, and two of the engineers. I can't be up here all the time, but I do have to be here a lot. And the lookouts have orders to call me at once if they sight another ship or an aircraft."

"And, as you say, you're the only navigator." *The only* human *navigator*, Grimes amended mentally.

The lookout came back to the bridge then, and Missenden took Grimes down to what was to be his cabin. It was a spare room, with its own attached toilet facilities, on the same deck as the captain's suite, which, of course, was now occupied by Missenden. It was comfortable, and the shower worked, and there was even a tube of imported depilatory cream for Grimes to use. After he had cleaned up he accompanied Missenden down to the saloon, a rather gloomy place paneled in dark, unpolished timber. Ellevie was already seated at one end of the long table, and halfway along it was an officer who had to be an engineer. Missenden took his seat at the head of the board, motioned to Grimes to sit at the right. A steward brought in cups and a pot of some steaming, aromatic brew, returning with what looked like two deep plates of fish stew.

But it wasn't bad and, in any case, it was all that there was.

After the meal Missenden returned to the bridge. Grimes accompanied him, followed him into the chart room, where he started to potter with the things on the chart table. Grimes looked at the chart—a small-scale oceanic one. He noted that the Great Circle track was penciled on it, that neat crosses marked the plotting of dead reckoning positions at four hourly intervals. He looked from it to the ticking log clock on the forward bulkhead. He asked, "This submerged log of yours—does it run fast or slow?"

"I . . . I don't know, Commodore. But if the sky clears and I get some sights I'll soon find out."

"You think you'll be able to?"

"Yes. I've always been good with languages, and I've picked up enough Tangaroan to be able to find my way through the ephemeris and reduction tables."

"Hmm." Grimes looked at the aneroid barometer—another import. It was still high. With any luck at all the anti-cyclonic gloom would persist for the entire passage. In any case, he doubted if Missenden's first attempt to obtain a fix with sextant and chronometer would be successful.

He asked, "Do you mind if I have a look around the ship? As you know, I'm something of an authority on the history of marine transport."

"I do mind!" snapped Missenden. Then he laughed abruptly. "But what could you do? Even if you hadn't given your parole, what could you do? All the same, I'll send Ellevie with you. And I warn you, that girl is liable to be trigger happy."

"Have you known her long?"

Missenden scowled. "Too long. She's the main reason why I'm here."

Yes, thought Grimes, *the radio officer of a merchant vessel is well qualified for secret service work, and when the radio officer is also an attractive woman* . . . He felt sorry for Missenden, but only briefly. He'd had his fun; now he was paying for it.

Missenden went down with Grimes to the officers' quarters, found Ellevie in her room. She got up from her chair without any great enthusiasm, took a revolver from a drawer in her desk, thrust it into the side pocket of her tunic.

"I'll go now," said Missenden.

"All right," she answered in a flat voice. Then, to Grimes, "What you want to see?"

"I was on this world years ago," he told her.

"I know."

"And I was particularly impressed by the . . . the ocean passage compasses you had, even then, in your ships. Of course, it was all sail in those days."

"Were you?"

Grimes started pouring on the charm. "No other

292

race in the galaxy has invented such ingenious instruments."

"No?" She was beginning to show a flicker of interest. "And did you know, Commodore Grimes, that it was not a wonderful priest who made the first one? No. It was not. It was a Baron Lennardi, one of *my* ancestors. He was—how do you put it? A man who hunts with birds?"

"A falconer."

"A falconer?" she repeated dubiously. "No matter. He had never been to the University, but he had clever artisans in his castle. His brother, whom he loved, was a—how do you say sea raider?"

"A pirate."

She took a key from a hook by the side of her desk. "Second Mate looks after compass," she said. "But Second Mate not here. So *I* do everything."

She led the way out into the alleyway, then to a locked door at the forward end of the officers' accommodation, to a room exactly on the center line of the ship, directly below the wheelhouse. She unlocked and opened the door, hooked it back. From inside came an ammonia-like odor. In the center of the deck was a cage, and in the cage was a bird—a big, ugly creature, dull gray in color, with ruffled plumage. It was obvious that its wings had been brutally amputated rather than merely clipped. Its almost globular body was imprisoned in a metallic harness, and from this cage within a cage a thin yet rigid shaft ran directly upward, through the deckhead and, Grimes knew, through a casing in the master's day cabin and, finally, to the card of the ocean passage compass. As Grimes watched, Ellevie took a bottle of water from a rack, poured some into the little trough that formed part of the harness. Then from a box she took a spoonful of some stinking brown powder, added it to the water. The bird ignored her. It seemed to be looking at something, for something, something beyond the steel bulkhead that was its only horizon, something beyond the real horizon that lay forward and outside of the metal wall. Its scaly feet scrabbled on the deck as it made a minor adjustment of course.

And it—or its forebears—had been the only compasses when Grimes had first come to this planet. Even though the Earthmen had introduced the magnetic compass and the gyro compass, this was still the most efficient for an ocean passage.

Cruelty to animals is penalized only when commerical interests are not involved.

"And your spares?" asked Grimes.

"Homeward spare—right forward," she told him. "Ausiphal compass and one spare—right aft."

"So you don't get them mixed?" he suggested.

She smiled contemptuously. "No danger of that."

"Can I see them?"

"May not? May as well feed them now."

She almost pushed Grimes out of the master compass room, followed him and locked the door. She led the way to the poop, but Grimes noticed that a couple of unpleasant looking seamen tailed after him. Even though the word had been passed that he had given his parole he was not trusted.

The Ausiphal birds were in a cage in the poop house. As was the case with the Tangaroa birds, their wings had been amputated. Both of them were staring dejectedly directly astern. And both of them (even though dull and ruffled their plumage glowed with gold and scarlet) were females.

Grimes followed Ellevie into the cage, the door to which was at the forward end of the structure. He made a pretense of watching interestedly as she doled out the water and the odoriferous powder—and picked up two golden tail feathers from the filthy deck. She straightened and turned abruptly. "What you want those for?"

"Flies," he lied inspiredly, "Dry flies."

"*Flies*?"

"They're artificial lures, actually. Bait. Used for fishing."

"Nets," she stated. "Or explosives."

"Not for sport. We use a rod, and a line on the end of it, and the hook and the bait on the end of that. Fishermen are always experimenting with different baits. . . ."

The suspicion faded from her face. "Yes, I remember. Missenden gave me a book—a magazine? It was all about outdoor sports. But this fishing . . . Crazy!"

"Other people have said it, too. But I'd just like to see what sort of flies I can tie with these feathers when I get home."

"If you get home," she said nastily.

Back in his cabin, Grimes went over mentally what he had learned about the homers, which was as good a translation as any of their native name, during his visit to Tharn. They were land birds, but fared far out to sea in search of their food, which was fish. They *always* found their way back to their nests, even when blown thousands of miles away by severe storms, their powers of endurance being phenomenal. Also, whenever hurt or frightened, they headed unerringly for home—by the shortest possible route, which was a Great Circle course.

Used as master compasses, they kept the arrowhead on the card of the steering compass pointed directly toward wherever it was that they had been born—even when that was a breeding pen in one of the seaport towns. On a Mercator chart the track would be a curve, and according to a magnetic or a gyrocompass the ship would be continually changing course; but on a globe a Great Circle is the shortest distance between two points.

Only one instinct did they possess that was more powerful, more overriding than the homing instinct.

The sex instinct.

Grimes had given his word. Grimes had promised not to do certain things—and those things, he knew, were beyond his present capabilities in any case. But Grimes, as one disgruntled Rim Runners' captain had once remarked, was a stubborn old bastard. And Grimes, as the Admiral commanding the navy of the Rim Worlds Confederacy had once remarked, was a cunning old bastard. Sonya, his wife, had laughed when told of these two descriptions of her husband, and had laughed still louder when he had said plaintively that he didn't like to be called old.

Nonetheless, he was getting past the age for cloak and dagger work, mutiny on the high seas and all the rest of it. But he could still use his brains.

Kawaroa's shorthandedness was a help. If the ship had been normally manned he would have found it hard, if not impossible, to carry out his plan. But, insofar as the officers were concerned, the two engineers were on alternate watches, and off-duty hours would be spent catching up on lost sleep. The left Ellevie—but she had watches to keep, and one of these two hour stretches of duty coincided with and overlapped evening twilight. Missenden was not a watchkeeper, but he was, as he was always saying, the only navigator, and on this evening there seemed to be the possibility of breaks appearing in the overcast. There had been one or two during the day, but never where the sun happened to be. And insofar as evening stars were concerned out here on the Rim, there were very, very few. On a clear evening there would have been three, and three only, suitably placed for obtaining a fix. On this night the odds were against even one of the three appearing in a rift in the clouds before the horizon was gone.

Anyhow, there was Missenden, on the bridge, sextant in hand, the lid of the chronometer box in the chart room open, making an occasional gallop from one wing to the other when it seemed that a star might make a fleeting appearance. Grimes asked if he might help, if he could take the navigator's times for him. Missenden said no, adding that the *wrong* times would be no help at all. Grimes looked hurt, went down to the boat deck, strolled aft. The radio shack was abaft the funnel. He looked in, just to make sure that Ellevie was there. She was, and she was tapping out a message to somebody. Grimes tried to read it—then realized that even if the code was Morse the text would be in Tangaroan.

He went down to the officers' deck. All lights, with the exception of the dim police bulbs in the alleyways, were out. From one of the cabins came the sound of snoring. He found Ellevie's room without any trouble; he had been careful to memorize the squiggle over her door that meant *Radio Officer*. He walked to the desk, put his hand along the side of it. Yes, the key was there. Or *a* key. But it was the only one. He lifted it from its hook, stepped back into the alleyway, made his way forward.

Yes, it was the right key. He opened the door, shut it behind him, then groped for the light switch. The maimed, ugly bird ignored him; it was still straining at its harness, still scrabbling now and again at the deck as it made some infinitesimal adjustment of course. It ignored him—until he pulled one of the female's tail features from his pocket. It squawked loudly then, its head turning on its neck to point at the potent new attraction, its clumsy body straining to follow. But Grimes was quick. His arm, his hand holding the feather shot out, steadied over the brass strip let into the deck that marked the ship's center line. But it had been close, and he had been stupid. The man at the wheel would have noticed if the compass card had suddenly swung a full ninety degrees to starboard—and even Missenden would have noticed if the ship had followed suit. (And would he notice the discrepancies between magnetic compass and ocean passage compass? Did he ever compare compasses? Probably not. According to Captain Dingwall he was the sort of navigator who takes far too much for granted.)

Grimes, before Missenden had ordered him off the bridge, had been able to study the chart. He assumed—he had to assume—that the dead reckoning position was reasonably accurate. In that case, if the ship flew off at a tangent, as it were, from her Great Circle, if she followed a rhumb line, she would miss the north coast of Tangaroa by all of a hundred miles. And if she missed that coast, another day's steaming would bring her into the territorial waters of Braziperu. There was probably some sort of coastal patrol, and even though surface and airships would not be looking for *Kawaroa* her description would have been sent out.

The rack containing water and food containers was on the forward bulkhead of the master compass room. It was secured to the plating with screws, and between wood and metal there was a gap. Grimes pushed the quill of the feather into this crack, being careful to keep it exactly over the brass lubber's line. He remembered that the male homer had paid no attention to the not-so-artificial lure until he pulled it out of his pocket. Had his own body odor masked the smell of it? Was there a smell, or was it some more subtle emanation? He had learned once that the male birds must be kept beyond a certain distance from the females, no matter what intervened in the way of decks or bulkheads. So . . . ? His own masculine aura . . . ? The fact that he had put the feathers in the pocket that he usually kept his pipe in . . . ?

He decided to leave the merest tip of the feather showing, nonetheless. He had noted that Ellevie went through her master compass tending routine with a certain lack of enthusiasm; probably she would think that the tiny touch of gold was just another rust speck on the paintwork.

He waited in the foul-smelling compartment for what seemed like far too long a time. But he had to be sure. He decided, at last, that his scheme was working. Before the planting of the feather the maimed bird had been shifting to starboard, the merest fraction of a degree at a time, continually. Now it was motionless, just straining at its harness.

Grimes put out the light, let himself out, locked up, then returned the key to Ellevie's cabin. He went back up to the bridge, looked into the chart room. It seemed that Missenden had been able to take one star, but that his sums were refusing to come out right.

The voyage wore on. It was not a happy one, especially for Grimes. There was nothing to read, and nobody to talk to except Missenden and

Ellevie—and the former was all too prone to propagandize on behalf of the Galactic Superman, while the latter treated Grimes with contempt. He was pleased to note, however, that they seemed to be getting on each other's nerves. The honeymoon, such as it had been, was almost over.

The voyage wore on. No other ships were sighted, and the heavily clouded weather persisted. Once or twice the sun showed through, and once Missenden was able to obtain a sight, to work out a position line. It was very useful as a check of distance run, being almost at right angles to the course line.

"We shall," announced Missenden proudly, "make our landfall tomorrow forenoon."

"Are you sure?" asked Grimes mildly.

"Of course I'm sure." He prodded with the points of his dividers at the chart. "Look! Within five miles of the D.R."

"Mphm," grunted Grimes.

"Cheer up, Commodore! As long as you play ball with the barons they won't boil you in oil. All you have to do is be reasonable."

"I'm always reasonable," said Grimes. "The trouble is that too many other people aren't."

The other man laughed. "We'll see what the Council of Barons has to say about that. I don't bear you any malice—well, not much—but I hope I'm allowed to watch when they bring you around to their way of thinking."

"I hope you never have the pleasure," snapped Grimes, going below to his cabin.

The trouble was that he was not sure. Tomorrow

might be arrival day at Port Paraparam on Tongaroa. It might be. It might not. If he started taking too much interest in the navigation of the ship—if, for example, he took it upon himself to compare compasses—his captors would at once smell a rat. He recalled twentieth century sea stories he had read, yarns in which people, either goodies or baddies, had thrown ships off course by hiding an extra magnet in the vicinity of the steering compass binnacle. *Those old bastards had it easy,* he thought. *Magnetism is straightforward; it's not like playing around with the tail feathers of a stupid bird.*

He did not sleep well that night, and was up on bridge before breakfast, with Missenden. Through a pair of binoculars he scanned the horizon, but there was nothing there, no distant peaks in silhouette against the pale morning sky.

The two men were up on the bridge again after breakfast. Still there was nothing ahead but sea and sky. Missenden was beginning to look worried—and Grimes's spirits had started to rise. Neither of them went down for the midday meal, and it was significant that the steward did not come up to ask if they wanted anything. There was something in the atmosphere of the ship that was ugly, threatening. The watches—helmsmen and lookouts—were becoming increasingly surly.

"I shall stand on," announced Missenden that evening. "I shall stand on. The coast is well lit, and this ship has a good echometer."

"But no radar," said Grimes.

"And whose fault is that?" flared the other.

"Your blasted pet priests'. *They* say that they won't introduce radar until it can be manufactured locally!"

"There are such things as balance of trade to consider," Grimes told him.

"Balance of trade!" He made it sound like an obscenity. Then: "But I can't understand what went wrong . . . the dead reckoning . . . my observed position . . ."

"The log could be running fast. And what about set? Come to that, did you allow for accumulated chronometer error?"

"Of course. In any case, we've been getting radio time signals."

"Are you sure that you used the right date in the ephemeris?"

"Commodore Grimes, as I told you before, I'm a good linguist. I can read Tangaroan almost as well as I can read English."

"What about index error on that sextant you were using?"

"We stand on," said Missenden stubbornly.

Grimes went down to his cabin. He shut the door and shot the securing bolt. He didn't like the way the crew was looking at the two Earthmen.

Morning came, and still no land.

The next morning came, and the next. The crew was becoming mutinous. To Missenden's troubles—and he was, by now, ragged from lack of sleep—were added a shortage of fresh water, the impending exhaustion of oil fuel. But he stood on stubbornly. He wore two holstered revolvers all the time, and the ship's other firearms were locked in the strong room. And what about the one that Ellevie had been waving around? wondered Grimes.

He stood on—and then, late in the afternoon, the first dark peak was faintly visible against the dark, clouded sky. Missenden rushed into the chart room, came back out. "Mount Rangararo!" he declared.

"Doesn't look like it," said Ellevie, who had come on to the bridge.

"It must be." A great weight seemed to have fallen from his shoulders. "What do you make of it, Commodore?"

"It's land," admitted Grimes.

"Of course it's land! And look! There on the starboard bow! A ship. A cruiser. Come to escort us in."

He snapped orders, and *Kawaroa's* ensign was run up to the gaff, the black mailed fist on the scarlet ground. The warship, passing on their starboard beam, was too far distant for them to see her colors. She turned, reduced speed, steered a converging course.

The dull *boom* of her cannon came a long while after the flash of orange flame from her forward turret. Ahead of *Kawaroa* the exploding shell threw up a great fountain of spray. It was Grimes who ran to the engine room telegraph and rang *Stop*. It was Ellevie who, dropping her binoculars to the deck, cried, "A Braziperuan ship!" Then she pulled her revolver from her pocket and aimed it at Missenden, yelling, "Terry traitor!" Unluckily for her she was standing just in front of Grimes, who felled her with a rabbit punch to the back of the neck. He crouched, scooped up the weapon and straightened. He said, "You'd better get ready to fight your faithful crew away from the bridge, Missenden. We should be able to hold them off until the boarding party arrives." He snapped a shot at the helmsman, who, relinquishing his now useless wheel, was advancing on them threateningly. The man turned tail and ran.

"You're behind this!" raved Missenden. "What did you do? You gave your word . . ."

"I didn't do anything that I promised not to."

"But . . . what went wrong?"

Grimes answered with insufferable smugness. "It was just a case of one bird-brained navigator trusting another."

The tidying up did not take long. Missenden's crew did not put up even a token resistance to be the boarding party sent from the warship. *Kawaroa* was taken into the nearest Braziperuan port, where her crew was interned pending decisions as to its eventual fate. Grimes and Missenden—the latter under close arrest—made the voyage back to University City by air. The Commodore did not enjoy the trip; the big blimp seemed to him to be a fantastically flimsy contraption and, as it was one of the hydrogen-filled craft, smoking was strictly forbidden.

He began to enjoy himself again when he was back in University City, although the task of having to arrange for the deportation of the sullen

Missenden back to New Saxony was a distasteful one. When this had been attended to Grimes was finally able to relax and enjoy the hospitality and company of the High Priest and his acolytes, none of whom subscribed to the fallacy that scholarship goes hand and hand with asceticism. He would always remember the banquet at which he was made an Honorary Admiral of the Ausiphalian Navy.

Meanwhile, his passage had been arranged on the Lornbound *Rim Cayman*, aboard which Missenden would also be traveling on the first leg of *his* long and miserable voyage home. It came as a surprise, therefore, when he received a personal telephone call from the Honorable Clifton Weeks, the Rim Worlds' ambassador to Tharn. "I hope that you're in no hurry to be getting home, Commodore," said the fat man. Grimes could tell from the Ambassador's expression that he hoped the reverse.

"Not exactly," admitted Grimes, enjoying the poorly concealed play of expressions over the other's pudgy features.

"Hrrmph! Well, sir, it seems that our masters want you on Mellise."

"What for, sir?" asked Grimes.

"Don't ask me. I'm not a spaceman. I didn't open the bloody world up to commerce. All that I've been told is that you're to arrange for passage to that planet on the first available ship. You're the expert."

On what? wondered Grimes. He said sweetly, "I'm looking forward to the trip, Mr. Ambassador."

Part Three

COMMODORE JOHN GRIMES was proceeding homeward from Tharn the long way around—by way of Groller, Stree and Mellise, by the route that he, in the old *Faraway Quest,* had opened and charted so many years ago.

On all the worlds he was still remembered. On Tharn the spaceport was named after him. In Breardon, the planetary capital of Groller, a huge statue of him stood in Council Square. Grimes had stared up at the heroic monument with some distaste. Surely his ears didn't stand out that much, and surely his habitual expression was not quite so frog-like. He made allowances for the fact that the Grollens, although humanoid, are a batrachian people, but he still inspected himself for a long time in a full-length mirror on his return to the ship in which he was a passenger.

And then *Rim Kestrel*, in which Grimes had taken passage from Tharn, came to Mellise.

Mellise was a watery world, fully four-fifths of its surface being covered by the warm, mainly shallow seas. The nearest approach to a continent was a long, straggling chain of islands almost coincident with the equator. On one of the larger ones was the spaceport. There was no city, only a village in which the human spaceport personnel and the Rim Confederacy's ambassador and his staff lived. The Mellisans themselves were an amphibious race; like the Earthly cetacea they returned to the sea after having reached quite a high stage of evolution ashore. They could, if they had to, live and work on dry land, but they preferred the water. They dwelt in submarine villages where they were safe from the violent revolving storms that at times ravaged the surface. They tended their underwater farms, raising giant mollusks, great bivalves that yield lustrous pearls, the main item of export. Their imports were the manufactured goods needed by an aquatic culture: nets, cordage, harpoon guns and the like. They could make these for themselves but, with the establishment of regular trade between themselves and the Confederacy, they preferred not to. Why should an essentially water-dwelling being work with fire and metals when pearl farming was so much more comfortable and pleasant?

Grimes rode down to the surface in *Rim Kestrel's* control room. Captain Paulus, the ship's master, was nervous, obviously did not like having his superior there to watch his ship-handling. But he was competent enough, although painfully cautious. Not for him the almost meteoric descent favored by other masters. His Inertial Drive delivered a thrust that nearly countered the planet's gravitational pull. The *Kestrel* drifted surfaceward like a huge balloon with barely negative buoyancy. But Paulus reacted fast enough when a jet stream took hold of the ship, canceling its effect by just the right application of lateral drive; reacted fast again when the vessel was shaken by clear air turbulence, pulling her out of the danger area with no delay. Nonetheless, Grimes was making mental notes. The efficiency of the spaceport's meteorological observatory left much to be desired; Paulus should have been warned by radio of the disturbances through which he had passed. (But he, Grimes, had made his first landing here before there was a spaceport, let alone spaceport facilities. He had brought the *Quest* down through the beginnings of a hurricane.)

The Commodore looked at the vision screen that showed, highly magnified, what lay aft and below. There were the islands, each one raggedly circular, each one ringed by a golden beach that was ringed, in its turn, by white surf. There was the cloudy green of shallow water, the clear blue of the deeper seas. Inland was the predominant purple of the vegetation.

Yes, it was a pleasant world, Mellise. Even here, out on the Rim, it could have been developed to a holiday planet, rivaling if not surpassing Caribbea.

If the Mellisans had been obliged to deal with the
Interstellar Federation rather than with the Rim
Worlds Confederacy, this probably would have
been the case. Grimes, whose first years in space
had been as an officer in the Federation's Survey
Service, knew all too well that the major Terran
galactic power was far more concerned with the
rights of other intelligent races in theory than in
practice—unless there was some political advantage to be gained by posing as liberator, conser-
vator or whatever.

He could see the white spaceport buildings now,
gleaming in the light of the afternoon sun, startlingly distinct against their backdrop of purple
foliage. He could see the pearly gray of the apron,
and on it the black geometrical shadows cast by
cranes and conveyor belts and gantries. He could
even see the tiny, blinking stars that were the three
beacons, the markers of the triangle in the center
of which *Rim Kestrel* was to land. He wished that
Paulus would get on with it. At this rate it would be
after sunset by the time the ship was down.

After sunset it was, and the night had fallen with
the dramatic suddenness to be expected in the low
latitudes of any planet. Overhead the sky was clear
and almost empty, save for the opalescent arc that
was the upper limb of the Galactic Lens, low on
the western horizon. Paulus had ordered all ports
throughout the ship opened, and through them
flowed the warm breeze, the scents of growing and
flowering things that would have been cloyingly
sweet had it not been for the harsh tang of salt
water. There was the distant murmur of surf and,

even more distant, a grumble of thunder.

"Thank you, Captain Paulus," said Grimes formally. "A very nice set-down."

And so it had been. Merchant captains, after all, are not paid to put their ships in hazard.

Port formalities were few. The Mellisans cared little about such matters as health, customs and immigration regulations. The port captain, a Rim Worlder, took care of all such details for them; and insofar as vessels owned by the Confederacy were concerned there was not even the imposition of port dues. After all, the levying of such charges would have been merely robbing Peter to pay Paul. The rare outside ships—the occasional Interstellar Transport Commission *Epsilon* Class tramp, the infrequent Empire of Waverley freighter, the once-in-a-blue-moon Shakespearian Sector trader—were, presumably, another matter. They would at least pay port dues.

Grimes sat with Captain Paulus and Stacey, the port captain, in Paulus' day cabin. Cold drinks were on the table before them. The Commodore was smoking his foul pipe, Paulus was nervously lighting one cigarette after another, and Captain Stacey had between his fleshy lips a peculiarly gnarled cigar of local manufacture. It looked as though it had been rolled from dry seaweed, and smelt like it. ("An acquired taste," Stacey had told them. "Like to try one?" They had refused.)

"Only a small shipment of pearls this time," Stacey said. "The pearl fishers—or farmers—are having their troubles."

"Disease again?" asked Paulus.

"No. Not this time. Seems to be a sort of predatory starfish. Could be a mutation. Whether it is or not, it's a vicious bastard."

"I thought, Captain Stacey," said Grimes, "that the people here were quite capable of dealing with any of the dangerous life forms in their seas."

"Not this new starfish," Stacey told him. "It's a killer." He sipped his drink. "The natives knew that you were coming here almost as soon I did, Commodore. Telepathy? Could be. But, sir, you are almost a local deity. Old Wunnaara—he's the boss in these parts—said to me only this morning, 'Grimes *Wannarbo*'—and a *Wannarbo* is roughly halfway between a high chief and the Almighty— 'will us help. . . .' Really touched by his faith, I was."

"I'm not a marine biologist," said Grimes. "But couldn't you, with your local knowledge, do something, Captain Stacey?"

"I'm not a marine biologist either, Commodore. It takes all my time to run the port."

And I recommended you for this appointment, thought Grimes, looking at the fat man. *I thought that this would be an ideal job for anybody as notoriously lazy as yourself. I thought that you couldn't do any harm here, and that you'd get on well with the Mellisans. But you can't do any good either.*

"They must produce pearls," stated Paulus, "if they're to pay for their imports. They've nothing else we want."

Nothing else that we want . . . thought Grimes.

But the Rim Confederacy is not alone in the galaxy. He said, "Surely, Captain Stacey, you've found out what sort of weapons would be most effective against these things. They could be manufactured back on Lorn or Faraway, and shipped out here. And what about protective netting for the oyster beds?"

"Useless, Commodore," Stacy told him. "The starfish just tear to shreds even the heaviest nets, made from wire rope. As for weapons—poison has always been effective in the past, but not any longer."

"We have to do something to help these people," Grimes said definitely. "And, frankly, not altogether from altrusitic motives. As you should know, both Waverly and the Shakespearian Sector are anxious to expand their spheres of influence. If they can help Mellise and we can't . . ." The unspoken words "you'll be out of a soft job" hung in the air between them.

"They seem to rely upon *you* to help them, sir," Stacey grumbled.

"And perhaps I can," Grimes told him. "Perhaps I can."

Perhaps he could—but, as he had said, he was not a marine biologist. Even so, he knew of the parallel evolution of life forms on all Earth-type planets. And in the course of his career he had tangled with unfriendly and hungry beasts on more than a century of worlds; he was still around and the hostile animals were not. Variations on familiar patterns or utterly alien, all had fallen victim to human cunning and human weaponry—and human savagery. Man, after all, was still the most dangerous animal.

He said good night to Stacey and Paulus, told them that he was going outside the ship to stretch his legs. He made his way down to the after air lock, then down the ramp to the smooth, clean concrete of the apron. He walked away from the direction of the administration buildngs and the human village, found a path that must lead down to the sea. On either side of it the feathery fronds of the trees rustled in the warm breeze. Overhead, Mellise's single moon, a ruddy globe with an almost unmarked surface, rode high in the sky.

Grimes came to the beach, to the pale, gently shelving stretch of coarse sand beyond which the surf was greenly luminescent. He kicked off his sandals and, carrying them, walked slowly down to the edge of the water. He missed Sonya.

He saw that a black, humanoid shape, outlined by the phosphorescence, was waddling ashore, splashing through the shallows. From its dark head two eyes that reflected the light of the moon stared at Grimes. The teeth glinted whitely in the long muzzle as it spoke. "*Meelongee*, Grimes *Wannarbo*." Its voice was like that of a Siamese cat.

"*Meelongee*," replied Grimes. He remembered that this was the word of greeting.

"You have come back." The English was oddly accented but perfectly understandable.

"Yes. I have come back."

"You . . . help?"

"I shall try."

The native was close to Grimes now, and the Commodore could smell the not unpleasant fishy odor of him. He could see, too, that he was old; in the moonlight the white hairs about the muzzle and the white patches of fur on the chest were plainly visible.

"You me remember?" There was a short, barking laugh. "No? I was cub when first you come to Mellise, Grimes *Wannarbo*. Now I am chief. My name—Wunnaara. And you, too, are chief—not of one skyship, but of many. I am chief—but known little. You are chief—but know much."

"The *Rim Kestrel* lifts tomorrow," said Grimes.

"But you will stay, *Wannarbo*? You will stay?"

Grimes made his decision. If there was anything that he could do he would be furthering the interests of the Confederacy as well as helping the natives of Mellise. Stacey, it was obvious, would not lift one fat finger. The ambassador, like the port captain, was a no-hoper who had been sent to a planet upon which no emergencies were ever likely to arise. Grimes had not yet met him, but he knew him by repute.

"I will stay," he told the Chief.

"Then I tell my people. There is much to make ready." Wunnaara slipped back into the water, far more silently than he had emerged from it, and was gone.

The Commodore resumed his walk along the beach.

He came to a shallow bay, a crescent-like indentation in the shoreline. There was somebody out there in the water swimming—and by the flash of long, pale arms Grimes knew that it was not a native. Too, there was a pile of clothing on the sand. Grimes quickly stripped. It was a long time since he had enjoyed a swim in the sea. He divested himself of his clothing without embarrassment. Even though he was no longer a young man his body was still compact, well-muscled, had not begun to run to belly. He waded out into the warm salt water.

Suddenly he was confronted by the other swimmer. Only her head and smooth, bare shoulders were visible above the surface. Her eyes and her wide mouth were very dark against the creamy pallor of her face.

"Can't you read?" she was asking indignantly. "Didn't you see the notices? This beach is reserved for ladies only."

Her accent was not a Rim Worlds' one; it was more Pan-Terran than anything. That would account for her indignation; only on parts of the home planet did the absurd nudity taboo still persist. But this was not the home planet.

Grimes said mildly, "I'm sorry. I didn't know." He turned to leave the water.

She said, "Don't run away. We can talk, at this depth, modestly enough."

"I suppose we can."

"You're from the ship, aren't you? But of course, you must be . . . let me see, now . . . I've a good ear for accents, and you haven't quite lost the good old Terran twang—Commodore Grimes, would it be?"

"Guilty," admitted Grimes. He was amused to note either that the tide was going out fast or that this companion had moved closer inshore. Her full breasts were fully exposed now, and there was more than a hint of the pale glimmer of the rest of her below the surface.

She said, "It's rather a pity that you're leaving tomorrow."

"I'm not leaving."

"You're not?" she asked sharply.

"No. I promised Chief Wunnaara that I'd stay to look into this plague of starfish."

"You promised Wunnaara . . ." Her voice was scornful. "But he's only a native, and has to be kept in his place. That's why I insisted on having this beach made private. I hated to think that those . . . *things* were spying on me, leering at me while I was swimming."

"And what about me, leering and spying?" Grimes asked sarcastically.

"But you're a Terran—"

"Ex-Terran, young lady. Very ex."

"—and we Terrans should stick together," she completed with a dazzling smile.

"I'm a Rim Worlder," Grimes told her severely. "And so must you be, if you're employed at the spaceport, no matter where you were born." He asked abruptly, "And what do you do, by the way?"

"I'm in the met. office," she said.

"Then I shall see you tomorrow," stated Grimes.

"Good!" Her smile flashed on again.

"I shall be calling in to register a strong complaint," the Commodore went on.

He attempted to step past the girl, intending to swim out to the first line of breakers. Somehow she got in his way, and somehow both of them lost their balance and went down, floundering and splashing. Grimes got to his feet first, pulled the young woman to hers. He was suddenly conscious, as she fell against him, of the firmness and the softness of the body against his own. It was all very nice—and all a little too obvious. But he was tempted, and tempted strongly. Then, but with seeming reluctance, she broke away from him and splashed shoreward, her slim, rounded figure luminous in the moonlight.

Her voice floated back to him, "I still hope that it's a pleasant meeting tomorrow, Commodore!"

It was not as unpleasant as it could have been. The girl, Lynn Davis, was second in charge of the spaceport's meteorological office. By daylight, and clothed, she was still attractive. Her hair was a dark, dull-gleaming blonde and her eyes were so deep a blue as to be almost black. Her face was thin and intelligent, with both mouth and nose a little too pronounced for conventional prettiness. There was a resemblance to Sonya, his wife, that strongly attracted Grimes; more than a physical likeness, it was a matter of essential quality. This, at once, put Grimes on his guard. Sonya had held the rank of commander in the Federation's Survey Service, and in the Intelligence branch at that. But now Federation and Rim World Confederacy worked together, shared all information, kept no secrets from each other.

Even so. . . .

Lynn Davis had all the answers ready. *Rim Kestrel* had been given no information on jet streams and clear air turbulence because there had been a breakdown of radar and other instruments. This, Grimes was made to feel, was *his* fault; the Rim Runners' Stores Department should have been more prompt in dealing with requisitions for spare parts. "And after all, Commodore," she told him sweetly, "*you* made the first landing here without any aid at all from the surface, didn't you?"

Grimes asked to see the instrument room. He thought that this request disconcerted her—but this was understandable enough. Any officer, in any service, likes to do things his own way and is apt to resent a superior's intrusion into his own little kingdom, especially when the superior is in a fault-finding mood. But she got up from behind her very tidy desk, led the Commodore out of the office and up a short flight of stairs.

At first glance the compartment looked normal enough; its counterpart could have been found at almost any human-operated spaceport throughout the galaxy. The deviations from the norm were also normal. On many worlds with a lack of recreational facilities the instrument room, with its laboratory and workshop equipment to one side of it, is an ideal place for hobbyists to work. The practice is officially frowned upon, but persists.

There was a tank there, a small aquarium, brilliantly lit. Grimes walked over to it. The only animal denizens were a dozen or so small starfish, brightly colored, spiny little beasts, unusually active. These, unlike their kind on the majority of worlds, seemed to prefer swimming to crawling as a means of locomotion, although they possessed, on the undersides of their limbs, the standard equipment of myriads of suckers.

"And who belongs to these?" asked Grimes.

"Me," she replied.

"Is marine biology your hobby?"

"I'm afraid not, Commodore. I just keep these because they're ornamental. They add something to the decor."

"Yes," he agreed. "Starfish." He walked to a bench where there was an intricacy of gleaming wire. "And what the hell's *this*?"

"A mobile," she told him. "Jeff Petersen, the met. officer, has artistic ambitions."

"And where is Mr. Peterson?"

"He's away. The crowd setting up the weather control station on Mount Llayilla asked Captain Stacey for the loan of him."

"Hmm. Well, I can't help feeling, Miss Davis, that if you and Mr. Peterson devoted more time to your work and less time to your hobbies you'd give incoming ships far better service."

She flared. "We never play around with our hobbies in our employer's time. And there's so little social life here that we must have something to occupy us when we're off duty."

"I'm not denying that, Miss Davis."

She switched on that smile again. "Why don't you call me Lynn, Commodore? Everybody else does."

He found himself smiling in reply. "Why not, Lynn?"

"Isn't that better? And, talking of social life, I'd like it very much if you came to my place some evening for dinner." She grinned rather than smiled this time. "I'm a much better cook than Mrs. Stacey."

That wouldn't be hard, thought Grimes. The Port Captain's wife, as he had learned that morning at breakfast, couldn't even fry an egg properly.

"Try to keep an evening open for me," she said.

"I'll try," he promised. He looked at his watch. "But I must go. I have an appointment with the Ambassador."

The Confederacy's Ambassador was a thin, languid and foppish man. In spite of the disparity in physical appearance he was cut from the same cloth as Captain Stacey. He was one of the barely competent, not quite bad enough to be fired but too lazy and too disinterested to be trusted with any major appointment. He drawled, "I can't order you not to stay, old man, any more than I can order you to stay. Let's face it—you pile on a few more G's (as you spacefaring types put it) than I do. But I still think that you're wasting your time. The natives'll have to pull their socks up, that's all. And tighten their belts for the time being—not that they have any belts to tighten. Ha, ha! You may have been first on this world, Commodore, but you haven't lived with these people as I have. They're a lazy, shiftless bunch. They won't stir a finger to help themselves as long as the Confederacy's handy to do it for them."

"And if the Confederacy won't," said Grimes flatly, "there's the Empire of Waverley. Or the Shakespearians. Or the Federation. Even the Shaara might find this planet interesting."

"Those communistic bumblebees? It might do the Mellisans a world of good if they did take over." He raised a slim, graceful wrist and looked at his watch. "Old Wunnaara's due about now. I don't encourage him—it takes *days* to get the fishy stink out of the Embassy—but he insisted."

"You could," pointed out Grimes. "have a room specially fitted for the reception of local dignitaries, something that duplicates, as far as possible, the conditions that they're used to."

"You don't understand, old man. It's taken me years, literally, to get this shack fitted and decorated the way that it should be. The *battles* I've had to fight with Appropriations! It's all a matter of keeping up a front, old man, showing the flag and all that. . . ."

A smartly uniformed Marine entered the elegant, too elegant *salon*.

"Chief Wunnaara, your Excellency."

"Show him in, Sergeant. Show him in. And attend to the air-conditioning, will you?"

Wunnaara was dressed for the occasion. His ungainly (on dry land) body was clad in a suit of what looked like coarse sacking, and riding high on a complicated harness-like framework was a tank, the contents of which sloshed as he walked. From this tank depended narrow tubes, connected to his clothing at various points. They dripped—both upon the cloth and upon the Ambassador's carpet.

A goggled mask, water-filled, covered his eyes and the upper part of his face. The smell of fish was very evident.

"Your Excellency," he mewed. "*Meelongee, Grimes Wannarbo, meelongee.*"

"Greetings," replied the Ambassador, and, "*Meelongee,*" replied Grimes.

"Your Excellency, Grimes *Wannarbo* has agreed to help. He come with me now, I show him trouble."

"Do you want to go through with this, old man?" the Ambassador asked Grimes. "Really?"

"Of course. Would you know of any scuba outfits on this island? I've already asked Captain Stacey, and he says that the only ones here are privately owned."

"That is correct, Commodore. I could ask the sergeant to lend you his."

"Not necessary, Grimes *Wannarbo,*" interjected the chief. "Already waiting on beach we have ship, what you call submarine."

"Good," said Grimes.

"You'd trust yourself to *that* contraption?" demanded the Ambassador in a horror-stricken voice. "It'll be one of the things that they use to take stores and equipment down to their farms."

"They work, don't they?"

"Yes, old man. But . . ."

"But I'd have thought, on a world like this, that the Ambassador would have his own, private submarine."

"I'm a diplomat, old man, not a sailor."

Grimes shrugged. He said formally. "With your

325

permission, your Excellency, I shall accompany Chief Wunnaara."

"Permission granted, old man. Don't get your feet wet."

The submarine had been pulled up on the beach, onto a ramp that had been constructed there for that purpose, that ran from the water to a low warehouse. Apart from its wheeled undercarriage it was a conventional enough looking craft, torpedo-shaped, with a conning tower amidships and rudder and screw propeller aft, with hydroplanes forward and amidships. A wooden ladder had been placed on the ramp to give access to the conning tower. Wunnaara gestured to Grimes to board first. The Commodore clambered up the ladder with a certain lack of agility; the spacing of the rungs was adapted to the Mellisan, not the human, frame. He had the same trouble with the metal steps leading into the submarine's interior.

When he was down in what was obviously the craft's control room he looked about him curiously. It was easy enough to get a general idea of what did what to which; the Mellisans, with no written language of their own, had adopted Terran English to their requirements. There were depth gauges, steering, hydroplane and engine controls, a magnetic compass. Inside an aluminum rather than a steel hull it should, thought Grimes, function quite satisfactorily. What had him puzzled was a bundle of taut bladders, evidently taken from some sea plant. Beside them, in a rack on the bulkhead, was a sharp knife. And he did not quite

approve of the flowerpot that was hanging to one
side of the steering gear, in which was growing a
vividly blue, fernlike plant. He recalled the conversation that he had had with Lynn Davis on the
subject of hobbies.

Apart from these rather peculiar fittings the little
ship was almost as she had been when built to
Mellisan specifications at the Seacraft Yard on
Thule: the original electric motors, a big bank of
heavy-duty power cells, a capacious cargo hold
(now empty) and no accommodation whatsoever.
He had noticed, on his way down through the
conning tower, that the compartment, with its big
lookout ports, could still be used as an air lock.

Wunnaara joined him, accompanied by another
native dressed as he was. The younger Mellisan
went straight to the wheel, from which all the other
controls were easily accessible. Wunnaara asked
Grimes to return with him to the conning tower.
The upper hatch, he saw, was shut now, but there
was an unrestricted view all around from the big
ports. And although the lower hatch remained
open there was ample room, on the annular platform, to walk around it. Wunnaara yelped some
order down through the opening. Slowly at first,
then faster, the submarine started to move, sliding
astern down the ramp on her wheels. She slipped
into the water with hardly any disturbance, and
when she was afloat at least half or her hull was
above the surface. Electric motors hummed and
she backed away from the beach, her head swinging to starboard as she did so. She came around
well and easily, and when she was broadside on to

the shore, starting to roll uncomfortably in the swell, the coxswain put the engines ahead and the wheel hard over to complete the swing. Then, after surprisingly little fuss and bother, she was headed seaward, pitching easily, her straight wake pearly white on the blue water under the noonday sun.

A red marker buoy indicated the location of the pearl beds. Quietly, without any fuss, the ship submerged, dropping down below the surface as her ballast tanks were filled. Grimes went back to the control room; always keenly interested in ships—the ships of the sea as well as the ships of space—he wanted to see how this submersible was handled. He was alarmed when, as he completed his cautious descent down the ladder, the coxswain snatched that nasty looking knife from the rack on the bulkhead. But the Mellisan ignored him, slashed swiftly and expertly at one of the seaweed bladders. It deflated with a loud hiss. Behind Grimes, Wunnaara hooted with laughter. When he had the Commodore's attention he pointed to the absurd potted plant hanging almost over the compass. Its fronds had turned scarlet, but were already slowly changing back to blue. Grimes chuckled as he realized what was being done. This was air regeneration at its most primitive, but still effective. These submarines, when built, had been fitted with excellent air regeneration plants but, no doubt, the Mellisans preferred their own. The oxygen released from the bladder brought with it a strong smell of wet seaweed which, to them, would be preferable to the odorless gas produced by the original apparatus.

Grimes watched the coxswain until Wunnaara called him back to the conning tower. He was impressed by the Mellisan's competence. He was doing things that in a human operated submarine would have required at least four men. Could it be, he wondered, that a real sea man must, of necessity, be also a first-class seaman? He toyed, half humorously, with the idea of recruiting a force of Mellisan mercenaries, to be hired out to those few nations—on those few worlds where there was still a multiplicity of nations—which still relied upon sea power for the maintenance of their sovereignty.

Back in the conning tower he forgot his not-quite-serious money-making schemes. The submarine—as he already knew from his inspection of the depth gauges—was not running deep, but neither was she far from the sandy bottom. Ahead, astern and on either side were the pearl beds, the orderly rows of the giant bivalves. Among them worked Mellisans—who, like similar beings on other planets, including Earth, were able to stay under water for a very long time on one lungful of air. Some of them, explained Wunnaara, were planting the irritant in the mantle of the shellfish. Others were harvesting the pearls from mollusks that had been treated months previously. These were taken to the underwater depot for cleaning and sorting and, eventually, would be loaded into the submarine for carriage to the spaceport. But, said the Chief, this would be a poor harvest. . . .

From his vantage point he conned the ship, yelping orders down to the coxswain. Finally they were drifting over a long row of opened bivalves. Considerable force had been employed in this opening, the not typical Mellisan care. They could extract the pearl without inflicting permanent injury upon the creature inside the paired shells; in many cases here the upper valve had been completely shattered. In most cases no more than a few shreds of tattered flesh remained. And in all cases what had been a pearl was now only a scattering of opalescent dust.

Now the submarine was approaching the high wire net fence that had been erected to protect the pearl farm. It looked stout enough to stop a ship of this class—but *something* had come through it. *Something* had uprooted metal posts embedded in concrete; *something* had snapped wire rope like so much sewing thread. It was not something that Grimes was at all keen to meet, not even in the comparative safety of this well-designed and -built submersible.

"You see?" mewed the Chief. "You see, Grimes *Wannarbo*?"

"Yes. I see."

"Then what do, Grimes *Wannarbo*? What do?" Under stress, the old Mellisan's English tended to deteriorate.

"I . . . I don't know. I shall have to see some of the starfish. Have you any in captivity, or any dead ones?"

"No. No can catch. No can kill."

There was a steady thumping sound, transmitted through the water, amplified by the hull plating.

"Alarm!" Wunnaara cried. "Alarm! Alarm! He shouted something in his own language to the coxswain. The submarine changed course, her motors screaming shrilly as speed was increased to full—or a little over. She skimmed over the flat sandy bottom, raising a great cloud of disturbed particles astern of her.

Ahead there was a commotion of some kind—a flurry of dark, almost human figures, an occasional explosion of silvery air bubbles, a flashing of metallic-seeming tentacles, a spreading stain in the water that looked like a frightened horse as she came full astern—and then she hung there, almost motionless, on the outskirts.

There were half a dozen of the . . . *things*, the starfish, and a dozen Mellisans. Through the now murky water could be seen the wreckage of practically an entire row of the bivalves—shattered shells, crushed pearls, torn, darkly oozing flesh. The odd thing about it all was the gentleness of the marauders. They seemed to be trying to escape— and they were succeeding—but at the same time were avoiding the infliction of serious injury upon the guardians of the beds.

And they were such flimsy things. Or they looked flimsy, as though they had been woven from fragile metallic lace. They looked flimsy, but they were not. One of them was trapped in a net of heavy wire handled by three Mellisans. Momentarily it was bunched up, and then it . . . expanded, and the wires snapped in a dozen places. One of them received a direct hit from a harpoon—and the weapon, its point blunted and broken, fell harmlessly to the bottom.

They were free and clear now, all of them, looking more like gigantic silvery snowflakes than living beings. They were free and clear, swimming toward the breached barrier, their quintuple, feathery arms flailing the water. They were free and clear, and although the Mellisans gave chase there was nothing that anybody could do about them.

"You see?" said the Chief.

"I see," said Grimes.

He saw, too, what he would have to do. He would make his own report, of course, to Rim Runners' head office, recommending that something be done on a government level to maintain the flow of commerce between Mellise and the Confederacy. And he would have to try to persuade that pitiful nong of an ambassador to recommend to *his* bosses that a team qualified to handle the problem—say marine biologists and professional fishermen from Thule—be sent at once to Mellise. But it would not be at once, of course. Nobody knew better than Grimes how slowly the tide runs through official channels.

But. . . .

What could he, Grimes do? Personally, with his own two hands, with his own brain?

There had been something oddly familiar about the appearance of those giant Astersidea, about their actions. There had been something that evoked memories of the distant past, and something much more recent. What was it? Lynn Davis' gaudy pets in the brightly lit aquarium? They swam, of course, and these giant mutants (if mutants they were) were swimmers, but there the similarity ceased.

"What do, Grimes *Wannarbo*?" Wunnaara was insistent. "What do?"

"I . . . I don't know," replied the Commodore. "But I'll do something," he promised.

But what?

That night, back in his room in the port captain's residence, he did his homework. He had managed to persuade Captain Stacey to let him have the files on all Rim Runners' personnel employed on Mellise, and also had borrowed from the Ambassador's library all six volumes of Trantor's very comprehensive *Mellisan Marine Life*. (Trantor should have been here now, but Trantor was dead, drowned two years ago in a quite stupid and unnecessary accident in the Ultimate Sea, on Ultimo, a body of water little larger than a lake.) Grimes skimmed through Trantor's work first, paying particular attention to the excellent illustrations. Nothing, nothing at all, resembled the creatures that he had seen, although most of the smaller starfish, like the ones he had seen in Lynn Davis' tank, subsisted by making forcible entry into the homes of unfortunate bivalves.

Then he turned to the files.

About half the spaceport employees were true Rim Worlders—born out on the Rim. The other half—like Grimes himself—were not, although all of them were naturalized citizens. Judging from the educational qualifications and service records of all of them, none of them would be capable of inducing a mutation. Grimes had hoped to turn up a biological engineer, but he was disappointed. And biological engineering is not the sort of thing that anybody takes up as a hobby; in addition to the years of study and training there is the quite expensive license to practice to obtain, and the qualifications for that are moral rather than academic or practical. Mary Shelley's Frankenstein is a permanent fixture in Man's mythology.

Feeling like a Peeping Tom, another permanent fixture, he leafed through Lynn Davis' service record. She was Terran-born, of course. Her real education had been at M.I.T., where she had graduated as a Bachelor of General Physics. After that she seemed to have specialized in meteorology. There had been a spell with Weather Control, North American Continent, and another spell with Weather Prediction, satellite-based. After that she had entered the service of Trans-Galactic Clippers as Spaceport Meteorological Officer. She had seen duty on Austral, Waverly, and Caribbea, all of them planets upon which T-G maintained its own spaceports. From Waverly she had gone to Caribbea—and on Caribbea she had blotted her copybook.

So, thought Grimes, *she's a compulsive gambler. She doesn't look like one. But they never do.* It was on Caribbea that she had become a regular habitueé of the New Port of Spain Casino. She had, of course, worked out a system to beat the wheel—but the system hadn't worked out for her. There had been the unhappy business of the cracking of the T-G cashier's safe, allegedly thiefproof, but (luckily) very few thieves held a degree in Physics. There had been the new banknotes, the serial numbers of which were on record, that had turned up in the safe of the casino's cashier.

After that—the Rim Worlds.

A pity, said Grimes to himself. *A pity. But it could have been worse. If she'd gone to Elsinore, in the Shakespearian Sector, where they're notorious for their gambling, she'd really be in a mess by now.*

He turned up the file on Peterson. The absentee meteorologist was another ex-Terran, and also had been employed with Trans-Galactic Clippers. Grimes noted with interest that Petersen had spent a few weeks on El Dorado, popularly known as "the planet of the filthy rich." (Grimes had been there himself as a young man, as a junior officer in the Federation's Survey Service.) It seemed that a T-G ship had called there on a millionaires' cruise, and T-G had insisted on sending its own spaceport personnel there in advance.

Women, not money, had been Petersen's trouble. Twice he had been named as correspondent in an unsavory divorce case. If the ladies had not been the wives of prominent T-G executives it wouldn't have mattered so much—but they had been.

There could be a connection, thought Grimes. *There could be. Both of them from Earth, both of them T-G. . . .*He shrugged away the idea. After all, it had been said that if you threw a brick at random aboard any Rim Runners' ship, the odds are that you will hit an ex-officer of the Interstellar Transport Federation's vessels.

So it went on—case histories, one after the other, that made depressing reading and, insofar as the quite serious crisis on Mellise was concerned, a shortage of both motive and opportunity. But money could be a motive. Suppose, tomorrow, a foreign ship dropped in, and suppose that somebody aboard her said to old Wunnaara, "*We'll* fix your starfish for you—in return for full trading rights. . . ."

And whatever else I am, thought Grimes tiredly, *I'm not a starfish fixer*.

He poured himself a stiff drink and went to bed.

She said, "I hear that you've been looking through the personnel files, John. That wasn't very gentlemanly of you."

"How did you hear?" asked Grimes. "My doing so was supposed to be as secret as the files themselves."

"There aren't any secrets on this bloody planet, in this tiny community." Her face, as she stared at him over her candlelit dining table, was hard and hostile, canceling out the effects of an excellent meal. "And did you find what you were looking for?"

"No."

"What were you looking for?"

"Somebody who's capable of doing a spot of biological engineering."

"Did you find anybody?"

"No, Lynn."

"What about the spaceport quack?"

"Frankly," said Grimes, "I wouldn't go to him with a slight head cold."

"Frankly, my dear, neither would I." She laughed, and her manner softened. "So you're still no closer to solving the Mystery of the Mutated Starfish."

"No."

"Then I'll solve it for you. There was a bad solar flare about a year ago, and our atmospheric radiation count went up no end in consequence. There's the answer. But I'm glad that you stayed on Mellise, John. You've no idea how hungry a girl gets for intelligent company."

"I'm glad that I stayed, Lynn. For personal reasons. But I really wish that I could help old Wunnaara. . . ."

She said, "I don't like His Too Precious Excellency any more than you do, John, but I often feel that he's on the right tack as far as the natives are concerned. Let them help themselves."

He said, "I discovered this world. I feel, somehow, that it's my direct responsibility."

She replied a little bitterly, "I wish that you'd start shedding some of your feelings of responsibility, *Commodore*. Don't worry so much. Start having a good time, while you can."

And I could, too, he thought. *With a quite beautiful, available woman. But. . . .*

She said, "It's a wild night. Hurricane Lynn—I named it after me. You aren't walking back to old Stacey's place in this, surely?"

He said, "It's time I was going."

"You'll be drenched," she told him.

"All right. Then go. You can let yourself out."

For a tall girl she flounced well on her way from the little dining room to her bedroom.

Grimes sighed, cursing his retentive memory, his detailed recollection of the reports from all the planets with which Rim Runners traded. But he had to be sure, and he did not wish to make any inquiries regarding this matter on Mellise. He let himself out of the little dome-shaped cottage, was at once furiously assailed by the wind. Hurricane Lynn had not yet built up to its full intensity, but it was bad enough. There were great sheets of driving rain, and with them an explosion of spray whipped from the surface of the sea.

Luckily the spaceport was downwind from the village. Grimes ran most of the way. He didn't want to, but it was easier to scud before the gale than to attempt to maintain a sedate pace. He let himself into the port captain's large house. The Staceys were abed—he had told them that he would be late—but Captain Stacey called out from his bedroom, "Is that you, Commodore?"

"Who else, Captain? I shall be going out again shortly."

"What the hell for?" testily.

"I have to send a message. An important one."

"Telephone it through to the Carlotti Communications Office from here."

"I want to make sure it goes."

Grimes faintly overheard something about distrustful old bastards as he went to his own room, but ignored it.

There was a very cunning secret compartment built into his suitcase. The Commodore opened it, took from it a slim book. Then, with scratch pad and stylus, he worked rapidly and efficiently, finishing up with eleven gibberish groups. He put the book back in its hiding place, pocketed the pad. Then he had to face the stormy night again.

The duty operator in the Carlotti Office was awake, but only just. Had it not been for the growing uproar of the hurricane, penetrating even the insulated walls, he would not have been. He reluctantly put down his luridly covered book and, recognizing Grimes, said, "Sir?"

"I want this to go at once. To my office at Port Forlorn. Urgent." He managed a grin. "That's the worst of space travel. It's so hard to keep track of dates. But my secretary will be able to lay on flowers for the occasion."

The operator grinned back. Judging by the way that he was making a play for that snooty Lynn Davis the Commodore must be a gay old dog, he figured. He said, a little enviously, "Your message will be winging its way over the light-years in a jiffy, sir." He handed the Commodore a signals pad.

Grimes put down the address, transcribed the groups from his own pad, filled in his name and the other details in the space provided. He said, "Let me know how much it is. It's private."

The young man winked. "Rim Runners'll never know, sir."

"Still, I prefer to pay," said Grimes."

He watched the miniature Carlotti Beacon—it

was like a Mobius Strip distorted to a long oval—turn on its mounting in the big star tank until it was pointing directly at the spark that represented the Lorn sun. He hoped that the big beacon on the roof of the building was turning, too. But it had to be. If it stopped, jammed, the little indicator would seize up in sympathy. In any case, it was shielded from the weather by its own dome.

The operator's key rattled rapidly in staccato Morse, still the best method of transmitting messages over vast distances. From the wall speaker blurted the dots and dashes of acknowledgment. Then the message itself was sent, and acknowledged.

"Thank you," said Grimes. "If there's a reply phone it through to me, please. I shall be at Captain Stacey's house."

"Very good, sir."

Grimes was relaxing under a hot shower when he heard the telephone buzz. Wrapping a towel around himself, he hurried out of the bathroom, colliding with Captain Stacey.

"It's probably for me," he said.

"It would be," growled Stacey.

It was. It was in reply to Grimes's signal which, when decoded, had read, *Urgently require information on solar flares Mellise sun last year local.* It said, after Grimes had used his little book, *No repeat no solar flares Mellise sun past ten years.*

Somebody's lying, thought Grimes, *and I don't think it's my secretary.*

Hurricane Lynn, while it lasted, put a stop to

any further investigations by Grimes. Apart from anything else, the sea people were keeping to their underwater houses, each of which was well stocked with air bladders and the carbon dioxide absorbing plants. He managed, however, to get back on friendly terms with Lynn Davis—or she with him; he was never quite sure which was the case. He found her increasingly attractive; she possessed a maturity that was lacking in all the other young women in the tiny human community. He liked her, but he suspected her—but of what? It was rather more than a hunch: there had been, for example, that deliberate lie about the solar flares. Grimes, who was an omnivorous reader, was well aware that fictional detectives frequently solved their cases by sleeping with the suspects. He wasn't quite ready to go that far; he had always considered such a *modus operandi* distinctly ungentlemanly.

Then Hurricane Lynn blew itself out and normally fine weather returned to the equatorial belt. Flying was once again possible, and Petersen came back to the spaceport from Mount Llayilla. Grimes didn't like him. He was a tall, athletic young man, deeply tanned, with sun-bleached hair and startlingly pale blue eyes. His features were too regular, and his mouth too sensual. The filed stories of his past amatory indiscretions made sense. And he was jealously possessive insofar as Lynn Davis was concerned. *She's nice, Commodore,* was the unspoken message that Grimes received, loud and clear. *She's mind. Keep your dirty paws off her.*

341

Grimes didn't like it, and neither did the girl. But the Commodore, now that the storm was over, was busy again. At least once daily he argued with the Ambassador, trying to persuade that gentleman to request the services of a team of marine biologists and professional fishermen. He composed and sent his own report to Rim Runners' head office. And, whenever conditions were suitable, he was out to the pearl beds with Wunnaara, at first in the little submarine and then in a skin diving outfit that the spaceport's repair staff had improvised for him. It was a bastard sort of rig, to quote the chief mechanic, but it worked. There was a spacesuit helmet with compressed air tanks, suitably modified. There was a pair of flippers cut from a sheet of thick, tough plastic. There was a spear gun and a supply of especially made harpoons, each of which had an explosive warhead, fused for impact. As long as these were not used at close range the person firing them should be reasonably safe.

Lynn Davis came into the maintenance workshop while Grimes was examining one of the projectiles.

"What's that, John?" she asked.

"Just a new kind of spear," he replied shortly.

"New—an' nasty," volunteered the chief mechanic, ignoring Grimes's glare. "Pack too much of a wallop for my taste. If you're too close to the target when one o' these goes off, you've had it."

"Explosive?" she asked.

"That's right."

She turned back to Grimes. "Are these safe, John?"

"Safe enough, as long as they're used carefully."

"But against starfish! Like using an elephant gun against a gnat!"

"There are starfish and starfish," he told her. "As everybody on this planet should know by this time."

"You think this will kill them?"

"It's worth giving it a go."

"Yes," she admitted. "I suppose so. . . ." Then, more briskly, "And when are you giving your secret weapon a trial?"

"There are a few modifications to be made," Grimes told her.

"They'll all be ready for you tomorrow morning," said the mechanic. "As promised."

She turned on her dazzling smile. "Then you'd better dine with me tonight, John. If you insist on playing with these dangerous toys there mightn't be another time." She laughed, but that odd, underlying note of seriousness persisted. She went on. "And Jeff will be out of our hair, I promise you that. There's a party on in the Carlotti Operations' Mess, and he *never* misses those."

"I've a pile of paper work, Lynn," Grimes told her.

"That can wait."

He made his decision. "All right, then. What time?"

"Whatever time suits you; 1800 hours, shall we say? For a few drinks first . . . ?"

"Good. I'll be there."

He dressed carefully for the dinner party, paying even more attention to the contents of his pockets than to the clothes themselves. He had one of his hunches, and he knew he'd need the things that he was taking from the secret compartment of his suitcase. There was the Minetti automatic, with a spare clip, neither of which made more than a slight bulge in the inside breast pocket of his jacket. There was the pack of cigarillos. (Two of the slim, brown cylinders possessed very special properties, and were marked in such a way that only Grimes would be able to identify them.) *Marriage to an Intelligence officer,* he thought, *has its points. Something is bound to rub off.* There was the button on his suit that was a camera, and the other button that was a miniaturized recorder.

On the way from his room to the front door he passed through the lounge where Captain and Mrs. Stacey were watching a rather witless variety program on the screen of their playmaster. The Captain looked up and around, his fat, heavy face serious. He said, "I know that it's none of my business, Commodore, and that you're technically my superior, but we—Lucy and myself—think that you should be warned. Miss Davis is a dangerous woman. . . ."

"Indeed, Captain?"

"Yes, indeed. She leads men on, and then that Jeff Petersen is apt to turn nasty."

"Oh?"

An ugly flush suffused Stacey's face. "Frankly, sir, I don't give a damn if you are beaten up for playing around with a girl young enough to be your granddaughter. But because you're Astronautical Superintendent of Rim Runners there'd be a scandal, a very nasty scandal. And I don't want one in *my* spaceport."

"Very concisely put, Captain. But I can look after myself."

"I hope that you can, Commodore. Good night to you."

"Good night, Captain Stacey."

Grimes let himself out. The pieces of the jigsaw puzzle were beginning to fall into place; his suspicions were about to be confirmed. He smiled grimly as he walked along the narrow street toward the row of neat little bungalows where Lynn Davis lived. Night was falling fast, and already lights were coming on in the houses. From open windows drifted the sound of music. The scene was being set for a romantic—romantic?—assignation.

Lynn Davis met him at her door. She was dressed in something loose and, Grimes noted as she stood with the lamp behind her, almost transparent. She took his hand, led him into her living room, gently pushed him down into a deep chair. Close by it was a tray of drinks, and a dish upon which exotic delicacies were displayed. Real Terran olives—and a score of those would make a nasty hole in the weekly pay of an assistant met. officer. Sea dragon caviar from Atlantia . . . pickled rock frogs from Dunartil . . .

The playmaster was on, its volume turned well down. A woman was singing. It was an old song, dating back to the twentieth century, its lyrics modernized, its melody still sweet with lost archaic lilt.

> *Spaceman, the stars are calling,*
> *Spaceman, you have to roam . . .*
> *Spaceman, through light-years falling,*
> *Turn back at last to home. . . .*

"Sherry, John?" asked Lynn Davis. She was sitting on the arm of his chair. He could see the gleam of her smooth flesh through her sheer robe. "Amontillado?"

He said. "You're doing me proud."

"It's not often I entertain such an important guest as you."

He sipped the wine from the fragile glass she had filled for him. She had measured her own drink from the same decanter. He did not think that there was anything wrong with it—any connoisseur would have told him, indignantly that there was *nothing* wrong with it—but at the first hint of muzziness he would smoke a cigarillo. . . .

She was leaning closer to him, almost against him. Her robe was falling open in front. She was wearing nothing underneath it. She said, "Aren't you hot? Why not take your jacket off?"

"Later, perhaps." He managed a quite creditable leer. "after all, we've all night."

"Why waste time?" Her mouth was slightly parted in frank invitation. *What the hell?* thought Grimes, and accepted. Her body was pliant in his arms, her lips on his warm and moist. But his mind, his cold, calculating mind, was still in full command of the situation. He heard the door open softly, heard feet sliding over the thick carpet. He pushed the girl away from him, from the corner of his eye saw her fall to the floor, a delectable sprawl of exposed, gleaming body and limbs.

"So," snarled Jeff Petersen. "So this is what you get up to, Mr. Commodore Dirty Old Man Grimes! What did you promise her, you swine? Promotion and a transfer to a better station?"

Petersen, Grimes noted, was not a slave to this instincts any more than he, Grimes, had been. Superficially his voice was that of the wronged, jealous lover, but there was an artificial quality in his rage.

Grimes said equably, "I can explain. . . ."

"Yes." Petersen was advancing slowly. "You can explain after I've torn off your right arm and beaten your brains out with it."

Suddenly the tiny pistol was in Grimes's right hand. It cracked once, and once only, a sound disproportionate to its dimensions. Petersen halted, staggered, staring stupidly. He swayed on his feet for long seconds and then crashed to the floor, overturning the low table, spilling wine over the sprawling body of the girl. She exploded up from the carpet like a tigress, all teeth and claws. Grimes was hampered by the chair in which he was confined but fought her off somehow. He did not want to use the gun again.

"You bastard!" She was sobbing. "You ruthless bastard! You killed him. And we were careful not to kill—not even the natives!"

"I didn't kill him," Grimes managed to say at

last, after he had imprisoned her hands behind her back, after he had clasped her legs between his own. "I didn't kill him. This pistol is loaded with anesthetic needles. He'll be out for twelve hours—no more, no less."

"He's not . . . dead?"

"Do dead men snore?" asked Grimes practically.

"I . . . I suppose not." Her manner changed abruptly. "Well, he asked for it, John, and this time he got it. Poor Jeff." There was little sympathy in her voice. "So . . ."

"So what?"

"So we might as well be hung for sheep as lambs. We might as well have the game as well as the name."

He said admiringly, "You're a cold-blooded bitch, aren't you?"

"Just realistic." She bent her head forward, but it was not to bite. After the kiss Grimes released her. She pulled slowly away from him, walked undulatingly to the door of the bedroom, shedding the torn remnants of her robe as she went.

Grimes sighed, then got up and followed.

She said, "That was good. . . ."

"It was."

"Stay there, darling, and I'll make us some coffee. We don't want to waste time sleeping."

A sleep, thought Grimes, *is just what I would like. The sleep of the just—the just after.*

He sprawled at ease on the wide couch, watched her appreciatively as she left him, as she walked gracefully to the door. In the subdued light she was all rosy bronze. In any sort of light she was, as he knew, beautiful. He heard a slight clattering from the kitchenette, imposed upon the still stertorous snores of the hapless Jeff. After a while she came back with a tray on which were a pot and two cups. She poured. "Sugar, darling? Cream?" The steam from the coffee was deliciously fragrant. He reached out for his cup, accidentally? put his fingers on the handle of hers. She gently pushed his hand away. "Mine hasn't sugar," she told him.

"You're sweet enough as you are," he said, asking himself, *How corny can you get?*

So he took three sips of the coffee that was intended for him, and at once felt the onset of heavy drowsiness, even though there was no warning flavor. He mumbled, "Like a smoke. . . . Would you mind, Lynn? In my pocket . . . on chair . . ."

She reached out to his clothing, produced the packet of cigarillos and his lighter. She, he already knew, did not smoke herself, which was just as well. She handed him the packet. In his condition, in the dim lighting, he could hardly make out the distinguishing mark. He hoped that he had the right one. Here and now, the special effects of the other one would be more spectacular than useful.

She lit the cigarillo for him, smiling condescendingly down at him. He inhaled the smoke, retained it for long seconds before blowing it out. He took one more sip of coffee, than let a dribble of the hot fluid fall on to his naked chest. He was careful not to wince. He mumbled indistinctly, then fell back against the pillows. His right hand, with the little smoldering cylinder between his fingers, fell limply onto his belly. He could smell the acridity of burning body hair, felt the sharp beginnings of pain. With a great effort of will he remained in his relaxed posture.

He heard her mutter, "I should let the old bastard burn, but . . ." Her cool, slim fingers removed the miniature cigar from his hand. He felt very grateful to her.

He heard her dressing, heard her walk rapidly from the bedroom. He heard, eventually, the front door open and shut. He gave her time to get clear of the house.

When he got down from the bed he expected to feel sick and dizzy, with drug and antidote still at war within his system. But he did not, although he was conscious of the minor burns. He dressed rapidly, checked his possessions. He was pleased to find that the Minetti was still in his pocket; probably whatever it was in the coffee was supposed to put him under for a longer period than the anesthetic needle-bullet that he had used on Jeff Petersen.

The street outside the house was deserted. Everybody was indoors, and everybody seemed to be having a party. He grinned. He had had one too. He walked briskly away from the spaceport, in the direction of the beach where he had first met Lynn Davis. The signs that had been affixed to the trunks of trees were a help. By what moonlight there was he could read, PRIVATE. LADIES ONLY. And how would she have managed, he wondered, if the other human ladies on Mellise had shared her views on outdoor nudity?

The beach was deserted. Backing the narrow strip of sand were the trees, and between their boles was undergrowth, affording effective cover. Grimes settled down to wait. He slipped the magazine from his automatic, exchanged it for the other one; the needle-bullets in this one were no more lethal than the first had been, but they differed from them in one or two respects. He took the remaining marked cigarillo from its packet, put it carefully into his breast pocket. This one had a friction fuse.

At last she came, walking barefooted over the sand, her shoes in her left hand, a heavy case in the other. She dropped the shoes, put the case down carefully. She opened it, then pulled out a silvery telescopic antenna to its full extent. She squatted down, making even this normally ungainly posture graceful, appeared to be adjusting controls of some sort. There was a high, barely audible whine.

Something was coming in from the sea. It was not a native. It came scuttling ashore like a huge crab—like a huge, five-legged crab. Then there was another, and another, and another, until two dozen of the beasts stood there waiting. For orders—or programming?

Grimes walked slowly and deliberately out from the shadows, his Minetti in his right hand. He said quietly, "I'm sorry, Lynn, but the game's up."

She whirled grotesquely like a Russian dancer.

"You!" she snarled, making it seem like a curse.

"Yes. Me. If you come quietly and make a full

confession I'll see to it that things go easy for you."

"Like hell I will!"

She turned swiftly back to the transmitter, kicking up a flurry of sand. The whining note abruptly changed to an irregular beat. And then the starfish were coming for him, slowly at first, but faster and faster. He swatted out instinctively at the leading one, felt the skin of his hand tear on metal spines. In his other hand was the gun. He fired—almost a full burst. The minute projectiles tore though the transmitter. Some of them, a few of them, were bound to sever connections, to shatter transistors. They did. There was a sputtering shower of blue sparks. The metal monsters froze into immobility.

But Lynn did not. She had her own gun out, a heavier weapon than Grimes's own. He felt the wind of her first bullet. And then, with one of the few remaining rounds in his magazine, he shot her.

He stood there, looking down at her. She was paralyzed, but her eyes could still move, and her lips, and her tongue. She was paralyzed—and when the drug took hold properly she would feel the compulsion to talk.

She asked bitterly, "How long will this last?"

"Days, unless I let you have the antidote."

She demanded, "How did you *know?*"

"I didn't *know*. I guessed, and I added two and two to make a quite convincing and logical four. Suppose I tell you—then you can fill in the details."

"That'll be the sunny Friday!"

"Will it?" Grimes squatted down beside her. "You had things easy here, didn't you? You and Jeff Petersen. Such a prize bunch of nongs and no-hopers, from the Ambassador and the port captain on down. I shouldn't have said that; I forgot that this is being recorded.

"Well, one thing that started to make me suspicious of you, especially, was that lie you told me about the solar flares. I checked up; there are very complete records of all phenomena in this sector of space in my office at Port Forlorn. Then there was the shortage of spares for your equipment—I remembered that the requisitions for electronic bits and pieces have been abnormally heavy ever since you and Mr. Petersen were appointed here. There was that ornamental tank of little starfish—and that so-called mobile almost alongside it. Petersen's hobby. The construction that, I realized later, looked very much like the tin starfish I saw raiding the pearl beds. There was the behavior of these same tin starfish: the way in which they attacked the bivalves with absolute viciousness but seemed very careful not to hurt the Mellisans.

"That tied in with the few weeks that Petersen spent on El Dorado.

"They have watchbirds there, Lynn, and similar semi-robots that function either on the ground or in the water. Animal brains in metal bodies. Absolute faithfulness and obedience to their human masters. As a skilled technician, Petersen would have been able to mingle, to a cerain extent, with the gifted amateurs who play around with that sort on El Dorado. He must have picked up some of their techniques, and passed them on to you. You two modified them, probably improved upon them. A starfish hasn't any brain to speak of, so probably you have the entire animal incorporated into your destructive servants. Probably, too, there's an electronic brain built in somewhere, that gets its orders by radio and that can be programmed.

"You were going to recall the local . . . flock, pack, school? What does it matter? . . . tonight, weren't you? For reprogramming. Some preset course of action that would enable them to deal with the threat of spears with explosive warheads. It wouldn't do to have tin tentacles littering the ocean floor, would it? When the Mellisans brought in the evidence even the Ambassador would have to do something about it.

"And, tonight being the night, I had to be got out of the way. Plan A failed, so you switched to Plan B. Correct?"

"Correct," she muttered.

"And for whom were you working?" he asked sharply and suddenly.

"T-G." The answer had slipped out before she could stop it.

"Trans-Galactic Clippers. . . . Why do T-G want Mellise?"

"A tourist resort." She was speaking rapidly now, in obvious catharsis. "We were to destroy the economy, the trade with the Confederacy. And then T-G would step in, and pay handsomely for rights and leases."

"And you and Mr. Petersen would be suitably rewarded. . . ." He paused. "Tell me, Lynn . . . did you enjoy tonight? Between the disposal of Jeff and the disposal of myself, I mean."

"Yes," she told him.

"I'm glad you said that. It makes what I'm going to do a lot easier. I was going to do it in any case; I always like to pay my bills." As he spoke, he pulled the cigarillo from his breast pocket, scratched the friction fuse with his thumbnail. The thing ignited at once, fizzed, ejected a bright blue pyrotechnic star. "I'm letting you go free," Grimes went on, "both of you. You will have to resign, of course, from the Rim Runners' service, but as T-G is your real employer that shouldn't mean any hardship. The records I have made"— he tapped the two buttons of his jacket—"stay with me. To be used, if required. Meanwhile my friends"—he turned to wave to Wunnaara and a dozen other natives who were wading up from the sea—"will dispose of the evidence. The story will be that they, without any outside aid, have succeeded in coping with the starfish plague. You will furnish them, of course, with transmitters like the one you used tonight so that your pets in other parts of the sea can be rounded up."

"Haven't much option, have I?" she asked.

"No."

"There's just one thing I'd like to say. That question you asked me, about my enjoying myself . . . I'm damned sorry this truth drug of yours made me give the right answer."

"I'm not," said Grimes.

It was nice while it lasted, thought the Commodore, *but I'm really not cut out for these James*

Bond capers, any more than I would be for the odd antics of any of the other peculiar heroes of twentieth century fiction. He filled and lit his pipe—he preferred it to the little cigars, even to those without the built-in devices—and looked out over the blue sea. The sun was warm on his naked body. He wished that Sonya were with him. But it wouldn't be long now.

Part Four

JOHN GRIMES WAS really homeward bound at last.

On both Tharn and Mellise he had been obliged to leave the ships in which he had taken passage when requested by the rulers of those planets to assist them in the solution of rather complicated problems. He had not minded at all; he had welcomed the prospect of action after too long a time as a desk-borne commodore. But now he was beginning to become a little impatient. Sonya, his wife, would be back soon from her galactic cruise and then the major city of Lorn would be—as far as Grimes was concerned— forlorn in name only. He was pleased that *Rim Jaguar* would be making a direct run from Mellise to Port Forlorn with no time-expanding calls *en route*. All being well, he would have a few days in which to put things in order prior to Sonya's homecoming.

It promised to be an uneventful voyage—and in deep space uneventful voyages are the rule rather than the exception. *Rim Jaguar* was one of the more modern units of Rim Runners' fleet, built for them to modified *Epsilon* Class design. She was well found, well manned and reasonably happy. Grimes was the only passenger, and as Rim Runners' Astronautical Superintendent he was given the run of the vessel. He did not abuse the privilege. He would never have dreamed of interfering, and he made suggestions only when asked to do so. Nonetheless he enjoyed the long hours that he spent in the control room, yarning with the officer of the watch, looking out through the wide viewports at the great, distant Galactic Lens, unperturbed by its weird, apparent distortion, the result of the warped space-time through which the ship was falling. He was Earth-born but, like so many spacemen who had made their various ways to this frontier of the dark, he belonged on the Rim, had come to accept that almost empty sky—the sparsely scattered, unreachable island universes, the galaxy itself no more than a dim-glowing ellipsoid—as being altogether right and proper and, somehow, far more natural than worlds in toward the center.

He was sitting in *Rim Jaguar's* control room now, at ease in his acceleration chair, his seamed, pitted face and his still youthful gray eyes almost obscured by the cloud of acrid smoke from his vile, battered pipe. He was listening tolerantly to the third officer's long list of grievances; shortly after departure from Mellise he had made it quite plain that he wouldn't bite and also that anything told to him by the ship's people would not be taken down and used as evidence against them.

"And annual leave, sir," the young man was saying. "I realize that it isn't always possible to release an officer on the exact date due, but when there's a delay of two, or even three months . . ."

"We just haven't enough personnel, Mr. Sanderson," Grimes told him, "to ensure a prompt relief. Also, when it comes to appointments I try to avoid putting square pegs into round holes. You know what *that* can lead to."

"The *Rim Griffon* business, sir?"

"Yes. Everybody hating everybody, and the ship suffering in consequence. A very sorry affair."

"I see your point, sir, but—" An alarm pinged sharply. "Excuse me."

It was the Mass Proximity Indicator that had sounded off, the only piece of navigational equipment, apart from the Carlotti Direction Finder, that was functional while the Interstellar Drive was in operation. Grimes swiveled his chair so that he could look at the globular tank that was the screen of the device. Yes, there was something there all right, something that had no business to be there, something that, in the screen, was only a little to one side of the glowing filament that was the extrapolation of the ship's trajectory.

Sanderson was speaking briskly into the telephone. "Control Room here, sir. Unidentified object 000 01.5, range 3,000, closing. Bearing opening."

Grimes heard Captain Drakenberg's reply. "I'll be right up, Mr. Sanderson."

Drakenberg, an untidy bear of a man, looked into the screen and grunted. He turned to Grimes. "And what do you make of it, sir?"

"It's *something*. . . ."

"I could have told you that, Commodore."

Grimes felt his prominent ears redden. Drakenberg was a highly competent shipmaster, popular rather than otherwise with his officers, but at times lacking in the social graces.

The third officer said, "According to Traffic Control there are no ships in this sector. . . ."

"Would it be a Rim Ghost?" asked the Captain. "You're something of an expert on them, Commodore. Would one show up on the M.P.I.?"

"Conditions would have to be exactly right," said Grimes. "We would have had to slip into its continuum, or it into ours. The same applies, of course, to any attempt to establish radio communication."

"We'll try that, sir," said Drackenberg bluntly. Then, to Sanderson, "Line up the Carlotti."

The watch officer switched on the control room Carlotti communicator, a miniature version of the main set in the ship's radio office, which was a miniature version of the huge, planet-based beacons. The elliptical Mobius Strip that was the antenna began to rotate about its long axis, fading into apparent insubstantiality as it did so. Sanderson threw the switch that hooked it up with the Mass Proximity Indicator. At once the antenna began to swing on its universal mounting, turning unsteadily, hesitantly in a wide arc. After its major oscillations had ceased it hunted for a few seconds, finally locked on.

"Pass me the microphone," Drackenberg ordered. Then he said, speaking slowly and very distinctly, "*Rim Jaguar* calling unidentified vessel. *Rim Jaguar* calling unidentified vessel. Come in, please. Come in, please."

There was a silence, broken by Grimes. "Perhaps she hasn't got M.P.I.," he suggested. "Perhaps she hasn't seen us."

"It's a compulsory fitting, isn't it?" growled the master.

"For the Federation's ships. And for ours. But the Empire of Waverley hasn't made it compulsory yet. Or the Shakespearian Sector." He got out of his chair, moved to the screen. "Besides, I don't think that this target *is* a ship. Not with a blip that size, and at this range. . . ."

"What the hell else can it be?" demanded Drakenberg.

"I don't know," admitted Grimes. "I don't know. . . ."

It hung there against the unrelieved blackness of Rim Space, a planet where no planet should have been, illuminated by a sun that wasn't there at all. There was an atmosphere, with cloud masses. There were seas and continents. There were polar icecaps. And it was real, solid, with enough mass to hold the ship—her Inertial Drive and her Mannschenn Drive shut down—in a stable orbit about it. An Earth-type world it was, according to *Rim Jaguar's* instruments—an inhabited world, with the scintillant lights of cities clearly visible scattered over its night hemisphere.

All attempts at communication had failed. The inhabitants did not seem to have radio, either for entertainment or for the transmission of messages. Grimes, still in the control room, looked with some distaste at the useless Carlotti transceiver. Until the invention of this device, whereby ships could talk with each other with shore stations regardless of range and with no time lag, psionic radio officers had always been carried. In circumstances such as these a trained telepath would have been invaluable, would have been able to achieve contact with a least a few minds on the planet below. Psionic radio officers were still carried by fighting ships and by survey vessels, but *Rim Jaguar* was neither. She was a merchantman, and the employment of personel required for duty only upon very special occasions would have been uneconomical.

She did not carry sounding rockets, even. Grimes, as Astronautical Superintendent of Rim Runners, had been responsible for that piece of economy, had succeeded in having the regulations amended. He had argued that ships trading only in a well charted sector of space had no need for such expensive toys. It had not been anticipated that an unknown planet—matter or anti-matter?—would appear suddenly upon the track between Mellise and Lorn.

But the construction of a small liquid fuel rocket is little more than a matter of plumbing, and the *Jaguar's* engineers were able to oblige. Her second officer—as well as being the ship's navigator he specialized in gunnery in the Confederacy's Naval Reserve—produced a crude but effective homing device for the thing. It was hardly necessary. The range was short and the target a big one.

The rocket was fired on such a trajectory that it would hit the night side while the ship was directly over the hemisphere. Radar tracked it down to the outer reaches of the atmosphere, where it disintegrated. But it was a normal, meteoric destruction by impact and friction, not the flare of released energy that would have told of the meeting of matter and anti-matter. That was that. The initial reports of the sighting, together with all the relevant coordinates, had already been sent to Lorn; all that remained now was to report the results of the sounding rocket experiment. Grimes was scribbling the message down on a signal pad, and Drakenberg was busy with the preliminaries of putting the ship back on to trajectory, when the radio officer came into the control room. He was carrying three envelopes, one of which he handed to the Captain, giving the two to the Commodore. Grimes knew what their contents would be, and sighed audibly. Over the years he had become too much of an expert on the dimensional oddities encountered out on the rim of the galaxy. And he was the man on the spot—just when he was in a hurry to be getting home.

The first message was from Rim Runners' Board of Management and read, *Act as instructed by*

Admiral Commanding Confederate Navy. The second one was from Admiral Kravinsky. *Carry out full investigation of strange planet.* Drakenberg, scowling, handed Grimes the flimsy that had been inside his own envelope. Its content was clear enough, *Place self and vessel under orders of Commodore Grimes, Rim Worlds Naval Reserve.*

"Keep the ship in orbit, Captain," ordered Grimes resignedly.

A dust mote in the emptiness, *Rim Jaguar's* number two lifeboat fell toward the mysterious planet. In it were two men only—Grimes and Sanderson, the freighter's third officer. There had been no shortage of volunteers, from the Master on down, but Grimes, although a high ranking officer of the Naval Reserve, was still an employee of a commerical shipping line. To make a landing on an unknown world with horse, foot and artillery is all very well when you have the large crew of a warship to draw upon; should the initial expedition come to grief there is sufficient personnel left aboard the vessel to handle her and, if necessary, to man her weaponry. But insofar as manning is concerned, a merchant ship is run on a shoestring. There are no expendable ratings, and the loss of even one officer from any department means, at least, considerable inconvenience.

Grimes's decision to take only Sanderson with him had not been a popular one, but the young man had been the obvious choice. He was unmarried—was an orphan. He did not have a steady girlfriend, even. Furthermore, he had just completed a period of Naval Reserve training and rather fancied himself a small arms expert.

Rim Jaguar, however did not carry much of an armory. Grimes had with him his own Minetti and one of the ship's laser handguns. Sanderson had one of the other lasers—there were only three on board—and a vicious ten millimeter projectile pistol. There were spare power packs and a good supply of ammunition for all weapons.

The third officer, who was handling the boat, was talkative on the way down. Grimes did not mind—as long as the young man kept his trap shut and concentrated on his piloting as soon as the little craft hit the atmosphere.

"This is a rum go," he was saying. "How do you explain it, sir? All that obvious sunlight, and no sun at all in the sky . . ."

"I've seen worse," Grimes told him. Like, he thought, the series of alternative universes he had explored—although not thoroughly—in that voyage of the *Faraway Quest* that somebody had referred to as a Wild Ghost Chase. And that other universe, into which he had quite literally blown his ship, the one in which those evil non-human mutants had ruled the Rim. On both of those occasions Sonya had been with him. She should have been with him now—not this lanky, blond, blue-eyed puppy. But that wasn't Sanderson's fault, and in any case Grimes did not think that he would find the young man lacking in any respect.

"I suppose," the third officer rattled on, "that it's all something to do with different dimensions. Here we're at the very edge of the expanding galaxy, and the barriers between continua must be stretched thin, very thin. That planet's popped through into our continuum, but only half through, if you see what I mean. Its primary has stayed put on the other side of the boundary. . . ."

"A fairish hypothesis," admitted Grimes. "It will have to do until we can think of a better one."

And, he told himself, *there must be a better one.* As far as he knew the difference between the universes were cultural rather than cosmological. There just couldn't be a planet here—or a sun with a family of planets.

"And I wonder what the people are like, sir. Would they be humanoid, do you think, or even human? They must be civilized. They have cities."

Grimes muttered something about plastic jungles.

"Not plastic, sir. They haven't radio, so the chances are that they don't run to chemical engineering. Concrete jungles . . . would that be better?"

Grimes allowed himself to suppose that it might be.

"You couldn't have timed it better, sir. That large town you decided on will be just clear of the terminator when we get down."

In the Federation's Survey Service, thought Grimes, we were drilled so that such timing became second nature. How had that instructor put it? "Make your first landing just west of the terminator, and unless some bastard chases you off you've the whole day to play silly buggers in."

"Better fasten seat belts, sir."

Grimes pulled the webbing taut across his body, snapped shut the buckle. In a boat fitted with Inertial Drive the ride down to the planetary surface should be a smooth one, provided that there was no atmosphere turbulence. But here there was no spaceport control to give information on meteorological conditions. He spoke into the microphone of the transceiver. "Commodore to *Rim Jaguar*. We are now entering exosphere. So far all in going as planned." He heard Drakenberg acknowledge.

The air below the boat was clear, abnormally so. The lights of the cities were like star clusters. For a brief second Grimes entertained the crazy idea that they *were* star clusters, that he and Sanderson had broken through into some other time and space, were somehow adrift in regions toward the heart of a galaxy. He looked upward for reassurance. But he did not, through the transparency of the overhead viewport, see the familiar, almost empty Rim sky. The firmament was ablaze with unfamiliar constellations. It was frightening. Had Sanderson, somehow, turned the boat over just as Grimes had shifted his regard? He had not, as a glance at the instrument panel made obvious. He had not—and below were still the city lights, and from zenith to horizon there were the stars, and low to the west was a great golden moon. Astern, the first rosy flush of dawn was in the sky.

His voice unemotional, deliberately flat, Grimes reported his observations to the ship.

Swiftly the boat fell through the atmosphere, so

369

fast that interior temperture rose appreciably. But Sanderson was a first class pilot and at no time did he allow the speed of descent to approach dangerous limits. Swiftly the boat fell, her Inertial Drive purring gently, resisting but not overcoming the gravitational field that had her in its grip. Through the morning twilight she dropped, and above her only the brighter stars were visible in the pale sky, and below her the land masses were gray-green rather than black, and the city lights had lost their sharp scintillance and were going out, street by street.

It was toward what looked like a park that Sanderson, on Grimes's instructions, was steering, an irregular rectangle of comparative darkness outlined by such lights as were still burning. There were trees there, the men could see as the boat lost altitude; there were trees, and there were dullgleaming ribbons and amoeboid shapes that looked like water, and featureless patches that must be clear level ground. Bordering the park were the towers of the city—tall, fantastically turreted and, when struck by the first bright rays of the rising sun, shining like jewels in the reflected radiance.

The boat grounded gently on a soft, resilient surface. Grimes looked at Sanderson and Sanderson looked at Grimes, and then they both stared out of the viewports. They had landed in the middle of the park, on what looked like a lawn of emerald green grass, not far from the banks of a stream. There were trees in the foreground, low, static explosions of dark foliage among which gleamed, scarlet and crimson and gold, what were either fruit or flowers. In the background were the distant towers, upthrusting like the suddenly frozen spray of some great fountain, an opalescent tracery against the clear blue sky.

"Open up, sir?" asked the young officer at last.

"Yes," said Grimes. An itemized list of all the precautions that should be taken before setting foot on a strange planet briefly flashed before his mind's eye, but he ignored it. And to wear a spacesuit in this huge, gorgeous garden would be heresy. But not all of his training could be dismissed so easily. Reluctantly he picked up the microphone, made his report to the ship. He concluded with the words, "We're going out, now, to make contact with the natives. You have your instructions, Captain."

"Yes, Commodore Grimes." Grimes wondered why Drakenberg should sound so anxious. "If I don't hear from you again twenty-four standard hours from now, at the latest, I'm to make a report directly to the Admiralty and await their orders." He hesitated, then brought out the final words with some difficulty. "And on no account am I to attempt another landing."

"That is correct, Captain Drakenberg. Over."

"Good luck, Commodore Grimes. Over and out."

Sanderson already had both air lock doors open and the cool breeze had eddied gently through the little cabin, flushing out the acridity of hot oil and machinery, bringing with it the scent of flowers, of dew-wet grass. There were birds singing outside and then, faint yet clear, the sound of a great clock somewhere in the city striking the hour. Automatically Grimes looked at his watch, made to reset it and then smiled at his foolishness. He did not know yet what sort of time it was that these people kept.

He was first out of the boat, jumping down onto the velvety turf, joined almost at once by Sanderson. "This is beautiful!" exclaimed the young man. "I hope that the natives come up to what we've seen so far." He added, "The girls expecially."

Grimes should have reproved him, but he didn't. He was too busy wondering what it was that made everything, so far, so familiar. He had never seen this world before, or any planet like it, and yet . . . How did he know, for example, that this city's name was Ayonoree? How could he know?

"Which way do we go, sir?" Sanderson was asking.

Which way? The memory, if it was memory, wasn't quite good enough. "We'll follow the stream," he decided.

It was a short walk to the near bank of the little river, along which ran a path of flagstones. The water was crystal clear, gently flowing. On it floated great lily pads, and on one of these sat a huge frog, all gold and emerald, staring at them with bright, protuberant eyes. It croaked loudly.

"It's saying something!" cried Sanderson.

"Rubbish!" snapped Grimes, who was trying to break the odd spell that had been cast over them.

But were those words that they could hear?

Follow stream stay in the dream.

Follow stream stay in the dream.

"You!" shouted Sanderson. "What do you mean?"

In reply the batrachian croaked derisively, splashed into the water and struck out slowly for the further shore.

So we follow the stream, thought Grimes. He set off along the path, the young man tailing behind. Suddenly he stopped. There was a tree, gracefully trailing its tendrillike branches almost to the water, to one side of the flagstones, another tree a few yards inshore from it. Between the trunks was a huge, glittering web. There was a spider, too, disgustingly hairy, as a large man's clenched fist, scuttling toward the center of its fragile-seeming net. And there was an insect of some kind, a confused fluttering of gauzy wings, snared by the viscous strands.

Grimes made to detour around the landward tree. After all, spiders were entitled to a meal, just as he was. Insofar as the uglier sides of Nature were concerned he tried to maintain his neutrality. He did not especially like spiders—but, in all probability, that oversized insect in the web was something even more unpleasant.

Behind him he heard Sanderson cry out, heard the hiss of his laser pistol and felt the heat of the beam that narrowly missed his right ear. The fleshy body of the spider exploded and hung there, tattered and steaming. There was a sickening stench of burned flesh.

Grimes turned angrily on the young man. "What the hell do you think you're doing? For all we know, spiders are sacred on this world!"

"More likely *these* are!"

Sanderson had pushed past Grimes and, with gentle hands, was freeing the trapped creature. "Look!" he was saying. "Look!"

The Commodore looked. This was not, as he assumed, an insect. It was humanoid, a winged woman, but tiny, tiny. Her lustrous golden hair hung to her waist, and beneath her filmy green robe was the hint of perfectly formed breasts. Her mouth was scarlet and her eyes blue, and her features were perfectly formed. She sat there in the third officer's cupped hands, looking up at him. Her voice, when she spoke, was like the tinkling of a little silver bell.

"Follow stream, and follow river,
When danger threatens do not quiver;
Follow stream to Ogre's Keep,
Wake the Princess from her sleep!"

"What princess?" demanded Grimes.

She turned to glare to him.

"Prince's servitors like you,
Should only speak when spoken to."

Sanderson was shocked. "This is the Commodore," he said severely to the winged being.

"Commodore, Schmommodore!" she replied sweetly—and then, with hardly a quiver of those impractical looking pinions, was gone.

"So you're promoted," said Grimes dryly. "And I'm demoted."

"All the same, sir, it was absolute sauce on her

part." Then he went on a little smugly. "The odd part is that I *am* a prince. My father was King of Tavistock, until they threw him out."

"And your great-grandfather," said Grimes, "who founded the dynasty, was a semi-piratical tramp skipper. I know the history."

"Do we follow the stream, sir?"

"Yes. It's as good a way to explore this world as any."

They followed the stream. Through the great park it led them, past enormous beds of fantastic, glowing flowers, through a grove of gaunt, contorted trees. The transition from parkland to city street was abrupt; suddenly there were cobbles underfoot instead of the worn flagstones, and on every hand towered multi-colored buildings, convoluted structures that made nonsense of all the laws of architecture and engineering.

People were abroad now, men and women, a great number of children. They were human enough in outward appearance at least, but there was an oddness about them, an oversimplification of all features, a peculiar blend of stylization and caricature. There was no vehicular traffic, but there were riders—some upon horses, some upon camels, some upon the lizard-like roadrunners indigenous to Tarizeel, some upon beasts that were utterly strange even to the widely traveled Grimes.

The two explorers marched on, ignored by the brightly dressed natives, ignoring them. They should, Grimes knew, have tried to make contact, which would not have been hard. From the scraps of conversation they overheard it was obvious that Anglo-Terran was the language of this planet. They should have demanded to be taken to the king, president or whatever authority it was that ruled this world. But it was not important. What was important was to find the Ogre's Keep, to awaken the sleeping princess. It was as though some outside power had taken control of them. The feeling should have been nightmarish, but it was not. Grimes was oddly grateful that somebody—or something—else was making the decisions that he should have been making.

The stream joined a river, and the path continued along the bank of the larger body of water, taking the two men clear of the city. They walked on steadily, feeling no fatigue, maintaining a brisk pace. They were away from the crowds of the city, met only an occasional pedestrian, and now and again a peasant man or woman pushing a barrow high-laden with produce in to market. One of these latter, a wizened, black-clad crone dragging a little cart fitted with pumpkins, accosted them. Raising high a skinny claw she declaimed in a cracked voice,

"Dare the dragon! Storm the Keep!
Save us all from endless sleep!"

"The dragon, madam?" inquired Grimes politely.

But she was given no time to answer him. From the cloudless sky crackled a bolt of lightning, dazzling, terrifying, striking the path between her and the two men. She waited, "I didn't say anything! I didn't say anything!" and was gone, scuttling toward the city, the cart bouncing along behind her, a trail of bruised and burst pumpkins in her wake.

"Somebody Up There doesn't like her," remarked Sanderson. Then, brightly, "Do you feel in the mood for dragon-slaying, sir?"

"Why not?" countered Grimes. After all, it would be no more outrageous than any of their other encounters to date. *Outrageous*? He repeated the word mentally. Where had he got it from? Nothing, so far, justified its use: the frog, the fairy in the spider's web, all the talk of ogres' keeps and sleeping princesses and dragons, it had all been perfectly natural. In any well-regulated world sleeping princesses were there to be awakened, and ogres' keeps to be stormed, and the dragons to be slain. Of course, the way he and the young prince were dressed was all wrong—more like peasants than like knights errant. But that could not be helped. Disguise was allowable.

"Shall we press on, Your Highness?" he suggested.

"Yes, Sir John. No doubt the dragon awaits us eagerly." Sanderson pulled the projectile pistol from its holster, spun it carelessly with his right forefinger through the trigger guard. "Methinks that our magic weapons will prove more efficacious than swords."

"Mehopes that you're right, Your Highness."

"Then come, Sir John. Time's a-wasting."

They walked on—and then, just ahead of them, Grimes saw a pontoon landing dock on the river. There was a ship alongside it, an archaic side-wheel paddle steamer, smoke issuing from its tall funnel. At the shoreward side of the stage was a notice board and on it, in big black letters on a white ground, the sign:

RIVER TRIPS TO OGRE'S KEEP.
HALF A FLORIN. VERY CHEAP.

"Your Highness," said Grimes, "let's take the boat and rest awhile, then face the dragon with a smile."

"Have you the wherewithal, Sir John, to pay the fare agreed upon?"

"I have a pass, Prince Sanderson. And so have you—your trusty gun."

Something at the back of the Commodore's mind winced at the doggerel and cried voicelessly, *You're a spaceman, not a character out of a children's book!* Grimes almost ignored it, tried to ignore it, but the nagging doubt that had been engendered persisted.

They marched on to the pontoon, their sturdily shod feet ringing on the planking, their weapons drawn and ready. Side by side, but with Sanderson slightly in the lead, they tramped up the gangway. At the head of it stood a man in uniform—and, incongruously, his trappings were those of a purser in the Waverley Royal Mail Line. He held out his hand. "Good knights, if you would board this ship, pay passage money for your trip."

"Varlet, stand back! The ride is free for this, the bold Sir John, and me!"

"And here, as you can plainly see," added Grimes, making a meaningful gesture with his Minetti, "is our loud-voiced authority."

"Sir, it speaks loud enough for me," admitted

the purser, standing to one side. As they passed him Grimes heard him mutter. "The Royal Mail could not be worse. *They* never made me speak in verse."

Grimes, who was always at home aboard ships of any kind, led the way down to the saloon, a large compartment, darkly paneled, with black leather upholstery on chairs and settees. At one end of it there was a bar, but it was shut. Along both sides were big windows, barely clear of the surface of the water. There were no other passengers.

Overhead there was the thudding of feet on planking. Then there was a jangling of bells, followed at once by the noise of machinery below decks. From above came the long mournful note of a steam whistle, and then came the steady *chunk, chunk, chunk* of the paddles. The ship was underway, heading down river. On either side the banks were sliding past, a shifting panorama of forest and village, with only rarely what looked like a cultivated field, but very often a huge, frowning, battlemented castle.

The rhythm of paddles and engines was a soothing one and Grimes, at least, found that it made him drowsy. He lolled back in his deep chair, halfway between consciousness and sleep. When he was in this state his real memories, his very real doubts and worries came suddenly to the surface of his mind. He heard his companion murmur, "Speed, bonny boat, like a bird through the sky. Carry us where the dragon must die."

"Come off it, Sanderson," ordered the Commodore sharply.

"Sir John, please take yourself in hand. Such

insolence I will not stand!''

"Come off it!" ordered Grimes again—and then the spell, which had been so briefly broken, took charge again. ''Your Highness, I spoke out of turn. But courtesy I'll try to learn.''

''My good Sir John, you better had. Bad manners always make me mad. But look through yonder port, my friend. Methinks we neareth journey's end.''

Journey's end or not, there was a landing stage there toward which the paddle steamer was standing in. Inshore from it the land was thickly wooded and rose steeply. On the crest of the hill glowered the castle, a grim pile of gray stone, square-built, ugly, with a turret at each corner. There was a tall staff from which floated a flag. Even from a distance the two men could make out the emblem: a white skull-and-crossbones in a black ground. And then, as the ship neared the shore, the view was shut out and, finally, only the slime-covered side of the pontoon could be seen through the window.

The paddle steamer came alongside with a gentle crunch and, briefly, the engines were reversed to take the way off her. From forward and aft there was a brief rattle of steam winches as she was moored, and then there were no more mechanical noises.

The purser appeared in the saloon entrance. ''Good knights, you now must leave this wagon. So fare you forth to face the dragon.''

''And you will wait till we are done?'' asked Grimes.

''We can't, Sir Knight, not on this run.

Come rain, come shine, come wind, come snow,
Back and forth our ferries go.
Like clockwork yet, sir, you should try 'em,
And even set your wristwatch by 'em.''

"Enough, Sir John," said Sanderson, "this
wordy wight will keep us gabbing here all night. In
truth, he tells a pretty tale—this lackey from the
Royal Mail!"

The spell was broken again. "You noticed too!"
exclaimed Grimes.

"Yes. I noticed. That cap badge with a crown
over the silver rocket." Sanderson laughed. "It
was when I tried to find a rhyme for *tale* that things
sort of clicked into place."

Grimes turned on the purser. "What the hell's
going on here?" he demanded.

"Alas, Sir Knight, I cannot say. *I cannot say*?"
The young man's pudgy face stiffened with resolu-
tion. "*No*! Come what may . . ."

Whatever it was that came, it was sudden. He
was standing there, struggling to speak, and then
he was . . . gone, vanished in a gentle thunderclap
as the air rushed in to fill the vacuum where he had
stood. Then another man stamped into the saloon,
in captain's uniform with the same familiar trappings.

"Begone, good knights," he shouted, "to meet
your fate! Get off my ship, I'm running late."

"Sir," began Grimes—and then that influence
gripped his mind again. He said, "Thank you for
passage, sir. Goodbye. We fare forth now, to do or
die!"

"Well said, Sir John," declaimed Sanderson.

"Well said, my friend. We go—to shape the story's end."

"I hope, good knights, you gallant two," growled the captain, "that story's end does not shape you." He led the way from the saloon up to the gangway.

They stood on the pontoon, watching the little steamer round the first bend on her voyage up river, then walked to the bridge that spanned the gap between landing stage and bank. Overhead the sky was darkening and the air was chill. The westering sun had vanished behind a bank of low clouds. Grimes, his shirt and slacks suddenly inadequate, shivered. *What am I doing here?* he asked himself. And then, quite suddenly, *Who am I?* It was a silly question, and he at once knew how foolish it was. The answer shaped itself in his mind. *I am the one they call Sir John, true comrade to Prince Sanderson.*

"We forward march," announced the Prince, "my cobber bold, to meet the perils long foretold. Up yonder hill, let us then, to beard the dragon in his den."

"The dragon wastes no time on fuss," remarked Grimes. "He's coming down, and bearding us."

Yes, the beast was coming down, either from the castle or from somewhere else atop the hill. It was airborne—and even in his bemused state Grimes realized that it should never have gotten off the ground. Its head and body were too large, its wings too small, too skimpy. But it was a terrifying sight, a monstrous, batwinged crocodile, its mouth, crowded with jagged teeth, agape, the long, sharp claws of its forefeet extended. It dived down on them, roaring, ignoring the laser beams that the two men directed at it, even though its metallic scales glowed cherry red where they scored hits. It dived down on them—and there was more than mere sound issuing from that horrid maw. The great gout of smoky flame was real enough, and Grimes and Sanderson escaped it only by diving into the undergrowth on either side of the steep path.

The beast pulled out of its dive and flapped away slowly, regaining altitude. The men watched it until it was only a darker speck in the dark sky, then realized that the speck was rapidly increasing in size. It was coming for them again.

Something was wrong, very wrong. In the fairy stories the dragons never kill the heroes . . . but this dragon looked like being the exception to prove the rule. Grimes holstered his laser pistol, pulled out his Minetti. He doubted that the little weapon would be of any avail against the armored monstrosity, but it might be worth trying. From the corner of his eyes he saw that Sanderson had out and ready his heavy projectile pistol. "Courage, Sir John," called the young man. "Aim for his head. We've no cold steel; we'll try hot lead!"

"Cold steel, forsooth!" swore Grimes. "Hot lead, indeed! A silver bullet's what we need!"

"Stand firm, Sir John, and don't talk rot! Don't whine for what we haven't got!"

Grimes loosed off a clip at the diving dragon on full automatic. Sanderson, the magazine of whose pistol held only ten rounds, fired in a more leisurely manner. Both men tried to put their shots into the open mouth, the most obviously vulnerable target. Whether or not they succeeded they never knew. Again they had to tumble hastily off the path just as the jet of flame roared out at them. This time it narrowly missed Grimes's face. It was like being shaved with a blowtorch.

He got groggily to his feet, fumbled another clip of cartridges out of the pouch at his belt, reloaded the little automatic. He saw that Sanderson was pushing a fresh magazine into the butt of his heavy pistol. The young man smiled grimly and said, "Sir John, the ammo's running low. When all is spent, what shall we do?"

"The beast will get us if we run. Would that we'd friends to call upon!"

"Many did give us good advice. If they gave us more it would be nice."

"What of the fairy Lynnimame?"

"And how, Sir John, do you know her name?"

The dragon was coming in again, barely visible in the fast gathering dusk. The men held their fire until the last possible moment—and it was almost the last moment for both of them. Barely did they scramble clear of the roaring, stinking flame, and as they rolled in the brush both of them were frantically beating out their smoldering clothing. The winged monster, as before, seemed to be uninjured.

Suddenly Sanderson cried out, swung to turn his just reloaded pistol on a new menace. It was Grimes who stopped him, who knocked his arm down before he could fire. In the glowing ovoid of light was a tiny human figure, female, with gauzy wings. She hung there over the rough, stony path. She was smiling sweetly, and her voice, when she spoke, was a silvery tintinmabulation. "Prince, your companion called my name. I am the fairy Lynnimame. I am she who, this very morn, from the jaws of the spider foul was torn. I pay my debts; you rescued me. I'll rescue you, if that's your fee."

"Too right it is, you lovesome sprite."

"Then take this, Prince. And now, good night."

She put something into Sanderson's hand and vanished. Before she flickered into invisibility Grimes, by the pale luminosity of her, saw what it was. It was a cartridge case, ordinary enough in appearance except that the tip of the bullet looked too bright to be lead. "A silver bullet!" marveled Sanderson. "A silver bullet. We are savèd. He'll play Goliath to my David!"

"Unless you load, you pious prig, he'll play the chef to your long pig!"

Hastily Sanderson pulled the magazine from the butt of his pistol, ejected the first cartridge, replaced it with the silver bullet. He shoved the clip back home with a loud *click*. He was just in time; the dragon was upon them again, dropping almost vertically. The first lurid flames were gushing from its gaping mouth when the third officer fired. The result was spectacular. The thing exploded in mid-air, and the force of the blast sent Grimes tumbling head over heels into the bushes, with only a confused impression of a great, scarlet flower burgeoning against the night.

He recovered consciousness slowly. As before, when he had dozed briefly aboard the river steamer, he was aware of his identity, knew what he was supposed to be doing. And then Sanderson's words severed the link with reality, recast the spell.

"Arise, Sir John! No time for sleep! We march against the Ogre's Keep!"

They marched against the Ogre's Keep—but it was more an undignified scramble up the steep path than a march. Luckily the moon was up now, somewhere above the overcast, and its diffused light was helpful, showed them the dark mass of briars that barred their way before they blundered into the thorny growth. Luckily they had not lost their weapons, and with their laser pistols they slashed, and slashed again, and slashed until their wrists ached with fatigue and their thumbs were numb from the continual pressure on the firing studs. For a long while they made no headway at all; it seemed that the severed, spiny tendrils were growing back faster than they were being destroyed. When the power packs in the pistols were exhausted they were actually forced back a few feet while they were reloading. It was Grimes who thought of renewing the attack with a wide setting instead of the needle beams that they had been using at first. The prickly bushes went up with a great *whoosh* of smoky flame, and the two men scrambled rather than ran through the gap thus cleared, and even then the barbed thorns were clutching at skin and clothing.

Then, with the fire behind them, they climbed on, bruised, torn and weary. They climbed, because it was the only thing to do. At last they were high enough up the hillside to see the castle again, black and forbidding against the gray sky. The few squares of yellow light that were windows accentuated rather than relieved the darkness.

They gained the rock-strewn plateau in the center of which towered the Keep. They stumbled across the uneven surface, making their way between the huge boulders, avoiding somehow the fissures that made the ground a crazy pattern of cracks. From some of these sounded ominous hissings and croakings and gruntings, from some there was a baleful gleaming of red eyes, but nothing actively molested them. And there was a rising wind now, damp and cold, that made a mockery of their rent, inadequate clothing, that whined and muttered in their ears like unquiet ghosts.

But they kept on at a staggering, faltering pace and came at last to the great iron-studded doorway. Barely within Sanderson's reach—and he was a tall man—was a huge knocker, forged in the semblance of a snarling lion's head. The young officer had to stretch to reach it; and as he put his hand to it, it moved of its own accord, emitting a thunderous clangor like an artillery barrage. *Boom, boom! Boom, boom! Boom!*

Almost as loud were the heavy footsteps that sounded thunderously behind the door. Almost as loud was the deep voice that asked, "Who on this night, so bleak and frore, disturbs the Giant Blunderbore?''

The double doors crashed outward. Standing there, silhouetted against the light, was a human figure. It was all of ten feet tall, and broad in proportion. It looked down at them, its eyes gleaming yellow in the black face, and bellowed, "Enter, Princeling! Enter, Knight! Ye shall be my guests tonight.'' Then, as the two men drew back, it went on, "Come in, come in! This is Liberty Hall—you can spit on the mat and call the cat a bastard!''

The lapse from rhymed couplets and the use of an expression that had never failed to annoy him snapped Grimes back to reality. He was Commodore John Grimes, of the Rim Worlds Naval Reserve, not Sir John, and he was supposed to be investigating this crazy planet. But the castle was real enough, as was the giant who loomed there in the open doorway, as were the bruises on his body that still ached, the scratches and burns that still smarted.

"What's the matter?'' he asked nastily. "Can't you find a rhyme for 'bastard'? And who are you, anyhow?''

"And who are you? All I know is that you are outsiders, and I'm supposed to stop you. Not that I want to. This damn foolishness has gone on too long. Much too long.''

From the sky thundered a great voice, "Blunderbore, your duty's plain! These prying strangers must be slain!''

The giant stared upward, growled, "—you. I've

had you, chum, in a big way.''

The anser was a sizzling bolt of lightning, a crackling streak of dazzling energy that should have incinerated Blunderbore where he stood. But he caught it with a huge hand, laughed and hurled it back like a flaming javelin, shouting, ''Try that on for size, damn you!''

''What's going on?'' Sanderson whimpered. ''What's going on here?''

''It's a long story,'' Blunderbore told him.

''It's a story, all right,'' agreed Grimes. ''The city of Ayonoree . . . the Frog Prince . . . the Fairy Lynnimame . . . and you, Blunderbore.'' Yes, it was all coming back to him, and it was all making a fantastic kind of sense.

''Can you be killed?'' Blunderbore was asking.

''I suppose so,'' said Grimes, conscious of the smart of his wounds. ''Yes, I fear so. We're the outsiders. We don't belong in the series, do we? And you and the others go on from installment to installment. . . .''

''Only because we're trapped. But come in. You have to wake the Princess. It's the only way out, for all of us.''

The huge man stood to one side as Grimes and Sanderson hurried into the castle. They were barely in time, were almost knocked from their feet by the wind from the crashing volley of great rocks that fell from the black sky. Splinters stung the backs of their legs painfully. Grunting, Blunderbore pushed past them, seized the two sides of the door in his big hands, pulled them shut just as another shower of boulders crashed against the stout, iron-bound timbers. "Hurry!" he shouted. "He's turning nasty!"

The giant led the way across the flagstone floor, to the far end of the enormous, gloomy hall. He staggered as he ran—and with cause. The very earth was growling beneath their feet, and each successive tremor was more violent than the last. From above came a crash of toppling masonry.

The air was thickening. Tendrils of yellow fog clutched at the running, stumbling men, and the writhing mist had substance. Half-seen, evil faces leered at them, distorted visages that were all teeth and dull-gleaming eyes. Vaporous claws reached out for them, solidifying as they did so. Behind Grimes Sanderson screamed, and the Commodore stopped and turned, slashing with his laser at the gelatinous obscenity that had the young officer in its grip. It piped shrilly as it disintegrated, stinking sulfurously.

"Hurry!" Blunderbore was still shouting. "Hurry!"

The stone floor was crackling underfoot, heaving and buckling, and from the high, vaulted ceiling ominous groans resounded. The castle could not withstand this punishment for long. The flaring torches were going out and there was a strong smell of escaping gas. Then, as a chance spark reignited the explosive mixture, there was a fiery blast that almost finished the destructive work initiated by the earthquake.

Almost finished.

But Blunderbore and the two spacemen were

still on their feet, somehow, and there were still walls around them, although crumbling and tottering, and over their heads the last stone arch still held, despite the torrential rain of rubble that was clattering upon and around it. Ahead of them was the great fireplace, into which the giant jumped without stooping. Then he bent slowly and fumbled among the dead ashes, and straightened even more slowly, the muscles of his naked back and arms bulging and glistening. He grunted as he came erect, holding before him an enormous slab of stone. He cast it from him—and the noise of its fall and its shattering was lost amid the general uproar.

Under the slab was a spiral stairway, a helix of rusty iron running down, and down, down to murky depths where an eerie blue glimmer flickered. The prospect was not an inviting one; how long would the walls of the shaft withstand the incessant tremors? Even so, the fire was yet to come, whereas the frying pan was becoming hotter and hotter. Great sheets of flame from the ruptured gas mains were shrieking across the ruined hall, and through them crashed increasingly heavy falls of debris. And the writhing phantasms were back, multiplying in spite of the geysers of burning, exploding gas, coalescing, solidifying, piping and tittering. They were insubstantial no longer; their claws and their teeth were sharp.

"Down with you!" bellowed Blunderbore. "Down with you! It's the only way!"

"You lead!" gasped Grimes, using his laser like a sword, slashing at the half-materialized things that were closing in upon them.

"No . . . I'll hold . . . them off. . . ." The giant had wrenched the great iron spit from its sockets on either side of the fireplace, was flailing away with it, grunting with every stroke. Tattered rags of ectoplasm clung to its ends, eddied through the smoke- and dust-filled air.

Grimes paused briefly at the head of the spiral staircase, then barked to Sanderson, "Come on!" He clattered down the shaking treads, his left hand on the outer guard rail, his pistol clenched in his right fist. The central column seemed to be trying to tie itself into a knot, but it held, although the steps were canting at odd angles. The walls of the shaft were starting to bulge inward.

Grimes ran—down, down, round, round— keeping his footing in spite of the earthquake shocks, in spite of his increasing dizziness. He ran, and after him ran the third officer. Up there above Blunderbore was still fighting; his joyous bellowing came rolling down on them like thunder, loud even above the clangorous destruction of the Ogre's Keep.

Down, down. . . .

Grimes staggered on, forcing his legs to move, to go on moving, taking great gasps of the damp, fetid air. Something barred his way, something long and serpent-like, with absurdly small forelegs, with curved poison-fangs and a flickering black tongue. The Commodore tried to stop, tried to bring his pistol up to a firing position, but could not. His impetus carried him on. Then he was *through* the monster; its body offered no more resistance than wet tissue paper.

Down, down. . . .

It was more of a fall than a run.

It was a fall.

Grimes thudded gently into something thick and soft, lay sprawled on the soft bed of moss, breathing in great, painful gulps. Slowly he became aware of his surroundings: the cave, lit by a soft, rosy radiance with no apparent source, the opalescent colonnades of stalactite and stalagmite, the tinkling, glittering waterfalls. He focused his attention upon his immediate vicinity. The Prince was still with him, was himself slowly stirring into wakefulness. Sir John knew where he was. This was the Witch's Cave, the home of the wicked Melinee.

She was standing over them, a tall woman, white of skin, black of hair, vividly red of mouth, clad in a robe of misty gray. In either hand she held a crystal goblet, bedewed with condensation. She murmured, ''Rest you awhile, good knights and true, and pray accept this cooling brew.''

Sanderson reached greedily for the vessel she held out to him—and Grimes, firing from his supine position, exploded it into a spray of splinters and acrid steam.

''It's not the mess,'' protested Sanderson, ''but it's the waste! I never even got a taste!''

''Prince, had we quaffed the witch's wine,'' Grimes told him, ''it would have turned us into swine.''

Melinee laughed, a low, throaty gurgle. ''You know too much, too much by far. But you'll be more fun the way you are.'' She looked at Sanderson as she said this. The invitation in her black eyes, her parted scarlet lips, was unmistakable.

The young officer reacted. He got gracefully to his feet, took a step toward the witch. He said gallantly. ''Who needs wine when you're around, beautiful?''

''Careful!'' warned Grimes.

''Have we been careful so far, sir? We've been collecting all the kicks—it's time that we got our paws on some of the ha'pence.'' Then, to the woman, ''Isn't there somewhere around here a little more private?''

She smiled. ''My bower, behind the waterfall . . .''

''Sanderson! I order you to keep away from this female!''

''*I* give the orders around here, old man,'' said Melinee sweetly. ''This is *my* cave, and whatever your rank may be it means nothing as long as you're on my property.'' She turned again to Sanderson. The filmy robe was already slipping down from one smooth shoulder and it was obvious that she was wearing nothing underneath it. ''Come,'' she murmured.

The admonitory voice boomed from the roof of the cavern. ''Melinee, you forget yourself!''

''I don't!'' she shouted. ''I'm remembering myself. I'm a real person, not a character in some stupid children's fairy story! If *you* can't write adult fiction, buster, *I'm* taking charge of the plot. I'm supposed to be stopping these men from going any further, aren't I? Then shut up and let me do it my way!''

"Melinee!"

"That's not my name, and you know it." She turned again to Sanderson. "Don't be shy, space-man. I'll show you just how wicked a wicked witch can be!"

"Mr. Sanderson!" Grimes's voice crackled with authority. "Leave that woman alone!"

The young man stood there, obviously thinking mutinous thoughts but not daring to express them. The woman stood there, looking at him, a contemptuous little smile curving her full lips. And then she turned, began to walk slowly and gracefully toward the waterfall. Her robe was almost transparent.

"Melinee!" The voice from the roof expressed entreaty as well as anger.

And why, Grimes asked himself suddenly, *should I be on his side?* He said aloud, but quietly, "All right, Mr. Sanderson. Go with her."

Sanderson shook his head bewilderedly. "First you tell me not to, and now you say that I can. . . . After all, we *are* on duty."

"Go with her," repeated Grimes. It was more of an order than a suggestion.

"But, sir . . ."

"Damn it all, when I was your age I didn't have to be told twice."

The Wicked Witch called over her shoulder, "Do as the nice man says, darling."

The third officer made a sort of growling noise deep in his throat, glared defiantly at the Commodore, then started after the woman. She had reached the shimmering curtain of the waterfall, was passing through it. As she turned to look back through the rippling transparency Sanderson quickened his pace. Grimes chuckled, pulled from his pocket the battered pipe that somehow had survived unbroken, filled it, then ostentatiously used his laser pistol as a lighter. It was a dangerous trick, but an impressive one.

From beyond the cascade came the sound of a crooning female voice. "Mirror, mirror on the wall, who is the fairest one of all?" Then there was a crash of splintering glass and a scream. "No! No! You can't do that to me! I'll fix you! I'll fix you, you . . . you fairy story-teller!"

Melinee burst back into the main cavern. She was shaking with murderous fury. "Look!" she yelled. "Look what that bastard did to me!"

Grimes looked. Sanderson looked. "But—" the latter started to say. Grimes interjected hastily, "It's shocking!" He was lying—as the mirror must have done.

"Come on!" she snarled. "This joke's gone on quite long enough!"

She led the way into her bower, through the curtain of falling water. As Grimes passed through it he heard behind him the clatter of falling stalactities, felt the brief wave of scalding heat as the waterfall flashed into steam. But it was too late to harm him, and the others were well clear.

On the far wall of the bower was the mirror—or what had been the mirror. Now it was only an elaborately molded golden frame set into the rock face. Melinee scrambled through it, ignoring the sharp edges that ripped her robe from hip to ankle.

Sanderson followed her, then Grimes. The tunnel beyond it was unpleasantly organic in appearance, a convoluted tube, with smooth and pinkly glistening walls, winding, pulsing underfoot, writhing.

Melinee ran on, sure-footed. Somewhere she had lost her sandals, had probably used one of them to smash the lying, libelous looking-glass. The men, in their shoes, slipped and slithered, but they kept up with her. Down they went, and down, losing all sense of direction, losing their footing, putting hands out to steady themselves against smooth, warm walls that shrank away from the touch. Down they went, and down, gasping in the hot air, suddenly conscious that the red-glowing walls were steadily contracting. Soon there would be no going any further ahead, and no turning back.

They were crouching, and then they were slithering on their bellies. Grimes, who had passed Sanderson while it was still possible, while there was still freedom of movement, suddenly found his way blocked, realized that the crown of his head was pressing against the soles of Melinee's bare feet. Faintly her voice came back to him. "We're there . . . at the air lock. But . . . I don't know how to open it. . . ."

"I . . . I have to crawl past you . . ." gasped Grimes. Then, urgently, "Make yourself small, woman! Breathe out!"

"I'll . . . try."

Like an earthworm in its tunnel—but with far less agility, far less speed—the Commodore edged forward. Somehow he managed to get both arms ahead of his body, clutched filmy fabric and the firm flesh beneath. He heard her give a little scream, but he ignored it. Cloth tore, and then he had a firm grip on her waist, just above her hips. His face was over her heels, and then pressing down on her ankles. Somehow he was still able to draw an occasional breath. His nose was sliding—but slowly, slowly—up the valley between her calves. He hunched his back, and the resilient wall above him gave a little.

He grunted as he wriggled forward. Somehow he negotiated her buttocks; then his fingers were on her shoulders. He pulled himself ahead, more rapidly now. He spat out a mouthful of hair, then slid his hands along her upreaching bare arms. And then there was metal, blessedly hard and solid to the touch—and touch was the only sense that he and to guide him.

Was this an air lock door? He did not know; he had only her word for it. And if it were, indeed, an air lock door, was it of the standard pattern? It had to be; otherwise the situation was utterly hopeless. Cramped as he was, Grimes could never get his laser pistol out of its holster—and even if he could its employment in this confined space might well prove fatal to himself and the others.

His fingers groped, scrabbled, feeling nothing at first but smooth, seamless metal. He had almost given up hope when he found what he was looking for: the neat little hole, large enough to admit a space-gloved digit. He had to squirm and contort himself to get his hand to the right angle. Under him Melinee whimpered a little, but did not complain.

The tip of his index finger crept over the faired rim of the hole, pushed into it, at first encountering nothing at all and then, after what seemed an eternity, smooth plastic. Grimes pushed, felt the surface give. He maintained the pressure, relaxed it, pushed again, and again, making "O" in Morse Code— "O" for Open."

He heard the faint whir of machinery, a noise that suddenly became louder. The inward opening door almost took his finger with it. And then he was in the air lock, closely followed by Sanderson.

Melinee had vanished.

Slowly Grimes and Sanderson walked through the silent, the too silent alleyways of the ship, fighting the lassitude that threatened to close down upon them, forcing their way through air that seemed to possess the viscosity of cold treacle. But they were not alone. In their ears—or in their minds?—sounded the croaking voice of the Frog Prince, the tinkling soprano of the Fairy Lynnimame, the husky whisper of Melinee. "You must not give in. You have come so far; you must not give in. Waken the Princess. Waken the Princess." And there was Blunderbore's urgent muttering, and the faint voices of the *River Queen's* captain and purser. "Wake the Princess. Wake the Princess."

They stumbled on, weakening, through the gelid air, the internal atmosphere that didn't even smell right, that didn't smell at all, that lacked the familiar taints of hot oil and machinery, of tobacco smoke and women's perfume, the clean, garden scents of the hydroponics deck. They staggered on, through alleyways and up companionways, fighting every inch of the way, sustained somehow by the fairytale characters whom they had encountered.

And Grimes knew what was wrong, knew the nature of the stasis that must, soon, make them part of itself, unless they reached the Mannschenn Drive room in time. He had read of, but had never until now experienced, the almost impossible balance of forces, the canceling out of opposing temporal precession fields that would freeze a ship and all her people in an eternal *Now*, forever adrift down and between the dimensions. That had been one of the theories advanced to account for the vanishing, without trace, of that Waverley Royal Mail liner ten standard years ago—the ship aboard which the writer Clay Wilton had been a passenger.

Grimes could remember, vividly, the blurb on the dust jacket of the book that he had bought as a present for the small daugher of a friend. "The last of the dreamers," the author had been called. He had skimmed through it, had laughed at the excellent illustrations and then, to his amazement, had been gripped by the story. It was about a world that never was and was never could be, a planet where sorcery was everyday practice, where talking animals and good fairies and wicked witches interfered in the affairs of men and women.

"You are beginning to understand," whispered Lynnimame.

There was the door ahead of them, with MANN-SCHENN DRIVE in shining metal letters above it. The door was closed, stubborn; it would not yield.

Human muscles were powerless against the stasis; human muscles with strength flowing into them from outside, somehow, were still powerless. The handle snapped off cleanly in Grimes's hand.

"Let me, sir," Sanderson was saying. "Let me try."

The Commodore stepped slowly to one side., his motions those of a deep-sea diver. He saw that the young man had his laser weapon out of its holster, was struggling to raise it against the dreadful inertia.

He pressed the firing stud.

Slowly, fantastically, the beam of intense light extruded itself from the muzzle, creeping toward that immovable door. After an eternity it made contact, and after another eternity the paint began to bubble. Aeons passed, and there was a crater. More aeons dragged by—and the crater was a hole. Still Sanderson, his face rigid with strain, held the weapon steady. Grimes could imagine that luminous, purple worm crawling across the space from the door to the switchboard. Then Sanderson gasped, "I can't keep it up!" and the muzzle of the pistol wavered, sagged until it was pointing at the deck.

We tried, thought Grimes. Then he wondered, *Will Wilton add us to his permanent cast of characters?*

Suddenly there was sound again—the dying, deepening whine of a stopped Mannschenn Drive unit, of spinning, processing gyroscopes slowing to final immobility. Like a bullet fired from a gun deflected after the pulling of the trigger, the laser

beam had reached its target. There was sound
again: fans, and pumps, the irregular throbbing of
the Inertial Drive, and all the bubble and clamor of
a suddenly awakened ship. From bulkhead speakers boomed a voice, that of the captain of the river
steamer. "Whoever you are, come up to the main
saloon, please. And whoever you are—thank
you."

Grimes sprawled comfortably in an easy chair, a
cold drink ready to hand. He had decided to stay
aboard this ship, the *Princess of Troon,* having
persuaded her captain to set trajectory for Lorn.
After all, he was already ten years late—a few
more weeks would make very little difference.
During the voyage the Commodore would be able
to question the *Princess'* personnel still further, to
work on his report. He was keeping young Sanderson with him. Drakenberg had not been at all
pleased when deprived of the service of a watch
officer, but the Commodore piled on far more G's
than he did.

Already Grimes was beginning to wonder if his
report would be believed, in spite of all the cor-
roborative evidence from the personnel of both
ships, *Rim Jaguar* and *Princess of Troon*. He recalled vividly the scene in the passenger liner's
main saloon when he and Sanderson had made
their way into that compartment. The stasis must
have been closed down while everybody was at
dinner; dishes on the tables were still steaming.

They had all been there: the frog-like Grollan,
the old lady who had been the peasant woman

encountered on the towpath, the pretty fragile blonde whose name should have been Lynn-imame, but was not; all of them looking like the characters in the illustrations to the Clay Wilton books. And there was the big—but not all that big—Negro, who was a physicist, not an ogre and the captain, and the purser. There was the beautiful woman who could have been the model for the Melinee in the pictures and who was, in fact, Mrs. Wilton. There were other officers, other passengers, and among them was Clay Wilton himself. He had the beginnings of a black eye, and a trickle of blood still dribbled from the corner of his mouth. Ship's staff had formed a protective cordon about him, but made it quite obvious that this was only because they had been ordered to do so.

After the first excitement there had been the conference, during which all concerned tried to work out what had happened, and why. Blundell, the big physicist—it had been hard not to think of him as Blunderbore—had said, "I've my own ideas, Commodore Grimes. But you, sir, are the recognized authority on Rim phenomena. . . ."

Grimes was flattered, and tried not to show it. He made a major production of filling and lighting his pipe. After he had it going he said, "I can *try* to explain. The way I see it is this. The ship went into stasis, and somehow drifted out from the Waverley sector toward the Rim. And out here, at the very edge of the expanding galaxy, there's always an . . . oddness. Time and space are not inclined to follow the laws that obtain elsewhere. Too, thought seems to have more power—physical power, I mean—than in the regions more toward the center. It's all part and parcel of the vagueness—that's not quite the right word—of . . . of everything. We get along with it. We're used to it.

"Look at it this way. You were all frozen in your ever-lasting *Now*, but you could still think, and you could still dream. And who was the most expert dreamer among you? It had to be Clay Wilton; after all, his publishers refer to him as 'the last of the dreamers.' Mr. Wilton dreamed out the story that he was working on at the time when your Mannschenn Drive went on the blink. Then he dreamed of the next story in the series, and the next, and the next. . . . Somehow a world shaped itself about his dreams. Out here, on the Rim, there must be the raw material for the creation of new galaxies. Somehow that world shaped itself, a solid world, with atmosphere, and vegetation, and people. It was real enough to register on all *Rim Jaguar's* instruments, even though it vanished when this ship came out of stasis. It was real enough, but, with a few exceptions, the people weren't real. They were little more than mobile scenery. The exceptions, of course, were those characters drawn from real life. And they led a sort of double existence. One body here, aboard the ship, and another body on the surface of that impossible planet, dancing like a puppet on Mr. Wilton manipulated the strings. Toward the end, the puppets were getting restive. . . ."

"You can say that again, Commodore," grinned Blundell.

"Yes, the puppets were getting restive, and

realized that they, too, could become puppet-masters, could use Mr. Sanderson and myself to break the stasis. And, at the same time, Mr. Wilton was trying to work us into his current plot.'' Grimes turned to the writer. ''And tell me, sir, did you intend to kill us?''

''Nobody dies in *my* stories,'' muttered the man. ''Not even the baddies.''

''But there has to be a first time for everything. That dragon of yours was far too enthusiastic. And so was your destruction of Blunderbore's castle.''

''I'd gotten kind of attached to the place, too,'' grumbled the physicist.

''I meant no harm.'' Wilton's voice was sullen.

''Don't you believe him!'' flared Mrs. Wilton—Melinee, the Wicked Witch. ''He has a nasty, cruel streak in him, and only writes the sweetness and light fairy-tale rubbish because it makes good money. But that trick of his with my mirror will be grounds for divorce. Any judge, anywhere, will admit that it was mental cruelty.''

''But what did you do to *me*?'' demanded the weedy little man, taking a pitiful offensive. ''You destroyed my world.''

But did we? Grimes was wondering. *Did we?*

Sanderson and the fragile little blonde had come into the small smoking room, had not noticed him sitting there; they were sharing a settee only a few feet from him.

''The really fantastic thing about it all, Lynnimame—I like to call you that; after all, it was your name when I first met you. You don't

405

mind, do you?" Sanderson was saying.

"Of course not, Henry. If you like it, *I* like it."

"Good. But as I was saying, the really fantastic thing about it all, the way that I fitted into old Wilton's story, is that I *am* a prince. . . ."

"But I think," said Grimes coldly as he got up from his chair, "that the Wicked Witch will be able to vouch that you're not a fairy prince."

And would they all live happily ever after? he wondered as he made his way to his cabin. At least he was finally on his way home.

There are a lot more where this one came from!

ORDER your FREE catalog of ACE paper-backs here. We have hundreds of inexpensive books where this one came from priced from 75¢ to $2.50. Now you can read all the books you have always wanted to at tremendous savings. Order your *free* catalog of ACE paperbacks now.

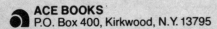

ACE BOOKS
P.O. Box 400, Kirkwood, N.Y. 13795

POUL ANDERSON